Thea pulled aside the lace panels covering her French doors and peered out onto the small semi-circular balcony that overlooked Central Park. Sure enough, something that *maybe* resembled a cat sat grooming himself on her wicker settee. The animal's fur, an odd assortment of earth tones and various shades of gray, was short in some spots, long in others. He looked as if a Persian had mated with both a Siamese and a calico, and the resulting genes couldn't make up their minds. "Strangest cat I've ever seen," she muttered. "All he needs is a few body piercings and he'd qualify as a feline Dennis Rodman."

"He's had a hard life."

Thea spun around. "I thought I told you to wait by the door."

Lucas Bennett shrugged. A sheepish grin settled over his face. "He doesn't like strangers."

"Really?" Thea flung open the doors, stepped onto the balcony, and took a seat next to the oblivious animal. The cat lifted his head, studied her for a split second, then climbed into her lap. Thea tossed its master a saccharine-sweet smile. Lucas Bennett glared at his pet, and this time *she* could read *his* thoughts.

Acclaim for *Hooking Mr. Right*

"*Hooking Mr. Right* was a real treat to read. I love this author's humor, and grasp of emotion in her characters. While there were funny moments (and I love those when I read), the relationship felt real and full of drama as it grew. And I loved the cat. All in all, a very entertaining story, and I will certainly search out more books by this author. – Christine Bush, romance author

"Dynamite story and oh so funny yet toughing in many moments. I highly recommend *Hooking Mr. Right*." – Amazon reviewer

Love this light and romantic story with a funny vibe and a good read for afternoon or evening fun. You'll enjoy this entertaining book." – Amazon reviewer

"Very nice story about two people with previous disappointments finding each other and moving to the place where they are prepared to take another chance. They were both sympathetic characters and I enjoyed getting to know them, as well as the delightful cat. As a bonus, when Thea is stressed she enjoys cooking delicious food and we are given some of the recipes at the end of the book. I can't wait to try the Double Chocolate Cherry Cream Cheese Brownies." – Amazon reviewer

Books by Lois Winston

Anastasia Pollack Crafting Mystery series
Assault with a Deadly Glue Gun
Death by Killer Mop Doll
Revenge of the Crafty Corpse
Decoupage Can Be Deadly
A Stitch to Die For
Scrapbook of Murder
Drop Dead Ornaments
Handmade Ho-Ho Homicide
A Sew Deadly Cruise
Stitch, Bake, Die!
Guilty as Framed
A Crafty Collage of Crime
Sorry, Knot Sorry

Anastasia Pollack Crafting Mini-Mysteries
Crewel Intentions
Mosaic Mayhem
Patchwork Peril
Crafty Crimes (all 3 novellas in one volume)

Empty Nest Mystery Series
Definitely Dead
Literally Dead

Romantic Suspense
Love, Lies and a Double Shot of Deception
Lost in Manhattan
Someone to Watch Over Me

Romance and Chick Lit
Talk Gertie to Me
Four Uncles and a Wedding
Hooking Mr. Right
Finding Hope

Novellas and Novelettes
Elementary, My Dear Gertie
Moms in Black, A Mom Squad Caper
Once Upon a Romance
Finding Mr. Right

Children's Chapter Book
The Magic Paintbrush

Nonfiction
Top Ten Reasons Your Novel is Rejected
House Unauthorized
Bake, Love, Write
We'd Rather Be Writing

Hooking Mr. Right

LOIS WINSTON

Writing as Emma Carlyle

Cover design by L. Winston

ISBN-13: 978-1-940795-16-4

"Women are like tea bags. We don't know our true strength until we are in hot water." – Eleanor Roosevelt

DEDICATION

To all the dreamers, may your dreams come true.

PROLOGUE

"Interested?"

Fighting to keep her lips from twitching with excitement, Hedda twirled a strand of angel hair pasta around her fork and studied the stylish but conservatively dressed woman sitting across the table from her. "Intrigued, to say the least."

"I thought you might be."

Hedda speared a shrimp and slid the food between her lips. Her companion waited patiently while she savored the mouthful and washed it down with a sip of Sauvignon Blanc, but Hedda's instincts—not to mention the white knuckled chokehold the woman continued to apply to her own wine glass—told a different tale. And raised Hedda's suspicions. "Why me?"

"You have the means."

"So do others. Have they already turned you down?"

The woman lifted her chin. "May I be frank?"

With a wave of her fork, Hedda motioned her to continue. "Please do."

"Rumor has it revenues are way down at *The Daily Post.*"

"As well as certain other places," said Hedda, stabbing her dining companion with the pointed insinuation.

Ignoring the interruption, the woman continued. "Our partnership would stimulate badly needed sales for the paper, which in turn would bring in more advertising dollars, moving you back into the black. Not to mention the boost to your own career."

"Or yours. Sales of your books would skyrocket."

The woman leaned back and smiled. "Precisely. I see it as a win/win situation for both of us."

Hedda couldn't argue with her reasoning. The stunt was a marketing gold mine for both of them. Gold? Hell, this idea was pure platinum. Why hadn't she thought of it? She smiled back. "You've got yourself a deal."

The woman relaxed her grip on her wine glass and raised it in a toast. As the stemware clinked, Hedda asked, "Did you have anyone in mind?"

"I hear Luke Bennett's available."

ONE

"The trouble lies in the Y chromosome." Thea took a sip of her coffee and glared across the black Formica-topped desk at her editor, waiting to pounce on Grace if she challenged her statement.

"How so?" Grace leaned back in her chair and sipped her own coffee. Over the rim of the cup an amused expression played across her face.

"Simple genetics, really. Women have two X chromosomes. Men have an X and a Y. Do you know what the definition of Y is?"

Grace set her coffee cup on her desk and raised her eyebrows. "No, but I suppose you're about to tell me."

"Y is an X with a broken leg."

Grace stared at her as if Thea had lost more than a suitcase in her recent, abrupt move from San Francisco to New York. "And your point?"

"Broken! Don't you get it? Defective!" Thea slammed her

hand onto a pile of unread manuscripts teetering on the corner of her editor's desk, nearly toppling the unwieldy stack onto the floor.

Grace grabbed for her cup, barely averting a brown tidal wave.

"Ergo," continued Thea, waving her hand in the air to punctuate her explanation, "there is no doubt that women are superior to men. No defective genes. Obviously, man was a rough prototype. God looked at Adam and said, 'I can do better than that.' Then he created Eve." She placed her cup on the edge of the desk, leaned back in her chair, crossed her arms over her chest, and offered her editor a triumphant smile.

"So this explains why you cancelled your wedding and hightailed it out of San Francisco? Defective male genes?" Grace shuddered. "Do me a favor, will you, Dr. Love? Keep these newly developed, radical theories to yourself. Unless, of course, you want to go from the *New York Times* Bestseller List back to an auditorium-size classroom packed with bored freshmen."

Doctor Love. Thea winced at the nickname the press had dubbed her secret alter ego, Dr. Trulee Lovejoy. In truth, she did wish she could return to the classroom and the comforting monotony of teaching Sociology 101 to less-than-eager first year students. Not that she possessed an all-consuming passion for her chosen career in academia, but with everything she had lost over the past few years, at least she'd still have her integrity. However, she could no more turn back the clock and regain her compromised professional ethics than she could restore her family's lost fortune. At least her popular how-to guides for finding the perfect mate had kept the collection agencies at bay.

"Some love expert! I couldn't even keep my own fiancé from sleeping with my sister." Thea raised her head and challenged

Grace. "Now aren't you glad I chose to publish under a pseudonym? Think of the public relations disaster I've averted. News flash: *Doctor Love Causes Coitus Interuptus after Catching Sister and Fiancé in Flagrante Delicto on Eve of Wedding. Update at eleven.*"

"Too erudite and wordy." Grace brushed away the imaginary headline with a wave of her hand. "Who'd understand all that Latin?"

Thea grimaced. "I can think of at least two people." Her brainy, Stanford-educated younger sister came to mind. As did her sister's equally brainy, MIT educated research partner who also happened to be Thea's ex-fiancé. Too late Thea had discovered Steve and Madeline were engaged in far more than metaphysical debates while researching distant solar systems and spatial anomalies.

"Yes, well..." Grace fidgeted in her chair, her gaze dropping to her lap.

"It's okay, Grace. I'm dealing with it. Putting three thousand miles between myself and them helps."

"Out of sight, out of mind?" Grace raised her chin and met Thea's eyes. "Come on, I know you better than that. You're hurting."

Thea exhaled a deep sigh and shrugged. "Guilty as charged." She glanced over at the large scheduling calendar covering half of one wall in Grace's office and laughed. The sound hung in the room, echoing with pain and resonating with irony.

"Just think, three weeks ago today my biggest concern was that the rehearsal dinner was getting cold because Steve was off in some corner deconstructing the theory of relativity. I used to dream we'd someday travel to Stockholm to pick up his Nobel Prize." She leaned forward, propped her elbows on the desk and scowled at her nearly empty mug. "It just never occurred to me that the award would be for causing my world to stop spinning on its axis."

Grace reached across her desk and patted Thea's hand. "Trust me. You're better off finding out the truth before the wedding rather than afterwards."

"Speaking from experience?"

"More than I like to admit. Maybe I should take some of Trulee's advice."

"Get real! If you have any sense, Grace, you'll let me out of my contract and forget about that third book. *Finding Mr. Right? Hooking Mr. Right?* I'm a fraud. I don't know the first thing about how to get a man and keep him. I'm a thirty-two-year-old sociologist with a lousy track record when it comes to the male species. How can you trust me to write credible books on the subject when I can't even trust my own judgment where men are concerned?"

Grace shrugged. "Maybe we both need to follow your advice. Others do and swear by your books. Besides, I'm not letting you out of your contract. Trulee Lovejoy is the best thing to happen to this company in years."

"Trulee Lovejoy." Thea shook her head. "What was I thinking? How did I ever let you talk me into that awful pseudonym?"

"If I remember correctly, I had a little help from a lady named Margarita. Several ladies named Margarita, actually. Besides, I'm hurt. You insisted on an alias, and I came up with the perfect *nom de plume* for you. After all, who would you believe when it came to matters of the heart, Dr. Trulee Lovejoy or Dr. Althea Chandler?"

Thea scowled. "Right now, I'd suggest you might have better luck with Lassie."

* * *

"Do you believe that woman's gall?" Lucas Bennett grabbed the morning edition of *The Daily Post* from his cluttered desk and flung it across the room. Leaning back in his chair, he stared up at the ceiling and raked his hands through his hair. "Why won't she leave me alone?"

"That woman?" asked his secretary, stooping to retrieve the scattered pages. She approached his desk, shaking her head in a scolding manner as she placed the newspaper on top of a stack of reports Luke needed to cover before the end of the day. "And just which *that* woman are you referring to this time? The ex-wife who walked out on you for her yoga instructor or the gossip columnist who has made you her newest pet project?"

Luke jumped to his feet, nearly toppling his chair backwards. Grabbing the paper, he held it inches from her nose and jabbed at the offending article with his index finger. "*This* woman, Margaret! The one who's turned my life into hell in the name of journalism. Since when is my personal life fodder for this rag that has the audacity to call itself a newspaper?"

"Ah." Margaret glanced at the column, "Guess number two—the reincarnation of Hedda Hopper, Louella Parsons, and Walter Winchell all wrapped up into one super celebrity sleuth. So what tantalizing tidbit has she unveiled in this morning's edition?"

Luke tossed the paper back onto his desk. "None. She's offering an all-expense paid week at La Spa to the lucky woman who reels in New York's most eligible bachelor!" He jabbed his thumb into his own chest. "That's me in case you had any doubts."

"Doubts?" Margaret smiled at him. "Never. So where do I sign up?"

Luke glared at her. "You can be replaced."

"Doubtful. No one else would last more than a day with you."

Luke knew she didn't mean it. Or maybe she did. He offered her an apologetic smile. Once a mild-mannered, unassuming guy, he had recently lost control of his life, thanks to a gossip columnist with ulterior motives. He found himself ill-equipped to handle the situation. At least Margaret understood. "You'd think I was a rock star or something, the way women are throwing themselves at me! Me! Do you believe it?"

He rounded his desk and paced across the thick Persian pile, wearing a path from one end of the room to the other. His voice filled with exasperation; his arms flailed. "Now it will only get worse. I never asked for this. Ever since I had the misfortune of meeting that sorry excuse for a reporter, my every move is detailed *ad nauseam*. She's stolen my life right out from under me. Everywhere I turn, I'm hounded by desperate single women with dollar signs in their eyes."

"Yes." Margaret smirked. "I'm certain it must be a terrible burden to be dubbed 'the stud who puts the man in Manhattan.'"

Stud! Luke shook his head in disbelief. He had never considered his physical attributes anything more than average. Average build. Average height. Average weight. He ran to keep in shape and prided himself on maintaining a well-groomed appearance. But a stud? As far as he was concerned, the only thing studly about him was the size of his investment portfolio, and he had always kept *that* a very closely guarded secret. "I'm no stud, Margaret. You know as well as I do that they're only after my money."

"*Déjà vu*, huh?"

"All over again."

All hell had broken loose three weeks earlier when he reluctantly accompanied his partners to a charity fundraiser at the Waldorf. Still nursing his wounds from his divorce, Luke had begged off. He had little interest in hobnobbing with celebrities during the best of times, let alone during one of the lowest points of his life. He'd offered to write a substantial check, but the firm's senior partners had insisted on his presence.

In hindsight Luke wondered if one of his partners' matchmaking wives had manipulated the situation behind the scenes, not to mention the table assignments. Luke found himself seated next to Henrietta Hopper, Hedda Two to her gossip column fans. She had adopted the name as an homage to Hedda Hopper, the late gossipeer of the first half of the Twentieth Century.

Although Luke divulged nothing of his personal life that evening, Hedda Two devoted her entire column to him in the next morning's edition of *The Daily Post*. Not only did she mention the recent demise of his short-lived marriage, she came too damn close for coincidence in estimating his net worth. Ever since that morning his life had become one continuous nightmare.

At times it felt as though every female in New York, available or not, was stalking him. Those not interested in him for themselves had daughters in mind. One octogenarian approached him during his morning run in Central Park, nearly tripping him with her cane in her zeal to thrust a photo of her great-granddaughter into his hands. Many of the offers he received were downright disgusting. Others, he was convinced, were anatomically impossible.

"In case you haven't noticed, Margaret, I'm after sympathy

here."

"I'll make a note, but you might want to take a look in a mirror one of these days, Mister I'm-No-Stud."

Luke glared at his forty-three-year-old secretary, and a twinge of envy consumed him. Happily married with two kids, Margaret possessed the one thing that continued to elude him. All the success and money in the world couldn't fill the void created by a lack of family.

If life were fair, his honest, thoughtful, fun-loving secretary would have an unmarried younger sister. Unfortunately, Luke wore the emotional bruises that proved life was anything but fair.

He thought he'd been on his way to happily-ever-after when he married Julie. But six months after saying "I do", he came home to find a my-lawyer-will-be-in-touch-with-your-lawyer note taped to the refrigerator. Not only had she left him without warning, she'd done it in the one way she knew would hurt him the most— a note on the fridge. Just like last time.

"It wasn't bad enough she announced my availability to every single woman in the tri-state area and suggested how-to books for snaring me. Now she's offering a grand prize to the winner!" Luke yanked his glasses from his face and began massaging the bridge of his nose.

He'd lost his desire for female companionship. The price had grown too steep. The only companion he now trusted was Cu. He felt relatively certain his cat wasn't harboring any hidden agendas. Besides, Cu couldn't care less about Luke's money as long as he had a constant supply of Feline Feast and clean kitty litter.

Margaret ducked around him and began straightening one of the many stacks of papers littering his cluttered desk. "How-to books?"

"She's mentioned them in each column. How could you miss it?"

Margaret tossed him one of her what-planet-are-you-from looks and pointed to herself. "Working mom, remember? Too much to do, too little time to do it. My Hedda updates come courtesy of your morning rants."

Luke repositioned his glasses on his face and reached for the paper. He scanned Hedda Two's column until he came to the offending paragraph. "Listen to this," he said. *"And don't forget, if you haven't purchased your copy already—and I can't imagine why not—run right out and pick up Dr. Trulee Lovejoy's new masterpiece,* Hooking Mr. Right. *You'd be hard-pressed to find better advice on how to hook Luke Bennett, and we all know he's as 'Mr. Right' as you can get."*

"Now you're really in trouble," said Margaret, moving from his desk to a stack of files scattered across the credenza at the side of the room. "Even I've heard of Dr. Trulee Lovejoy. She's been at the top of the bestseller lists for ages."

"You're kidding. Dr. Trulee Lovejoy. What kind of name is that?" He scowled at the paper. "Sounds like a topless dancer, if you ask me. Or worse."

"Well, I wouldn't know," she said, glancing up from the folders she had begun to sort and file. "Never having met any topless dancers...or worse."

"*Hooking Mr. Right.*" Luke snorted. "What is it? Ten easy steps to becoming a successful gold-digger? I can just imagine what this Dr. Trulee Lovejoy looks like." He paused for a moment, studying the ceiling. "Hmm...let me guess. A silicone Barbie doll, right? Big hair. Big tits. Pea brain."

Margaret closed the file cabinet, shrugged her shoulders, and shook her head in another one of those scolding gestures that told him he was acting like a jerk. "Nice image, Luke, but if you're looking for confirmation, forget it. From what I've heard, she's pretty reclusive. She doesn't have her picture plastered across her book jackets like most of those pop psych gurus, and she refuses to do talk shows or book signings. What I can tell you is women swear by her books."

"Just what I need," muttered Luke. He slumped back down in his chair and lowered his head into his hands.

* * *

Luke's mood worsened steadily as the day progressed. By the time he left his office on Wall Street and flagged a cab, he was snarling. Before Hedda Two had turned his life into Hades on the Hudson, he'd had taken the subway to and from his uptown apartment. The trip was both quick and economical—two things a taxi ride wasn't. And although cost was no object, his father had brought him up to respect both time and money. Some old habits refused to roll over and play dead. But Hedda had put a halt to his underground transport when she mentioned his propensity for subway transit in one of her columns. The next day three dozen women were waiting to ambush him on the platform.

Now, thanks to Hedda Two and a meandering detour due to road repairs, he sat stuck in a traffic jam on the fringes of the theater district. The taxi had inched forward less than half a block in the past fifteen minutes with no indication that it would speed up any time soon. Impatient to get home, he rapped on the Plexiglas partition. "Pull over. I'll get out here." He handed the cabby a twenty. "Keep the change."

After slipping on a pair of mirrored sunglasses, Luke flipped up the collar of his trench coat and plowed his way through the pre-theater crowds on their way to dinner. At first, he intended to head over to the Port Authority and pick up the A or C train, but as he approached the subway entrance, he decided to swing north. With a pleasant breeze stirring the early spring air and the crowds blessedly unaware of his identity, he decided to walk. Cooped up behind his desk all day, he needed the exercise.

His euphoria over his anonymity didn't last long. As he approached Fifty-fifth Street, his senses sprang to attention. Waiting for a light to change at Fifty-seventh, his suspicions grew, and his anger increased exponentially. By Fifty-ninth Street he was absolutely certain the woman several yards behind was following him.

As his apartment on Central Park West came into view, Luke stepped up his pace. He switched his briefcase from his left to his right hand and hazarded a quick glance over his left shoulder. Although he had managed to increase the distance between them, the woman was still following behind, maintaining a brisk pace.

This has gone too far, he told himself as he ducked into the lobby of his building. *It's time to circle the wagons and make a stand.*

* * *

On the walk back from the offices of Wordsmith Press to her Central Park West apartment, Thea mulled over her lengthy conversation with Grace. Once they had exhausted the topic of Thea's cheating ex-fiancé and backstabbing sister, her cancelled wedding, and Thea's subsequent flight from San Francisco to Manhattan, she and her editor had spent hours brainstorming— or more accurately, arguing—over the direction of her next book. A book Thea was contractually bound to write whether she wanted to or not.

In the end the meeting had concluded with nothing resolved.

The discussion came to a halt when Lucy, Grace's assistant, rapped on the office door. "Sorry to interrupt, Grace, but you have that meeting scheduled upstairs."

Grace glanced at her watch and scowled. "Sorry, Thea. Damn bean counters. When they snap their fingers, we're all required to form a Conga line and dance to their tune." She rose from behind her desk and gathered a stack of files. "We'll have to continue this another day. In the meantime, give my suggestion some serious thought. I'm convinced it's the right angle for your next book."

Thea hated the idea, and the more thought she gave it, the more she hated it. Grace was pushing for something Thea stood firmly against, a "Dear Trulee" book filled with readers' pleas for help and Doctor Lovejoy's responses.

Ever since the publication of *Finding Mr. Right*, Trulee had received a tremendous amount of fan mail. However, many of the letters that arrived for her at the publishing house were desperate pleas for help. Thea had steadfastly refused to answer them. She wasn't qualified to offer personal advice that could impact a stranger's life. It was bad enough the public believed the slop she dished out in her books. Instead, she requested that her publisher send out a form letter suggesting the writers seek out a competent therapist. Now Grace wanted a compilation of the best of those letters along with Thea's personal advice. No way.

But with her next deadline looming, she needed to come up with an idea that both appeased Grace and satisfied her contractual obligations. And she needed to find that idea quickly. Otherwise, she'd have to capitulate to Grace's demand and compromise herself even further.

Thea stepped up her pace, the slightly crisp spring breeze and much needed exercise refreshing both her muscles and her mind.

In an absurd way the early evening along the streets of Manhattan reminded her of home. If she closed her eyes to the hordes of people and her ears to the cacophony of traffic, she could almost smell San Francisco Bay on the breeze blowing in off the Hudson River. Almost. Once her olfactory glands filtered out the car exhaust, diesel fumes, overcooked hot dogs from the street vendors, and uncollected trash lining the sidewalks.

The trek from her publisher's midtown offices wasn't daunting, though, and as she turned into the lobby of her building, she decided she'd continue to walk until the weather grew too cold come winter. Only next time she'd have to remember to wear her Nikes and a soft pair of terry socks instead of bare feet and espadrilles.

It was her last thought before a menacing figure stepped from the shadows and blocked her path.

TWO

Thea froze. The unbidden images of every mugging she'd ever read about in the papers or seen on the news flashed across her brain. The man stepped closer. Mirrored sunglasses masked his eyes. His mouth was set in a hard, menacing line. She backed up until the cold marble wall hit her body. He advanced. Placing a hand on either side of the wall inches from her head, he leaned forward until his nose nearly touched hers.

"This ends now!" he said, his voice deep and menacing. "I'm going to make you an example to all those other man-hungry predators stalking me."

"Get away from me!" Thea found her voice, but her words came out as a whimper rather than the roar she wanted, fear preventing her from filling her lungs with the air she needed to scream her head off.

How did this maniac get inside the building? And where the hell was the doorman? Thea tried to duck under his arm, but he countered by anticipating her move and shifting his body. Why didn't he just grab her purse and run? Isn't that what muggers did? Unless he wasn't interested in money. He had said something about making an example of her. Thea stiffened her body and swallowed back a moan of panic. This was no time to lose her wits.

The man glanced over his shoulder. "Melvin, don't just stand there," he yelled. "Call the police!"

Melvin? The doorman? Where was he? Thea craned her neck to the side and spied the doorman hovering in the corner. Her mugger was on a first name basis with her doorman? Something didn't add up. She glanced back at the man. Since when did muggers wear Burberry trench coats? Thea took a deep breath, found her voice, and yelled at the top of her lungs, "Melvin, get this jerk off me!"

The doorman stepped from the shadows and inched forward, wringing his hands in front of him. His voice quivered as he spoke. "Mr. Bennett, sir. I'm afraid you've made a terrible mistake."

"I haven't made any mistake. This woman's been stalking me for half a mile. I want her arrested."

"But, sir —"

"The police, Melvin!"

"Please, Melvin, do as he says," pleaded Thea. "And when the police arrive, you can tell them how he assaulted me. There's going to be an arrest, all right. I want this gorilla thrown behind bars where he belongs!"

The man turned back to her. "Nice try, little lady, but I haven't laid a hand on you, and you're the lawbreaker here. Stalking *and* trespassing."

"Trespassing? I live here!"

"What?"

Her statement shocked him into dropping his arms and

stepping back. Bracing herself, Thea drew her right knee up and caught him in his privates.

"Ow!" He dropped to his knees, cupping his hands over his groin.

Thea backed away from him. Tossing aside her purse and canvas tote, she spread her legs and feigned an aggressive kickboxing stance she'd once seen demonstrated on the evening news. With any luck he wouldn't guess she had no idea what she was doing.

"You live here?" he repeated, his voice several octaves higher as he staggered to his feet.

Thea didn't bother answering. Instead, she narrowed her gaze and pressed her lips into a tight grimace. Then she shifted her weight forward to what she hoped was an offensive maneuver of sorts.

The man turned to Melvin. The bewildered doorman nodded in agreement. "This is Dr. Chandler, Mr. Bennett. She moved in about two weeks ago."

The man's jaw slackened. All at once Mr. Hyde transformed into Dr. Jekyll. "Please forgive me, Dr. Chandler," he said, tentatively taking a step toward her, his right hand extended. "You see, I've had some problems lately with some marriage crazy women, and —"

"Don't come any closer," said Thea. Bracing herself against a massive marble column, she warned him off with an outstretched palm. "Just keep your distance. I don't know who you are or what your problem is, mister, and frankly, I don't care. But if you ever come near me again, you'll find yourself slapped with a restraining order so fast you won't know what hit you!"

"But you don't understand. I —"

Thea didn't give him a chance to continue. Stooping to retrieve her purse and canvas tote, she shot him one parting glare full of daggers. Unfortunately, the gesture lost all its impact as she lost her balance. Thea's feet headed north; her torso lurched south. Her arms flailed wildly to regain her footing. His hands shot forward, grabbing her by the wrist and shoulder just in time to keep her from landing face first on the floor.

"Take it easy," he said, dropping his one hand from her shoulder.

Thea stared blankly at the man's fingers still wrapped around her wrist. Angry over his absurd accusations and embarrassed by her own clumsiness, she wanted nothing more than to flee to the quiet of her own apartment. She took a deep breath that failed to steady the turmoil roiling inside her. "Don't touch me," she said, her voice sounding nearly as wobbly as her legs felt. Refusing to look at him, she jerked her wrist free of his grasp, squared her shoulders, and spun on her heels—smack into the marble pillar.

For a split second her world turned black. Then, it spun dizzily on its axis. Thea blinked back the stars dancing before her eyes.

"Are you all right?" He placed both hands on her shoulders, steadying her as she swayed.

No, she wasn't all right, but she'd be damned if she'd let him know it. With supreme effort she fought back tears of pain and frustration. Forcing herself not to feel for the egg-sized lump she was certain had sprung up on the side of her head, she squared her shoulders once more, raised her chin, and marched across the lobby to the elevator, ignoring both him and his question.

He followed.

Thea stared straight ahead, glaring at the man's reflection in the polished brass, her own grim countenance rebounding off his mirrored sunglasses. *She* didn't understand? Oh, she understood all right. He was just another full-of-himself hunk of a macho male with a caveman mentality. Act first. Think later. If at all.

She studied her own reflection, engaging in a mental conversation with the woman staring back at her—the plain looking woman who wore no makeup, whose straight brown hair was pulled back into a sensible ponytail. *Well, Dr. Trulee Lovejoy, you really know how to bring out the best in the male species, don't you?* One short, ironic laugh escaped through her pursed lips.

"Is something funny?"

A soft ding announced the arrival of the car. "More than you could possibly know," she mumbled, stepping inside as soon as the doors slid open.

"I fail to see the humor in what just occurred in the lobby," he said, his voice filled with remorse. "I acted horribly, and I do wish you'd let me explain. This was a terrible misunderstanding. I'm offering you my sincerest apologies."

Misunderstanding? Thea responded with a frozen glare that rivaled the Mendenhall Glacier.

He sighed, pushed the button for the twelfth floor and turned to face her. "Your floor?"

"A misunderstanding? How dare you try to assuage your conscience that way, you Neanderthal!" Her fury caused her voice to rise to the level of a soprano who had inhaled helium. "What do you do when you actually have an argument with someone? Pull out your Uzi?"

"If you'd only allow me to explain, you'd understand." He sighed again, this time heavier. "Floor?" he repeated.

"Same," she muttered.

He whipped off his glasses and stared down at her. "You live on *my* floor?"

His floor? Great. Her gaze fixed on the brass doors, she refused to look at him as she spoke. "I wasn't aware you owned it."

The antiquated Otis elevator seemed to take even longer than normal, creaking and lumbering its way up the twelve stories before finally coming to a halt. He stepped aside to let her exit first.

She turned left.

He followed.

Well, your luck is holding, as usual, Althea. It isn't bad enough he has to live on the same floor, he's even on the same wing!

It got worse.

When Thea stopped at her door to search for her keys, he continued down the hall—to the next apartment!

"It appears we're next-door neighbors," he said, inserting his key in the lock.

He stepped over the threshold and shut the door behind him before she could close her gaping mouth.

* * *

Through supreme effort and with the aid of years of yoga classes and daily meditation working in her favor, Grace forced her body and facial features to remain calm. Inwardly she seethed at the group of suits sitting across the polished cherry conference table from her. A summons from the "Iceberg Trio" as they were called behind their backs—Goldberg, Landisburg, and Brayburgh—always meant trouble for her.

The three Armani-clad bean counters of Wordsmith Press. Grace studied the skinflints as they positioned files and spreadsheets in front of themselves. Classic oxymoron, she thought, or better yet, oxy-morons. Their tightfisted control of Wordsmith's purse strings made Shylock look like a philanthropist, but you'd never know it from the twelve-hundred-dollar designer suits draping their flabby bodies.

As if on cue from a hidden conductor, The Icebergs leaned back in their chairs and cleared their throats. In unison. Grace held her breath as the inquisition commenced. She refrained from showing any trace of emotion as Goldberg, the head Iceberg, stated the purpose of the meeting. No small feat, considering his demand.

When he finished, all three stared at her expectantly. Grace removed her hands from her lap and placed them, fingers interlaced, on the table. She leaned forward slightly. "We have a signed contract with the author," she reminded them, leveling her gaze on each of the three men in turn. "One that specifically states she will not make any public appearances to promote her books and that her image will not be used in any media advertising. She was quite specific in her desire to remain anonymous. Upper management, marketing, *and* the legal department all signed off on this with the purchase of the first book."

Goldberg twisted his thin lips into a condescending smile. "Then I suggest you find a way to convince the author to renegotiate that particular clause in her contract, Ms. Wainwright."

Grace leaned back in her chair and folded her arms across her chest. "This makes no sense. She's consistently on the bestseller lists. Her books are flying off the shelves. Have you seen the increased sales numbers since Hedda Two began touting them? We've never had such a huge success."

"Hedda's column only runs in New York and less than a dozen other papers in the tri-state area," said Goldberg. "She doesn't have national syndication. Women in Tupelo and Topeka don't give a flying fig about Hedda Two and her New York celebrity twaddle. We need to increase sales throughout the country."

"She'll never agree to this."

"Let me give you a little incentive, then." He nodded to Landisburg on his right.

Landisburg opened the folder in front of him and leafed through a stack of papers until he found the one he wanted. He cleared his throat, then began to read a list of recent Wordsmith Press titles. "*Deauville Diary. Life in the Service of the Lord, the Autobiography of a Small-Town Southern Preacher. Beating the System.*"

"All bought by you, Ms. Wainwright," said Brayburgh, weighing in for the first time.

Grace winced. Talk about a run of bad luck, and none of it her fault. Shortly after publication, it was discovered that the author of *Deauville Diary*, a memoir of the author's bittersweet love affair with a Frenchwoman, had never set foot in France. During the year he supposedly spent in Deauville, he was selling used cars in Peoria. And who wanted to buy a book by a prevaricating used car salesman? Apparently, very few people, judging from the book's dismal numbers.

Then there was *Life in the Service of the Lord, the Autobiography of a Small-Town Southern Preacher.* A very spiritually uplifting book. Too bad Reverend Strothers didn't practice what he preached. His penchant for little boys came to light during a book tour through Texas. The Reverend got fifty years, and Wordsmith got stuck with fifty thousand unsold books.

Beating the System? The text was about gambling, but the writer had made one huge mistake. He hadn't gambled on the real author discovering his plagiarism. Now Wordsmith was embroiled in a multi-million-dollar lawsuit.

And Grace was responsible for all three losses. Which was why she was doing her damnedest to promote the hell out of her only recent winner while staying within the bounds of her contract with Thea.

"Do you have any idea how much these books have cost the company, Ms. Wainwright?" asked Goldberg.

She didn't know the exact number, but she figured adding in the litigation, Wordsmith stood to lose millions. "You have no right to blame me for this. I'm an editor, not a private investigator. Each of those books was well-written and would have sold if not for extenuating circumstances."

"Those extenuating circumstances have pushed us way down in the red for the year," said Landisburg.

"What does that have to do with Trulee Lovejoy?"

"Everything," said Brayburgh. "Hers are the only books that are keeping us afloat. We're a small press. We can't afford the losses we've sustained." He paused for a moment before adding, "Thanks to you."

Yoga classes or no yoga classes, meditation or no meditation, Grace had reached her saturation point. She slammed her fists on the table, rattling the water glasses, and shouted at the three bean counters. "You're making me a scapegoat! You have no right."

"On the contrary," said Goldberg. "We're offering you the opportunity to redeem yourself and cover your losses."

Grace glared at him. "Right. How will getting Trulee to reveal her true identity do that?"

"We send her on a nationwide tour," said Landisburg. "She hypes those books on every TV and radio station from here to L.A. Sales will triple. Maybe even quadruple."

"And if she refuses?" asked Grace.

"Then we'll just have to make some personnel cuts," said Goldberg. "Beginning in the editorial department."

* * *

Her mouth agape, Thea stared down the empty hallway for a good minute after her next-door neighbor, AKA Mr. Neanderthal, let himself into his apartment. Finally, she turned to her own door and struggled with her key, wincing from the pain in her wrist when she twisted the knob. Damn him! This was all his fault. If he hadn't confronted her like some self-righteous, steroid-driven caveman, she wouldn't have gotten so peeved that she lost her equilibrium. Confrontational men had a way of unbalancing her, figuratively and so it seemed, literally. Now she was left to suffer the consequences—a bruised wrist from his *gallant* attempt to keep her from falling and a headache threatening to consume the five boroughs of New York.

Tears sprang to her eyes. What the hell was she doing in New York, anyway? She'd never felt so miserable. Well, actually, she had. The moment she walked in on her sister and her ex-fiancé sprang to mind as one of the lower points in her life. At the time she masked her pain with anger. Now that the anger had had time to diffuse, she was beginning to second-guess her rash three-thousand-mile move.

At least if she'd stayed in San Francisco, she'd have friends to help her pick up the pieces of her fractured life. All she had in New York was a sore wrist and a torturous headache. Not to mention a growing pain in the lower part of her anatomy—otherwise known as her newly discovered next-door neighbor.

Maybe he traveled a lot, and she wouldn't bump into him very often. Yes, and maybe if she wished really hard, she'd sprout wings and fly to Venus.

Thea yanked the key from the last of the three locks and slammed the door behind her, taking extreme pleasure, despite her growing headache, in the reverberation that traversed the length of the wall. She hoped he heard it. And felt it. Men! Maybe she'd title her next book *Men—Not Worth the Effort*. Or *Get a Dog Instead*. But somehow, she didn't think Grace would go for either of those suggestions.

Trulee Lovejoy was supposed to help women catch men, not convince them the testosterone-laden brutes weren't worth the trouble. The problem, though, was that Trulee's alter ego, Dr. Althea Chandler, had lousy judgment in men. As far as Thea was concerned, the half of the population that possessed the defective Y chromosome wasn't worth the effort. Case in point: ex-fiancé, Dr. Stephen J. Ross.

The ringing phone drew her attention away from her vindictive musings. Tossing her purse, tote, and keys on a chair, she reached for the receiver. The moment she heard the voice on the other end, she wished she hadn't.

"Althea, this has gone on too long. You had no business running off like that. I need you back here."

Thea wasn't surprised by her sister's demand. Madeline lived in her own private world of quarks and neutrinos. And adultery. In her mind what occurred the night before Thea's aborted wedding was no more than a slight misunderstanding, certainly not something to keep Thea from shouldering her family responsibilities.

Struggling to keep all emotion from her voice, Thea responded to her sister's demand. "I'm not coming back, Madeline."

"You're holding a grudge, Althea. Mother wouldn't have liked that. This is your home." Madeline choked back a sob that Thea suspected was well scripted. "Please, Thea," her sister whined. "I didn't mean for this to happen. I said I was sorry, didn't I?"

Thea sighed. She had allowed herself to be manipulated for too long—first by her parents, then her sister. And where had it gotten her? She'd been used and abused—mentally, emotionally, and financially. No one appreciated the sacrifice she had made in the name of family, not that anyone except Grace knew the nature of that sacrifice. Still, enough was enough. "Mother is dead," she reminded Madeline.

Her sister sniffled. "That doesn't mean you can walk away from your obligations. Everything's a mess. Bill won't speak to me. He wants a divorce. You won't come home. Why are you all doing this to me?"

Me? Did her sister actually believe she was the victim in this B-movie soap opera? But, of course. Thanks to her parents, Madeline had grown up believing the world revolved around her. Camilla and Frederick Chandler may have had the best of intentions, but they'd created a monster. "You brought this on yourself, Madeline."

"I said I was sorry! What more do you want?"

"I want you to leave me alone." Thea slammed the phone into its cradle. Her mother's rule against slamming echoed in her head, but as she had told her sister, Camilla Chandler was dead. Her oldest daughter no longer felt constrained nor needed to abide by her mother's dictates.

Thea headed for her computer, but quickly changed her mind. She was beginning to see stars again, and she wasn't certain she could navigate the keyboard with her sore wrist. Instead, she opted for two aspirins and an ice pack. Alternating the pack between her wrist and head, she slumped onto the sofa and stewed over the call from her sister.

With eight years between them, Madeline's birth had disrupted Thea's comfortably settled role as an only child. Compounding the situation, the Chandler's second daughter was born a genius. Although Thea was herself a bright child, her status in the family rapidly plummeted.

While most toddlers were struggling to walk without tripping over their own feet, Madeline Chandler taught herself to read. By the age of eight she had mastered calculus. At twelve she was enrolled at Stanford. She graduated with a doctorate in astrophysics before she was old enough to vote.

Thea was told repeatedly that Madeline had been blessed with a rare gift, and as a member of the family, Thea had an obligation to help nurture her sister's genius. From the beginning, Madeline was treated like royalty, surrounded by doting parents and an older sister who jumped through hoops to do her bidding. And Thea jumped without complaint. Because Madeline was special, and it was expected. And most of all because Thea was the responsible daughter.

Now her parents were gone, and Thea was left to suffer the consequences of their overindulgent attitudes toward her younger sister. Genius aside, Madeline was a spoiled brat who thought nothing of hurting the sister who had sacrificed so much for her. Thea had reached her saturation point. She would no longer act as Madeline's enabler.

She picked up the phone and dialed her San Francisco attorney. After being connected, she outlined her wishes to him.

Thea heard the lawyer's disapproval in his voice. "Are you certain you want to do this, Althea?"

"I've made up my mind, Arthur. I'm making a new life for myself in New York. I won't be returning to San Francisco. I want a clean break."

"If that's your decision."

"It is."

"I'll draw up the papers and overnight them to you to sign. This is a very generous gift. Your sister will be quite surprised."

"Yes, she will," agreed Thea. She hung up the phone. Madeline was in for the surprise of her life—and a rude awakening.

Thea didn't hate her sister. Over the years she had come to understand that Madeline was a victim. They both were. Each sister in her own way had suffered at the hands of well-meaning, but misguided parents. In allowing Madeline total freedom to explore her genius, they had crippled her. Only Madeline was too self-absorbed to realize it.

As hurt as Thea was by her sister's betrayal, she wasn't acting out of a need for revenge. Madeline wouldn't understand that now but maybe in time. Someday she might even thank Thea. Not for the house. Thea had no doubt Madeline would quickly lose the one remaining piece of their joint inheritance. Thea was sacrificing the house she loved to a greater good. Independence was the true gift she was offering her sister—the one gift Frederick and Camilla Chandler had inadvertently denied their daughter. The question was—would Madeline be wise enough to understand that?

The aspirins were beginning to have their desired effect on her headache. The stars swimming around her eyes receded into the firmament. Reaching for a two-week-old copy of *New York Magazine* that she'd purchased shortly after her arrival and had yet to browse, Thea pushed aside all thoughts of her sister and aimlessly flipped through the pages.

Until she came across the *Gotham* section.

And saw a photo of the man who had pinned her up against the lobby wall moments earlier.

The picture wasn't large—only about two by two inches, and he appeared with several others. But that was him, all right. Thea read the caption out loud. *"Recently dubbed 'The Most Eligible Bachelor in Manhattan' by* Daily Post *columnist Hedda Two, Luke Bennett of Porter-Sachs-Bennett, seen with partners Sean Porter (left) and Jerome Sachs (right) chatting with Hollywood's latest sweetheart Jennifer Annenberg at the Waldorf gala fundraiser for Cystic Fibrosis."*

And I'm sure he hated every moment of it! Just look at that unhappy grin stretching ear to ear. Why, the man was positively drinking up the attention.

Man-hungry predators. His words sprang to her mind. When he confronted her in the lobby, he'd referred to her as one of the man-hungry predators out to get him. She glanced once more at the predatory way he eyed Jennifer Annenberg, and suddenly everything made sense to her. Luke Bennett was New York's celebrity *du jour*, and he was using his newfound fame to bag himself a Hollywood megastar—while every unattached female in New York City tried to snare him. And he'd assumed she was one of them.

Thea cast the magazine aside. Leaning back, she closed her eyes. Thankfully, judging from the company he kept, there was little chance of her and Luke Bennett traveling in the same circles. Jennifer could have him.

* * *

Sometime later the buzz of the intercom startled Thea awake. She shook the grogginess from her head, then waited for her eyes to focus before staggering to the call box and pushing the button. "Yes?"

Melvin's voice boomed over the intercom. "Flower delivery for you, Dr. Chandler."

"Thank you. Send him up, please."

Thea fished around in her purse for a couple of singles to tip the deliveryman. Flowers. Most likely a peace offering from Madeline, one her sister could ill afford if her husband had walked out on her. Poor Bill. Madeline had always taken his love and devotion for granted—as she had everyone's in her life. Now she had the audacity to think a few dozen flowers would erase the hurt and repair the damage her selfish actions had caused. How typical!

At the sound of the doorbell, Thea cradled the ice pack between her stomach and sore wrist and swung the door open with her good hand. An enormous floral arrangement confronted her, completely obliterating the upper half of the deliveryman. Or was it a woman? Either way, she couldn't handle the massive arrangement with one functioning arm.

"Thank you," she said, silently cursing her sister's fiscal recklessness. But Thea wasn't surprised. Even at their bleakest moment, when they were two steps away from foreclosure and bankruptcy, her mother had faced financial ruin by going shopping. Madeline came by it naturally. "Would you mind bringing them into the living room?" she asked, stepping aside to let him—or her—enter.

Him, she decided, following from behind. Definitely a very well defined him with broad shoulders that tapered to a pair of denim-clad slim hips and tight buns. Thea sighed. No use fantasizing. She'd sworn off men and for good reason. The deliveryman bent to place the arrangement in the center of her newly purchased antique wormwood and wrought iron coffee table, then straightened and turned.

"You!"

THREE

To Thea's dismay, Tight Buns was none other than The Neighbor from Hell. Heat infused her cheeks, and she prayed he interpreted it as anger and not the embarrassment she actually felt over her abruptly deflated fantasy.

"I knew you wouldn't let me in to apologize."

Damn right! She pointed to the floral arrangement. "Are those flowers from you, or did you tackle the deliveryman?"

"They're from me."

"Then kindly take them and leave. I want nothing to do with either you or your flowers."

He didn't answer her. With a sharp intake of breath and a look of horror settling across his face, he stared at her ice pack draped wrist. "Did I do that?"

"No. I treat myself to an ice pack and an espresso everyday at this hour. Of course, you did it!"

He muttered something under his breath that sounded like half apology and half expletive-laced self-flagellation. Then, before she realized what was happening, he grabbed her good arm above the elbow—with extreme delicacy, she noted, as though he were afraid of inflicting further damage—and urged her in the direction of the door. On the way, he reached down and retrieved her keys and purse from the chair where she'd tossed them earlier. "We're getting that X-rayed," he said. "It could be broken."

"Let go of me!" Thea tried to wriggle from his grip, but her effort was only halfhearted. Suddenly all the fight drained from her. She ached. Physically and emotionally. And she was tired. Tired of making decisions. Tired of shouldering burdens. Tired of being taken for granted. Tired of being used. If Luke Bennett wanted to take her to the hospital for X-rays, let him. After all, he was responsible for the physical part of her pain.

Now if only someone would offer to take care of the emotional part.

* * *

Luke glanced at the woman seated beside him in the cab. Although she tried hard to hide it, he could tell she was in severe pain. Thankfully, her wrist was only badly sprained, but the doctor discovered she'd also suffered an extremely mild concussion from her collision with the marble column. A subsequent battery of tests ruled out any serious damage—no swelling, no fluid on the brain. After several additional hours of monitoring, she was allowed to leave.

Stubborn woman. If she'd only listened to reason, none of this would have happened. Granted, he'd jumped to the wrong conclusion, but under the circumstances, it was understandable, wasn't it? Any rational person would think so. Wouldn't he?

Still, maybe he had approached her with a bit too much forcefulness in the lobby. He'd frightened her. Which had been his objective, of course, but that was when he thought she was one of *them*. And even if she had been one of them, he hadn't intended the encounter to result in physical injury. He wouldn't harm a ladybug, let alone a lady. But she didn't know that. So, from her point of view, he supposed her reactions were justified.

Technically the injuries were her own fault, though, not his. He was only trying to keep her from falling when she lost her balance, and slamming her head into the column...well, he could hardly be blamed for that. She knew the column was behind her. Why hadn't she looked where she was going?

Still, Luke felt like a first-class heel. Menacing verbal assaults weren't normally part of his makeup. At least they never had been before that duet of witches destroyed his life—his two-timing ex-wife and that gossipmonger columnist. Hell, his friends often jokingly referred to him as Clark Kent because of his mild-mannered nature. So what had happened to him? Lately when he looked in the mirror, he no longer recognized himself. Worse yet, he was quickly growing to dislike the face staring back at him.

He exhaled a lungful of annoyance and broke the frigid silence hanging between them. "You're a doctor," he said. "Didn't you realize you might have a concussion?"

"I'm not that kind of doctor."

"So what kind are you?"

"If you must know, I have a doctorate in sociology."

"You're a professor?"

"I was."

"And now?"

"I write."

"Sociology books?"

She shot him a look that was the silent equivalent of "duh."

Luke decided against any further attempts at conversation. He wondered if there were monasteries for wealthy, reluctant-bachelor stockbrokers. However, as much as he craved the solitude, he wasn't certain he'd take to the austerity. Or the poverty. And then there was the issue of celibacy. Even though he'd recently sworn off women, a man did have his needs.

They sat in silence for the remainder of the taxi ride back to the apartment building.

* * *

At her door Thea inserted her key in the first of the three locks, then turned to Luke. She supposed she owed him a thank-you for escorting her to the hospital, but then again, she wouldn't have a sprained wrist or a concussion if it weren't for him. In the end, though, her upbringing won out, and she forced the words out over her lips as she unlocked the second deadbolt. "Thank you."

"Your injuries are my fault," he said, a hangdog expression settling over his features. "It was the least I could do."

Exactly what she'd been thinking but having him voice her thoughts took her by surprise. "Yes, well, that *is* true." Still groggy from the whack to her head, Thea paused for a moment before continuing. "Perhaps next time you won't overreact and jump to the wrong conclusion." She unlocked the final deadbolt and stepped over her threshold. "Good night, Mr. Bennett."

To her shock he had the audacity to brace the door with his arm and follow her inside.

"Where do you think you're going?" she asked, trying to shut the door on him.

"Doctor's orders. You're not supposed to spend the night alone."

"I can take care of myself, thank you."

"What if you pass out? The doctor said you might experience some subsequent dizziness."

"I won't. I'm going straight to bed. Good night, Mr. Bennett."

He refused to budge. Instead, he grabbed the door out of her hand and closed it behind him. "And if you get up in the middle of the night?"

Thea was tired of arguing. Tight buns aside, Lucas Bennett was the most irritating, obstinate man she'd ever met. "I'm calling the police."

He reached inside his jacket pocket and offered her his cell phone. "Be my guest. And give my regards to the precinct captain."

She couldn't win. "Let me guess. Army buddies?"

"Best friends since grade school. P.S. Eighty-seven."

Just her luck. She studied the imposing man filling her entry hall and grimaced. Physical force was definitely out of the question—even if she had the use of both arms. He towered a head above her and outweighed her by at least sixty pounds. Maybe more.

Her gaze rested for a moment on the muscular arms crossed over a solid chest, then traveled down to his flat stomach. His front looked as good as his rear. She stole a quick glance back up at his face. She hadn't paid much attention to his features earlier, but now she saw that the picture in *New York Magazine*, a minuscule headshot, hadn't done him justice. The minute image had failed to capture the rugged set of his jaw, a mouth meant to capture and devour, and a pair of crystal blue eyes that stared at her with an intensity that sent Tom, Dick, and Harry, the three acrobats who lived in her belly, rappelling down her intestines.

Thea tore her gaze from his, her head suddenly dizzy but not from any concussion. No man had ever rattled her to such an extent. Without warning, an alien force had invaded and gained control of her body. Dr. Althea Chandler, the rational thinking, Vassar educated Ph.D., had suddenly transformed into a love-struck adolescent and all because Lucas Bennett had a face and physique that made Brad Pitt look like an also-ran. Summoning up great effort, Thea forced herself to remember that a) she didn't like the man standing in front of her, and b) she had sworn off all men.

Luke cleared his throat. Thea felt the heat rising to her cheeks. "Seen enough?"

I will not let him do this to me! She pursed her lips and glared at him, refusing to succumb to the intense reaction he'd stirred in her. Instead, she chalked the carnal response up to post-Steve trauma, Trulee Lovejoy guilt, three weeks' worth of little sleep, the lobby fiasco, and a lack of caffeine. "I was merely gauging my ability to forcefully remove you with only one usable arm."

"Uh-huh." He leaned one shoulder against the wall, his arms still crossed over his chest, and offered her a knowing smile. "Tell me, just what *do* you call that form of self-defense you practice? The one you used downstairs? Kick-ballet?"

So much for her acting abilities. She hadn't fooled him for a moment. Thea threw her arms up in surrender—no easy feat, considering one was in a sling—and retreated to the living room, collapsing onto the sofa. He followed behind her, taking the chair on the opposite side of the coffee table.

"Just make yourself right at home," she said, punctuating the statement with a wave of her good arm and a mega-dose of sarcasm.

"Thank you." He smiled pleasantly, as if they were the best of friends. Then he reached for the portable phone sitting on a pile of magazines and began punching in a series of numbers.

"Just what do you think you're doing?"

"Ordering us some dinner. I haven't eaten yet, and I have a feeling neither have you."

"I'm not hungry." Actually, she was, but she'd be damned if she'd break bread with him. The Neanderthal eyed her with skepticism while he rattled off a list of Chinese dishes to someone named Mrs. Ling.

"Ten minutes," he said, replacing the phone. "They'll deliver."

Thea scowled. They sat in silence, staring at each other over the massive floral arrangement. The contest of wills lasted all of five minutes before her eyelids drooped closed.

* * *

Luke watched Dr. Chandler sleep. Awake, she came across as a feisty ball of anger, but sleep softened her harsh edges and transformed the harridan into a peaceful, almost childlike angel. For the first time he noticed her creamy skin, devoid of makeup, with its delicate sprinkling of freckles across the bridge of a pert nose, the long lashes that kissed high cheekbones, the Cupid's bow lips that turned upward into a slight smile.

He fought a sudden overwhelming urge to release her light brown hair from the tight confines of the no-nonsense fabric-covered elastic that pulled it severely off her face. Instead, he clasped his hands tightly over his knees and tried to visualize her silky hair draped softly over her shoulder and across her breast.

He tried to remember the color of her eyes but couldn't. His own anger, first at her, then himself, blocked such details from his mind. Until now. Now he had time to study the woman at his leisure, and he found her to be a pleasant sight. Unfortunately, Luke knew from bitter experience that pretty packages often contained bombs that left permanent scars. Besides, Dr. Chandler had already proven that behind her soft exterior lay a waspish personality.

Luke rose and wandered around the room, a combination living-dining room much like his own. Although he could well-afford a larger apartment in a fancier high-rise, he chose to remain in the unpretentious, Prohibition-era building.

The caustic-tongued Dr. Chandler, however, dressed in a severe navy suit, struck him as a chrome and glass minimalist—someone who'd be more at home in one of Trump's garish modern monstrosities. He had expected to find her apartment done in sharp lines and harsh angles—stark, no-nonsense furniture that complemented her personality. To his surprise he discovered an eclectic mix of cozy antiques and a profusion of color. Overstuffed furniture covered in a riotous mix of red, blue, green, and purple plaid and floral fabrics exuded a welcoming warmth.

At the opposite end from the sitting area stood a rustic looking table with six unmatched chairs and a sideboard. Luke stood over the table, running his hand along the smooth pine slab. He was instantly reminded of his grandparents' home where he'd spent summers as a child. A similar table and chairs had been the focal point of his grandmother's bustling kitchen. The memory filled him with a combination of sweet longing and aching emptiness.

Luke returned to the sitting area. As in his apartment, floor-to-ceiling built-in bookcases lined the far wall. An assortment of books and antique china occupied half the shelves. The remainder were still bare, waiting for the contents of the half dozen cartons stacked off to one side. Two of the boxes were labeled *knickknacks*, the rest *books*.

Luke strode down the hall in search of Dr. Chandler's bedroom, finding it where he'd expected. Her apartment was a mirror image of his. Their bedrooms shared a wall, their heads resting each night mere inches from one another. He chuckled, wondering how that information would sit with her. Not well, he imagined.

Scanning the pink and white lacy bedroom, Luke found it difficult to reconcile the strident, take-no-prisoners image Dr. Chandler projected with her soft, gracious surroundings. Either her bluster and lion's roar were false bravado, or the woman was one giant contradiction of terms. Whichever the case, Luke was finding her obvious disinterest in him a welcome change from the simpering airheads he now dodged on a daily basis.

Too bad they'd gotten off on such a bad footing. He didn't like the idea of being on less-than-friendly terms with his new neighbor, but after their initial run-in and her subsequent hostility, he doubted there was much chance of maintaining a casual friendship.

Tossing aside a pile of embroidered throw pillows, he turned down the patchwork quilt that covered her bed and returned to the living room.

Luke lifted Dr. Chandler into his arms. As he carried her down the hall to her bedroom, she snuggled against his chest. Her scent—a combination of orange blossoms and vanilla—wafted around him. He inhaled deeply, enjoying the sensation and was suddenly struck by how good she felt in his arms—warm and soft and somehow very right. He hadn't held a woman in his arms in a long time. The thought unnerved him and brought him to his senses. He'd sworn off women. For good reason. And this woman was definitely not someone who should be making him forget that vow.

He deposited Dr. Chandler on her bed and despite himself, chuckled softly as he bent to remove her shoes. Definitely a contradiction of terms, he thought, glancing back at the almost military cut of her suit. Luke slipped the casual rope and canvas shoes from her bare feet, drew the quilt up around her, and headed for the kitchen.

Rummaging through her kitchen cabinets, he found the makings for coffee. Thankfully, the good doctor owned an espresso machine. The night stretched long in front of him. He was already drained from first a long day at the office, then the verbal sparring he'd endured due to his initial, explosive confrontation with his new neighbor. To remain awake to monitor her, he'd need something far stronger than Mr. Ling's green tea.

A few minutes later, the intercom buzzer signaled the arrival of his dinner. After paying the delivery boy, Luke poured the double shot of espresso into a mug and carried the steaming beverage and takeout containers back to the living room, hoping to find something of interest on TV. He scanned the room. Where the hell was her television? She had to own a television! *Everyone* owned a television.

He set his coffee and dinner on an end table and walked down the hall, popping his head into each of the spare rooms. The smaller of the two, the one originally meant to serve as maid's quarters, was in the process of becoming her office. An L-shaped workstation, complete with computer and printer, wrapped around two walls of the room. File cabinets lined a third wall. A small wooden bookcase, filled with computer manuals and assorted textbooks, rounded out the room's furnishings.

Luke moved on to the second, larger room, set up as a guest bedroom—assuming any guest could circumnavigate his way around the stacks of cartons littering the floor. Neither room contained a television.

Grumbling to himself, he stalked back to the living room. Maybe he could find a page-turner among her enormous collection of books—Grisham, King, Clancy—anything to hold his interest and keep him awake.

Beginning at one end of the wall, he quickly scanned the titles, grimacing at row after row of "chick" books. Historicals. Tearjerker romances. The collected works of Jane Austen and the Brontë sisters. He moved farther down the rows of shelves, fairing no better. Poetry—everything from Shakespeare's sonnets to Emily Dickinson and Keats. Luke muttered under his breath and moved on. More Shakespeare, this time his complete plays. A set of encyclopedias. *Did anyone still use physical encyclopedias?* Next came the cookbooks—several dozens of them. Of all the choices of reading matter, those held the most promise. His rumbling stomach agreed.

Only two shelves of books remained. Luke doubted they'd prove any more alluring, but he planted his feet in front of them and began reading the spines.

What the hell! The anger built slowly at first, but as he read title after title, his body grew more rigid, his pulse quickened, and his blood pressure skyrocketed into the danger zone.

One by one Luke read the titles through clenched teeth. *How to Make a Man Fall in Love with You. The Path to 'I Do'. How to Snare a Millionaire.* He found that one particularly interesting! *Casting Love Spells, Reeling in Lovers. The Art of Seduction. Flirt with Him Today, Marry Him Tomorrow.* Three dozen books, all on the same subject. As far as he was concerned, there could be but one reason for a woman to have such a collection.

And then he saw them. *Finding Mr. Right* and *Hooking Mr. Right* by Dr. Trulee Lovejoy. Luke pulled both books from the shelf and grabbed a seat. He no longer feared falling asleep, not when he found himself in possession of the enemy's arsenal. His hunger forgotten, he flipped open to the first page of the first chapter of the first book.

Lucas Bennett planned on staying one step ahead of Dr. Chandler and every other conniving female in New York. Forewarned was forearmed.

* * *

Thea woke feeling groggy and disoriented. She twisted her neck and stared at the digital display of her alarm clock. Three-o-five. She had no recollection of getting into bed. The last thing she remembered was a ridiculous contest of wills between herself and her next-door neighbor. What was his name? Bennett. Lucas Bennett. Slowly, it all came back to her. The city's newly crowned stud-muffin had refused to leave her apartment. They had been staring down one another over that enormous arrangement of yellow roses he brought her.

And now five hours later, she found herself in bed. Thea flung aside the quilt, exhaling a sigh of relief over finding herself fully clothed—minus her shoes. Swinging her legs over the edge of the bed, she slowly drew herself upright. No wobbles. No dizziness other than the lightheadedness that comes from an empty stomach. The last thing she remembered consuming was a cup of coffee nearly ten hours earlier. As if on cue, her stomach erupted in loud protest. Tom, Dick and Harry, her tummy acrobats, demanded sustenance. Barefoot, she headed for the kitchen.

* * *

Luke was finishing up the last chapter of *Hooking Mr. Right* when he heard Dr. Chandler enter the kitchen. After hours of silently seething, he was ready for a showdown with her. He grabbed both Dr. Lovejoy books and stormed into the kitchen, gaining a small measure of satisfaction from her startled reaction to his appearance.

"What are you still doing here?" she cried, jumping at the sight of him. "You nearly scared me to death!"

"So, you weren't following me!" he roared. "Maybe you'd care to explain these!" He waved the books in her face. "And the dozens of others lining your bookcase!"

FOUR

Dr. Chandler stared at the volumes Luke waved in front of her nose. A slightly flustered expression crossed her face, confirming his suspicions.

"I don't know what you're talking about," she said, pushing the titles aside.

Luke didn't believe a word of her protest. He opened one of the books and began reading, *"Chapter Two. The Closer the Better. If you want Mr. Right to notice you, you have to place yourself in situations where you will constantly run into each other. Take a position at the same firm or at least in the same office building. Join his health club and show up to exercise when he does—in your sexiest Spandex, of course. And best of all, move as close as possible—even if it means bribing the leasing agent or president of the co-op board.'"*

Her eyes grew wide, and she exploded in laughter. "You are the most egocentric, delusional male I've ever had the misfortune of meeting! Do you really think any woman would go to all that trouble to meet you? Or anyone? Allow me to clue you in on something, Casanova. You're not worth the effort. No man is."

Luke smirked. "Oh, really. Then perhaps you'd care to account for your enormous library with such titles as *A Thousand and One Ways to Get Him to the Altar* and *Make Him Beg for More and More and More*." He tossed the books onto the kitchen counter, spread his legs, crossed his arms over his chest, and waited, daring her to explain away the evidence. "Me thinks the lady doth protest too much."

She shook her head, her eyes now filled with disbelief. "You really do have a habit of jumping to the wrong conclusions, don't you, Mr. Bennett?" She pushed him aside and marched into the living room. He followed, watching as she searched the bookcase, then removed a slim, brown leather-bound volume and threw it at him. "Read it," she said.

Luke stared at the title of the scholarly looking work. "*A Study of the Popularity and Proliferation of Advice, Self-Help and Personal Improvement Books Written by Self-Proclaimed Experts in the Field of Human Relations* by Althea L. Chandler." He glanced over at the other books on the shelf, chagrin replacing triumph. "And those?"

"Research."

"Research," he repeated, grimacing at the sound of the word. "Of course." She was right. He *had* jumped to an erroneous conclusion. Again. Jeez! Hedda and her army of desperate, unattached women had turned him into an irrational, arrogant bastard. And he'd taken all his frustration out on his totally innocent new neighbor. No wonder she considered him a Neanderthal. He'd given her little reason to assume otherwise. Luke shrugged his shoulders and offered her a sheepish grin. "I don't suppose another dozen roses might help?"

Now it was Dr. Chandler's turn to assume a militant pose. She placed her uninjured hand on her hip, raised her chin, and glared at him. "Hardly."

"Two dozen?"

She wasn't amused by his attempt to diffuse the situation with a bit of humor. Her eyes narrowed. Her lips pursed into a thin line. She drew in a sharp breath through her nostrils and exhaled forcibly before she spoke. "The only thing that would help, Mr. Bennett, is for you to leave. I don't *want* you here, and I don't *need* you here. As you can see, I'm perfectly recovered from our earlier encounter."

She walked over to the front door, undid the three deadbolts, and swung the door open. Waving her arm toward the hallway, she addressed him. "*If* you don't mind."

As he walked past her, he decided he liked her a whole lot better when she was sleeping.

He also noticed her eyes for the first time. They were filled with fire and the most incredible shade of deep violet he'd ever seen.

* * *

Thea slammed the door behind him. Too late, she remembered the hour and hoped she hadn't wakened half the building. Her mother would turn over in her grave.

Ladies do not slam doors, Althea.

Thea leaned against the wall and rubbed her temples. She didn't want to think about the past. The memories were too painful, but the more she tried to tamp them back into the recesses of her brain, the more they reared their ugly heads. Conflicting emotions sparred within her. She had loved her mother, and deep down she knew her mother had loved her. But try as she might,

Thea had always fallen short in her mother's eyes.

Camilla Chandler, an anachronous throwback to gentler times, had possessed a catalogue of a thousand-and-one archaic rules for proper ladies. She'd spent half her life trying her damnedest to instill them in her oldest daughter, but no matter how hard Thea worked at pleasing her mother, she never got it right.

Camilla's rules echoed in her head. *Ladies do not raise their voices. Ladies do not make a scene. Ladies do not question their elders. Ladies do not. Ladies do not. Ladies do not.* Thea was guilty of breaking them all.

It didn't matter that she was the responsible daughter who compromised her own professional integrity to save her family when they teetered on the brink of financial ruin. In her mother's eyes she was a failure.

Honestly, Althea, I don't know what I'm to do with you. Why can't you be more like your sister?

Well, maybe she had never mastered *Camilla's Rules for Young Ladies*, but *she* was the daughter who'd committed the ultimate sacrifice to protect her mother and sister. Too bad neither of them would ever know it. Not to mention appreciate it.

She wondered how Camilla, a woman who had lived her life obsessed with making the right impression, would have reacted to Madeline's adultery. Thankfully, Camilla hadn't lived to witness the night before Thea's aborted wedding. If the cancer hadn't killed her mother, the ensuing social scandal certainly would have.

Thea wandered into the kitchen and gathered up the books Luke Bennett had tossed on the counter. *Trulee Lovejoy*. She stared at the two bestsellers, her contract with the devil. Her mother would have been appalled. Talk about things a well-bred lady should not do! Camilla died never knowing how much she owed to Trulee Lovejoy.

Scowling at the books, Thea headed for the living room and shoved them back onto the shelf. Her mother's outdated antebellum sensibilities had cost them nearly all her father's fortune. If Camilla had lived more in the present than the past, Thea never would have had to prostitute herself writing such garbage. As it was, she thanked God that her literary joke struck gold, enabling her to save the house and pay for Camilla's costly medical treatments.

Thea often wondered if she would have compromised herself had Camilla not been diagnosed with cancer or had she known the excruciatingly painful and expensive experimental treatments would neither save nor prolong her mother's life, but the speculation filled her with guilt. She had been the responsible one. Her mother had been ill. Her father's money had disappeared. *Someone* had to do *something*. *She* had to do *something*. Her sister was...Thea frowned...useless in the best of circumstances.

Madeline's genius was her excuse for not sharing any of the burden. After all, both Thea and Madeline had been raised to believe that Madeline couldn't cloud her mind with petty day-to-day details. According to the Canon of Frederick and Camilla Chandler, Madeline's *raison d'être*—twenty-four hours a day, seven days a week, three hundred sixty-five days a year—was to ponder, and eventually unlock, the mysteries of the universe. The minutiae and detritus of daily life were left to lesser life forms—like Thea

So Madeline sat and pondered and thought deep thoughts. And as Thea had recently discovered, occasionally found time to engage in a few less-than-noble endeavors with her research partner, AKA Thea's ex-fiancé Steve.

As much as Thea felt used and unappreciated by her mother and her sister, they were still her family—the only family she had after her father died. She couldn't turn her back on them, especially under such devastating circumstances. After all, she was the dependable one.

Returning to the kitchen, she poked at the discarded, half-empty cartons of cold Chinese takeout littering her kitchen table. Just like a man, she thought, tossing the glutinous leftovers into the trash.

Thea yanked open the refrigerator door and retrieved the pan of double chocolate cherry cream cheese brownies she'd baked the day before. She frowned at the half-empty pan. Not good enough. Not by a long shot. She reached into the freezer for a carton of Chunky Monkey and dumped the nearly full pint on top of the brownies. Climbing back in bed, she proceeded to consume all seven hundred gazillion calories.

The late Camilla Chandler would definitely not have approved.

* * *

As Luke stepped inside his apartment, Cu greeted him with an angry yowl.

"Missed me, did you?" He stooped to lift the cat into his arms. Cu eyed him suspiciously, withholding his usual sandpaper-tongued greeting. "Hey, give me a break, will you? It's been a long day."

The cat hissed once, then sprang from Luke's arms and headed toward the kitchen. Luke followed. He found Cu standing over his empty food dish, his chin raised in an accusing manner.

"Guess I'm in the doghouse with you, too." He reached for a

can of Feline Feast. The cat, a stray of extremely questionable background, was normally a real pussycat. He demanded little besides a constantly filled food dish. However, a lack of Tabby Treats apparently awakened his savage ancestry.

Cu hopped onto the counter, his nose inches from the humming can opener. "Don't get too close," warned Luke. "You might lose a whisker. Or worse."

Taking half a step backwards, Cu lowered his head onto his outstretched paws and continued to monitor Luke's progress. As soon as the flaky fish and chicken medley was scooped into his dish, he attacked it with the relish of a monk coming off a ten-day fast.

Luke shook his head, chuckling as he watched the food disappear. Cu was always good for comic relief. And Lord knew, he could stand a good laugh or two after the day he'd just lived through.

After filling another dish with dry Tabby Treats and refreshing Cu's water bowl, Luke headed for his bedroom. With any luck he might squeeze in a few hours' sleep before morning. He stripped down to his jockey shorts, cracked open the balcony French doors, and tumbled into bed.

Deep violet eyes filled his dreams.

* * *

Grace paced back and forth from one end of her cramped apartment to the other, stepping around and over stacks of submissions she'd printed out and taken home over the past six months but had yet to read. If she didn't prefer reading while soaking in the tub, she'd have far less clutter, but she'd once learned the hard way not to mix her laptop with a bubble bath. So if the next Stephen King or J.K. Rowling lurked within those reams of paper, they'd just have to wait. She had a bigger problem right now.

The Icebergs made it perfectly clear her job security rested on getting Thea to capitulate and out herself as Trulee. As much as Grace understood Thea's need for anonymity, she had her own troubles. And bills. Keeping two kids in college was a constant juggling act. Well-paying editorial jobs weren't exactly a dime a dozen these days. If she lost her job at Wordsmith Press, who knew if she'd find another position?

"Sometimes life as a single parent really sucks," she muttered to the four walls. "Especially when your slime ball ex has a penchant for writing rubber checks." She glared across the room at the overdraft notice sitting atop a stack of unpaid bills. He'd done it to her again. And there wasn't a damn thing she could do about it. According to his voice mail message, the weasel was off sunning himself in Capri with his latest jailbait girlfriend.

Funny how Dick-head always managed to find money for himself but never for his own kids. But wasn't that the reason she'd divorced him in the first place? She and the kids had always placed last on his list of priorities—well after himself, his business, his friends, his mistress *du jour*, his Lamborghini, his Catamaran, and his season tickets to the Yankees. Not necessarily in that order.

Taking him to court proved pointless. Slick Dick always kept one step ahead of her and everyone else. All his toys technically belonged to the corporation owned by his equally sleazy father. As such, his playthings weren't considered assets in the divorce settlement. And although Dick ran the company for Dick-head Senior, he was listed on the books as an employee who received a modest salary.

She had walked away with the apartment and little else other than a small monthly child support check and his written agreement to cover half their daughters' tuition when the time came. His payments, though, were erratic at best and rubber at worst.

Grace had no choice but to convince Thea to change her mind. But how? Thea had nothing to gain by coming forth and everything to lose. If word leaked that Dr. Trulee Lovejoy was actually esteemed sociology professor Dr. Althea Chandler, Thea could kiss her academic career goodbye. It would be like discovering the chair of the English literature department at Harvard secretly wrote category romance. No self-respecting university would look twice at her.

But Grace and Thea had forged a friendship that extended beyond the boundaries of the editor/author relationship. Grace alone was privy to Thea's secret double life and the reason behind it. When circumstances forced Thea to relent and agree to sell the *joke* that had never been meant for publication, the two women entered into a working alliance that became the Chandler family's salvation. Now Grace needed Thea to play savior—or more appropriately, martyr—to save *her* job and *her* ass.

Grace doubted the bonds of friendship stretched that far. After all, if the situation were reversed, she doubted she'd sacrifice her career for a friend. For one of her kids? Of course. She'd lay down her life for her daughters. But give up her career for a friend? Highly unlikely. So she was back to Square One.

She marched down the hall to her bedroom, flopped on the bed, and stared up at the slowly revolving ceiling fan. "Shit! Shit! Shit!" she screamed, pummeling the mattress with her fists. Talk about a no-win situation. She was screwed. Plain and simple. No way would Thea agree to step forth as Trulee. What was the point of even asking?

* * *

Luke woke to find he'd slept well into midmorning. He was shaved, showered, and half-dressed before he realized it was Saturday. He considered going for a run, but Hedda and her minions had pretty much stripped him of that pleasure. Luke ran as much for emotional cleansing as physical exercise, but his last few attempts had resulted in more chaos than peace of mind, requiring the diversionary tactics of a Navy SEAL. Besides, at this late hour, he suspected at least a dozen women were camped out across the street waiting to pounce on him the moment he exited the building.

He nudged the French doors open another several inches and peeked out. One. Two. Three. Four. Five. Six. Only half a dozen females. One pair, a group of three, and a loner lingered outside the stone wall surrounding Central Park. At the moment, all eyes were trained on the building lobby, waiting, no doubt, for the most eligible bachelor in Manhattan to make an appearance.

Luke muttered a few choice expletives before stepping back into the room. He weighed his options—house arrest or running a gauntlet of desperate spinsters. Neither held much appeal. *Damn woman!* He'd like nothing better than to get his hands around Hedda Two's neck. *And* that Dr. True Love or whatever the hell her name was. The last thing he needed was some pseudo-shrink offering a game plan to every unattached female in the city. Why in hell couldn't they all just leave him alone?

"Do I look like some goddamn lottery prize?" he asked Cu. It was then that Luke noticed the cat wasn't stretched out atop his customary perch on the mahogany armoire. And he hadn't kept him company while he shaved, either. "Cu?" Luke poked his head into the bathroom. No cat.

He strode down the hall, checking the rooms on either side before getting to the kitchen. Cu's bowl of Tabby Treats remained untouched from last night. Luke grew worried. Cu always gobbled up his overnight snack before morning.

He began a systematic search. One by one he checked under and behind every piece of furniture, inside each closet and cabinet, repeatedly calling his pet's name. No cat.

He headed back to the bedroom. Cu liked to sun himself on the balcony. Had he slipped out without notice? Luke poked his head around the door and quickly scanned the small landing, hoping none of the women on the street below saw him. They might know which building he lived in, but to his knowledge they were ignorant as to which apartment. He intended to keep it that way.

The balcony contained a large clay pot with a dead hydrangea and one slightly rusty wrought iron porch chair but no cat. Luke was stymied. Cu couldn't have slipped out of the apartment. His front door was bolted from the inside. He was about to close the French doors when he happened to glance to his left.

"Cu!" Luke groaned. How the hell had his cat managed to get onto his neighbor's balcony? And why did it have to be *that* neighbor? Cu, looking for all the world like feline royalty, sat ensconced in the center of a flowery cushioned wicker chair—on Dr. Althea Chandler's balcony! And damn if he didn't look pleased with himself!

Luke gauged the distance between the railings of his balcony and Dr. Chandler's. Not even Evil Kneivel's cat could jump that far. A stringcourse, jutting out no more than four or five inches, ran across the façade of the building where the railing met the wall. The ledge was far too narrow for a person but apparently adequate enough for a curious daredevil cat. "Smart move, Cu," called Luke. "You're really pushing those nine lives of yours. Now get back here."

Cu lifted his head and yawned.

"Damn it, Cu! Don't make me come get you." The cat, ignoring his pleas, stood and stretched. Then settling back down, he began to groom himself.

"This is just terrific," muttered Luke, flailing his arms and glaring at his cat. Still half-dressed for work, he stormed back into the bedroom before any of the Ladies' Surveillance Squad noticed him. The last thing he wanted to do after last night was have another run-in with his new neighbor. *Thanks a lot, Cu!*

Luke postponed the inevitable as long as possible. He first changed into a pair of jeans and a Mets sweatshirt. Then he made himself a cup of coffee, hoping Cu would come to his senses and return while he fortified himself with caffeine. Three cups later Luke's eyeballs were floating, and Cu was still preening on Dr. Chandler's balcony.

Gritting his teeth, he left his apartment and headed down the hall. At Dr. Chandler's door, he paused before knocking, grimacing at the sounds of off-key caterwauling coming from inside the apartment.

* * *

Thea had awakened early. Although her head no longer hurt, her wrist still throbbed. Maybe she shouldn't have removed the support bandage last night before returning to bed, but she wasn't certain which bothered her more—the elasticized fabric or the injury it protected. She had intended to spend the weekend unpacking the remainder of her cartons, but the aftermath of her run-in with Mr. Attack-First-Send-Roses-Later scuttled those plans. After downing a few aspirin, she opted for a leisurely morning of show tunes, a bowl of oatmeal with raisins, and a cup of cappuccino. She was in the middle of helping Mary Martin wash that man out of her hair when the doorbell rang.

She wasn't expecting company. She knew no one in Manhattan except her editor, and Grace wasn't the kind of woman to show up unexpectedly early on a Saturday morning. Besides, the doorman was supposed to announce visitors before allowing anyone entry beyond the lobby.

Thea approached her front door with suspicion. "Who is it?" she asked, peering through the peephole, but the question proved redundant. She could see who it was, and the sight of him did not please her. "What, no roses?" she asked, swinging open the door as he announced himself.

"I've come to collect my cat," he said.

Dumbfounded by his statement, Thea could only stare at her neighbor in bewilderment. *His cat?* She wondered if her ears had suffered some damage from yesterday's concussion. Why would he think she had his cat?

"He's on your balcony," he continued.

"You have a cat?"

He nodded.

"And he's on my balcony?"

Now he stared at her. "Are you all right?"

"Of course, I'm all right. Why wouldn't I be?"

"Because you don't seem to comprehend what I'm saying. Maybe you're having complications from the concussion. Have you experienced any dizziness? Ringing in the ears?"

Great! Now he's reading my mind. Thea cradled her re-bandaged wrist with her good hand and leaned against the door. "He's not some kind of commando attack cat, is he?"

Lucas Bennett eyed her as if she'd suddenly lost her mind. "What?"

"Well, considering his master, I just thought maybe you'd trained him to prey on innocent women."

He exhaled forcibly. "He's as gentle as a lamb."

"Opposites attract, huh?" Thea debated for a moment. "Wait here." She threw him a don't-take-another-step-closer look and headed down the hall.

He followed her anyway.

Thea pulled aside the lace panels covering her French doors and peered out onto the small semi-circular balcony that overlooked Central Park. Sure enough, something that *maybe* resembled a cat sat grooming himself on her wicker settee. The animal's fur, an odd assortment of earth tones and various shades of gray, was short in some spots, long in others. He looked as if a Persian had mated with both a Siamese and a calico, and the resulting genes couldn't make up their minds. "Strangest cat I've ever seen," she muttered. "All he needs is a few body piercings and he'd qualify as a feline Dennis Rodman."

"He's had a hard life."

Thea spun around. "I thought I told you to wait by the door."

Lucas Bennett shrugged. A sheepish grin settled over his face. "He doesn't like strangers."

"Really?" Thea flung open the doors, stepped onto the balcony, and took a seat next to the oblivious animal. The cat lifted his head, studied her for a split second, then climbed into her lap. Thea tossed its master a saccharine-sweet smile. Lucas Bennett glared at his pet, and this time *she* could read *his* thoughts.

"How in the world did he get over here?" she asked, glancing across to his balcony. "Surely, he didn't jump that distance."

"I'm assuming he used that." He pointed to the stringcourse. "Never did it before. I can't imagine what got into him last night. I'm sorry for the inconvenience, Dr. Chandler." He bent down to scoop up his pet, but the cat had other ideas. Scampering off Thea's lap, he darted into the bedroom.

They found him curled up in the center of her bed. The cat, his chin lifted in defiance, studied his master as if daring him to make a move. Lucas Bennett gritted his teeth and muttered something that sounded halfway between a growl and a curse. He leaned over the bed, his arms outstretched to scoop up the wayward animal. The cat had other ideas. He bounded over his master's left arm, jumped onto the floor, darted between his legs, and made a beeline under the bed.

Thea bit down on her lower lip to stifle a laugh. "Doesn't like strangers?" She flung her one good hand onto her hip. "If you ask me, your pet doesn't seem too fond of *you*, Mr. Bennett. Do you mistreat him?"

"Do I look like someone who goes around mistreating animals?"

Thea answered by raising one eyebrow, then glancing down at her sore wrist.

"Damn it! That wasn't deliberate," he said. "I was trying to keep you from falling."

"I wouldn't have lost my balance if you hadn't accosted me in the first place."

"That was a misunderstanding." He combed his fingers through his hair and shook his head. "I tried to explain if you'd only given me a chance. I thought you were one of *them*. I said I was sorry, didn't I?" When she met his question with stony silence, he stormed around to the other side of the bed and lowered himself onto the rug.

One of them? He had used that phrase last night, as well. The man sounded paranoid-delusional. Finally, her curiosity got the better of her. "Them? Who is this *them* you keep referring to?"

He raised his head to answer her. "Hedda Two's Army of the Unattached. Look out your window. Several of her soldiers are down there right now."

Thea stepped back onto the balcony. "How do you know they're waiting for you?" she asked.

"The tall one in the navy power suit jumped into a cab with me two days ago and offered to walk on my back—among other things. And the chubby one with long black hair came up behind me at the bank on Wednesday and made a suggestion that I am certain, Dr. Chandler, would turn you a lovely shade of scarlet." He reached under the bed. "Damn it, Cu! Enough of this. Come out of there."

Thea walked back across the room. Kneeling on the opposite side of the bed, she stuck her head underneath. The cat was in the middle, beyond Luke's reach. Was it her imagination, or did the punk-rock cat look as though he were enjoying the situation? She could swear she saw a Cheshire grin spreading across his face. Thea stretched out her hand to him. "Here, puss. Come on, baby." When he ignored her, she turned her attention to his owner. "You named your cat after a letter of the alphabet?"

"It's his nickname. Two letters—C and U, and I didn't name him. He came named."

"Came? He was a gift?" Thea chuckled. "Someone has an

interesting sense of humor."

"He wasn't a present."

Thea laughed once more. "Must be that magnetic personality of yours." She nodded toward the window. "Attracts all sorts of strays."

"It hasn't worked on you." He inched his way farther under the bed but still couldn't reach the cat.

"Ah," retaliated Thea, ignoring the cut, "but the real question is, did it work on Jennifer?"

"Who?" He jerked his head up, banging it on the bed frame. "Ow!"

"Watch your head," advised Thea. "Jennifer Annenberg. There's a photo of the two of you in *New York Magazine*. I'm sure you've seen it. The one where you're practically drooling on her dress? Don't tell me it isn't framed and hanging in your apartment!"

He dragged himself out from under the bed. Leaning against the wall, his long legs stretched out in front of him, he folded his arms across his chest and roared with laughter. "You're jealous!"

"Hardly," said Thea, standing up on the other side of the room. "As far as I'm concerned, she's welcome to you. I'm not interested in any male attachments, and even if I were, you're definitely not my type."

He looked stung. "You don't like me, do you?"

Thea crossed her arms over her chest. The man was as dense as concrete. "Not particularly. I prefer my men with egos slightly narrower than my door frames."

"Ouch." He grimaced, but his expression was as phony as a three-dollar bill. She could see it in the twinkling mirth of his baby blues. "I'm really not such a bad guy once you get to know me."

"I wasn't planning on getting to know you, Mr. Bennett."

"Good! Have dinner with me, then."

FIVE

"Are you out of your mind?"

Luke found the suggestion quite logical. As a matter of fact, the more he thought about it, the more he saw his new neighbor as the answer to his problem. "Actually, there's a method to my madness, doctor." If Hedda and her horde thought he was involved in a relationship, he'd no longer be considered fair game. Having made her disinterest in him crystal clear, Dr. Chandler was the perfect choice for the deception. Now all he had to do was convince her to go along with his plan.

"You're new to the city, right?"

"What if I am?"

"Any friends here?" Her downturned expression answered the question for him. He pressed on. "And, forgive me, but you don't strike me as the sort of woman who feels comfortable going out to dinner and theater alone."

She scowled at him. "Your point, Mr. Bennett?"

"I have a problem. I'm practically a prisoner in my own

apartment. I'm followed the moment I leave by Dr. Lovejoy-toting crazies. You need an escort. I need someone to help me foil Hedda the Matchmaker. I'm proposing a solution that would aid us both. No strings attached." He studied her as she mulled over his offer.

"But we don't like each other," she said, knowing he'd *really* hate her if he ever discovered the truth about Dr. Trulee Lovejoy.

"I'm willing to call a truce if you are. And throw in a dinner for good measure. Let's see where we go from there."

Thea picked at the edge of her bandage. Finally, she nodded. "All right, Mr. Bennett. We did get off to a poor start, and I'd much prefer a friendly neighbor to a hostile one." She held out her good hand. "I'm willing to give it a try if you are. The truce, that is."

"Luke," he said, taking her hand, "and we'll discuss the rest over dinner."

Thea eyed him skeptically. She was too battle scarred to trust any man, least of all him. Still, she *was* new in town, and she *did* hate going out alone. How he had discerned that bit of information from their brief encounters was something she didn't care to dwell on, though. The thought of being that transparent to anyone—especially a man—didn't sit well with her. However, for the past two weeks she'd suffered cabin fever in a city of nine million people with scores of theaters and museums beckoning.

Damn him! He had read her like a book. Thank goodness it wasn't one she'd written.

"It's only a dinner, doctor."

An evening out sounded tempting. She glanced up at him. Big mistake. Those large crystal blue eyes of his sucked her in like a whirlpool. All at once Tom, Dick, and Harry, her tummy acrobats, took flight, but this time they weren't bouncing on their internal trampoline. They were soaring through the air without a safety net.

Stop it! The last thing in the world she needed was to be swept off her feet by a good-looking Lothario who only wanted to use her. And Luke Bennett *did* intend to use her. His offer was nothing more than a business arrangement. Yet, Thea found herself mesmerized by his translucent azure eyes and slightly knit brow. The boyish way his dark blond hair flopped over his forehead reminded her of a youthful Robert Redford.

Whoosh! Tom took flight, executing a mile-high triple somersault. That did it. Fearing she'd regret her decision, but unable to stop herself, she caved. "Please call me Thea," she said, nodding her acceptance.

He offered her a thousand-watt smile, his brow unknitting. "Thank you, Thea."

Cu pranced out from under the bed and jumped up into Luke's arms. "Oh, so we're pals again, are we?" Cu responded with a tongue-sanding to his chin.

A sparkle of light danced around the cat's neck, catching Thea's attention. Her fingers reached for the heart-shaped gold pendant dangling from his collar. Flipping it over, she read the engraved word. "Cupid?" Thea bit her lower lip to keep from laughing, but the attempt proved futile. *Luke Bennett's cat is named Cupid?* Unable to stop herself, she exploded in a fit of giggles. "You're kidding."

"I told you I didn't name him." A flush of embarrassment worked its way up his neck.

She studied the cat, now the picture of contentment in his master's arms. Cupid stared back at her. In his amber and yellow-flecked eyes she read a myriad of emotions. Mirth. Understanding. And...and challenge? *You're losing it, Althea. He's only a cat.*

But, like some omnipotent seer, the scruffy looking reject continued to focus his attention on her. Then he jutted his chin up in acknowledgement as if he'd read her thoughts.

Forgetting she believed in neither superstitions nor anthropomorphics, Thea shot the cat a silent message. *Don't even think of it!*

Cu responded with a loud purr.

* * *

Shit! Shit! Shit! Madeline stamped her foot and glared at the mail as it slid through the door slot and landed on the floor. With a swift kick, she sent the envelopes sailing across the hardwood, releasing a host of dust bunnies that flew up and attacked her nose. She sneezed. Once. Twice. Three times. Damn dust! She swatted at the motes floating in front of her face. Like she needed something else to deal with! Her eyes teared, and the growing stack of unopened mail she'd consigned to a pile under her mother's neoclassic sideboard blurred.

Another deluge of envelopes fell through the slot. More bills. She didn't have to open them to know. They emitted sinister vibrations like the ominous music that signaled impending doom in a Wes Craven horror flick. And just what was she supposed to do about all these past due notices? Bill had cut off all her credit cards. Her checking account hovered in the very low triple digits until next payday, and even then, it wouldn't grow by much, certainly not enough to sustain her and pay for the upkeep on the house.

Fat tears spilled down her cheeks and plopped onto the floor. Madeline sank to her knees, swiped at her eyes, and sniffed back a sob. She was all alone and didn't know what to do. *Why me?* Hadn't enough gone wrong in her life over the past three weeks? She didn't deserve this. It wasn't supposed to work out this way. Everyone had deserted her. Everyone hated her. Her sister. Her husband.

And then there was Steve. She cringed at the thought of him—and her own stupidity. The coward had seen no reason to stick around and help clean up the fallout, either. He'd also seen no reason to cash in the honeymoon tickets, even though there hadn't been a wedding. Within hours of the elephantine mound of shit hitting the wind tunnel, he secured himself an invite to do a guest lecture at the University of Hawaii. She hadn't heard from him since.

"Take me with you," she had begged.

He shrugged. "Sorry, Madeline. The invitation is only for me."

"I'm your research partner, damn it!"

"But I'm the senior researcher, remember? Besides, I think we need to cool things for a bit if we want Thea and Bill to come to their senses, don't we?"

Madeline stared at him in disbelief. "You honestly expect them to forgive and forget?"

"Thea and Bill are both very charitable people. You'll see. In a few months everything will be back to normal. Thea and I will be married, and you and Bill will be back together. This has all just been a miniscule hiccup in the cosmos of our lives."

"And after they forgive and forget, we take up where we left off?"

He tilted her chin up and kissed her cheek. "Of course, darling."

His words were the shower of ice water she needed to come to

71

her senses. *Bamboozle me once, shame on you; bamboozle me twice, shame on me.* For a genius, she could be pretty damn stupid. Had she ever stopped to think through her harebrained scheme? Of course not. And she had no one to blame but herself.

She never meant it to go as far as it had, but from the very beginning, nothing had worked according to her plan. She quickly found herself wallowing deeper and deeper in her own self-created quagmire of duplicity. The more she struggled to extricate herself, the farther under she sank. Now her sister and her husband had both turned against her. She supposed she deserved it, though. She was such a loser. Some genius! Ha! Look what all that genius had gotten her.

A third pile of mail fell through the slot. "Enough!" She pounded the floor with her fists and kicked her feet, sending up another cloud of dust. "I suppose if I tape the mail slot closed, you'll just deliver the lot by carrier pigeon down the chimney, right?" She waited for a response from the mailman, but either he hadn't heard her shout through the thick oak door, or he chose to ignore the crazy lady rattling around alone in the huge Victorian house on the hill. Jeez! She was turning into a caricature of some goddamn Gothic heroine. All she needed was a chatelaine dangling from her waist.

The thought sobered her. Madeline pulled herself to her feet and turned her back on the mail. She'd go to the lab and lose herself in her work. Maybe when she returned home, Thea and Bill would be back where they belonged, and everything would return to normal. Minus Steve.

But where would she go once Steve returned from Hawaii? The research grant belonged to him. So in essence, the lab belonged to him, too. But forget the lab. Madeline didn't even want to chance running into him on campus, let alone continue working on the same research project with him.

She chuckled past the lump in her throat. Ironic how things worked out. She'd gotten exactly what she'd wanted but at a far steeper price than she ever anticipated having to pay. Her grand plan had backfired and blown up in her face. Thea and Bill were right about her. She was incapable of dealing with anything but the most abstract computations.

Yet, if nothing else, one good thing had come out of the debacle she created. Steve was dead wrong about her sister. Thea would never take him back, and Thea owed her little sister big time for unmasking the weasel. Maybe someday Thea would even thank her for sparing her far greater heartache. But she doubted even Thea was capable of that much forgiveness.

* * *

Dinner! Thea scowled at the outfits lining her closet, Luke's parting words echoing in her brain. *Wear something nice.* That was *after* he'd given her well-worn neon yellow Mickey Mouse warm-ups a disapproving once-over. What had come over her? How could she possibly dress for dinner when she could barely struggle into sweats with one functioning arm? And damn it, whose fault was *that*? She had two working arms before Mr. Jump-to-Conclusions attacked her.

Okay, so he hadn't really attacked her, and maybe if she hadn't been such a klutz, she'd still have the use of both arms. But if Lucas Bennett hadn't jumped to conclusions in the first place, she wouldn't have gotten flustered and lost her balance, and he wouldn't have had to grab for her when she started to fall.

Wear something nice! He made it sound as if she were some hick bumpkin whose wardrobe would send those *What Not to*

Wear hosts into cardiac arrest! Well, she'd show him. *Yeah, right! Get a grip, Althea.* She stared at herself in the full-length closet mirror. Reality stared back at her. Who was she kidding? Every time she slipped into anything that wasn't sensible or practical, she felt like a twelve-year-old playing dress up. Madeline was the Chandler sister with the face and figure for Versace. Thea's body, better suited to an adolescent, screamed Sears Roebuck. Hardware department.

She rifled through the garments. Other than splurging for the trappings of an aborted wedding, Thea hadn't purchased any clothes besides an occasional pair of pantyhose or underwear in nearly five years. And even then, to save money she chose Walmart over Victoria's Secret for anything that remained concealed beneath her dresses and suits. Most of her wardrobe consisted of conservative outfits for teaching and a never-worn ivory crepe de Chine suit she had planned to wear on the way to her honeymoon. She deliberately left her rehearsal dinner outfit and wedding gown behind in San Francisco.

Thea removed the ivory suit from her closet and tossed it onto the bed. If Tom, Dick, and Harry decided to perform one of their gymnastic routines during dinner, the outfit would remind her of what happened the last time she allowed her emotions to control her brain. *Think defective Y chromosomes*, she ordered herself, but the gray matter rebelled and conjured up an image of Luke Bennett's sexy blue eyes, instead.

What the hell is the matter with you, Althea? Was she turning into a masochist? Hadn't she learned her lesson with Steve? She stomped over to her bureau and removed an ivory lace camisole and a pair of pantyhose from the drawer.

Under normal circumstances, Thea could shower and dress in

under twenty minutes. This evening the task took nearly two hours. Forty-five minutes of that devoted to one-handed combat with a battalion of pantyhose. She managed to ruin two pairs before finally succeeding in wriggling a third onto her feet, up her legs, and over her hips without twists, tears, or runs.

She gave up on her hair in under five minutes. No matter how she struggled and contorted, sophisticated twists required two hands. Sighing, she brushed her hair back and held it in place with a mother-of-pearl headband.

She was applying lipstick when the doorbell rang.

"Ready?" asked Luke when she swung open the door.

Thea fought back a grimace. She hadn't expected a my-you-look-ravishing-this-evening, but after the struggle she endured to dress up for him, the least he could do was notice the improvement over Mickey Mouse. Especially since the suit cost nearly as much as one of her monthly installments to the IRS. Instead, Luke focused his attention on the arm she held cradled against her midsection.

He pointed to her wrist. "Aren't you supposed to keep that in a sling?"

"It hurts my neck. Besides, the Dior sling is at the cleaners, and you specifically requested something on the elegant side."

"You have any silk scarves?" he asked, stepping into her apartment and closing the door behind him.

"Yes."

"Go get one."

"Excuse me?"

Luke either didn't hear or chose to ignore the sarcasm in her voice. He merely refined his initial order. "Preferably a large square."

Thea headed for the bedroom, uncertain why she was complying without so much as a peep but doing so just the same. Like Camilla's obedient daughter. But she no longer had to please Camilla, and she sure as hell didn't have to please Luke Bennett.

As Thea rooted through her drawers, anger bubbled in her gut. *O.K., Althea, what would Trulee recommend in such a situation?* Nothing came to mind. Her *expert* persona had deserted her. She found a scarf and returned to the living room with it. Like a good girl.

"Planning on making something disappear?" she asked, tamping down her frustration with a caustic remark.

"Only your discomfort." Luke took the pastel paisley square from her hand. Holding the silk at opposite corners, he flipped the square into a triangle. "Hold your hair back," he said, stepping behind her.

When Thea lifted her hair, he whipped the scarf over her head and under her forearm. "How's that?" he asked, adjusting the knot to sit on her shoulder.

"Fine." More than fine. She couldn't feel the knot, and the silk didn't chafe her neck the way the rough cotton had. "Thank you."

Luke stepped back, studied her, then nodded. "The moment I saw that suit, I knew it needed accessorizing."

All Thea's anger and frustration immediately dissolved into one explosive burst of laughter. *Look who's overreacting now, Althea!* Sometimes, as the great Sigmund Freud had suggested, a cigar is just a cigar. Maybe it was time to jettison some of her West Coast baggage. "And just where did you acquire such fashion know-how?"

"Eagle Scouts. Along with a full knowledge of first-aid and knot tying." He opened her apartment door. "Shall we?"

Thea stepped across the threshold and didn't protest when Luke took the key from her hand and locked her door. The man she had taken an instant dislike to twenty-four hours earlier had just diffused all her anger. Maybe she had misjudged him. Everyone had rotten days, and from what she could gather, Luke had had his share of them lately. As had she. Maybe he wasn't such a jerk after all.

* * *

"A cab please, Melvin," said Luke as they entered the lobby.

"Yes, Mr. Bennett." The doorman's head whipped from side to side, eyeing Luke, then Thea, but he kept his face emotionless. She could only imagine what he must be thinking after yesterday's altercation.

As they stepped outside, Luke hooked his arm around her waist. Thea immediately stiffened. "Mr. Bennett!"

He pulled her closer and whispered in her ear. "I don't mean to be fresh, but you'd be doing me a huge favor if you went along with this."

Luke's lips brushed against the rim of her ear. Thea's knees buckled. Her body melted into his. Tom, daredevil stomach acrobat that he was, shot out of a cannon. He ricocheted around Thea's stomach then lodged in her throat—her extremely dry throat.

"Across the street," whispered Luke.

"Across the street," she repeated, the words not making sense to her.

"They're across the street," he said.

Then she saw them—the same six women he'd pointed out to her that morning. They were *still* loitering on the sidewalk in front of the park, but now Thea was close enough to see their faces, and they were definitely *not* happy campers.

Meanwhile, Luke had buried his face in her hair. His fingers played a concerto up and down her spine. Her legs turned to linguini, a second cannon blast jettisoned Dick, and she fought to swallow the sigh of pleasure threatening to escape from between her lips.

Then the taxi pulled up.

"Thanks," said Luke after they were settled in the back seat of the cab. "Maybe they'll take a hike now."

Thea was too rattled to speak. Heat flushed her neck and cheeks. She knew it had all been an act for Luke, but the emotions he released in her were very real. And that scared the hell out of her. She shifted her weight, placing several extra inches between the two of them. "So," she said, finally finding her voice. "I take it Jennifer's on location?"

"What?" Luke shot her an odd look.

"Well, obviously you wouldn't need me to play-act with you if your new girlfriend were available."

"New girlfriend?" Luke shook his head. "My dear Dr. Chandler, if I had a girlfriend, do you think I'd be in this mess?"

"Oh." Thea looked away in embarrassment. "She turned you down. I didn't know. I'm sorry."

Luke reached for her chin and turned her to face him. "What in God's name are you babbling about?"

"Jennifer Annenberg, of course. The way you were drooling over her in that magazine picture, I just assumed —"

"You just assumed? You, the woman who has accused *me* of jumping to the wrong conclusions, *just assumed?* Ha!" He fell back against the seat, whipped off his glasses, closed his eyes, and massaged the bridge of his nose. "Three weeks ago I was a nobody," he muttered. "And by God, I'd give just about anything to go back to being one."

He repositioned his glasses and turned back to her. "Now, doctor, it's time for a bit of your own medicine. First." He held up one finger and waved it under her nose. "I am *not* dating Jennifer Annenberg or any other celebrity. I never have, and I never intend to. Second." His middle finger joined his extended index finger. "I spent less than twenty seconds in her company that night, and then only because one of my partners, who grew up next door to her father, insisted on introducing me. And finally." His ring finger shot up. "I was *not* drooling over her. I was eyeing the appetizer buffet behind her because I hadn't eaten all day and was starving!"

Thea groaned. Twice in less than ten minutes. Luckily, Luke was unaware of her first transgression. "You're right," she said, forcing the words over the humble pie caught in her throat. "I need to practice what I preach."

"Not a bad idea," said Luke, still glaring at her. Then he softened and smiled that boyish smile of his. His eyes twinkled back to life. "Think we can start over?"

"I'll try if you will." She extended her hand. "Friends?"

"Friends." He clasped her hand between both of his.

Take a break! Thea silently yelled at Tom, Dick, and Harry.

* * *

Luke's choice of restaurant surprised Thea. For someone who claimed to enjoyed anonymity, he'd chosen an establishment with a reputation that extended clear across the continent. Dinner for two at Le Cirque cost as much as a week's worth of groceries for an average family. Thea doubted that many of the women chasing Luke dined at Le Cirque. If they had that kind of money, they wouldn't need to pursue him or any man. The men would be pursuing them. And Luke certainly had no need to impress her. After all, this was hardly a date. Thea shrugged off her questions and perused the menu, determined to enjoy the meal.

"I'd recommend the lobster," suggested Luke.

Lobster? He might not need to impress her, but he obviously had no qualms about spending a king's ransom to feed her. She glanced over the menu. "You've been here before?" Although they lived on Central Park West, their building, last modernized decades ago, was not considered one of the elite addresses on the Upper West Side. Thea could hardly afford elite, not with her financial commitments. She expected anyone who dined often at Le Cirque to reside in a far more prestigious building.

"We often take clients here. Mostly for lunch, though."

"You treat your clients well."

"When someone is entrusting you to invest millions of dollars, you can't exactly take him to the corner hot dog vendor for lunch."

"No, I don't suppose so." She glanced across the table as he studied the wine list, and it occurred to her that she knew next to nothing about Lucas Bennett—other than his bachelor status, which had somehow led to his recent unwelcome celebrity status. "You're an investment banker?" she asked.

"A partner in a brokerage firm."

That explained how he could afford Le Cirque, but what about the apartment? Thea started to ask, but the tight set of Luke's mouth told her any further questions were unwelcome. Instead, she glanced back down at the menu and mumbled, "Lobster sounds fine."

But it wasn't. Although the meat was removed from the shell, Thea had completely forgotten about her sprained wrist. She hadn't needed both hands to eat her escargot appetizer or baby spinach with goat cheese salad. Neither had required a knife. The entree, on the other hand, did. She stared down at the lobster and frowned.

"Is something wrong with your dinner?"

"No, just my brain." Thea sighed. She held up the knife. "I wasn't thinking."

He held out his hand. "Neither was I. Pass your plate. I'll cut it up for you."

"I feel like a two-year-old," she said, complying. A flush of embarrassment crept up her neck and into her cheeks. "I doubt many of Le Cirque's patrons need their dinners cut up for them."

Luke chuckled, but the merriment that had crossed his face quickly dissolved. "Damn!" he said, ducking his head. A scowl, with craters the size of the Grand Canyon, replaced his laugh lines.

"What's wrong?"

"That woman is here, and she's heading this way."

SIX

"That woman?" Thea glanced over her shoulder in the direction of Luke's glare. An outrageously overdressed Amazon, complete with feathered turban and fox stole—head attached—zigzagged her way toward their table. Waving an opera-length gloved arm in their direction, she periodically stopped to plant a kiss on someone's cheek or toss off a few *bon mots*. Everyone seemed to know her, and everyone seemed to covet her attention. Except Luke. Although he had plastered a sickly smile across his face, he looked as though he'd like to crawl under the table and dig a hole to China.

"Who is she?" asked Thea, mesmerized by the Auntie Mame character playing to the audience of diners.

But before Luke could answer, the woman was upon them. "Luke, darling! How nice to see you!" She pulled out a chair and joined them at the table. Leaning in Luke's direction, she tapped her cheek with a ring-clad index finger. Much to Thea's amusement, Luke obliged with a quick peck. "You naughty boy," she continued. "Where have you been hiding?"

"Hiding? There's nowhere to hide in this city. Not when you have half the female population stalking me, Hedda." He finished cutting Thea's lobster into bite-sized pieces and passed the plate back to her.

Hedda? So this was the infamous reporter Luke claimed had turned his life upside-down. Thea had expected...well, she wasn't really certain what she had expected, but definitely not a seventy-something overbearing caricature of a nineteen-thirties era *grande dame.*

The woman laughed boisterously. The fox bounced up and down against her shoulder. "Admit it, darling. You're loving every minute of it!"

Luke offered her a less than sincere smile. "Loved, Hedda. Past tense." He gestured toward Thea. "As you can see, I am no longer in need of your unsolicited services."

Hedda now turned her attention toward Thea, and it was Thea's turn to cringe. "Congratulations, my dear!" She motioned to the plate Luke had handed back to her. "You're a quick study. I see you already have him well-trained." Then she glanced at Thea's silk sling, and her eyes grew wide with curiosity. "However did you injure your arm? Or is it really injured?" she added in a stage whisper, accentuating the question with a conspiratorial wink.

Trained? Thea glanced over at Luke, but instead of bailing her from Hedda's inquisition, he remained silent, his expression shuttered. What had he gotten her into? "Why would I fake an injury?" she asked, turning back to Hedda.

"Chapter Ten," said Hedda, whipping an all-too-familiar looking book from her voluminous handbag and proceeding to flip rapidly through several dozen well-worn pages. "'*Now That*

He's Hooked, Train Him to Treat You Like the Princess You Are.'"
She eyed Thea skeptically. "You *have* read *Hooking Mr. Right*,
haven't you, my dear?"

Read it? She wrote it! Every single stupid word on all two
hundred and fifty-seven pages. But neither Hedda nor Luke knew
that, and Thea intended to keep it that way. She hesitated, her
words tripping over themselves. "I...um...that is...uh —"

"Oh, my dear, Trulee's books are a must for every woman. You
simply *have* to have a copy. Here." She shoved the book into
Thea's hand. "It's even autographed. See?" She grabbed the book
back and flipped it open to the inside cover. "'*To Hedda, my dear
friend and sister in romance. With love from Dr. Love, Trulee.*'" She
handed the book back to Thea and held up two fingers, side-by-
side. "We're this close," she bragged. "She's like a daughter to me."

What! Thea nearly fell off her chair. *I've never met you in my
life, lady!*

"That explains a lot," muttered Luke.

Thea felt Tom, standing atop a galloping stallion, wobble
unsteadily. She offered the book back to Hedda along with a smile
of regret, while fighting to keep a civil tongue in her mouth.
"Thank you, but I can't accept this, Miss Hopper. It has too much
personal sentiment attached to it. I'm sure I can find a copy at the
bookstore."

"Nonsense!" Hedda waved the book away. "You need it, and I
can always get another."

"She most definitely does *not* need it," said Luke, finally
coming to Thea's aid, but his voice sounded tight and controlled.
Too controlled.

Hedda's face brightened. "Oh? Then this is it? Our grand prize
winner?" She turned to Thea, patting her on the hand.

"Congratulations, my dear. You *are* a fast worker." Hedda then proceeded to root around in her purse, finally retrieving a pen and notebook. "What did you say your name was?"

"She didn't," said Luke.

Hedda swung her attention back to Luke. Shaking her head, she reprimanded him with a tsking noise. "You are being rather truculent this evening, Lucas. How can I tell my readers your fiancée's name, when I don't know it myself?" She returned to Thea, waiting for a response. "And I want to know about your arm, too," she added.

Luke answered for her. "Just tell them the hunt is over. She injured her arm wrestling me to the ground."

Hedda shook her head. "Now, Luke. Sarcasm? From you? Besides, I don't see a ring." She addressed Thea once more. "Chapter Twelve. *Engagement Rings, the Bigger the Better*. Or was it Chapter Nine?" She tapped her pen against her lower lip and stared up at the ceiling as if expecting the answer to be written above her. Then she waved the pen in the air. "Whatever." She tapped the book, still sitting between them on the table. "Just look it up."

"I'll do that," said Thea.

Luke shot her a glare punctuated by a snort.

"And keep in mind," continued Hedda. "You can't collect your prize until you get him to the altar. And of course, I get a wedding exclusive for my paper."

"Prize?" Thea felt as though she had stepped into the middle of an alternate universe. What was this woman babbling about? She glanced from Hedda to Luke. The poor man looked ready to explode. Or commit murder. But he obviously understood Hedda's reference.

"The all-expense paid week at Le Spa, of course," said Hedda. "To the lucky woman who lands New York's most eligible bachelor. Don't you read my column?"

"I'm afraid not," said Thea.

Hedda's voice, a mixture of indignation and bafflement, climbed three octaves. "But that's not possible! *Everyone* reads my column!"

"Apparently not," said Luke, his body relaxing, the hint of a smile spreading across his face. "Which is one of the reasons I fell in love with her."

Fell in love with her! That wasn't part of their agreement. Thea was beginning to suspect she'd sold her soul to the devil for an expensive dinner—a dinner which was growing colder by the minute.

As if reading her thoughts, Luke pointed to his plate. "If you'll excuse us, Hedda?"

"Of course." Hedda glanced at her copy of *Hooking Mr. Right*. After a brief hesitation, she picked up the book and rose, her expression a study in bewilderment, as if her entire world had just collapsed around her. The idea that someone in New York didn't hang on her every word seemed inconceivable to the gossip columnist. Thea almost felt sorry for her.

"Well, that went better than I could have hoped," said Luke, stabbing a piece of lobster meat onto his fork. He dipped it in a pool of clarified butter and plopped the morsel into his mouth.

Suddenly, everything made perfect sense to Thea. Her devious next-door neighbor had set her up. What an actor! He *knew* Hedda would be at Le Cirque this evening. Once again, she'd allowed herself to be used. *Idiot!* What had she expected? Hadn't he come right out and said he wanted her to help him fool Hedda?

And hadn't she agreed? Thea pushed the food around on her plate. She no longer had any appetite for the pricey meal. Or Luke Bennett. If she'd realized what he was getting her into, she never would have agreed to his little game of Fool the Gossip Columnist. Fresh from a two-timing fiancé and a broken heart, she didn't need a fake engagement pouring salt in her still festering wounds.

Tom lost his footing, slipped from his perch, and was trampled by the stallion.

* * *

"I suppose I'll need to get you a ring now," said Luke, unlocking Thea's door for her. The corners of his mouth dipped into a scowl.

She stepped inside, barring him entrance. "I hardly think that's necessary," she said.

"Of course, it's necessary. Now that Hedda thinks we're engaged, she'll get suspicious if you're not wearing an engagement ring the next time she runs into us."

"There isn't going to be a next time, Mr. Bennett," she said, attempting to close the door on him.

Luke grabbed hold of the door and stepped inside the apartment. "Mr. Bennett? What's gotten into you? We had an agreement. You can't back out now!"

Thea shook with indignation. "You never said I'd have to pretend to be your fiancée! You set me up tonight!" She had kept her resentment in check through the remainder of the dinner, not wanting to cause a scene, but all the anger that had built inside her from the moment Hedda left their table now threatened to explode in one huge sob of humiliation.

For some reason she couldn't fathom, she felt nearly as betrayed as when she'd stumbled upon Madeline and Steve. Maybe it was the word *fiancée* that had triggered the volatile emotions. Maybe it was when Luke so blithely lied about falling in love with her. She didn't know, and she didn't care. Thea closed her eyes and took a deep breath, trying to hold on to her last vestige of control.

"How else did you expect me to get Hedda off my back?" he asked. "Did you honestly think she'd call off her army just seeing us having a casual dinner together? For God's sake, Thea, you could have been a client for all she knew!" He raked his hands through his hair and sighed in exasperation. "I'm sorry. I thought you understood."

"Apparently not, but that's your fault, not mine. You should have been more specific."

Luke's jaw dropped. "Does this mean you're refusing to go out with me again?"

She nodded. "I can't pretend to be someone I'm not." *I already spend too much of my life doing that.*

"You can't do this to me!" he cried. "We had an agreement."

To him? He sounded as selfish as Madeline. Did all of humanity think Thea's sole purpose on Planet Earth was to make everyone else's life easier? What about her life? Her needs? When was someone going to consider her feelings? "I think you'd better leave," she said, opening the door.

"This is just great," muttered Luke. "Thanks for nothing." He spun around and stormed down the hall.

Thea slammed her apartment door, then marched down the hallway to her bedroom, fighting back the tears that stung at her eyes. She struggled out of her clothes, ripping the third pair of pantyhose that evening. Staring at the shredded nylons, she finally allowed the tears to fall.

She couldn't imagine why an egotist of a man she'd met little more than twenty-four hours ago could make her feel so miserable. It made no sense. Maybe her turbulent emotions were a delayed reaction over her San Francisco nightmare. Maybe she was transferring her feelings of anger over Steve's betrayal to Luke. Maybe it was only PMS. All she knew for certain was she felt miserable.

A scratching sound drew Thea's attention away from her anguish and to the French doors. "Not you again," she said, pulling aside the lace curtains to find Luke's sorry excuse for a cat pressing his nose up against the glass.

Thea opened one of the doors. Cupid entered as if he owned the place. He sidled up to Thea, rubbing his coat against her bare legs. "I suppose he sent you," she said, stooping to lift the cat with her good arm. Cupid responded by licking the salty tears from her cheeks.

A moment later she heard pounding at her front door. "Just as I thought," she said to the cat. "You're an accomplice." She placed Cupid on her bed and slipped on her robe. Still barefoot, she scooped up the cat, draped him over her shoulder, and headed down the hall.

"I suppose you've come for this," she said, swinging the door open and shoving Cupid at Luke. "Pretty cheap trick getting your cat to do your dirty work."

Luke looked at her as though she were stupid. Or crazy. "You obviously don't know the first thing about cats, doctor. You can't train them like dogs." He exhaled, emitting a sound that was half snort and half growl. "Besides, he was already on your balcony when I got home."

"Then I suggest you keep your French doors closed."

"I like fresh air!"

"This is New York City, Mr. Bennett. There is no *fresh* air!" Thea slammed the door in his face and started crying all over again.

She cried late into the night, periodically falling into a restless sleep that found her back on that fateful night before her wedding. Everything had appeared so perfect. Too perfect. And she'd been too naïve and too stupid to see through that false guise of perfection.

* * *

Thea surveyed the dining room, the table set with her late mother's best silver and Rosenthal china, the catering staff waiting in the wings to serve the rehearsal dinner, but Thea sensed that something very important was missing. Then it hit her. The groom. She hadn't seen Steve since they returned from church nearly an hour earlier.

A white-gloved waiter carrying an empty hors d'oeuvre tray passed her on his way to the kitchen. A moment later the caterer appeared at Thea's side. "If you're ready, Dr. Chandler, we can begin serving dinner."

"Five minutes." She offered the woman an apologetic smile before heading for the living room. Knowing Steve, he was off in some corner deconstructing the theory of relativity with one of his ushers, all members of his astrophysics team. Hopefully, she'd find him before they whipped out their laptops and rolled up their sleeves.

Thea made a mental note to hide Steve's computer before tomorrow's ceremony. She chuckled, imagining the write-up on the society page of the San Francisco Examiner. "The wedding of Berkeley Professor Althea L. Chandler to Dr. Steven J. Ross was postponed for several days while the groom solved an equation that revealed the secrets of the universe."

Entering the living room, Thea craned her neck, nervously

searching the crowded room before settling her attention on her sister's husband. "Bill, have you seen Steve? Dinner's ready, and I can't find him."

"I saw him out by the pool a few minutes ago." He nodded in the direction of the French doors that led to the patio. "With Madeline."

"Oh, great!" Thea flapped her arms in frustration. "If they've gotten into another one of their metaphysical debates, we'll all starve to death."

"We could sit down without them."

Thea offered her brother-in-law her best withering look. "You don't think the rest of the guests would find it a bit odd that the groom and matron-of-honor were missing from the rehearsal dinner?"

Bill shrugged. "Give up, Thea. Half the time they're not here when they are here. You and I will never be able to compete with sub-atomic particles. Sometimes I wonder why the two of them bother with us."

"Because they love us." She tucked an errant piece of hair from her French twist behind her ear as she left Bill and wove her way through a roomful of guests.

Standing at the edge of the top tier of the multi-level patio, Thea scanned the pool area. Someone had flipped on the outdoor sound system. Chopin fluttered on the gentle breeze. Festive white lights danced across the surface of the calm water. There was no sign of either Steve or Madeline.

Thea glanced up at the sky. The night was perfect as only a San Francisco night could be. A full moon held court over a myriad of stars. Off in the distance the Golden Gate created the perfect backdrop. Softened to an impressionistic blur by the ever-present, low-lying night fog, the bridge and its surroundings looked like a

Monet painting.

Heading down the stairs and around the pool, Thea smiled. She loved this house. This view. The sacrifice she'd made to keep her family home was worth everything it cost her. Tomorrow, after the sun had burned through the fog, she'd stand at the other end of the garden in the orchid-decorated gazebo and share an arms-entwined champagne toast with the man she loved.

The man whose deep baritone voice she now heard as she passed the cabana.

Thea swung open the door. "Hey, you two, dinner's..."

* * *

Thea woke with a start, her heart pounding, her limbs trembling, her eyes encrusted with dried tears. She squeezed her eyelids shut, trying to force away the horrid sight of her naked sister lounging like a diva on the cabana chaise. And Steve, equally bare, looking like a little boy caught with his pants down. Correction. Not down—off and lying in a heap on the floor. She remembered how a quickly withering part of his anatomy had pointed toward them.

The nightmarish image fresh in her mind, Thea began sobbing all over again until she cried herself back to sleep, only to awaken once again, when she opened the cabana door.

* * *

The next morning the cat was back on her balcony.

* * *

Luke was beside himself. He'd heard her crying most of the night. The sobs tugged at him, and it was all he could do to keep himself from returning to her apartment door. But he knew that would only make the situation worse. If Althea Chandler realized that the wall separating their headboards wasn't the least bit soundproof, she'd most likely die of embarrassment.

For the life of him he failed to understand how he could possibly be the cause of such heartache. They barely knew one another. Besides, he'd been up front with her from the start. Maybe she was unstable. Or maybe, as Julie had accused, he was extremely dense when it came to women. Thanks to his ex-wife, he certainly had a track record to prove that particular hypothesis.

To make matters worse, he again had to retrieve his traitorous cat. For the third time! After all Luke had done to rescue and nurse Cu back to life, this was the thanks he got! He stood on his balcony clenching a cup of coffee between his hands and glared over at Benedict Arnold. *Ingrate!* Cu hissed at him, then went back to grooming his private parts. "Real gentlemanly behavior, Cu. Wait 'til the vice squad hears about this."

He glanced at the empty sidewalk across the street. Maybe the estrogen brigade had gotten the message after seeing him with Thea last night. Surely the lack of desperate women who'd made a habit of gathering at the park wall had nothing to do with Hedda. He knew her Sunday column had been written and printed well before last night's dinner. The news of his *capture* wouldn't appear until the Monday morning edition of *The Daily Post*.

Unfortunately, Luke knew his reprieve would be short-lived. Once Hedda discovered he really wasn't engaged, she'd probably notify every major network, and the bounty hunters would be back, hungry as ever. Unless he could convince his unhappy neighbor to sign back on.

Cu hopped off the chair. Luke saw Thea's balcony door swing open. He ducked back into his bedroom, not wanting her to see him. She already suspected him of employing forced cat labor. He saw no point in adding fuel to her suspicions. "You might as well come in," he heard her tell Cu.

Luke gritted his teeth and marched down the hall, uncertain what to expect, but knowing he had to retrieve his errant pet. He didn't need any more problems with his new neighbor. He paused outside her door, listening to the music coming from within. Once again, a familiar Broadway piece was being butchered by an off-key vocal accompaniment. Poor Dr. Chandler couldn't carry a tune to save her life.

A germ of an idea began percolating within Luke. He knocked.

Thea immediately opened the door. Without a word she thrust Cu into his arms and started to slam the door in his face. Luke was ready for her. "Wait, please!" He forced his foot over the threshold to keep the door open. "I owe you an apology."

Thea hesitated. The corners of her mouth were pulled taut, her posture tense, but her eyes were red-rimmed, evidence of her teary night. Before she could speak, the phone rang. She ignored it.

"Aren't you going to answer that?" asked Luke when she continued to stand at the door, staring at him. The phone rang a second time, then a third.

Thea shook her head.

The answering machine clicked on. "You have reached the phone of Dr. Althea Chandler. I am unable to take your call at the present time. Please leave a message at the sound of the tone, and I will return your call as soon as possible. Thank you."

There was a short, high-pitched beep followed by a loud sigh. Then a male voice spoke her name. "Althea?"

SEVEN

Thea froze. Color rushed to her cheeks, and she squeezed her eyes shut, but she seemed incapable of moving. "Darling, please pick up the phone. How many times do I have to call and leave the same message? We have to talk about what happened. This isn't like you, running off the way you did, acting so stubborn. It's childish and beneath you."

He sighed a second time, the sound louder and more frustrated. "I've said I'm sorry. We both have. Madeline is beside herself. You and Bill are overreacting. It meant nothing, darling. Really. You have to believe me. It was just something that got out of hand. You know, the heat of the moment. Pre-wedding jitters, that's all. Or maybe it was something Madeline and I had to get out of our systems. But it's over, Thea. I promise, it will never happen again. I want you to come back. We both do. We need to put this little misunderstanding behind us and get on with our lives. Please, Thea?"

After a third sigh that smacked of annoyance, the caller hung up. The machine clicked off. Thea stood ramrod straight, her fists balled, her eyes still closed. Her lower lip trembled slightly, and Luke knew she was trying to keep from crying in front of him.

So this bastard was the cause of last night's crying jag, not him. Relief washed over Luke. He was surprised she hadn't rushed over to the machine and turned it off as soon as she recognized the caller. His message wasn't meant for a stranger's ears, but Thea hadn't moved. Whatever had happened between them, the mere sound of his voice had apparently paralyzed her beyond reason. Luke reached out and gently wrapped his fingers around her upper arm. "What did he do to you?" he whispered.

Her eyes flew open. She stared at him as if surprised by his presence.

"You look like you could really use a friend right now."

She closed her eyes once more and slumped against the wall. "Do you have any idea what it's like to have someone you love stab you in the back?" she whispered.

As a matter of fact, he did. And he knew what it felt like to have your world come crashing down around you because of it. He closed the door, led her into the living room, and sat her down on the couch.

Cu jumped out of his arms and settled on her lap. She began stroking his fur. "I'm sorry," she said, not looking up at him. "I didn't mean to fall apart like that. I'm fine now. Thank you."

She wasn't fine, though. She was in a state of emotional shock. In the background the singer on the CD launched into a vindictive tirade.

I hate men.

I can't abide 'em even now and then....

Luke chuckled at the timing. Thea raised her head and offered him a tentative smile, but she looked lost and vulnerable. Too vulnerable. Luke's heart, the one he thought no longer had room for women in general and any woman in particular, went out to her. He knew the pain she felt. All too well. He'd been there. "Why don't I fix you a cup of tea?" he offered.

She didn't protest.

He left her with Cu, returning a short time later with two steaming mugs. Handing one to her, he settled himself in one of the chairs on the other side of the coffee table and waited for her to speak.

Thea took a sip of the tea, sighed once, then spoke into the cup. "That was my ex-fiancé on the phone. Three weeks ago, the night before our wedding, I discovered him and my sister in...in...." She paused.

Luke finished the sentence for her in as delicate a manner as he could. "A compromising position?"

She nodded.

"Do you still love him?"

Her head shot up. Angry violet flames flickered in her eyes. She tightened her grip on the mug, her knuckles growing white. "I stumbled upon them during the rehearsal dinner. Twenty people witnessed my humiliation, and he has the unmitigated gall to call it a misunderstanding! Could you forgive and forget such a betrayal?"

Luke cursed under his breath. At least Julie left him a note on the refrigerator. She hadn't taken out an ad in *The Times*. "No," he answered her, staring into his own cup. "I know for a fact I couldn't."

Her expression changed to one of question. Luke knew from experience that more than anything, right now Althea Chandler needed a kindred spirit, someone who had lived through the pain eating away at her. "My ex-wife did something similar. Only not as public."

She lowered her gaze once more, her words now nearly a whisper. "So Hedda's bound and determined to get you back up on the horse?"

Luke nodded. "But like you, I'm not interested in getting burned again." He allowed his words to sink in, then added, "And don't think for a moment that the infamous Hedda Two has orchestrated her little campaign out of the goodness of her romantic heart. This is all about money."

Thea's head sprang up. "Money?"

"Money. Nothing else. *The Daily Post* is on the verge of bankruptcy. The paper's columnists are resorting to any methods they can to increase circulation. Their jobs are on the line."

"I'm sorry I overreacted."

Luke dismissed her apology with a wave of his hand. "It was my fault. Had I known what you were going through, I never would have suggested the ruse."

Thea smiled, this time a little deeper. "Hello, Mr. Bennett. Nice to meet you, and by the way I recently discovered my fiancé is sleeping with my sister."

"Luke," he reminded her, but he was glad she was able to make a small joke. The singer on the CD had long since finished her anti-male tirade and moved on to a love song.

"You like Broadway musicals?" he asked.

Thea nodded.

"When my wife left, my partners made it their business to keep me from falling into an abyss of self-pity."

"Did it work?"

Luke shrugged. "Not really." Thea's expression went from hopeful to crestfallen. "But Sean and Jerome aren't the most creative guys in the world. After all, they're stockbrokers."

"So are you," Thea reminded him.

"But a highly creative one who happens to know how to get his hands on two tickets to the three o'clock matinee of the hottest show in town."

Thea immediately perked up. "The new Sondheim?"

"Interested?"

"But I heard it's sold out for the next six months."

Luke rose. "I'll pick you up at two. Let's go, Cu." The cat jumped off Thea's lap and followed him back to his apartment.

Now all he had to do was kill someone for two tickets to a sold-out show.

* * *

Luke felt extremely pleased with himself. After a grueling two hours on the phone, calling in favors, he secured two orchestra seats to that afternoon's performance. It cost him five times the normal box office rate, but if it meant Dr. Chandler would continue with their charade, it was well worth it. Of course, she'd made no such promise, but he was hoping his efforts would pay off, and he could ease her back into the subterfuge.

"Enjoying the show?" he asked during intermission. Dumb question. She positively glowed.

"Yes. Very much. Thank you."

He pressed his campaign ever so slightly, knowing she couldn't possibly turn him down after the gift he'd given her. "Would you accuse me of ulterior motives if I offered to buy you dinner tonight?"

The corners of her mouth turned up into a soft smile. "With

or without Hedda?"

"Touché." Luke chuckled. "How about if you pick the restaurant? If she happens to show up, it will be your fault, not mine."

* * *

Thea picked a deli on Seventh Avenue known for its enormous sandwiches and lack of upscale atmosphere.

"I would have sprung for Sardi's or The Four Seasons," he said, biting into his corned beef special, then washing it down with a long draught of icy beer.

She shrugged. "Those tickets must have cost you a fortune. Not to mention last night's dinner. Besides." She quickly perused the room. "I doubt this is one of Hedda's haunts. The only celebrities here are framed and hanging on the walls. Not much in the way of dirt for a gossip columnist to dig up."

Luke loved a good deli sandwich, but he rarely got the chance to indulge in one. Power lunches and cold cuts didn't mix, and Julie had turned her nose up at such establishments, labeling the food unfit for human consumption. He shook his head and exploded in a hearty laugh.

Thea eyed him suspiciously. "What's so funny?"

"Not funny. Refreshing. Amazingly refreshing."

Her expression shifted to one of confusion. "I don't understand."

"Half the unattached women in this city are chasing me, hoping I'll become Prince Charming to their Cinderella, and here you sit concerned about the cost of a dinner I'm treating you to!"

She shrugged again. "I'm not chasing you. Besides, I don't see the connection."

Of course, she wouldn't see the connection. Althea Chandler

was unlike any woman he'd ever known. In the short time since meeting her, he'd come to discover she was both thoughtful and honest to a fault. Unlike other women, he suspected she possessed not a deceitful bone in her body. "I suppose it's just nice to be around someone who isn't harboring any ulterior motives. I haven't come across that very often in the women I've known."

Her face grew somber, and she toyed with her food, pushing the coleslaw around her plate with her fork. "Maybe you've known the wrong women."

He couldn't disagree. "Sometimes we have no choice."

* * *

Like Superman hiding behind the guise of Clark Kent or Batman masquerading as Bruce Wayne, Thea hid her alter ego from the world. Her contract with her publisher stipulated no personal publicity—no book signings, no talk shows, no photos. Self-exploitation was bad enough. She tried to keep her conscience as clear as possible, continually reminding herself of the reason behind the deception.

Now that she had severed herself from the burden of maintaining the family house in San Francisco, she could finally glimpse an end to the duplicitous life she'd led the past several years. Even with the expense of the New York apartment, she expected her next book to earn enough to obliterate the remainder of her mother's debts. Her ultimate goal, returning to scholarly pursuits without anyone being the wiser, now seemed within reach.

And yet, for some reason, that thought didn't trigger the rush of relief she expected it to. She had no idea why, but discomfort washed over her each time she looked toward the future. She hated being Trulee. Hated the sham. Why did the thought of returning to her old life produce such ambivalent feelings?

As she and Luke strolled back uptown after leaving the deli, her internal turmoil fused with Luke's praise—praise she didn't deserve—and churned into an acid mix that burned her with shame. *I suppose it's just nice to be around someone who isn't harboring any ulterior motives.* Not harboring ulterior motives? If he only knew. Dr. Althea Chandler held the title of Queen of the Ulterior Motive!

And then there was the second title, equally shameful, which now blazed in foot-high neon pink letters before them for all the world to see.

Luke had suggested a leisurely walk rather than returning directly to their apartment building, and she hadn't paid attention to the direction he'd taken. If she had, she would have steered them away from this particular corner. Now it was too late.

He'd stopped in front of the Barnes & Noble window display. His hands clenched at his sides, his body rigid, he glared at the huge sign hanging above the pyramid of heart-embellished books. *Hooking Mr. Right by Dr. Trulee Lovejoy, Queen of Romantic Advice.* "There should be a law against women like her," he muttered.

Thea shuddered. *Don't panic,* she ordered herself, cradling her injured arm. *He has no way of knowing the truth.* She choked back a lump of anxiety and forced a normal inflection into her voice. "Some countries have such laws," she said, "but putting aside the First Amendment for a moment, why the hostility toward this one author?"

He flailed his arms, gesturing wildly in a manner she'd come to recognize as his frustration mode. He stared at her as though she'd recently arrived from another planet, not another city. "She's destroying my life," he nearly screamed, catching the momentary attention of several passersby.

Thea studied the angry man at her side. He wore mirrored aviator glasses that hid his eyes. A baseball cap, its brim pulled forward, shadowed his face. No one had recognized him at the theater or the deli. She was beginning to wonder how much Hedda's columns had actually affected his life and how much was Luke's own paranoia. Granted, she'd seen the women staked out across the street from their apartment building, but she'd counted only a handful, not a horde.

"If you're referring to the swarms of women out to snare you, I thought Hedda was responsible for that. Where does Dr. Lovejoy fit in?"

"Isn't it obvious? Hedda recommended that damn book as a way to snare me. Last night she practically admitted the two of them are in cahoots. I'll bet Hedda's getting a hefty endorsement fee from the publisher to shill that drivel for them." He pointed at the window. "There, look! Two more recruits!"

Thea watched as a couple of young women lifted books off the pile, thumbed through a few pages, then tucked the copies under their arms and headed for the cash register.

"The book is titled *Hooking Mr. Right*, not *Hooking Mr. Bennett*. You may find this hard to believe, Luke, but you aren't the only eligible bachelor in Manhattan, let alone every woman's dream catch."

Luke snorted. "It doesn't matter. That woman is single-handedly setting feminism back two centuries. She should have her license revoked."

Ms. magazine had used the exact same words in a blistering editorial attack on Trulee. Of all the negative comments made about her books, this one stung the most. Inside Thea shrieked her apology—to *Ms.* and the world. *I didn't mean to! It was a joke!* A joke she'd cash in on to bail out her mother.

But the joke was on her. Instead of taking her first *advice* book as the tongue-in-cheek parody she'd written, the public fell for her phony advice to the lovelorn—hook, line, and proverbial sinker.

Initially, Thea had written the first book and sent it off to a publisher to prove her thesis—that anyone could call herself an *expert* and get published in the field. The book was pure spoof. At least she thought so. Then the double-whammy family crisis had hit.

Several days later, Grace called with a contract offer. The offer stood even after Thea came clean and admitted the book was a satire and her reason for writing it. Grace didn't mind. After that conversation Thea signed the contract, expecting the publisher to merchandize *Finding Mr. Right* as a lampooning of the genre. Much to her chagrin, the marketing executives decided otherwise, and that decision sealed her fate as the reluctant love expert.

Now along with all her other baggage, Thea dealt with the guilt of the joke no one else got, and she found herself in the damning position of defending the phony words of a phony woman. She stared at Luke's reflection in the window. "Just because you don't agree with her advice —"

"You're not condoning this garbage, are you?" He paused for a moment, scowling at her. "Exactly what did you write in your dissertation?"

Thea looked away, softly speaking to the plate glass window instead of him. "I set out to prove that most of the advice books on the market today are written by self-proclaimed authorities with little or no education in their field, then show how the books affect society."

"And did you?"

Did she ever! Thea hesitated for a moment before answering, still not looking directly at Luke. "We live in a society of instant gratification. The public is more than willing to plop down twenty-four ninety-five for an immediate solution to their problems, whether it's excessive weight, a bad marriage, out-of-control teenagers, or..." She paused, glancing at him over her shoulder, "...loneliness."

"Problems like that don't happen overnight," said Luke. "They develop over time. And they rarely get solved by reading one book. Any sensible person knows that."

"True." Thea finally worked up the courage to face him. "But desperate people often lack common sense and become a marketer's dream. The writers of these books capitalize on that. Most people can afford a few dollars for a book but not the hundreds or even thousands of dollars that a good therapist charges. They see that a doctor has authored a book offering a quick solution to their problem, and they grab it like a lifeline."

"So, you're telling me these books are all written by frauds?"

She shrugged. "Not all. There are a percentage of books written by well-qualified experts, but too many are written by authors with dubious credentials, and the unsuspecting public has no way of differentiating between the true authorities and the charlatans."

"There are laws to protect the public against things like that. A person can't practice medicine without a license."

"They're not prescribing drugs, only offering theories and advice," she explained, fearing she sounded apologetic. "*Their* theories. *Their* advice. For the most part those who claim to be doctors, are doctors—only not necessarily in the fields of medicine or the social sciences."

"What do you mean?"

She sighed. "I'll give you an example. Have you ever heard of Dr. Michael Resnikoff?"

"I've seen him on TV. He writes parenting books, doesn't he?"

"Yes, but he's neither a psychologist nor a pediatrician, although most people believe he is."

"Are you saying he's not a doctor?"

"Oh, he's a doctor, all right. He holds a doctorate in art history from a small college in upstate Minnesota."

"What a fraud! Someone should stop him. He's duping the public."

"And that isn't?" Thea pointed to a perfume advertisement on the side of a bus shelter. "If I wear that perfume will a hunk on a white steed sweep me off my feet? The model on that poster says so."

"But that's just Madison Avenue hype. You can't compare the two."

"Can't I? Both the ad and the book are peddling improved self-image. 'Buy me and you'll look better.' 'Buy me and you'll feel better.' For some people the perfume works like a placebo. And for some the book gives them the courage or validation they need to make changes in their lives, hopefully for the better. After all, much of self-image is no more than mind over matter."

Luke's expression told her he wasn't buying into the theory. All the same, she pressed forward. "In Dr. Resnikoff's case, he's simply putting down on paper common sense childrearing techniques many people have used for decades. You don't need a degree in medicine to know that spoiling a child creates a monster. He may be leading the public on about his credentials, but his advice is sound."

"So why do I sense a *but* coming."

"Because that's not always the case with these self-help authors. However, since we live in a country with free speech and anyone can claim to be an expert on something, it boils down to a case of *caveat emptor*. Let the buyer beware."

"Point taken," conceded Luke.

"It gets worse, though. Unfortunately, some of these advice books can be downright dangerous. That same model, the one hawking the perfume? She wrote a bestselling diet book this year, *The Super Model's Super Diet*. An anorexic seventeen-year-old with no credentials or background in nutrition is telling America's youth how to eat. That's the real problem as far as I'm concerned, not Dr. Trulee Lovejoy and her advice on how to catch a man."

Luke muttered a few choice expletives under his breath. "In other words, some of these authors are the modern-day versions of snake oil salesmen."

Thea turned back to the window before nodding. Put that way, she was no better than the vultures she had hoped to expose. But she knew that already, no matter how pure her intentions. She had only wanted to rescue her family. Although she hadn't prostituted herself to get rich, she was just as guilty.

"I guess, had I thought about it, I would have figured that out," said Luke. "I've never bought a self-help book. Hell, I've never even *thought* about buying a self-help book."

"Few men do. Most buyers are women."

"Who are being taken advantage of by greedy bastards making a buck off their problems."

"No one ever said life was fair," she mumbled, as much to herself as to Luke. "But remember, no one is twisting anyone's arm to buy these books, either." She uttered that last sentiment in a vain attempt to assuage her own guilt. It didn't work. It never had in all the times she tried to convince herself. So she steered the conversation back to him. "I think you're suffering from a classic case of transference, Luke."

"How so?"

"Good old Psych 101. In your eyes Trulee Lovejoy is responsible for your problems because Hedda is plugging her book as a means to trap you. Guilt by association."

"But Hedda admitted —"

"Hedda only admitted that she and Trulee were friends, and who knows how true that is?"

"She had an autographed copy of her latest book."

"Which she could have inscribed herself." *I certainly didn't autograph it to her.* "All you have is Hedda's word concerning the friendship. But put that aside. What if they are friends? Trulee didn't set out to make your life miserable. Consider how long it takes from the time an author pens a book until it arrives on store shelves."

"I suppose that's true. I guess I have overreacted." Luke's expression grew sheepish. "I seem to be doing a lot of that lately."

Thea offered him a smile of understanding. "Your anger toward Hedda is justified, but it's unfair to take your frustrations out on Dr. Trulee Lovejoy. She's an innocent bystander."

"You win. I'm acting like an ass."

With that admission, Thea went out on a limb. "Besides, I think her books are fun."

"What!" Luke's eyes widened. He stared at her as if she'd just admitted to enjoying jumping out of airplanes. Without a parachute. "After what you've just told me about these pseudo-shrinks?"

Thea forced a chuckle and admitted to Lucas Bennett what only her editor knew. "Because I believe Trulee's books were written as parody. She's poking fun at books like *The Rules*. The only problem is, few people get the joke."

Luke grew thoughtful. "Hmm...I never considered that. They were definitely over the top. But they're not being marketed as parody."

And therein lies my problem. And the source of my guilt.

The conversation left Thea with a terrible case of self-loathing, but as she had so often in the past, she assigned the feelings to her ever-expanding vault of unaddressed emotions and hoped the mix wasn't brewing an ulcer. Arriving at her apartment, she slipped into her best Pacific Heights hostess manners and offered Luke a cup of coffee.

"For the road?" he asked.

Thea glanced down the hallway. "It *is* a long trip, and you *did* have a beer with dinner. I wouldn't want you growing drowsy along the way." She also wasn't ready for the evening to end, but she didn't tell him that. Thea knew the moment she was alone, Tom, Dick, and Harry would pry open the locked box, and she'd be wallowing in self-pity. Her three acrobats possessed a spiteful streak which they gleefully unleashed with ever increasing frequency.

Unfortunately, Luke declined her offer. "Another time. I have a meeting in D.C. tomorrow morning, and I need to go over some papers before turning in."

* * *

Liar! Cursing himself, Luke entered his own apartment. True, he did have an appointment with the Senate Banking Committee the next day, but it was scheduled for noon, and he was so well prepared, he could give the presentation with his eyes closed. So why had he refused her invitation? Wasn't he the one who wanted to cultivate the friendship? Althea Chandler was the perfect buffer between him and Hedda's marriage-crazy troops.

However, thirty-five years of experience with the opposite sex had convinced him that women usually said what they thought men wanted to hear. And when they found someone with more power, more wealth, or more celebrity, they left. Thea showed no interest in any of those attributes, and that fascinated him, even if his own painful experiences had convinced him all women harbor ulterior motives.

Only today he'd discovered that Thea was someone he'd like to cultivate for other reasons—reasons he'd foresworn. Her eyes captivating him. Like a mood ring, they changed from violet to periwinkle to lilac to deep purple, reflecting her emotions. Several times during the matinee, he found himself watching her rather than the stage, enjoying the exuberance of her expression and the sparkle in those magnificent eyes more than Sondheim's newest songs.

Then there was her body, slim and youthful with just the right amount of curve in all the appropriate places—no matter how well she attempted to hide the fact behind that Marian-the-Librarian dress she'd worn today. Hers was a body meant for skimpy black nothings, not buttoned-to-the-collar shirtwaists. Luke groaned, the idea of Thea wearing a satin and lace teddy created a most unwelcome feeling in his lower anatomy. He forced his thoughts elsewhere.

Sex aside, he also appreciated Thea's values. And her mind. She possessed well-thought-out opinions and had no qualms about voicing them. The more he mulled over her comments, the more he realized how right she was about his irrational rancor toward Dr. Trulee Lovejoy. His current problems stemmed from Hedda's need to promote herself, not Dr. Lovejoy's guides for the lovelorn.

Subconsciously, he'd transferred blame to the elusive author because it was safer than tackling the powerful gossip columnist. Luke's father had raised him to be a gentleman, and gentlemen don't throttle gossipmongering pains in the butt—as much as he'd like to. Besides, he had to be careful concerning how he responded to Hedda. She commanded a strong following. A few well-chosen words in her column could wreak havoc on his business. Luke had to place his partners and their clients above his personal situation.

Cu rubbed against his pant leg and meowed. "Need some attention?" H scooped the cat into his arms. Cu nuzzled his muzzle into Luke's shoulder, purring his contentment. "So what's your assessment of our new neighbor, Cu?"

The cat leaped out of his arms and ran into the bedroom. Luke followed, finding him pawing at the French doors. "Yeah, I agree. It's stuffy in here." He swung open the door. Cu immediately darted across the threshold, sprang onto the stringcourse, and scampered down the narrow ledge to the next balcony.

"I suppose it's my fault for asking the question." Shaking his head in amazement, he watched as the cat pawed at Thea's door. "You're making a real pest of yourself," he told the cat.

Thea's door opened. "You again?" The overture to *The King and I* streamed from her apartment, the rich notes drifting toward him on the soft evening breeze. She stepped onto the balcony. She'd shed her shirtwaist for a calf-length nightshirt. In the waning light of dusk, he could just make out the image dancing across her breasts—the logo from *A Chorus Line*. Althea Chandler certainly loved her musicals.

"I'm training him to be a cat burglar," he called to her.

Thea lifted Cu into her arms and walked over to the railing. "Cute. Did the former residents of this apartment own a cat? Maybe he misses a companion."

"No pets, no kids. And to my knowledge they never once stepped foot onto their balcony in the three years they lived here." He raised his hands, palms up. "I swear Cu never did this before Friday night. Not once."

She whispered something to the cat, then turned back toward her apartment. "I'll meet you at the door," she called over her shoulder.

EIGHT

Thea awakened the following morning to a ringing telephone and a warm body curled up next to her—a warm, purring, furry body.

"How in the world...?" Cupid lifted his punk-rock head and raised one eyelid, exposing a sleepy amber eye. He yawned, oblivious to her confusion, then lowered his head onto his paws and returned to his dreams. "I'm going to start charging you rent," she muttered, grabbing the phone on the fourth ring. "Hello?"

"Did I wake you?"

"Grace?" Thea twisted to check the bedside clock. *Seven-thirty?* Why would Grace call so early on a Monday morning—especially since they'd spent all of Friday afternoon meeting over her next book. She propped herself up against the headboard. Cupid, awakened once again by the movement, hopped onto her lap. "Is something wrong?"

"No, I'm just so excited, I couldn't wait to call you from the office. Have you seen *The Daily Post* this morning?"

"I haven't even seen my first cup of coffee yet. And I don't get

The Daily Post."

"Coffee can wait," said Grace. "Run out and pick up the paper. And see if you can get your hands on a copy of Friday's edition. Your guardian angel is causing sales of your books to skyrocket."

"What?"

"You've heard of Hedda Two, haven't you? The gossip columnist?"

Thea groaned.

"Hey, don't be so judgmental. She has a huge following, and she wields a lot of power in certain circles. People in New York listen to her as much as the rest of the country used to watch *Oprah.* Anyway, she's been recommending your books lately."

Thea already knew about Hedda's promotion of her books. Her sprained wrist was a direct result of Hedda's *recommendations.* She dreaded hearing what the plumed matriarch of gossip had written after their Saturday evening encounter at Le Cirque. Tom, Dick, and Harry began their morning calisthenics. Thea took a deep breath. "What did she write?"

"Well, you have to understand a bit of the background here. There's this very rich, good looking stockbroker whose wife walked out on him a few months ago, and Hedda's been trying to find him a new wife and —"

"I know all about Luke Bennett, Grace."

"You do?"

Thea gripped the hem of her quilt. Harry gripped her intestines. "The column, Grace. What did Hedda write in her column?"

"Well, first, you have to know that Hedda has offered a week at Le Spa —"

Thea cut her short. "I know. I know. What did she write?"

Grace sighed, no doubt slightly miffed that Thea wanted her to skip the dramatic prologue and get right to the heart of the matter. "She writes," said Grace, "and I quote, '*The early bird gets the worm...and maybe the man. My sources tell me copies of* Hooking Mr. Right *flew off bookshelves from Battery Park to the Bronx over the weekend, but those of you who dragged your feet better be speed-readers. The race is heating up, ladies. Yours truly had the pleasure of dining with Mr. Most Eligible and his date Saturday evening, and I have to tell you, darlings, it appears the lovely brunette has an edge over the rest of you at the moment.*'"

Had the pleasure of dining with...? Hedda certainly knew how to stretch the truth. Thea's first impulse was to set Grace straight about the table-hopping Butinsky, but she quickly decided against it.

Grace was already bound to one major secret, albeit reluctantly. She fought a losing battle to have Thea promote the Trulee Lovejoy books. Think of the publicity that would be generated if the *lovely brunette* Hedda referred to in her column turned out to be none other than Dr. Trulee Lovejoy herself. Confronted with such a situation, Grace might be tempted to forget an old promise Thea had forced her to make in exchange for increased profits on her number one bestseller.

"Anyway," said Grace, "we need to talk."

"About Hedda Two? Why?"

"No. About you."

"Me?" Grace's ominous tone raised Thea's suspicions. "What about me?"

Grace hesitated. "I don't want to discuss it over the phone. We need a face-to-face."

"About what?"

"Something came up at the office Friday after you left. Can we meet for lunch?"

"Grace, if this has to do with strong-arming me into that *Dear Trulee* book idea of yours —"

"No, it's got nothing to do with that. Lunch? Noon at Café Allegra? It's on Seventy-second off Madison."

Thea agreed. With trepidation. Grace never pussyfooted. If she had anything to say, she said it. And why had she chosen a restaurant so far from Wordsmith's Westside Midtown offices? Something was definitely up, and Thea had a bad feeling about it.

She hung up the phone and snuggled under the quilt with the cat. "You have any idea what it's like to live a life of lies, Cupid?" The cat swiped her cheek with his rough tongue and meowed. His body vibrated with a loud purr. Thea sighed. "No, I don't suppose you do."

* * *

Grace arrived at Café Allegra twenty-minutes ahead of schedule. She was working on her second Bloody Mary, still at a loss as to how she'd convince Thea to save her editor's ass, when her designated savior walked through the door.

She pointed to the sling. "What happened to your arm?"

Thea slipped into the booth. "Sprained wrist. It's nothing." She eyed Grace. Eyed the nearly empty Bloody Mary glass. Eyed Grace again. "You never drink at lunch."

Grace shrugged, aware that Thea knew Wordsmith's policy concerning alcohol. No drinking during daytime meetings with authors and agents. The publisher expected his editors to come back from lunch with clear heads, not zombied out and incapable of completing a full day's work. Which was why Grace had chosen a restaurant far from the office. No chance of running into someone from Wordsmith all the way uptown. This afternoon she needed a mega-dose of liquid courage for her meeting with Thea. She drained the remains of her drink and signaled the waiter for another. "Chalk it up to extenuating circumstances."

Thea's eyes grew wide. "What's going on?"

Grace stared into her empty glass, sighed, and shook her head. "I'm in deep shit."

Thea reached across the table and placed her hand over Grace's. "How can I help?"

Grace smiled ruefully. She knew Thea would soon regret uttering those four little words. "Maybe you should have a drink first."

Thea took a deep breath and studied Grace for a moment before nodding. When the waiter brought Grace's third Bloody Mary, Thea ordered a glass of Moscato. The two of them sat in silence, Grace alternately sipping her drink and nibbling a celery stalk. She refused to make eye contact until the waiter returned with Thea's wine, then waited until after Thea took several sips before telling her about Friday's meeting with The Icebergs.

At first, Thea said nothing, her glass poised halfway to her lips. She just stared at Grace. In bewilderment. As if Grace's words hadn't registered. Then she slowly set her wineglass down. With her palms flat on the table, Thea leaned forward and spoke under her breath to keep her words and her anger from carrying to the other tables. "Oh, no, Grace. No! No! No! We have a binding contract. You agreed. No publicity. No photos. No public appearances. Nothing."

"I know, and I wouldn't ask if my job wasn't on the line." She gulped down the rest of the Bloody Mary. "They're going to fire me if I don't get you to go along with this."

Thea shook her head. "There's got to be another solution. Some other way to generate more revenues without my involvement."

"I tried. The Icebergs said it wasn't good enough."

"What wasn't good enough?"

"Hedda's campaign to marry off Luke Bennett by using your books?"

"What about it?"

Grace sat a little straighter in her chair and tapped her index finger to her chest. "My idea."

"Omigod!" Thea turned a garish shade of pea green, made all the more sickly by the way it clashed with her aqua turtleneck sweater.

Grace frowned at her. "Why get so upset? I scored a terrific PR coup, and it didn't cost a cent. Sales of your books have skyrocketed in the New York metro area. Problem is, the Icebergs want that same kind of sales spike throughout the country, and Hedda's column isn't syndicated nationwide."

"And what if it were? Do you really envision hordes of desperate, single women grabbing copies of my books, hopping on planes, and heading to New York to snare themselves an eligible hunk?"

Grace shrugged. "Stranger things have happened. After all, we live in the age of reality TV."

"What about the cost to Luke Bennett? You're destroying his life. Not to mention what you're doing to mine."

"Don't be ridiculous, Thea." She dismissed the accusations with a wave of her half-eaten celery stalk. "Luke Bennett is eating up all the attention, and none of this has anything to do with you."

"And just where do you get your insider info? From Hedda Two?"

"Of course. Hedda knows everything about everyone."

"I wouldn't be so sure about that."

"Well, be that as it may, you can see I tried my damnedest to avoid dragging you into this, but the Icebergs have given me no choice."

"I can't, Grace. You know I'd do anything else for you but not this."

Grace slammed her empty glass onto the table. "Damn it! I saved your ass when you had nowhere else to turn, Thea."

"And I'll always owe you for that."

"Damn right. Now it's payback time. I can't afford to lose my job, and you're the only person who can prevent that. You have to come out as Trulee."

"No, I've prostituted myself enough in print. I can't. I won't do it in public."

"Please, Thea, I'm begging you."

She shook her head. "Look, Grace, I don't want to be Trulee. I never did. I want my old life back, and I intend to get it back just as soon as I pay off the creditors and the IRS. Then goodbye Trulee Lovejoy. No more books. That was the deal."

"It still could be. No one's asking you to write any more than your three-book contract."

Thea slumped back against the banquette. "But I wouldn't be able to return to teaching. I've destroyed my credibility as a sociologist. Going public blows my cover. What college or university would hire me? How would I earn a living?"

Although Grace had agreed to the no publicity arrangement, she never understood why Thea would choose teaching an auditorium full of uninterested freshmen over the celebrity and wealth of life as a bestselling author. Women gobbled up her books like chocolate at a PMS convention. As Trulee Lovejoy, Thea could write her own ticket. "But you're earning a fabulous living now. You could just keep writing more books."

Thea scowled at her. "I hate writing those books. You know that. Besides, even if I agreed—which I won't—it would never work. I'm no actress. I'd never be able to pull it off."

Grace dismissed her objection with a wave of her Bloody Mary glass. "Of course, you could. You wrote the books, didn't you? You wouldn't be talking about anything you hadn't already written."

"It's not the same. Maybe I could manage to get through a book signing without making a fool of myself, but you're talking speaking engagements, radio call-in shows, television talk shows. Can you honestly picture me on *The View*? On *Ellen*? On *Late Night*? People think Trulee is some outgoing, vivacious *femme fatale*. Look at me. I'm a colorless mouse. A timid Plain Jane."

"Don't be ridiculous. You're stunning. Besides, looks never hampered Doctor Ruth."

"Doctor Ruth compensated with a quirky personality—something else I lack." Thea held up her hand to stop another protest. "I'm telling you, your publicity blitz would wind up a publicity nightmare. Believe me, I'm doing you a favor by refusing."

Grace's heart sank. Thea had a point. Deep down, Grace knew it wouldn't work, even if by some miracle Thea agreed. Thea was too much of an introvert to pull off the type of promotional campaign The Icebergs had in mind.

Grace sighed. She was doomed. Farewell Park Avenue apartment; hello unemployment line. And her kids could kiss their Ivy League educations goodbye. "But if you refuse to do it, what am I going to do?"

Thea threw her arms up in the air. "I don't know, Grace. Tell them I'm agoraphobic."

"Oh yeah, they'll really buy that—even if they know what it means, which I seriously doubt. These guys only understand numbers. They're not interested in excuses."

"Then tell them I have leprosy."

"Right. Far more believable."

"So hire a shill."

"Yet another workable solution. And just how am I going to justify *that* on my expense account?"

Thea threw her head back against the banquette and released a frustrated, forceful exhale. "Then you do it, Grace."

* * *

Luke returned from Washington hot and surly. The day had started off with an unexpected and less than friendly grilling by an overbearing junior senator. It went downhill from there, culminating in a ride back to New York on the Acela from Hell—complete with dead air-conditioner and a forty-five-minute mechanical delay outside of Princeton.

Of course, he hadn't helped his mood by picking up a discarded copy of that morning's *Daily Post* during the breakdown and discovering his ploy to thwart Hedda's campaign had backfired on him. Instead of calling off her army after seeing him dining with Thea on Saturday night, she'd rallied her single soldiers to redouble their efforts.

The woman knew good publicity when she saw it. Hedda needed increased newspaper sales to save the paper and thus, her job. She wasn't about to call off the battle against Luke just because she thought he was taken. Short of Luke waving a marriage license under her gossip sniffing nose, Hedda planned to milk her crusade for all it was worth and for as long as possible.

By the time Luke arrived at his apartment, all he wanted was a cold shower and an even colder beer. What he got was a note taped to his front door.

Cupid came to visit. Again.

Luke debated ignoring the note until he freshened up, but he was afraid if he entered his apartment, he might collapse and not get up again until morning. The tone of Thea's note led him to believe she wasn't exactly pleased by her uninvited houseguest. After Hedda's latest column, the last thing he wanted to do was alienate his neighbor. Again. He needed her friendly cooperation now more than ever. With a heavy sigh, he spun on his heels and trudged back down the hall.

When Thea opened her door at the sound of his knock, the music of Andrew Lloyd Webber spilled into the hall. Luke briefly wondered if the orchestral recording of *Cats*, was in honor of her apartment crasher. But it was the rich Italian aroma mingling with the notes that captured his attention, sending his taste buds into a state of ecstasy, and reminding him he hadn't eaten anything in over six hours. After taking a quick mental inventory of the limited contents of his refrigerator, he wondered if he might somehow wrangle a dinner invitation.

"Do you feel as rotten as you look?" she asked.

"Worse." *And incredibly hungry.* "I hope Cu wasn't too much of a pain." He bent down and scooped the cat into his arms. "What the hell's gotten into you lately?" he asked the cat. Cu responded with a loud meow.

"I found him in my bed this morning," Her eyes had deepened

to the color of eggplant. Was that eggplant Parmesan he smelled? He'd prefer veal or chicken, but he'd settle for eggplant.

He raised one eyebrow, studying first the cat in his arms, then the woman standing beside him. Thea looked furious. Cu looked smug. Luke found the situation comical. He chuckled. "Lucky cat."

Thea pierced him with an icy glare and a deep scowl. Humor usually diffused tension. Not this time. The lady was definitely not amused. Luke had a vision of his veal-chicken-eggplant Parmesan flying out the window. He wondered if week-old Chinese takeout was safe to eat.

"Sorry," he muttered, faking contrition he didn't feel. After all, what was the big deal? His cat liked her. She should feel honored. Cu didn't bestow his considerable charms on just anyone. Especially members of the opposite sex. He either ignored or acted hostile toward every woman Luke brought to the apartment. The cat and his ex-wife, members of the same mutual animosity society, had barely tolerated each other. "I've had a rough day," he added. *And I'm hungry!*

"Cheer up." She offered him a cold smile. "Tomorrow's bound to be worse."

"How pleasantly cynical of you, doctor."

She waved her good arm in the air. "I get that way when I'm forced to tote kitty litter and canned tuna three blocks with one functioning arm. How about closing your balcony door the next time you go out?"

True, he should have thought to close the door, given Cu's new balcony-hopping habit, but damn it, who the hell asked her to play the role of martyr? "Why didn't you just stick him out on your balcony and close the door? He knows where to find his food and litter."

"Tell that to your cat," she yelled at him, her voice raising several octaves. "I *did* put him out on the balcony. He didn't go home. Instead, he made such a racket, I thought someone might call the police!"

"This is New York City, *doctor*. The police have better things to do."

"Thank you for the civics update, *Mr. Bennett*! Now if you'll be so kind as to remove both yourself and your cat from my apartment, I would like to eat my dinner in peace." Instead of waiting for a response, she grabbed his arm and pushed him into the hall, slamming the door behind him.

"So much for staying on friendly terms," he told Cu. "And dinner."

He walked into his apartment and headed straight for the refrigerator and the leftover Chinese takeout. A blue green fuzz coated the Kung Po Shrimp Ding.

* * *

Damn! She hadn't meant to sound so strident and confrontational, but after Grace's lunchtime two-fisted atom bomb attack, she couldn't stop seething. Still, it wasn't fair to take her anger over Grace out on Luke. He was the innocent victim of her machinations.

Thea groaned. *My God, if he ever finds out Trulee's true identity, he'll kill me.* Grace's little PR stunt made it look like Thea and Hedda were in cahoots. If the truth came out, how could she possibly convince him otherwise? Talk about guilt by association.

Then there was his cat. In truth, she didn't mind Cupid's visits, but snuggling under the quilt with him this morning had triggered a pervasive loneliness that clouded the remainder of her day, making Grace's bombshell all the worse.

Not that she'd experienced many bright days over the last several weeks but waking to a cat in her bed had been a real bummer—especially when she should have been snuggling with her new husband. Not that *that* was ever going to happen now. Stroking Cupid's fur, she had envisioned herself growing old, a lonely spinster dressed in lace-edged, high-collared lavender dresses with only a cat for a companion.

And then there was her liquid lunch with Grace. They never got around to ordering any food. The discussion—if you could call it that—ended when Thea stormed out of the restaurant. Just what she needed in her life—more guilt. Talk about a no-win situation. Putting aside her implied culpability in Luke's unsettling predicament, if she agreed to help Grace, she ruined her life. Refuse and she ruined Grace's life.

She owed Luke an apology. He wasn't at fault here. Steve was. And Madeline. She couldn't even place any blame on Grace for her collusion with Hedda or for trying to renege on their deal. The bean counters had blackmailed Grace into a corner. No. As far as Trulee was concerned, she had no one to blame but herself. After all, she opted to compromise her ethics and take the easy way out. Grace dangled the gold coins under her nose, but no one had forced Thea to grab the bag.

Thea had noticed the way Luke's gaze had kept darting toward the kitchen. He had practically drooled on his rumpled pinstripe. She suspected Melvin the doorman heard his grumbling stomach twelve floors below.

She checked the contents of the oven. Sauce bubbling, cheese browned to a golden perfection, her veal Parmesan with mushrooms and baby spinach set off a loud protest in her own stomach. Tom, Dick, and Harry, connoisseurs of Italian cuisine, were demanding their dinner. With their propensity toward red sauce and pasta maybe she should have named them Tomasso, Federico, and...what *was* the Italian form of Harry? Enrico? Thea shrugged. She had a more pressing problem at the moment. Adjusting the light under a pot of linguini, she turned her attention to the dilemma.

Her sprained wrist had healed well enough to prepare the meal with only a bit of minor inconvenience. She had compensated. Besides, at the time she'd been more concerned with doing something to take her mind off her troubles, and cooking always worked as a panacea for whatever troubled her.

As a child, she had constantly gravitated to the kitchen whenever her loneliness consumed her, or her unladylike behavior triggered a reproachful lecture from her mother. A deep bond developed between her and Yolanda Marie, her family's French-Italian cook. While her parents ignored her and fussed over Madeline, Thea received the attention she craved from Yolanda Marie—along with cooking lessons from the master Cordon Blue chef.

Years later, she still sought and found solace in the kitchen, the only place where she had complete control over her world. The only place where she could truly be herself.

Thea had placed the food in a small casserole, which proved easy to slip into the oven single-handed. Removing the piping hot dish was an entirely different problem. She opened the oven door, pulled out the wire rack containing her dinner, and bit down on her lower lip while she mulled over her limited options.

The most sensible course of action was to knock on Luke's door, invite him to dinner, then have him lift the baking dish onto the counter. Sensible, but smacking of ulterior motive. He'd think she only invited him because she couldn't remove the dish herself. Strike that idea. She wasn't about to offer him an apology with strings attached.

Thea plopped into a kitchen chair, propped her elbow on her knee, and cupped her chin in the palm of her good hand. She stared at the veal Parmesan. She frowned at her bandaged wrist. The seconds ticked away.

Three minutes later she was still scowling alternately between her wrist and the meal. "Oh, the hell with it!" She rose to her feet. "It's not going to grow legs and walk out of the oven." She slipped her arm from the sling and donned a couple of oven mitts. Holding her breath and gritting her teeth, she lifted the dish out of the oven. The pain proved bearable. Barely.

Ten minutes later, after downing a couple of aspirin to offset the renewed ache in her wrist, she stood in front of Luke's door. Balanced between her hip and good arm, she held a large wicker basket complete with main course, a plastic container in which she had placed the drained linguini, another filled with Caesar salad, a small loaf of Italian bread, and a bottle of chilled Asti Spumanti.

She rang the doorbell with her elbow.

* * *

After a quick shower, Luke sat sprawled half-naked on his living room couch, nursing a beer and a grudge. Too tired to go out for dinner and too hungry to wait for a takeout delivery, he looked forward to a can of soup with as much relish as a dieter looks forward to a stalk of celery. At the sound of his doorbell, he glanced over at Cu, who sat preening himself on top of the coffee table. "Can't be your favorite doctor with her standard complaint," he muttered. "Unless you've discovered some way to clone yourself."

Cu scampered off his perch and followed Luke to the door. "Must be Mrs. Lillibridge," he told the cat. The kindly widow across the hall looked after Cu whenever Luke traveled. A diabetic who sent weekly shipments of freshly baked goodies to her grandchildren, she often pressed Luke into service as her official taste tester. Luke hoped she had spent the day baking up a storm. "One minute," he yelled, dashing into the bedroom for a robe. He couldn't greet Mrs. Lillibridge wearing nothing but a pair of boxers.

Only when he flung open his front door, it wasn't Mrs. Lillibridge standing in the hallway.

Thea looked nervous and terribly unsure of herself. "I...I wasn't very nice to you before. I was upset about something, and I had no right to take it out on you."

Luke eyed the basket balancing awkwardly on her hip and nodded. *Food! Yes! Delicious smelling Italian food!* He reacted to the aroma like one of Pavlov's dogs. Trying to hide his excitement, he raised one eyebrow and jutted his chin toward the basket. "Roses?"

"Dinner. If you'd like some. It's nothing fancy, but you looked hungry before, and there's more than enough for two."

Thank you, Lord! Luke reached for the basket. Damn, it was heavy. "How did you manage this with your arm in a sling?"

Thea ignored his question, silently following him toward the kitchen.

Luke set the basket on the counter and turned to confront her. "Well?"

"I...um...I...." Thea stared at him. Her mouth gaped open. Her skin deepened to a shade of dark rose. Her large violet eyes grew even larger before she darted her gaze away from him and to the far side of the room.

Luke glanced down. His robe had come undone, exposing Joe Boxer's bright yellow smiling face, complete with strategically placed large red tongue. "I wasn't expecting company." He turned and dashed down the hall. "Be right back," he called over his shoulder.

He chuckled as he slipped into a pair of jeans and a T-shirt. He might have expected such a reaction from Mrs. Lillibridge, but not Dr. Althea Chandler. How could a woman who owned a library of reference works with titles like *The Female Orgasm—A Woman's Right, A Man's Duty* blush over a loose-fitting pair of boxer shorts?

He returned to find she had already set the dining room table with his good china, crystal, and silver. He found her in the kitchen dividing the salad into two bowls. The bread sat on a cutting board, awaiting slicing. The wine bottle, still corked, sat beside it, as did a plastic container of pasta, but the large, covered dish remained in the basket. He lifted it out and carried it into the dining room, setting it on the trivet she'd placed in the middle of the table.

Thea followed with one of the salad bowls. "Would you open the wine and slice the bread?" She appeared somewhat more at ease than she had a few moments ago, and her skin had reverted to its normal peachy hue, but she still avoided making eye contact with him.

After Luke sliced the bread and uncorked the wine, he carried them both to the table. He was surprised to find she had lit a pair of candles. "Nice touch." He motioned to the flickering tapers standing tall in his grandmother's antique Waterford candlesticks.

Thea shrugged her shoulders and offered him a slight smile. "One candle in an empty Chianti bottle is more traditional, but you seem to be low on empty wine bottles."

"And checkered tablecloths. I'll have to remedy that before next time." He pulled out a chair for her. "However, there's more than one way to transform a Manhattan apartment into an Italian bistro."

He crossed the room to the bookcases along the far wall and withdrew a CD from his massive music collection. "One Italian tenor coming up." He inserted the disc into the player. Within moments Andrea Bocelli filled the room with his sonorous rendition of *Con Te Partirò*.

"What shall we drink to?" asked Luke, filling both wine glasses.

"Getting through the evening without an argument?"

"I'll drink to that." He handed her one of the glasses then clicked the rim of his glass gently against hers. "Touché, doctor!"

After only one bite Luke knew he'd entered gastronomic heaven. "Is this homemade Caesar dressing?"

Thea nodded. "I whipped it up while I was waiting for the linguini to cook."

"I don't see any anchovies."

Thea scrunched up her nose. "Sorry. I never could develop a taste for anchovies."

Luke laughed. "Good. Neither could I." He had dined in some of the finest restaurants in Europe and the States. Many of them prepared their award-winning Caesar salads at tableside, but none could compare to the dressing Thea whipped up while waiting for the linguini to cook. Even if she did leave out the anchovies. He raised his salad-laden fork in an appreciative toast. "Brava." Then he motioned toward the main course. "The heavenly smell that has tortured me for the past half hour, from scratch, as well?"

"Veal parmesan with mushrooms and baby spinach. Mostly from scratch. I cheated on the marinara sauce. I thought I had some in the freezer, but I didn't, so I used a jar from the gourmet shop down the street and added some fresh tomatoes."

Luke glanced at the main course. "I suppose I can forgive you that. You must enjoy cooking." Try as he might, he could not envision his ex-wife *whipping up* anything other than a dinner reservation at a chic restaurant. All their expensive cookware, along with the china, crystal, and silver, had gone unused throughout their short marriage. When he made the mistake of asking why she'd insisted on purchasing them, Julie had rolled her eyes and answered, "Really, Luke, what would people think?"

"I find cooking creative...and stress-reducing."

Luke placed the empty salad bowls on the sideboard and lifted the lid to the baking dish. He filled a plate for her and one for himself, cutting her meat into bite-size pieces before handing it to her. "Stress-reducing," he repeated. "What had you so upset that you spent the day chopping garlic and tomatoes? Get another call from the creep? What was his name, Bill?"

"Steve," she said. "Bill's my brother-in-law. Soon-to-be ex-brother-in-law," she corrected herself, "and no, Steve hasn't called since yesterday morning."

"So what happened?"

Distress washed across Thea's face. She stared down at her plate. "It was work related. I'd rather not discuss it."

Luke decided not to push the subject. The last thing he wanted was this wonderful dinner ruined by another misunderstanding. He took a bite of the veal, thin strips that she'd rolled with a spinach, chopped mushroom, and ricotta filling, then baked in a marinara sauce topped with Parmesan. If he thought he'd gone to heaven from her Caesar dressing, the veal confirmed it. "This is absolutely incredible."

"I'm glad you like it."

"Like it?" Luke stared at her in amazement. She had referred to this gourmet feast as *nothing fancy*. Was it possible she didn't realize what a gift she had? "My God, woman, you're wasting your talents. You should be writing cookbooks, not sociology texts."

She blushed at the compliment. He wished she'd stop doing that. There was something too innocent and sweet about the way she reacted to him at times—when she wasn't yelling at him—something that reminded him of all those Jane Austen books on her shelves. To Luke's dismay, he found her rosy cheeks triggering another form of hunger within him, one that thin strips of veal in marinara sauce would not appease.

Thankfully, the doorbell rang.

"If we're lucky," said Luke, rising from his chair, "that might be dessert."

Thea looked perplexed. "How? You didn't know I was coming."

"Neither did Mrs. Lillibridge, but she's the only other person who would ring my bell without going through Melvin, and she generally comes bearing something sweet and chocolaty."

"Mrs. Lillibridge?"

"The elderly lady across the hall. You haven't met her yet?"

Thea shook her head.

Luke found it odd that Mrs. Lillibridge, the building's unofficial Welcome Wagon hadn't stopped by to greet her newest neighbor. When he'd purchased his apartment, she brought over enough casseroles and pies to fill his freezer. "Then you're in for a treat. Mrs. Lillibridge is a treasure."

Luke headed over to the front door and swung it open.

"Hello, Lucas, dear." Mrs. Lillibridge hand him a platter of chocolate meringue cookies. "I stopped by earlier in the day, but no one answered. I wanted you to sample the chocolate peanut butter brownies I baked for the twins. I think I may have added too much sugar by mistake, and with you not in, I had to ask Melvin to taste them for me, and you know how he is." She stopped to catch her breath, then sighed. "The man inhales anything, regardless of quality. I do hope they weren't too sweet."

"I was down in D.C. on business." He bent to peck her cheek. "And I'm sure the cookies were delicious. Come inside. There's someone I want you to meet." He ushered her into the living room. "I don't believe you've met our newest neighbor." Luke motioned from Thea to Mrs. Lillibridge. "Dr. Althea Chandler. Mrs. Beatrice Lillibridge."

Thea rose and extended her hand. "How do you do?"

"Oh, not very well at all, my dear." To Luke's dismay Mrs. Lillibridge pulled out a chair and made herself at home.

Thea shot him a worried glance. He shrugged helplessly. "Tea, anyone?" he asked, removing the dinner plates.

"That would be lovely, dear," said Mrs. Lillibridge. "Calamity is always easier to face with a nice hot cup of tea, you know."

"Calamity?" Luke studied the elderly woman. Diabetes aside, she appeared as spry and healthy as she always did. "You're not ill, are you, Beatrice? Dr. Chandler isn't a medical doctor."

"Heavens no, Lucas. I'm fine. You're the one with the problem, dear. Not me."

NINE

"Me?" Luke gaped at his elderly neighbor.

"Tea before troubles, Lucas." Mrs. Lillibridge wagged her finger at him. "And brewed, mind you. None of those little bags you try to pawn off on me."

"Yes, ma'am." Luke headed off to the kitchen, his arms laden with dirty dishes.

Cu jumped up into the elderly woman's lap. "Hello, there, dear one. And how are you today?" She stroked the cat's multi-colored, multi-length fur with her gnarled fingers. "Ugly, isn't he?" she whispered to Thea, winking one rheumy eye. "But he's such a charmer. And smart."

"So I've noticed." Cupid raised his smug head in her direction. She swore he understood every word of the conversation.

"I'm sorry I haven't had a chance to welcome you to the floor," continued Mrs. Lillibridge, her silver head bobbing, "but...." She glanced toward the kitchen. "Well, under the circumstances, with having made up my mind, there hardly seemed much point in establishing a new relationship only to end it so quickly. But the children are growing so fast, you see, and a visit here and there is never enough. Why, they hardly remember me from one time to the next, and I just can't have that, now can I?"

"No, of course not." Thea didn't have a clue what the woman was babbling about, but she decided agreeing was the most judicious course of action. Hopefully, Mrs. Lillibridge's prattle would make more sense to Luke.

He returned several minutes later carrying a large tray laden with tea fixings, two empty plates, and a third containing several bakery cookies. He divided the chocolate meringue cookies between the two plates, keeping one for himself and handing the other to Thea.

"You're not having any?" she asked Mrs. Lillibridge.

"Beatrice has diabetes," said Luke, placing the bakery cookies in front of the older woman. "Sugar free," he assured her. "From the shop around the corner."

Mrs. Lillibridge smiled at him and then sighed deeply. "You are a sweetheart, Lucas, and so very thoughtful. I'm going to miss you."

"Miss me? You're leaving?"

"I'm afraid so. As I was just explaining to our new neighbor here." She fluttered a hand in Thea's direction. "I've decided to move to Florida. I know I swore I'd never leave the city, but the truth is, the cold really got to me this past winter. I'm not as young as I used to be, you know. And now that Susannah's husband..."

She turned to Thea. "Susannah's my daughter," she explained, taking a sip of the tea Luke handed her. "Anyway, now that Collin's accepted a transfer to Tampa, if I join them—and Luke, you know how much they've been after me to move in with them—well, I'd get to spend all that time with my grandchildren. They won't be young forever, you know. Pretty soon they'll be off with their friends all the time...." Her voice trailed off, her eyes growing apologetic and asking for understanding.

"When are you planning to move?" asked Luke.

Mrs. Lillibridge took a deep breath, holding it for a moment before releasing it in a gush. She appeared somewhat chagrined as she answered. "Friday."

"Friday!"

"I know it's not much notice, and I realize this is a terrible inconvenience to you, Lucas, what with your traveling and all, but Susannah has a chance to go with Collin on a business trip to Paris, and they haven't had a vacation—just the two of them, that is— in so long, what with their move and the twins being so young. I'm sure if you try, you'll be able to make other arrangements for your sweet little pussycat." She bent her head and planted a kiss on Cupid's fur before continuing. "I am going to miss you, too," she told the cat.

Then she turned back to Luke. "There's that wonderful pet hotel downtown, you know, and even though you don't like boarding Cu, I'm sure they have very nice people running it. They received a wonderful write-up in *The Times* several weeks ago."

"I'll manage," said Luke, not sounding too happy, but he smiled at Mrs. Lillibridge. "Don't worry yourself about it. I'll miss you, though. So will Cu."

"And I'll miss both of you, dear." She reached over and patted his hand. "You have no idea how difficult a decision this has been for me. Why, you're practically family to me, Lucas."

She turned to Thea. "He's been like a son to me ever since he moved in. I couldn't ask for a more thoughtful neighbor." Then her face brightened. Her light gray eyes twinkled, and the corners of her mouth turned up in a huge smile of satisfaction. She slapped the table with the palm of one hand. "Why, of course! Why didn't I think of that before? Dr. Chandler, you wouldn't mind, would you, dear?"

Thea's head was spinning from the woman's mile-a-minute monologue. *Mind what?* "I...."

"There, see! Of course she wouldn't," said Mrs. Lillibridge, placing the cat in Thea's lap. "Then it's all settled." She rose. Luke joined her. "Now I really must be going. You two young people enjoy the rest of your evening. Don't bother showing me out, Lucas. I know the way." She smiled broadly and waved to Thea as she headed toward the door. "Nice meeting you, dear."

"She doesn't come up for air very often, does she?" asked Thea after she heard the front door close.

"No," said Luke, "and she's really left me in a bind." He scowled as he gathered up the tea things and headed toward the kitchen.

"How so?" Thea set Cupid on the floor and followed Luke into the kitchen.

"Mrs. Lillibridge has looked after Cu ever since I found him. I have to go out of town for a week on Monday, and I was counting on her. As usual."

"What about that pet hotel she mentioned?"

Luke placed the dishes in the sink and turned to face her. "When I found Cu, he was being attacked by a pack of strays. By the time I chased off the other cats he'd been badly mauled. The trauma left him terrified of other animals. When I take him to the vet, I have to make a special appointment before or after regular office hours so there are no other pets in the waiting room."

She bent down to pet the cat who'd followed them into the kitchen and was sidling up against her ankles. "Poor baby." So that's why Cupid looked like a refugee from a punk rock concert. He was more the victim of gang violence than the product of a genetic stew.

She looked up at Luke. He was filling the sink with soapy water. His distress over the well-being of his pet touched her. She'd never known a man capable of such compassion toward a helpless animal. Luke showed more faithful devotion toward Cupid than Steve had shown toward her. She wondered what that said about her and her lack of insight into the human psyche. She had misjudged both men, nearly making the mistake of her life with one of them. "I'll take him," she said.

Luke shook his head. "No. Just because Mrs. Lillibridge offered your services —"

"*I'm* offering my services," she corrected him. "Mrs. Lillibridge has nothing to do with it. Besides, I already have the kitty litter," she reminded him, "and he does seem to prefer my apartment to yours, lately."

Luke stared at her. "You're serious?"

She nodded.

"It would be a tremendous relief knowing he was with someone he liked. You really wouldn't mind?"

"Not at all."

"I'll give you a key. I wouldn't want him to get too used to your place. Or your bed," he added, smiling sheepishly. "And I'll make sure there's plenty of food and litter before I leave so you don't have to lug any back from the market."

"I'd appreciate that."

"How about an after-dinner drink?" He grabbed a dishtowel

and wiped his hands.

Thea pointed toward the sink. "What about all those dirty dishes?"

He shrugged. "They're not going anywhere." He reached for her hand, gently urging her to follow him back to the living room. "Baileys or brandy?"

* * *

Grace arrived at her office first thing Tuesday morning to find a fluorescent green Post-it note stuck to her computer screen. In thick black marker, Goldberg, the head Iceberg, had scrawled: *See me as soon as you get in.* She closed her eyes and took three deep courage-plucking breaths. This was it. Showdown time.

"Hey, you okay?"

Grace's eyelids sprang open. Lucy, her assistant, stood in the doorway, staring at her. "Fine," she assured her, but the word rang false in her ears.

"See the note from upstairs?"

Grace scowled. "How could I miss it?" She smoothed an imaginary wrinkle from her pencil skirt, grabbed her briefcase, and headed for the door. "You know where to find me," she said, with a backwards glance to Lucy.

"Nice outfit," Lucy called after her.

Grace dipped her head, her gaze skimming down her torso to take in the cherry red raw silk Dolce & Gabbana suit and matching dagger-heeled Jimmy Choo boots. The deep V-cut of the jacket exposed a substantial amount of cleavage. The ultra-short skirt revealed a considerable amount of thigh. Definitely not her usual business attire. She last worn the suit to a celebrity-studded literacy fundraiser luncheon at The Plaza, but on that day, she'd brought the outfit to work and changed prior to leaving for the event.

Today she specifically chose the sexy garment to draw attention to her every God-given curve. She knew she looked spectacular and at least ten, if not fifteen, years younger than her nearly half a century. Red was her color, a brilliant contrast to her jet-black hair and smoky gray eyes. She'd spent two hours dressing this morning, making certain every stroke of makeup, every wave of her shoulder length hair, every angle of her body made a statement.

Moments later she stood outside Goldberg's office. After a final deep breath, she rapped on the door, grabbed the knob, and entered the bean counter's lair without waiting for his response. "You wanted to see me?"

Goldberg waved her in, his attention remaining focused on the spreadsheet on his desk. Grace cleared her throat. He grimaced before looking up, but when he finally did cast a glance in her direction, the expression on his face told her she had nothing to worry about.

Grace offered him her sexiest come-hither smile. *Let the games begin.*

* * *

In the past five years Porter-Sachs-Bennett had expanded to include main branches in Atlanta, Dallas, and San Francisco. Each month one of the firm's three partners spent a week in another location. Prior to the monthly trips, Luke put in long hours of preparation. Because Monday's Senate testimony had shortened his week by a day, he arrived home Tuesday evening well after nine o'clock.

A quick glance around the apartment told him he was alone. He dropped his briefcase on a chair in the living room and headed next door to retrieve his wayward cat.

"You work long hours," said Thea, greeting him at her door. "Have you eaten?"

Luke scooped Cu into his arms. "Is that an invitation?" He'd stopped at Mr. Ling's Chinese à Go-Go for a container of Hunan Beef and fried rice, but after last night's feast he'd gladly forego Mr. Ling's specialty for anything his neighbor whipped up.

"I've already eaten," she said, "but I couldn't help noticing your empty refrigerator last night. Would you like an omelet?"

Did he detect a note of enticement in her voice, or was he merely looking for an excuse to accept her invitation? "My cat has already imposed enough for both of us," Of course, he could have prevented that by closing his balcony door this morning. Had he left it open in the hope that he'd have to retrieve Cu this evening? He knew damn well he had. But why? That question had puzzled him much of the day as his mind strayed from monthly branch reports to the memory of a fascinating pair of violet eyes.

"It's no imposition."

Those damned amethyst eyes were now staring up into his, and Luke had to remind himself he'd sworn off women. But then he remembered that Thea was safe. Unlike the obstacle course of women he dodged on his way to work this morning, she had no desire to drag him to the altar. She was merely being neighborly.

Cu swung his head in the direction of Thea's voice, nodded and purred. Then he offered Luke a loud meow, which Luke interpreted as *Don't be a jerk. The lady's a damn gourmet chef.*

"Cu says I'd be a fool to decline."

Once he tasted the omelet—stuffed to overflowing with tomatoes, mushrooms, and sweet peppers—he knew the cat had been right.

* * *

Thea spent most of the next day staring at a blank computer screen. If she didn't get something written soon, she'd miss her deadline and be forced to return the advance she'd already divided up between the IRS, her mother's doctors, and the hospital. However, try as she might, she couldn't bring herself to slip back into the persona of Dr. Trulee Lovejoy and write more lies. She had seen firsthand how her concocted psychobabble wreaked havoc in one man's life. How many other people, besides Luke, had she inadvertently harmed to save her family?

A call from the remaining member of that family interrupted her self-castigation.

"Althea," cried Madeline, nearly hysterical, "you have to help me! I can't handle this! I need you!"

Her sister sounded so distraught that Thea wavered momentarily before quickly reminding herself why she'd put three thousand miles between them.

"I don't know what to do!" A loud sob punctuated Madeline's words.

Thea glanced at the calendar. The third week of the month signaled the arrival of bills. The electric company, the phone company, the cable service, the pool service, the security monitoring service, the lawn service—everyone expected payment by the first of the following month.

In happier times Thea, Madeline, and Madeline's husband Bill had lived under one roof. Although Thea shared the financial responsibilities of the house with Madeline, Bill paid his wife's share. But Bill and Madeline were divorcing, and since Thea had signed her half of the house over to her sister, Madeline was now solely responsible for its upkeep. And the stately Pacific Heights structure had a way of drinking up money like a parched camel.

Although Madeline was considered one of the country's foremost astrophysicists, she reaped little financial reward from her genius. Because she refused to teach, preferring to concentrate entirely on her research, she received a minimal stipend from the university. She also applied for few grants, spurning all corporate funding. Her father had warned her against unscrupulous industrial giants who might take advantage of her genius. Thus, she'd turned down every position ever offered to her in the private sector. Now that Madeline was without her husband's financial support, she'd have to make some difficult decisions if she wanted to keep the house.

"I can't make it stop," whined Madeline, "and everything's getting ruined! I called Bill, but all he did was yell at me, and you're not here, and I don't know what to do!"

Thea sighed. Same old refrain. Maybe she should get an unlisted phone number. "Try growing up, Madeline."

"How is that going to stop the water?"

What in the world was her sister babbling about? "What water?"

"The water! Damn it, Althea, haven't you been listening to me? There's water everywhere! I'm up to my ankles in it!"

"Where?"

"In the laundry room. Why won't anyone help me? It's pouring out into the kitchen and the breakfast nook and the sun porch and...."

"Did you turn off the main?" asked Thea.

"Main what?"

Although intellectually brilliant, due to her pampered upbringing, Madeline lacked the basic coping skills that most children develop by the time they reach adolescence. Madeline could solve the most complex mathematical equation, but she had no idea how to deal with a ruptured pipe.

Thea directed her sister to the water main shutoff valve. "Did the water stop?" she asked.

"Yes."

"O.K., now call a plumber."

"I can't right now. I have work to do at the lab, and I'm already late. I'll call tomorrow."

Thea took a deep breath and silently counted to ten. "You can't wait, Madeline. You have no water until the pipe is repaired. Do you understand what that means? No toilets. No bath. Not even a glass of tap water."

"I can't take a bath?"

Madeline was known to soak for hours in the bathroom Jacuzzi. She claimed she did her best thinking with steamy water bubbling around her. Were all geniuses as stupid as her sister? "Call the plumber, Madeline! And mop up the water before it ruins the floors and furniture. The wet-vac is in the laundry room utility closet."

"The plumber can do that when he comes."

Right! Deciding it was best to let Madeline discover some things on her own, Thea hung up the phone and turned her attention back to her blank computer screen.

Cupid jumped onto her desk and pranced across the keyboard, producing the only characters to appear on her monitor in the past several hours. Thea stared at the undecipherable message on the screen. "Makes about as much sense as anything I've ever written," she told the cat.

He meowed in agreement. Thea pulled a Tabby Treat from her skirt pocket and held it out for him. Cupid scarfed down the dry snack, jumped onto her lap, and nosed his way into her pocket searching for more. Finding none, he voiced his displeasure with a boisterous yowl.

"We all have to learn to live with disappointment." Pushing the cat from her lap, she hit the delete key, erasing his journalistic musings. When the screen was once again blank, she leaned back in her chair and scowled at the blinking cursor. "So now what?"

Instead of a flash of insight hurling down from the heavens, Thea heard the rattle of dishes on the drain board. "Those *were* clean!" she yelled, raising her voice loud enough for the cat to hear her.

Thea wasn't used to four-legged beasts walking across her kitchen counters. If Cupid were going to make himself a regular visitor, one of them was going to have to change some habits. As she headed for the kitchen, she had an uneasy feeling she knew which of them it would be.

Due to Madeline's allergies, Thea had never owned a pet other than a couple of goldfish she'd won at a street fair. Five-year-old Madeline dubbed them Goldencrantz and Gildenfish, which her parents had thought quite clever—no matter that they were Thea's fish. After all, how many five-year-olds read *Hamlet*, let alone could devise goldfish pun names based on two minor characters?

Unfortunately, a week later Madeline decided Goldencrantz and Gildenfish were suffering from homesickness. To help them return home, she flushed them down the toilet, and that was the end of Thea's pets. Until Cupid decided to adopt her.

Once the cat had lured her away from the computer and into the kitchen, Thea remained there, spending the rest of the day baking bread. According to Yolanda Marie, bread baking was a powerful tonic for emotional distress.

"You should write a cookbook," a teenage Thea once told her. "Zen and the Art of Sourdough."

From that day on, whenever an unhappy Thea wandered into the kitchen, Yolanda Marie would ask, "*Eez le zourdough day, oui, ma petite zourpuss?*" Then without another word, she'd set aside her work and pull out the bread makings.

Today was definitely a *zourdough* day, even if Thea had no sourdough starter and had to settle for making a few loaves of French bread. With her wrist nearly healed, she found pounding the dough helped her vent her frustrations over Trulee and Madeline as well as deal with the deep-seated anger the goldfish memory had triggered.

At the time, although she'd been upset over losing her fish, she understood Madeline's reason for setting them free. Now, nineteen years later and in light of everything else which had happened, she wondered if her sister had acted out of compassion or spite.

The more Thea dwelled on Madeline's treachery, the more she began to reevaluate her sister's past behavior. She slammed her fist into a lump of elastic dough, sending a cloud of flour into the air. What a blind fool she'd been!

* * *

Madeline stared at the dead phone in her hand. Althea had hung up on her. Again. Bill had hung up on her earlier. They both hated her. She splashed her way to the kitchen table and slumped into a chair. "No one would care if I drowned in this mess," she cried to the four walls. She lowered her head onto her crossed arms and sobbed until her throat grew raw.

Try growing up. Althea's words rang in her head like a dirge.

Bill's accusations chimed in, *I loved you, Madeline. We both did, and look how you repaid that love? You're nothing but a spoiled, selfish brat! I'm through with you. Steve can have you.*

But she didn't want Steve. She wanted her husband back. And her sister. She'd sacrificed so much and for what? A freedom she now realized wasn't worth the price she'd paid for it. "Some genius I am. Give me two choices, and I'll always pick the wrong one," she muttered between sobs. An imbecile could have pointed out the holes in that half-assed scheme of hers, but, as usual, she hadn't considered the ramifications of her behavior. She acted without thinking because she was incapable of logical thought anywhere but in her work. Genius? Hell, she was more an idiot savant!

"Well, screw it!" She kicked back the chair, flinging up a spray of water. The lab was the only place where she ever felt grown up. The only place she was respected and treated like an adult. The only place she truly belonged. So that's where she'd go. She grabbed her purse off the counter and headed for the door, but her sister's words screamed louder in her head. *Try growing up.* Madeline hesitated in the hallway. She turned and stared back at the pool of water covering the kitchen floor. *Try growing up.* Althea wouldn't leave the house in this state. Neither would Bill. *Try growing up.*

She tossed her purse back on the counter, picked up the phone, and called the plumber. Luckily, her organized sister had a list of emergency numbers hanging by the phone. Then she splashed her way back into the laundry room and dragged the wet-vac out of the closet. Thea was right. As usual. It was time Madeline grew up.

Madeline plugged in the wet-vac and flipped the power switch. A torrent of water flew up and drenched her from head to toe. She yanked the plug from the wall and stared at the traitorous machine. "Vac!" she screamed at it. "You're supposed to suck up the damn water, not spout off like Old Faithful!" Then she noticed the second switch. One position for blowing out, one for sucking up. "Given two choices...," she muttered.

* * *

That evening Thea delayed eating her own dinner until Luke arrived to fetch Cupid. Although she found the cat to be a much-needed diversion from her problems, she was lonely for human company and hoped the scent of freshly baked bread and homemade bouillabaisse would entice Luke to stay.

She needn't have feared.

"Keep this up, and I'll become your slave for life," he said, dipping a crusty chunk of French bread into the thick seafood stew.

"Fine. You can start by cleaning the cat hairs off my kitchen counter. Do you have any idea how difficult it is to knead bread with a cat swiping at the dough?"

Luke scowled at the animal in question. Cu was draped across the back of Thea's couch. His tail swished to and fro, keeping time to an old Jerome Kern ballad, but his amber gaze remained fixed on the soup tureen in the middle of the table. "You could have sent him packing. You spoil him."

"And you don't? You could close your balcony door, you know."

He shrugged. "But then I wouldn't have an excuse to come here. I'd miss getting berated *and* fed."

"Then it's true." She smacked the table with her palm. "You and that cat are in cahoots!"

Luke raised his hands in submission. "Guilty as charged, ma'am. I knew the moment I accosted you in the lobby that you were the answer to my gastronomic needs."

"Yes, well, keep it up, and you won't have to worry about something else."

"What's that?"

She pointed at the nearly finished loaf of bread. "Another few helpings of that bread and Hedda will take you off her A-list. Who ever heard of a hunk with a spare tire?"

Luke reached for the remaining chunk of bread and saluted her with it. "To chubbiness," he declared, reaching for the butter, "and the privacy it brings."

Thea lowered the wine glass she had raised in answer to his toast and studied Luke. Frown lines settled at the corners of her mouth.

"What's wrong?"

She shook her head. "I'm puzzled. You have the city's foremost gossip columnist turning you into a celebrity, and you're running for the hills. Most men would love being in your position, but not you. You go as far as asking a stranger to pretend to be your fiancée in an attempt to put a halt to it. Why?"

Cu leaped off the sofa, scampered across the hardwood floor, and jumped onto his lap. Luke tore off a piece of bread and offered it to the cat. As Cu licked the butter, Luke stroked his fur and mulled over how he wanted to answer Thea. She was right. Most men would give anything to be in his position. But he wasn't most men. He'd already been burned twice. "I'm not sure you'd understand."

"Why is that?"

"Because you're different from most women I've known. You, Dr. Chandler, don't have a dishonest bone in your body. I, on the other hand, have had the misfortune of loving two extremely deceitful women."

Thea's brow knit together. "Two?"

Luke struggled to keep his voice flat and unemotional. "When I was eight years old, I arrived home from school to find a note taped to the refrigerator door. Seemed my mother wanted more out of life than my hardworking father could provide."

Thea gasped. "She abandoned you?"

"For a wealthy lover. I haven't seen her since." He paused, took a deep breath, and then continued. "My wife, knowing how my mother hurt me, also left a note on the refrigerator door. Only she also emptied a few bank accounts before running off to Nepal with her yoga instructor."

TEN

For the remainder of the week, Luke ate well, but Thea's soul grew progressively more tormented. She ignored her computer and her impending deadline, choosing instead to spend each day in her kitchen rather than in her office. She needed the Zen, but no matter how many hours she spent cooking and baking, she found little inner peace. Instead, she fretted the days away while a line from Shakespeare repeated over and over in her head like a broken record. *Oh, what a tangled web we weave, when first we practice to deceive.*

Luke admired integrity—a trait which, unbeknownst to him, she sorely lacked. She had deceived him about her writing career and hated herself for doing it. Yet, if she confessed her alter ego's identity, she risked destroying their blossoming friendship, and that would be most painful of all.

That aside, she couldn't face another rejection. Not from a man, even if their relationship *was* purely platonic. On the other hand, her conscience couldn't take any more lies. She found herself trapped in a damned-if-I-do-damned-if-I-don't conundrum. And Grace had compounded her problems by concocting that little publicity stunt with Hedda.

On Friday Luke arrived for dinner waving two tickets for the next evening—Sarah Brightman and Michael Crawford in concert at Carnegie Hall. "A thank-you for helping me through this past week. I normally exist on fast food the week prior to a business trip. Both your cooking and your company were far more enjoyable."

He placed the tickets in her hand, folding her fingers around them, then added a caveat. "I have to warn you, though. This is a benefit concert."

"Meaning?"

"Hedda. Chances are she'll be there."

"Hedda," Thea grimaced. She could feel Tom, Dick, and Harry dragging out their trampoline. Accepting Luke's invitation meant agreeing to continue with his charade. Was she willing to forego a once-in-a-lifetime performance to protect a principle she'd already repeatedly sacrificed?

She had told him she couldn't pretend to be someone she wasn't. What he didn't know was that she already lived that lie on a daily basis. As far as charades went, Dr. Althea Chandler was the queen of the hoaxsters. "I'll wear a suit of armor."

Except, she didn't own a suit of armor, or anything else suitable for such an evening. She might have gotten away with chain mail sooner than wearing the same outfit she worn to dinner the previous Saturday night. Hedda was the kind of woman who'd remember such a detail. Thea wasn't the least bit bothered by that, but she had no desire to embarrass Luke by giving the gossip maven the opportunity to devote her next column to Luke

Bennett's fiancée's fashion *faux pas*. Hedda or no Hedda, she probably couldn't get away with wearing her ivory suit, anyway.

As patrons of the symphony, her parents had often attended similar benefits in San Francisco, often taking their two daughters. Her father had always worn a tux, her mother an evening gown, their daughters equally elegant in junior-set formal wear.

"Is it black tie?" she asked, hoping he'd say no, but doubting she'd have such luck. After all, nothing else in her life was going right. Why should this?

"Of course."

What did she expect? Thea handed the tickets back to him. "I'm afraid I'll have to pass." Cupid rubbed up against her leg. His plaintive meow echoed the disappointment she fought to hide from Luke. "I left my gowns in San Francisco."

"But not your heart," he reminded her. "The stores are open tomorrow."

As if it were that simple. Thea shook her head. The move, far more expensive than she'd anticipated, had maxed out her credit cards and left her counting pennies until her next royalty check arrived.

Of course, splurging on the antique coffee table for her living room hadn't helped. She rationalized that extravagance by filing the receipt under *Sanity Preservation*. After all, compared to the cost of a psychiatrist, the coffee table was a bargain, and a piece of furniture would never hurt her the way her ex-fiancé had.

When the going gets tough, go shopping? So, maybe she did have a bit of her mother in her after all. She really couldn't afford the antique, and never should have purchased it. Even with the expense of the house off her back, she still felt only steps away from a bread line. Of course, if she didn't get her act together before her publishing deadline, she'd be standing smack in the middle of that line.

A formal gown, even one from Macy's rather than Saks or Bergdorf, was out of the question. Thea shook her head. "I can't."

She had never been much of an actress. In high school she was far more comfortable working behind the scenes than on stage. She got away with pretending to be Trulee only because Trulee stayed hidden from the public. Otherwise, she never could have pulled off the deception. Consequently, she was hardly surprised when Luke zeroed in on her reason for turning him down.

"Finances tight?"

Thea nodded. "I'm afraid I squeezed the last drop of blood out of the proverbial stone when I bought my apartment. I probably should have taken something in Brooklyn or Queens, but...." She shrugged. "After living all my life in Pacific Heights, I guess I'm just a snob at heart. Besides, the moment I saw this place, I fell in love with it."

"Which is why I stay," said Luke. He paused for a moment, combed his fingers through his hair, then rubbed his jaw. "I don't suppose you'd allow me to buy you a dress for tomorrow night, would you?"

"Out of the question."

"You'll be missing a wonderful concert."

Yes, she would, but in the greater scheme of her life, this was a relatively minor disappointment compared to the others she had dealt with. "*C'est la vie.* If I'm lucky, public television will record it for broadcast at some later date."

"Or we could reach a compromise."

Thea eyed him skeptically. Cupid positioned himself between their feet, his head swinging back and forth like a spectator at a tennis match. "What sort of compromise?"

"A loan. You can reimburse me when you get back on your feet."

The offer sounded tempting, but the last thing she needed was more debt hanging over her head. "No. It's a generous offer, but I already have quite a few debts. I'm sorry."

"Then how about if you work off the cost of the dress?"

"Excuse me?"

Ignoring her, Luke walked into the kitchen. Thea followed, Cupid scampering close on her heels. She watched as Luke grabbed a pencil and scratch pad from the holder next to the telephone. "Dinner, five nights. Let's see." He tapped the eraser end of the pencil against his chin. "There was veal Parmesan Monday." He made a notation on the pad. "An omelet Tuesday. Bouillabaisse Wednesday. Steak Diane yesterday."

He glanced up from his scribbling. "And tonight?" Luke filled his lungs. "Definitely garlic something-or-other." He grabbed a potholder and lifted the lid from a pan simmering on the stove. "Shrimp scampi?"

Hands on hips, Thea nodded.

He scrawled an additional line onto the page. "Then there's Cu-sitting Monday through Friday of next week." At the sound of his name Cupid jumped onto the counter and nuzzled Luke's arm. He brushed the cat's paw aside and jotted several more notes, then made a flourish of tallying up the total before handing her the paper.

Thea skimmed what he'd written, gasping when she read the bottom line. "*For services rendered, seven hundred dollars*! You can't be serious!" She ripped the sheet in half and tossed it into the trash. "I'm not some charity case, Luke Bennett. Even in New

York fast food doesn't cost sixty-five dollars a meal."

"You didn't cook fast food. Besides, I'd be hard-pressed to find comparable meals anywhere in Manhattan for less than that amount."

"A sixty-five-dollar omelet? Not even at Le Cirque, Luke. And seventy-five dollars a day to feed your cat? You could almost get a hotel room for that!"

"Hardly. This *is* New York, as you're so fond of reminding me. And in New York, that's the going rate at the local Tabby Towers." He waved toward the phone. "Give them a call if you don't believe me."

Rather than reaching for the phone, Thea crossed her arms over her chest and glared at him. "That's not the point."

Luke smirked at her warrior-like stance. The hint of a chuckle lurked behind his words. "It's been a long day, Thea. Let's not debate semantics."

He may as well have patted the top of her head and said, *why don't you just give in and do it my way, so we can get on with dinner.* The message was the same. He found her objections not only groundless but also amusing!

Luke reached into his pants pocket, pulled out his wallet, and began counting out hundred-dollar bills. "Now, you can either accept payment for the dinners and an advance on taking care of Cu next week, or you can decline. I certainly can't force you to go shopping, but you know damn well you want to see that concert, and I want to take you."

He held out the money. Thea stood firm.

"Don't be stubborn about this. Go buy a dress, and make us both happy." He slammed the bills onto the counter, then folded his arms across his chest, mimicking her aggressive posture. A challenge emanated from his clear blue eyes.

Cupid sniffed at the bills, eyed Luke, then snorted.

Feeling manipulated, Thea scowled first at the money, then Luke. Anger roiled inside her—along with a certain acrobatic threesome who were hell bent on creating the ulcer that devoured Cleveland. She turned away from him. "Friendship doesn't come with a price tag. Was I wrong to think we were becoming friends? Is this still just an *arrangement*? Luke gets his phony fiancée, and Thea gets an occasional night on the town?"

"Is that what you think?"

She spun around to confront him. "I don't know what to think! Part of me is very angry and hurt right now. I don't want your pity, Luke Bennett, and I certainly don't want to be used by you."

"And the other part?"

His words were spoken without emotion. She looked up into his eyes, expecting coldness. Instead, she found a warmth that permeated her soul and melted her rage. The unexpected feelings took her by surprise. "I don't know," she whispered, shaking her head.

Luke stepped closer. Only a hair's breadth separated their bodies. He reached up and brushed a lock of hair off her cheek. The intimacy of the act sent a shiver of pleasure—or was it warning?—skittering down her spine. "My ex-wife often accused me of being insensitive. Maybe she was right. I handled this poorly. I only wanted to help."

Yes, she knew that now. His eyes told her before his words. Still, she felt confused. She was the giver, the doer, the protector. She spent her life sacrificing for others. Luke had turned the tables on her. Seven hundred dollars might not constitute a sacrifice to him, but still, she wasn't used to having someone consider her needs. Did her violent reaction stem from decades-old bruises that had nothing to do with him? "Why?"

"Because that's what friends do." He picked up the money and placed it in her palm, then gently folded her fingers over it, cupping her hand in both of his. "Will you do me this favor? As a friend?"

Thea nodded. In the back of her mind, she sensed something had changed, but she wasn't certain what or how or why. She only knew she liked the feel of her hand in his and didn't want it to end. "As a friend," she repeated, her eyes focused on their joined hands.

Cupid nestled his head against their hands and purred.

* * *

The next morning Thea stood in front of her dresser, eyeing the seven one-hundred-dollar bills Luke had pressed her into accepting. Although she'd grown up wealthy, the last several years had given her an entirely new perspective on the value of a dollar. She picked up the bills and scowled at them. Every fiber in her body rebelled against spending a king's ransom for a dress she'd wear for an evening.

And what if there were future invitations, as she anticipated there might be? No, as she now *hoped* there might be. Would Luke insist on clothing her each time? Friend or no friend, she couldn't allow that. "The bucks stop here," she mumbled, shoving the bills into her wallet.

He expected her appropriately dressed for the evening, and she would be. But the bills hadn't come with any strings attached. Seven hundred dollars could either purchase one moderately priced gown at an upscale department store or an entire wardrobe if a girl knew where to shop.

And Thea knew where to shop.

She had stumbled upon Repeat Performance while exploring Greenwich Village soon after her move to Manhattan. The secondhand clothing shop, with its appealing window display of classically elegant garments, caught her attention as she strolled down Bleecker Street that day.

Thea grabbed a light jacket and headed downtown.

An hour later she stood in front of a full-length mirror, admiring the black silk Donna Karan that draped her body. Never in a million years would she have believed she could wear such a dress, but the saleswoman had insisted she try it on.

"You're perfect for Donna Karan," said the clerk who'd picked out the garment after sizing up Thea's figure. "That gown was made for you."

And so was the price. Thea glanced at the tag pinned to the side seam. Fifty dollars. At this rate she could afford...she scrunched up her nose and did a little quick mental arithmetic...fourteen gowns! "I'll take it," she said, amazed at how good she looked—and felt. Maybe Madeline wasn't the only Chandler daughter who could wear Versace. "What else can you suggest?"

Over the next several hours Thea tried on a wide range of formal and cocktail length gowns, finally settling on two of each along with a black beaded shawl, an untailored champagne colored shantung jacket and two pairs of never worn Ferragamo heels.

"Many of our *suppliers* are shopaholics," confided the saleswoman with a wink as she wrapped up Thea's purchases. "You know the type. They spend their days spending their husband's money, then never get around to wearing half of what they've bought."

Thea knew the type all too well. Her mother had given new meaning to the term *shop till you drop*—even after all their money had disappeared.

She left the boutique laden down with several shopping bags. The total bill came to two hundred eighty-one dollars and twenty-five cents. If she needed additional outfits later, she now knew where to shop. If not, she planned on returning the substantial balance to Luke.

* * *

"Lovely," said Luke when he arrived at her apartment later that evening. He crossed his arms over his chest and nodded approvingly. "You did well."

Thea spun around, showing off the outfit from all angles. "Very well." Grabbing the beaded shawl off a chair, she wrapped it around her shoulders and preceded Luke out the door.

* * *

The evening included an after-concert dinner where Thea found herself seated at a table with Luke's two business partners and their wives. He introduced her as Dr. Althea Chandler, a friend.

"Where do you practice?" asked Sean Porter, the firm's senior partner, a tall, scholarly looking man with a full head of silver white hair that he wore trimmed just above his collar.

"I'm a professor of sociology. Up until last semester I taught at Berkeley, but I've taken a sabbatical to do some writing." Luke's partners and their wives didn't need to know the sabbatical was actually an emergency personal leave. No, more an escape than a leave.

"So you're only here temporarily?" asked his wife, a petite brunette with an infectious smile.

Hardly. As much as she loved San Francisco, the city held too many painful memories for her. For better or worse, New York was now her home. "I'm not certain about my future plans at this point. I like Manhattan. I've thought about applying for a position at one of the colleges or universities in the city. Maybe NYU or Columbia. If either has any openings."

"Jerry's on the Board of Trustees at Columbia," said Sean, motioning to the third partner in the Porter-Sachs-Bennett triumvirate. "I'm sure he'd be happy to put in a good word for you."

Jerome Sachs looked like the Mutt to Sean Porter's Jeff, or the Hardy to his Laurel. Whereas the senior partner appeared to spend several hours a week in a gym, Jerome, the middle partner, obviously spent the same amount of time or more at Dunkin' Donuts. Thea pegged his age at about forty-five, somewhere halfway between Luke and Sean, and quickly concluded he removed his full head of jet-black hair each night before retiring. Looks aside, though, he was as charming as Sean. He nodded in agreement. "Absolutely."

"What are you writing?" asked his wife, a stunning blonde, easily ten years younger and half a head taller than her husband.

Thea hesitated. "I...um...I'm expanding on my dissertation." But not in the way she'd originally intended. Her two scholarly volumes on the subject, published by small university presses, lay moldering in some warehouse—if not a landfill—while Dr. Trulee Lovejoy ruled the bestseller lists.

"Thea's uncovered some interesting facts about all those psycho-babble authors flooding the bookstores," said Luke. "Like that Trulee Loveless."

Thea cringed.

"Lovejoy," said Barbara Porter. "Trulee Lovejoy."

Luke shrugged. "Whatever."

"Well, of course, I've never read her books," said Diane Sachs, "but I've heard many women credit her with helping them find the perfect mate."

Luke snorted. "Desperate women relying on deception. What basis is that for a lasting relationship?"

Thea picked at her appetizer. Tom, Dick, and Harry raced around the Indianapolis Tummy Speedway. Suddenly, the crab mousse didn't look the least bit appetizing. She placed her fork on her plate and smiled weakly. "I thought you'd gotten past that, Luke."

He turned to her. "You might see it as parody, Thea, but the fact remains most women take the books at face value. They don't get the joke."

"What joke?" asked Barbara.

"Thea thinks the books were written as a lampoon."

"Really?" asked Diane. "What makes you think that?"

"You'd have to read them with an objective eye," said Luke. "Unfortunately, most people don't."

"Is that so bad?" asked Diane. "I'd imagine the women who buy her books are just insecure and need a little help in socialization skills."

"Somehow, Di, I don't think insecurity is a problem for the women chasing me. Not when they begin a conversation with a verbal résumé of their sexual prowess."

Thea felt the need to defend her alter ego against such a ludicrous accusation. She had *never* suggested any woman behave in such an audacious manner! "I don't believe I remember seeing any such advice in either of Trulee's books, Luke."

"Does it matter? What she suggests is nearly as bad."

One eyebrow raised, Barbara turned first to Luke, then Thea. "You mean you've both actually read her books?"

"As research," said Thea.

"And you, Luke?" asked Diane. "What's your excuse for reading *Finding Mr. Right* and *Hooking Mr. Right*?"

"How else am I to stay one step ahead of the vultures?"

Diane switched her attention back to Thea. "Ever meet her?"

Every time I stare into the mirror. Thea sidestepped Diane's query with a non-committal reply. "She's very reclusive."

"No longer," said Diane. "According to this morning's paper, she's about to launch a nationwide promotional tour. She's kicking it off Monday at Barnes & Noble. The flagship down on Union Square."

Luke swore under his breath. "Great. Just what the country needs."

"Poor Luke," said Barbara, patting his hand. She turned to Thea. "I take it you know all about Hedda Two and her campaign to find him a new wife?"

Thea stared past Barbara, her gaze focused on Diane. Surely, the woman had gotten her information wrong. She'd turned Grace down, and Grace had made no further attempt to cajole her into agreeing to the publicity junket. So what the hell was going on? Had Grace gone ahead and hired a ringer to act as Trulee?

"Thea?" She blinked Barbara back into focus. "I asked if Luke's told you about Hedda?"

"Oh, yes." She glanced nervously at Luke. "He certainly has." Thea had spied Hedda earlier at a table across the room and wondered what would happen once Hedda began table-hopping.

"According to last Monday's column, Hedda claims you've found someone, Luke," said Diane, casting Thea a questioning glance. "Is it true?"

Luke pierced Diane with a cold glare and a hard scowl. "I don't know why you bother to read that drivel." He then turned his attention back to his salad, placing a forkful of endive in his mouth to signal the end of the conversation. At least as far as he was concerned.

Thea watched as Diane and Barbara exchanged knowing glances. What had Luke gotten her into? Not to mention himself. Last Saturday night he'd led Hedda to believe she was his fiancée. How did he expect to explain his way out of this situation once Hedda confronted them? And how could he not have known that the situation would arise?

Yes, he'd told her Hedda might be at the concert. However, he'd failed to mention his partners and their wives would also be in attendance and joining them for dinner. Had he deliberately set her up again or just not thought through the situation? After last night Thea wasn't certain what to believe about Luke Bennett.

As it turned out, she didn't have long to wait. The plumed newsmonger arrived between the salad and entrée. "And how are my three favorite princes of Wall Street?" she asked, tossing air kisses at each of the partners. She completely ignored Diane Sachs and Barbara Porter, zeroing in on Thea instead. "Heavens, my dear! You're still ringless!"

Here it comes. The proverbial excrement is about to hit the fan.

Hedda turned on Luke. "This is totally unacceptable, Lucas Bennett. After all, you're not some impoverished Bohemian! What exactly is your excuse for not giving your fiancée an engagement ring?"

"Fiancée?" Four pairs of eyes turned first on Thea, then Luke. The males' faces were filled with astonishment, their wives with satisfied smirks.

"What the hell's going on here, old boy?" asked Sean. "You announce your engagement to Hedda before telling your closest friends?"

"Don't any of you read my column?" wailed Hedda. "I announced Luke's engagement last Monday."

Poor Luke. He turned to Thea, his eyes begging for a miracle, but she merely shrugged her shoulders. As far as she was concerned, he had only one course of action available to him. "Time to come clean?"

He sighed. "I suppose."

But his explanation was hardly what she expected. He addressed his business associates and their wives. "We were planning on telling you all later this evening. As for bigmouth, here," he nodded toward Hedda, "she ambushed us last Saturday night."

He wrapped one arm around Thea's shoulders, drawing her close to him. With his free hand he clasped her tightly laced fingers and raised them to his lips. "Right after my darling said yes."

ELEVEN

He'd done it to her again! Not wanting to make a scene, Thea swallowed back both her anger and a groan, delivering instead a strained smile to the two other couples at the table. She wondered if Luke knew that he was only making a bad situation worse. Lies were like rabbits. They multiplied at the speed of light. She had firsthand experience and guilty conscience to prove it.

Luke placed her trembling hands back in her lap, then brushed his lips against her ear. "Go along with me, please," he pleaded in a whisper that only she could hear. "We'll straighten this out after Hedda leaves."

Drawing deep within herself, Thea mustered what little acting ability she possessed. Nodding, she gazed lovingly into her "fiancé's" eyes. In the background she heard the other two couples offering their congratulations. Turning to them, she smiled her acceptance.

"But what about the ring?" insisted Hedda.

"Yes, where's your diamond?" asked Barbara.

"I don't want one," said Thea, feeling relieved that she could finally offer something of truth to the conversation. Hedda gasped. Everyone except Luke stared at her as though she'd suddenly sprouted a second head. Wearing a puzzled expression, his gaze was fixed on their still joined hands nestled in her lap.

"Nonsense!" Hedda snorted her objection. "You can't mean that. With his money he should buy you the Hope diamond. Don't make excuses for him."

Luke released her hands. Raising his head, he spoke directly to Hedda. His voice was subdued yet forceful. "The Hope diamond isn't for sale, and if my beloved tells me she doesn't want an engagement ring, then she means it. This is the most honest woman I've ever known."

Hedda pursed her lips. She glared first at Luke, then at Thea, not bothering to hold back her apparent annoyance at the two of them.

Keeping a smile firmly plastered on her face, Thea blinked, fighting the tears gathering behind her eyes. The others would think she was overcome by Luke's words. Only she knew how much his praise pained her.

"Coming from Luke," said Jerome, "that's the highest of compliments. You must be one very special lady." He lifted his glass. "To Dr. Althea Chandler, the best thing to ever happen to our Luke."

"Here! Here!" said Sean.

"Welcome to the family," added Barbara.

"I'll second that," said Diane.

Hedda smiled down at Thea. "Dr. Althea Chandler," she repeated. "Well, it took a while, but I finally have what I came for." She swept the table with a dramatic wave of her arm. "Enjoy your dinners," she said, then spun on her heels and headed back toward her own table.

Once Hedda left, Luke explained his backfired ruse to the rest of the members of the table.

"So you and Luke aren't involved?" asked Barbara, a note of disappointment filtering through her words.

"Only as neighbors," said Thea. "We barely know each other." So why was she having difficulty focusing on anything beyond the lingering feel of his lips against her fingers or the way his breath had kissed the rim of her ear?

"Great acting job," said Sean, "but I'm afraid you've dug yourself into a crater, old man. Excuse the mixed metaphor, but once Hedda sinks her claws into a story, she milks it until the cow runs dry."

A chill of foreboding slithered up Thea's spine. *I finally have what I came for.* Hedda's parting words rang in her ears.

Luke removed his glasses and massaged the bridge of his nose. Tension lines creased his forehead. "Hedda isn't really interested in finding me a wife," he said.

His partners and their wives stared at him.

"Could have fooled me," said Jerry.

"No, this entire campaign is more about her than me. I'm simply a means to an end."

"I don't understand," said Diane.

Luke took a sip of his wine before explaining. "These columns of hers are increasing readership for a nearly bankrupt daily—besides generating publicity for her."

"Of course!" The expression of puzzlement disappeared from Diane's face. "Even if the paper folds, she's hopefully created enough exposure for herself to get picked up by one of the other large publishers."

"But she's already in other papers, isn't she?" asked Barbara.

"Syndicated in the northern suburbs, Long Island, Jersey, and Connecticut," said Luke. "If *The Daily Post* folds, the syndication dries up. Those papers can't afford her on their own."

"She needs a city paper as a backer," added Diane.

"Or television?" suggested Barbara. "I've often wondered why she hasn't been signed for an entertainment segment on one of the network newscasts or the tabloid shows on Fox or cable."

"Yes, but at whose expense?" asked Thea, knowing they all thought she meant Luke and not her.

* * *

By the time they arrived back at their building, Thea's head was spinning, her emotions in a state of turmoil. Luke's deceit. Her chaotic feelings about him. Hedda's ambush. Grace's bombshell of her connivance with Hedda. It was all too much for her to deal with at once, and in the cramped confines of the elevator, Luke's closeness set her nerves even further on edge. She couldn't wait to escape to the relative calm of her own apartment.

"Thank you," he said after she unlocked her door. "Things got a bit out of hand there for a while. You were a terrific sport about the whole thing—especially the ring." He chuckled. "And you saved me a bundle."

Was he really that dense? Once again, he'd placed her in an awkward position, and all he cared about was the cost of a diamond ring! "I wasn't thinking of you," she said, her voice tight with suppressed anger. "I have no intention of wearing a token of a phony engagement."

"Well, it was quick thinking on your part, anyway. I hope the concert made up for the fiasco that followed."

"Truthfully?" Or should I be polite and lie? Thank you, Luke. It was a lovely concert and worth all the humiliation you subjected me to afterwards!"

He stared blankly at her. "Humiliation? Thea, when did I...."

She waved her arms in frustration. "You don't get it, do you? You have no idea how you embarrassed me in front of your friends."

Luke's mouth fell open. "I'm sorry. I had no idea...." He stopped mid-sentence, his attention fixed on the solitary tear that had escaped from the corner of her eye. She reached to swat it away, but he grabbed her hand. With his other hand he reached out and captured the tear on the tip of his index finger and stared at the droplet of moisture.

"I've hurt you," he said, his gaze meeting hers. "I never meant to do that." He sighed heavily, his features growing contrite. "I'm such a jerk. I wasn't thinking."

"No, you weren't."

"Again."

She nodded. "Again."

He released another heavy sigh and hung his head. "What I did was incredibly thoughtless and selfish. Believe it or not, I do know how even the most benign lie can devastate someone else. I'm sorry, Thea." He paused for a moment, reaching for her hands and clasping them between both of his. "Even though I don't deserve it, can you find it in your heart to forgive me? Please?"

Thea stared at their joined hands. That same mixture of pleasure and warning traversed her limbs and rippled along her spine. His words melted her anger. She lifted her chin and studied his face. The pain in his eyes touched her. His apology was so heartfelt and sincere, how could she not forgive him?

She knew from firsthand experience how easy it was to get sucked into a quagmire of deceit. She now knew Luke well enough to accept that his behavior, although sometimes thoughtless, was never calculated. He hadn't deliberately set out to hurt her. He just hadn't thought through the consequences of his actions. Like her. She'd never meant to hurt anyone, either.

Thea nodded. "I forgive you."

Luke exhaled a sigh of relief. "Thank you for being so understanding." He reached out and cupped her cheek with the palm of his hand. Their eyes met for the briefest of moments, his gaze penetrating her soul before he bent his head and captured her lips with his.

Thea's lips parted in invitation, an invitation Luke quickly accepted. His tongue joined his lips in skimming, tasting, exploring. And then his hands joined his lips and tongue. The fingers of one hand strummed and caressed her neck and collarbone, sending shivers of pleasure coursing through her body. His other hand loosened her twist of hair and threaded his fingers through the silken strands. She shivered with pleasure. With need.

He drew her closer and whispered her name, his voice husky with desire, and she melted farther into him. Wrapping her arms around his neck, all her inhibitions and hesitancy slipped away, and she began her own journey, skimming, tasting, and exploring right back, her body melded to his.

When a moment later Luke suddenly broke the kiss and stepped back, he left her overwhelmed with confusion. And much more. Emptiness. Longing. Desire. With one kiss he'd shattered the universe as she knew it. With one kiss he'd changed everything between them. Forever. She stared back up at him and saw the same roiling emotions playing across his face.

Neither spoke. Neither moved. Time stood still, and something changed between them. Something unspoken and undefined, but they both knew a monumental shift had just occurred in their world. Luke may have initially intended the kiss as an affectionate gesture between friends, a thank you for her forgiveness and understanding. But from the moment their lips met, it had taken on an entirely different meaning. A spark ignited, surprising them both with its unexpected, incendiary intensity. Thea saw it in Luke's eyes, and she felt it flowing through her own body like molten lava, hot and thick and consuming everything in its path. Consuming her with a need she didn't want to feel ever again.

Luke cleared his throat. "I'd better go." His body told a different story. She'd felt it in the press of his torso against hers, in the organ that sprang to life against her belly the moment their lips met. He didn't want to leave any more than she wanted him to. His gaze bore into her, waiting for her to protest, waiting for another, more encompassing invitation.

An invitation she couldn't give no matter how much her body throbbed with need. Not yet. Not until she confessed everything to him. And then she doubted he'd still want her the way he did at this moment. Thea nodded. "Good night."

* * *

Thea paced back and forth in her apartment for hours that night, trying to understand the Voodoo that had invaded her body. With one kiss Luke Bennett transformed her Rock of Gibraltar foundation into a quivering mile-high mound of Jell-O. Steve's kisses had never unleashed such wanton passion within her. No man's had.

She'd previously experienced desire—or what she'd thought

was desire—but nothing in her past—albeit, limited—relationships with men came close to the explosive force triggered by Luke's one kiss. Until a few hours ago she would have scoffed at the notion, deriding the romance novels that spoke of such nonsense. Her rational mind had refused to accept that *any* kiss could trigger such unbridled emotion. Boy, had she been wrong.

The few hours of sleep she managed that night produced unwanted dreams of a man she'd do well to keep at a safe distance—both in the real world and the world of her subconscious. Only in her dreams, Luke Bennett was anything but at a safe distance. In the dreams that played over and over in her mind throughout the night, neither of them had stopped with that one kiss.

Thea woke with a start. The sandman's world had lost its safe haven status the night she stumbled upon Madeline and Steve in the pool house. Now another uninvited vision had taken up residence in her slumbering brain, its various permutations torturing her as they danced behind her closed lids.

She kicked aside the quilt and greeted the rising sun. Maybe she could exorcise her unwelcome thoughts and images with a good physical pounding to her body. If nothing else, with any luck, she'd exhaust herself to the point of collapsing into a dreamless stupor. Stripping off her nightgown, she pulled on her neon yellow Mickey Mouse sweats, slipped on a pair of socks and sneakers, and headed out the door.

As soon as Thea entered Central Park, she broke into a sprint, joining countless other runners taking advantage of the cool, early morning hour. Only the others seemed to know what they were doing. Thea hadn't run since high school when a mandatory lap around the track preceded each period of physical education.

Taking off like the proverbial bat out of hell, she forgot about the need for warm-up stretching exercises. She gave no thought to pacing herself. And she hadn't remembered to bring a bottle of water.

Fifteen minutes into her run, panting for air, Thea collapsed on a bench. A stitch pierced her right side, a spasm cramped her left calf. The water fountain twenty yards down the path beckoned, but twenty yards might have been twenty miles for all the good it did her. She broke out in a cold sweat as a tarp of dizziness blanketed her. Fighting to stave off a wave of nausea and the blackness that threatened the edges of her brain, she slumped forward, closed her eyes, and rested her head on her knees.

"Here. Drink this."

Still panting, Thea forced her eyelids open and stared at the most perfect set of male limbs she'd ever seen. Skin pulled taut over corded muscles, not an ounce of flab or fat. No knobby knees. Only the tan coloring and light dusting of blond hair told her she stared at flesh and blood, not one of Michelangelo's marble masterpieces.

Her gaze traveled upward. A skimpy pair of black nylon running shorts fluttered in the breeze, whipping around upper thighs that framed one incredibly large, firm....

When Thea didn't reach for the water, Luke tipped her head back and held the pull-spout to her lips, squeezing the bottle gently to produce a trickle of water. "Slow sips. Don't guzzle. You'll cramp."

Luke had seen Thea collapse onto the bench as he rounded the path on his way back from his morning run. She was easy to spot. Her bright yellow Mickey Mouse sweats stood out like a nun at a Rave. No one who knew the first thing about running would don such heavy clothes on a morning like this, much less run without water. "What were you doing?" he asked.

She raised her head and blinked. Her sallow complexion blanched white before a rosiness crept back into her cheeks. Her tongue darted across her parched lips. "Exercise." The word came out on a dry raspy gulp of breath.

"Like hell. Killing yourself is more like it. You're dehydrated. Don't move." He grabbed a rag from his waistband and jogged down the path toward the fountain. A moment later he returned and placed the damp, cool cloth on the back of her neck.

Luke settled onto the bench, leaned back, and exhaled his frustration. Damn! After a sleepless night, he'd spent the last hour and a half running to rid himself of the hunger this woman unleashed in him after he'd made the mistake of kissing her. Little good it had done him. One look at her this morning and those cravings had returned. Tenfold.

* * *

When Luke left for Atlanta Sunday evening, Thea breathed a sigh of relief. She needed some space between them to sort out the jumble of confusing emotions roiling inside her. His unexpected, but hardly unwelcome, goodnight kiss the evening before had completely shattered what little equilibrium she still possessed. Although relatively short but by no means chaste, Luke's kiss had branded itself into her soul. This morning's attempt to rid herself of the sensuous images running rampant through her mind backfired big time. Now every time she closed her eyes, she saw those magnificent legs. It had taken every ounce of discipline she possessed to keep from reaching out and stroking them this morning. With her tongue.

Luke's kiss and her uncontrollable response had multiplied by a factor of gazillion her distress over her predicament. Thea needed time to find a solution that would abate her moral crisis over Trulee without causing Luke to despise her for deceiving him. "And when I'm finished doing that, I'll find a cure for cancer and break the light barrier," she told Cupid. "One is just as doable as the others."

The cat hopped onto her lap and studied her with those disconcerting amber eyes of his. "I swear, Cupid, there are times I think you know a hell of a lot more than the rest of us. So why don't you help me out here, huh?"

The cat answered by curling into a ball and offering her a deep, vibrating purr before falling asleep.

"And after all I've done for you. Ingrate."

Once again, that night Thea slept fitfully. After a series of X-rated dreams, she woke with a whopping case of *Bennett on the Brain*, and her thoughts were anything but platonic. The early morning phone call from her editor only added to her anxiety level.

"My God, Thea, I have to rely on Hedda Two to learn you're Luke Bennett's mystery fiancée? Is that why you jumped all over me last week? What the hell's going on? How can you get yourself engaged to a man you've known less than two weeks? Especially after what happened to you in San Francisco. Have you flipped?"

Thea rubbed the sleep from her eyes and yawned. "Good morning, Grace. I can't tell you how much I look forward to these early Monday morning chats."

"I'm beginning to worry about you, Thea. Maybe you should see a therapist. This is not normal behavior—especially for you."

Thea sighed. Grace's underlying message came across loud and clear: Sensible Dr. Althea Chandler never acted capriciously.

"Look, Grace. I'm not engaged to Luke Bennett, okay? So stop worrying."

"But according to Hedda...."

"I know." Thea proceeded to explain how Luke had cajoled her into acting as his accomplice to thwart Hedda and how the plan had backfired in his face.

"And yours, I'm afraid," said Grace. "Wait till you see today's column. You're treading on thin ice here, babe. Does he know about Trulee?"

"No, of course not!"

"You know, Thea, you could have found another way to forget Steve. You really didn't have to jump from one soap opera into another."

"It's worse than that," she admitted, the realization hitting her like a Mack truck. She tried to shake off the feeling, telling herself it was only infatuation. She was merely suffering from a delayed case of Post-Romantic Stress Syndrome. It was all Steve's fault.

"How could it be much worse?"

The rational side of Thea's brain fell by the wayside, drowned out by a sea of love hormones. And why? Because another man had kissed her? No, not just another man. One very specific man whose kiss she could still feel from the quiver in her lips all the way down to the tingle in her toes. "I think I'm falling in love with him, Grace."

Her editor groaned. "You're right. It's worse."

"By the way, Grace, not to change the subject or anything, but is there something you want to tell me about Trulee?"

Grace cleared her throat. "You heard?"

"So it's true? I can't believe you actually hired someone to pose as me!"

There was a long pause on the other end of the phone. "Uhm, I didn't exactly *hire* anyone."

"What do you mean? Are you sure you can trust this person?"

"Oh, I can trust her."

"So who is she?"

"Me?"

"Grace!"

"What else could I do, Thea? My job was on the line, and you suggested it. You should have seen the expression on Goldberg's face when I fessed up. You'd think he hit the lottery."

"I also suggested telling him I had leprosy. For God's sake, Grace, I wasn't serious!"

"You're angry."

"Yes. No." Was she? Thea thought for a moment. Now she had something else complicating her life. Just what she didn't need at the moment. "Hell, I don't know, Grace. Better you than me, I suppose, but it just adds another layer of lies to an already rickety tower of deceit. At some point it's all going to come crashing down on top of me. On top of *us*."

"You left me little choice, Thea."

"I suppose."

"Will you come to the book signing today? I could use the moral support."

"You're going to need a lot more than moral support."

"What do you mean?"

"I hope you spent the weekend committing those two books to memory. Trulee has a legion of fans who know every chapter by heart."

On the other end of the line, Grace sounded like she was about to be sick.

Thea hung up the phone and walked into the bathroom. Catching a glimpse of herself in the mirror, she was shocked by her lovestruck expression. How could she look like a starry-eyed adolescent when her world was crumbling around her? She attempted to regain control of her mind and body with a stern lecture. *Get real, Althea! You can't be falling in love with Luke Bennett. You barely know the man, and besides, the jury's still out as to whether you even like him.*

No, that was no longer true. She *did* like Luke, perhaps, too much, now that she'd gotten to know him—even with his propensity for throwing her to the lions. Just one lion, really, and she understood he did that out of desperation. And not completely thinking things through. Yet another annoying male trait she chalked up to the defective Y chromosome.

Or was it? Hell, even she was guilty of acting without thinking. Had she only realized what she was getting herself into with that first book...but there was little point beating that dead horse. Under the circumstances, she knew she'd do it all again in a heartbeat. Her mother had needed her help. And after all, she was the responsible daughter.

Besides, she could understand Luke's frustration. Hedda was enough to drive any sane person over the edge. And he *had* apologized afterwards. Thea pressed her fingers against her lips and closed her eyes, remembering the form his apology had taken.

Anyway, her sin was far worse. She should have come clean to him about Trulee that first night before their relationship had time to develop. They would have parted enemies, but wasn't it better to be stabbed in the front by an enemy than in the back by a friend? Thea felt like a rat—a hypocritical rat trapped inside an exercise wheel. No matter how hard she tried to escape, she only ran faster and faster in the same tight circle of lies.

* * *

Thea stood at the entrance to the Union Square Barnes & Noble and stared at the large black and white blowup poster taped to the window. A seductive looking Grace, her neckline dipped low enough to reveal cleavage meant to reawaken the dormant hormones of a catatonic octogenarian, smiled back at her. Superimposed over Grace's breasts, bold lettering stated: *Today only. Noon to 2pm. Meet Dr. Trulee Lovejoy, author of the national bestselling husband-hunting guides,* Finding Mr. Right *and* Hooking Mr. Right.

Thea pulled open the door and stepped inside. Another poster, this one twice as large, stood on an easel directly in front of her. Behind the easel, a line of women, their arms laden with copies of both of her books, snaked around the tall bookcases lining the first floor. Thea glanced at her watch. Eleven forty-five. The book signing didn't begin for fifteen minutes, and already the store was packed with autograph seekers.

"The end of the line is over there." A saleswoman grabbed two books off a table next to her, offered them to Thea, and motioned to the right with her chin.

Thea shook her head and waved away the books. "Thanks, but I'm not here for the signing." She skirted the crowd, heading for the front of the line and her formerly sane editor.

Grace found her before she found Grace. "God, am I glad you're here!"

TWELVE

Although Grace wore the same outfit and jewelry from the photograph, she looked anything but seductive at the moment. She looked frazzled, pasty, and ready to barf. She grabbed Thea's hand and yanked her behind a rack of New York City sightseeing books. "Did you see that line? I can't do this! What was I thinking?"

Exactly what Thea had been wondering ever since Grace dropped her bombshell that morning, but she bit back the I-told-you-so comment that perched on the edge of her tongue. They were in this together. With the publication of the first Trulee book, Grace became Thea's reluctant accomplice. Now, Thea was forced to become hers. Because if Grace failed at this ruse, all hell would break loose, and that was the last thing either of them needed.

"Okay." Thea fought to keep her own voice calm, even if she felt anything but calm. One of them had to figure a way to get Grace through this, and by default, that someone was she. "Take a deep breath."

Grace inhaled a ragged breath and hiccupped it out. "Great!" She hiccupped again. "Just what I need!"

In spite of herself, Thea giggled.

"I'm glad you—hic—find this amusing— hic."

Thea shrugged. "It's either laugh or cry, Grace. Sometimes you just have to bow to the absurd. And you have to admit, Doctor Love, the hiccupping how-to guru, is more than a little absurd."

With that, Grace burst out laughing. "I'm certifiable. I need another drink."

Thea detected no alcohol on Grace's breath, but that meant nothing since Grace usually drank vodka. "Another? How many have you had?"

"Not nearly enough. How the hell am I going to get out of this?" The laughter subsided, the hiccups disappeared, and reality once more confronted them.

"You're not. Just smile and sign your name. I mean, my name. No. Jeez! I mean Trulee's name. Thank them for coming and buying the books, and whatever you do, *don't* answer any direct questions."

"Dr. Lovejoy?" Thea and Grace both turned to find a store employee rushing over to them. "Oh, there you are," she said to Grace. "It's time to start. Isn't it wonderful how many women showed up for the signing?"

Grace offered the woman a weak smile. "Wonderful."

"Come along then. As soon as I introduce you, I'm going to check with our other stores and have them messenger over whatever stock they have on hand. We're already running low, and the signing hasn't even started yet. We haven't had a turnout like this since Madonna's last book." She spun on her heels and headed back in the direction she'd come.

"Show time," said Thea. "Ready?"

After a reluctant nod, Grace filled her lungs, holding the breath for a moment before exhaling slowly. She took two steps toward the center of the store before stopping and turning back to Thea. Panic colored her face green. "I can't!"

"Yes you can. Think yoga." Thea grabbed her by the shoulders and spun her around.

Grace reached for Thea's hand and squeezed. "Promise me you'll stay close."

Thea squeezed back. "I promise."

Grace, looking for all the world like Marie Antoinette as she ascended the steps to the guillotine, headed toward the table. God save the queen, thought Thea, following several paces behind her. *And while you're at it, God, I could use a little help, too.*

As soon as Grace arrived at the table, the special events coordinator gave her—or rather, Trulee—an introduction that caused the assembled women to break out in raucous applause. Some even whistled and whooped like jocks at a sporting event.

The first person in line approached the table, grabbed Grace's hand, and gave it an enthusiastic shake. Grace produced a staged smile in return. Extracting her hand, she reached for a pen, bent her head, and signed her first autograph.

Thea held her breath, fearful Grace might suffer a momentary lapse and sign *Grace Wainwright* instead of *Trulee Lovejoy*. She leaned forward and read over Grace's shoulder: *Trulee Lovejoy.* Short and simple. No salutation. *Good*, thought Thea. *Less of a chance to screw up.*

"Oh." The woman on the other side of the table frowned at the signature. "Could you write something personal, maybe? Like, *To*

Rosemary, Love from Doctor Love?"

"Uhm, sure." Grace scrawled the requested words above the signature. Then she snapped the book closed and handed it back to the woman. "Thanks for coming."

"I'd like that inscription, too," said the next woman in line, "but *To Michele.* With one *l.*"

So much for short and sweet, thought Thea.

As the line of women slowly inched their way up to the table to collect their autographs, Thea noticed that either Grace had reached deep enough within herself to draw on her years of daily yoga or the vodka had begun taking hold. She couldn't tell which, but as Grace settled into her role, her body relaxed a bit and the sickly green pallor faded from her face.

"I just loved your first book," said the next person in line as she handed over a copy of *Hooking Mr. Right.* "I followed all your advice and found my Mr. Right. Now I need to learn how to hook him." She sighed. "He won't look twice at me!"

"Well, this should help," said Grace, flipping open the book.

"That's what I'm hoping—could you sign that, '*To Mindy, my biggest fan?*'—but what if I follow all your advice, and he still doesn't ask me out? Or what if he does but then never calls again? Will your book tell me how to make Jason fall in love with me? I'll just die if he doesn't! I know he's my soul mate, but how do I get him to realize that?"

Grace, her mouth agape, stared at the young twenty-something. The line of women, previously abuzz with chatter, had quieted. Everyone had turned her attention to Mindy and Grace, waiting for Dr. Trulee Lovejoy to offer Mindy the recipe for Love Potion Number Nine.

Grace tossed a frantic glance in Thea's direction.

Thea ignored her and studied her feet.

"Well, you know," said Grace, turning back to Mindy, "my friend and I were discussing that very subject just this morning over coffee. Weren't we?" She reached back and tugged at Thea's skirt, forcing her closer to the table. "She's having some man troubles of her own, and she asked me, 'Trulee, what if I follow all your advice, and Mr. Right still refuses to cooperate?'" She tilted her head up and locked her gaze on Thea. "And what did I tell you, Thea?"

Thea's mouth dropped open. She stared back at her *friend*. So much for telling Grace not to answer any direct questions. Grace had taken her advice, all right. Taken it and Mindy's question and lobbed them both squarely back at her, putting her on the spot in front of a crowd of more than a hundred Trulee devotees.

She glanced out across the room. A blurry sea of expectant faces awaited her reply. A vision of Steve and Madeline swam before her eyes. Her Mr. Right had definitely turned out to be Mr. Wrong. Mr. All Wrong. She lifted her fingers to her lips, lips that still tingled in remembrance over the press of Luke's kiss, and her head once again spun with conflicting emotions. About him and the secret she kept from him.

"Thea?"

"Sometimes Mr. Right turns out to be Mr. Wrong," she whispered, half to herself.

"Exactly," said Grace. She raised her voice, repeating Thea's statement for the crowd to hear. "That's what I told her. Sometimes Mr. Right is really Mr. Wrong."

"But I know Jason is my Mr. Right," whined Mindy. "I just need you to tell me how to convince him of that."

"If you follow the advice in *Hooking Mr. Right*, everything will work out for you—*if* Jason is really your Mr. Right. But you have to accept that he might not be, and in that case, why waste your time trying to transform a man who will never change?"

Grace's voice had filled with scorn. Thea wondered if she was thinking of her own failed marriage and the ex-husband she not so fondly constantly referred to as Dick-head.

"You can't force someone to love you if the chemistry isn't there," continued Grace, warming to the topic. "Maybe you need to reread *Finding Mr. Right*. It's possible Jason isn't Mr. Right. Not your Mr. Right, anyway."

Mindy fought back tears. Her lower lip trembled. "But I love him!"

"I don't think you do," said Grace. "I think you're infatuated with Jason and in love with the idea of being in love." She handed Mindy her book. "How old are you? Twenty? Twenty-one?"

"Nineteen."

Grace dismissed her with a wave of her hand. "Honey, you're not old enough to know what love is. Come back and talk to me after you've grown up."

The next person in line squeezed a dazed Mindy out of the way and handed over her copy of *Hooking Mr. Right*. "So how do you know if Mr. Right is really Mr. Wrong?" she asked.

Grace flipped her hair over her shoulder and tossed a wide grin in Thea's direction. Her eyes twinkled. "You'll have to buy my next book," she said to the woman. "*Mr. Right or Mr. Wrong?*"

Grace's sudden public disclosure of her next book bothered Thea, especially since the idea had come off the top of Grace's head only moments earlier and didn't involve any prior discussion with Thea. However, *Mr. Right or Mr. Wrong?* appealed to her. Far more than a Dear Trulee book. She could live with *Mr. Right or*

Mr. Wrong? And once she wrote it, her bargain with the devil would be fulfilled, and she'd regain her freedom. And figure out how to come clean to Luke.

Over the next two hours, Thea watched as Grace transformed Dr. Trulee Lovejoy into a Howard Stern/Dr. Phil melded clone. Gone were any remnants of self-doubt or stage fright. Grace, drawing on what Thea believed were years of built-up hostility toward her ex-husband and a driving need to keep her job, blossomed in her new role like a rose in time-lapse photography. The women who had come to meet Dr. Love ate up every word of her in-your-face advice. No one seemed to notice or care that her tone and style were worlds apart from that of the writings of Dr. Trulee Lovejoy.

A star was born. Or a monster. Thea wasn't sure which, but she had little time to dwell on Grace's new career. As she slipped out of the bookstore, leaving Grace to her adoring fans, Thea caught a glimpse of a cab pulling away from the curb. In the back seat sat a woman in a peacock feather festooned purple cloche.

* * *

That night Thea set up the small portable television that had remained packed since her move. Grace—or Trulee—was scheduled to make a guest appearance on *The Late Show*. Thea was relieved to see she rattled off the Top Ten List, then left. No *tête-à-tête* with the host. Just The Top Ten Uses for Chocolate Fudge Sauce, suggestions *not* taken from either of Thea's books but supplied by the staff writers. Ice cream wasn't mentioned.

In spite of herself, Thea laughed at a few of the uses Grace ticked off—especially the one about packing a jar of the stuff in your three-year-old's backpack when he goes to visit Daddy and his trophy tramp in their newly furnished McMansion. That one sounded more like Grace than the staff writers, and Thea wondered if they had used her input in compiling the list.

But even after a good laugh, Thea had trouble sleeping that night. Although Grace seemed to be handling her role well, too much could still go wrong. Thea didn't need another complication in a life already entangled in a gargantuan Gordian knot of lies and deceptions.

And then there was the Hedda factor. Had she been the woman Thea saw driving away from the bookstore? If so, did Grace know she was there? Had she informed Hedda beforehand? Hedda knew Grace as Trulee's editor, not Trulee. Grace couldn't admit she was a mere doppelganger. Not to a gossip columnist. That would blow the ruse wide open.

Thea tossed and turned all night. Thoughts of Hedda led her to thoughts of Luke. She had come no closer to solving her Luke Problem. She'd compounded it. Falling in love with Luke Bennett was a bad idea. A very bad idea.

* * *

The following morning Thea picked up the copy of yesterday's newspaper and read the title of Hedda's Monday column for the hundredth time. *Luke Bennett's Mystery Fiancée Unmasked.* No matter how often she read it, the words still made her cringe. It hadn't taken Hedda long to discover the embarrassing circumstances behind Thea's abrupt departure from San Francisco. She wondered which one of her so-called *friends* had blabbed and how much the culprit had charged for the juicy details.

Or was the blabbermouth her sister? She wouldn't put it past Madeline. She'd already proven herself to be a Judas. One way or another, someone had spilled the beans, and now all of New

York's five boroughs and many of the outlying suburbs were privy to her humiliation at the hands of her sister and her ex-fiancé.

Reliable sources tell yours truly that Dr. Chandler recently broke off her engagement to noted physicist Dr. Steven J. Ross when she caught him diddling her kid sister the night before the wedding. Naughty, naughty, Dr. Ross.

But take heart, ladies. This whirlwind courtship between Dr. Chandler and our Luke is nothing more than a rebound romance for both. Keep the faith, my stoic soldiers of romance and happily-ever-after endings. We can't allow our most eligible bachelor to be snared by an outsider, can we?

Thea tossed the newspaper onto the end table and headed for the kitchen to refill her coffee cup. If Hedda's sleuthing had uncovered the debacle in San Francisco so quickly, how long before she unearthed her other secret? Not to mention whatever Hedda had written after seeing Thea so chummy yesterday with the woman everyone now thought of as Dr. Trulee Lovejoy.

Thea looked forward to the morning paper as much as she looked forward to her next gynecology exam. Both were necessary evils she couldn't avoid.

"What am I going to do?" she asked Cupid, as she head for the freezer instead of the coffee pot. She scooped out a large spoonful of Ben & Jerry's Cherry Garcia and nibbled at the ice cream. When Cupid began stalking the carton, she carefully picked the chocolate chunks from what remained on her spoon and offered him a taste of the ice cream. The cat quickly lapped up every bit of the sweet confection, then whined for more.

"No way, José. You're already a fat, spoiled pussycat, not to mention a huge distraction." She tossed the ice cream spoon into the dishwasher, returned the half-empty carton to the freezer, and hoisted the cat under her arm. "I have work to do, and you're going back to your own apartment for a few hours so I can do it. Or try to, at least. *Mr. Right or Mr. Wrong?* summons."

Cupid yowled a protest.

"I fully agree, but I haven't got much choice, do I? For the time being, it's Trulee or the welfare rolls." Cupid wriggled in her grasp as she locked her door, then headed down the hall to Luke's apartment.

"Forget it," she told the cat as she unlocked Luke's door. "I've made up my mind." She unceremoniously dumped Cupid inside. "Now behave yourself."

The indignant cat arched his back and hissed once before stalking off. Thea closing the door behind him and headed for the elevator, steeling herself for whatever she'd find in Hedda's latest column.

* * *

Had he, without wanting to, found the woman of his dreams? This was the question that plagued Luke during the flight from New York to Atlanta. Without realizing it, Dr. Althea Chandler was taking a blowtorch to his frozen heart.

Whoa, Casanova! Losing his head once to a whirlwind courtship should be lesson enough for any man. He wasn't so stupid he'd make that mistake twice, was he? In hindsight and after much wound licking, Luke had come to realize he'd never loved Julie. He loved the idea of being in love. And being loved in return.

Too late he discovered that Julie had loved his money, not him. She craved excitement and the jet set life he spurned. She may have ditched him for her yoga instructor, but Luke later discovered the pundit of pecs was far from just a yoga guru. He not only owned a friggin' chain of fitness centers that stretched from Los Angeles to Long Island, but he was a celebrity in his own right, counting among his close friends the likes of more than a few A-list celebrities.

Julie had set her avaricious green eyes on steeper heights than Luke was willing to scale. As far as he was concerned, good riddance to her.

But Thea was as different from Julie as the sun was from the moon. At first, he'd seen his new neighbor as merely a means to an end—someone he didn't particularly like but would tolerate to get Hedda and her man hunters off his tail. Then he'd gotten to know her. And enjoy her. And suddenly, Luke found himself thirty thousand feet up and suffering from a massive case of Thea Withdrawal.

He never should have kissed her.

I can't let this happen. Damn it, I've known the woman less than two weeks. He wasn't thinking with his head. Another part of his anatomy had taken over his brain. *It's only physical need*, he told himself. *You've been without for too long.* Besides, there was no indication that the feelings, even libido driven ones, were mutual. She, too, had been badly burned and had made it quite clear she wanted nothing more than friendship from him—*platonic* friendship.

Still, Thea had allowed him to kiss her. And *he* had broken off the kiss, not her. And he could tell she was as rocked and shaken by that kiss as he'd been. Rocked and shaken into speechlessness.

But Thea didn't strike Luke as a woman who'd engage in occasional no-strings attached recreational sex. If he were smart, he'd douse a bucket of ice water over his growing lust and start thinking of her as a sister. Or better yet, a *Sister*—complete with habit and wimple.

If only he hadn't kissed her.

Luke closed his eyes and relived that kiss. She'd been angry with him Saturday night, and he couldn't blame her. He wasn't so dense that he hadn't noticed. And her anger *was* justified. He *had* used her—and then used her again when he stood at her door and realized how much he yearned for a taste of her.

Except that one short kiss only sent his taste buds into sensory overload and fueled his desire for more. Much more. Then, the following morning when he'd seen her punishing herself to the brink of collapse, he was poleaxed by her fragile vulnerability. He wanted to scoop her up in his arms, carry her to a secluded mossy knoll, and...*Damn it, Bennett. Don't go there!*

* * *

Grace forced a strained smiled across the table at her interrogator. No matter what Hedda Two called it, this was far from a friendly lunch interview. The woman was digging too deeply, asking too many probing questions. And she kept bringing up Thea—as if she suspected something and was waiting for Grace to confirm her suspicions.

"I met your friend recently," said Hedda.

Grace eyed her over the rim of her Bloody Mary glass. "My friend?"

"Dr. Althea Chandler. Interesting woman."

"What makes you think she's a friend of mine?"

Hedda smiled in a way that sent a chill up Grace's spine. "Don't play coy with me, darling. I was at your book signing yesterday."

"Oh." Grace drained her glass and signaled the waiter for

another.

"How long have you two known each other?"

"Several years, but I don't see what that has to do with anything."

Hedda raised both eyebrows high enough to skim the bottom of the short veil edging her shocking pink pillbox hat. "Years? Funny how she didn't mention knowing you when I offered her a copy of your book."

Grace grabbed the chance to turn the tables on Hedda. "Was that the evening you claimed you and I were as close as a mother and daughter? Forgive me if I've had a lapse of memory, but I believe we've only met once before, and at that point you didn't know I was the author of the Trulee books. You only knew me as Trulee's editor."

Instead of showing any signs of embarrassment over getting caught in her lie, Hedda bristled. "I should think you'd be grateful for all the free publicity I've given you!"

"Even if it means stretching and embellishing the truth to suit your needs?"

"And you haven't, Dr. Lovejoy? In that respect we're very much alike, you and I."

Grace stared at her from over her glass. "How so?"

"We both exploit and manipulate for personal gain."

Grace ignored the barb. "I'm here to discuss my book tour, not my friends and their personal lives."

"Yes, your book tour. The mysterious Dr. Trulee Lovejoy finally surfaces. What made you come out of hiding after all this time? Two years on the bestseller lists. Not a drop of personal promo. No one knew who you were or what you looked like, and now all of a sudden, a cross-country, whirlwind promotional campaign. Why now?"

Grace shrugged. She'd expected the question. "If you're looking for some dark conspiracy, there is none. It was purely a marketing decision to create buzz. And it worked. How many other authors get the kind of turnout we had Monday?" She sat back in her chair and smiled at Hedda. "Of course, your resounding endorsement of my books in your columns has certainly helped."

"Yes, but don't you find it more than a bit coincidental that the bachelor I chose—the very bachelor you so conveniently suggested—is suddenly engaged to your friend? A friend who was about to marry someone else only a few weeks ago."

Grace knew the engagement was a ruse to get Hedda off Luke's back, but she didn't let on. "Yes, isn't it? Funny how life works out. I suppose that old cliché about a small world really is true."

"Indeed." Hedda pressed on. "Tell me, darling, exactly how do you two know each other, being that she just moved here from San Francisco?"

Grace glanced at her glass. She could use another drink but feared the vodka might loosen her tongue. She needed to keep tight control of how she responded to Hedda. This was one interview she'd protested but to no avail. Hedda wielded too much power. The publicity department had insisted. Grace weighed her limited options. Better to walk out on the interview than say something she'd later regret. She gathered up her purse and jacket. "I told you I'm not discussing my friends. If you have questions about Thea Chandler, I suggest you ask her."

"I did. She's not talking."

"Then I suggest you drop it." She rose from her seat, ready to walk out on the interview.

Hedda offered her an apologetic smile and patted the table. "Sit, Trulee. You win. Tell me about your next book."

* * *

Thea didn't need empathic abilities to know something was wrong the moment she opened Luke's apartment door. The stereo was blaring some God-awful he-done-her-wrong country twang. Luke was partial to jazz and classical music. She doubted he owned anything recorded in Nashville. Then there were the half dozen Louis Vuitton suitcases scattered between the foyer and living room. Luke had stopped at her apartment to say goodbye before leaving for the airport. His luggage had consisted of a Tumi overnighter and his laptop case.

Suddenly, an ear-splitting scream came from the bedroom, drowning out the hapless vocalist. "Damn it! I swear I'll kill you, you sonofabitch!"

Thea heard something hard hit the wall. Cupid yowled. Seconds later she heard him racing down the hall, his claws clicking a rapid staccato against the hardwood floors. Rounding the corner into the foyer, he vaulted onto one of the suitcases, then leaped into her arms.

"Come back here you vile four-legged Satan!"

Cupid bared his claws and hissed at the woman's shrill voice. A moment later she, too, rounded the corner, stopping short when she saw Thea. "Who the hell are you?"

"I could ask you the same question," said Thea, cradling the angry cat. "Along with asking what you think you're doing in Luke Bennett's apartment."

The woman narrowed her eyes at Thea. "For your information I happen to live here. I'm Luke Bennett's wife."

So this was Julie! Thea studied the scantily clad woman. Her tall, well-endowed body trembled with rage. Luke had said she ran off to Nepal with some guru in search of spiritual enlightenment. Judging from her tirade, Thea doubted Julie had found any.

"I'm Luke's neighbor," she said, managing to keep all emotion from her voice. "I'm taking care of his cat while he's out of town."

"You?" Julie raked Thea with a cold, dismissive scowl. "What happened to old lady Lilli-what's-her-name?"

Thea clutched Cupid closer to her chest. With one disdainful glance, Julie had pricked Thea's Achilles heel. Julie's expression announced in no uncertain terms what she thought of Thea. Julie was gorgeous and knew it. Thea was plain and definitely no threat to her. Issues of inadequacy already hounded her. She wouldn't let this contemptible woman add to her lack of self-worth.

Tom, Dick, and Harry had other ideas, though. They started to pry open the box containing all of Thea's insecurities. *No!* She mentally slammed the lid back in place, refusing to let Luke's ex-wife get the better of her. "Lillibridge," she said, matching Julie's glower. "Her name is Mrs. Lillibridge, and she moved."

"Well, you're a lousy replacement. Look what that monster did." She held out a handful of shredded red silk. "This is a Valentino. Or it was," she shrieked, "before that damn cat sank his claws into it."

Julie shook the fabric under Thea's nose. Droplets of water flew from her midnight black hair, sprinkling the torn garment, Thea, and the cat. Cupid hissed in protest, swiping at the negligee. Julie yanked her arm back, but Cupid had already grabbed hold of the silk. Another rent resounded in the tension-filled room.

"Damn you!" Julie flung what was left of the nightie to the floor and lunged at Cupid. Thea stepped back but not quickly enough. With another menacing hiss, Cupid bared his claws and struck.

"Oww!" Julie grabbed her wrist. "He attacked me!" she cried, pointing to a thin crimson welt scratched across her flesh.

"You attacked him," said Thea. "Cupid was only defending himself."

"How dare you!" Julie placed her hands on her hips. Hate-filled green eyes speared Thea. Her rapid breathing forced her breasts to bob up and down, straining against her black lace teddy. "Get that cat out of here, or I'll call the pound and have him put out of my misery."

Stroking Cupid's head, Thea tossed Julie one last look of loathing and turned to leave.

"Wait!" Her hand on the doorknob, Thea paused but refused to turn around. "When is my husband due back?"

"Friday." Thea stepped into the hall and slammed the door behind her. Not until she returned to her own apartment did she realize Julie had continually referred to Luke as her husband, not her ex-husband.

* * *

As branch visits went, Luke's trip to Atlanta ranked as one of the most unproductive business trips of the past year. And it was all Thea's fault. Every time he tried to concentrate on a report or chair a meeting, he found his mind drifting. He saw her face everywhere he looked, heard her voice no matter who was speaking to him.

Never had he allowed his private life to encroach on his professional life. Even during the upheaval of his divorce, he'd been able to compartmentalize his emotions, placing his anger over Julie's betrayal on hold during the hours he spent at his office.

The idea that Thea held the power to intrude so completely

into his thoughts frightened him. He didn't want to start caring for her in the way his mind and body were responding. He didn't want to care about another woman in that way ever again, but he was helpless to control either his thoughts or his hormones. And *that* made him angry. It was definitely all her fault, whether she knew it or not.

He stewed about Thea and the way she made him feel throughout his long trip back to New York—a very long trip, thanks to mechanical problems that grounded his flight in Charlotte, North Carolina. By the time the airline called in another jet and got the passengers safely to La Guardia, the normally short flight had taken over six hours. His taxi didn't pull up in front of his apartment building until past one in the morning.

Hot, tired, and hungry, Luke paused momentarily in front of Thea's door. If he'd heard the slightest sound seeping out into the hallway, he would have knocked, but her apartment, along with the rest of the floor, was bathed in silence. He continued on to his own door.

Luke dropped his suitcase and laptop in the foyer and continued down the darkened hallway. Stepping into his bedroom, he flipped on the overhead light.

"Hello, darling."

Momentarily paralyzed, he stared blankly at the naked woman sprawled across his bed. When he finally found his voice, he roared at her, "What the hell are you doing here?"

THIRTEEN

Luke's bellowing voice startled Thea awake. Through the bedroom wall she heard his anger. In a gush of relief, she expelled the breath she'd figuratively held since her run-in with Julie. For four days she'd worried how Luke would react to his ex-wife's sudden appearance—if Julie were indeed his *ex*-wife. The woman who'd taken over the apartment next door didn't seem to think so, but Luke's violent outburst allayed Thea's fears. The man was definitely not happy.

The yelling died down. A moment later he pounded on her door. Thea grabbed her robe, shoving her arms through the sleeves as she ran barefoot down the hall.

"When the hell did she show up?" he demanded by way of greeting.

"Shh!" She grabbed his arm and hauled him inside, closing the door behind him. "How many other neighbors do you want to wake up?" She cocked her head to the side, sized him up with a quick nod, then smiled. "By the way, it's nice to see you, too, even if you do look like day-old death warmed over. Have a nice trip, Luke?"

He grunted an unintelligible reply.

Thea took his hand and led him into the living room. Luke collapsed onto the sofa. He leaned his elbows on his knees and stared up at her. God, she looked inviting—especially after the unwelcome sight he fled moments earlier. She stood inches from his knees, her hands on her hips, her figure draped in a lightweight yellow cotton robe that did little to hide the soft curves beneath it.

Her soft violet eyes filled with sympathy. "Not what you expected to come home to, is it?"

Luke leaned back against the sofa, sighed deeply, and shook his head, but he couldn't tear his eyes from the sight of the woman standing barefoot before him. As his gaze meandered down Thea's body, all the frustrations of the past several days came to a head. His own traitorous body began responding in a decidedly ungentlemanly way. He wondered if she had any idea of the havoc she wreaked in him. Only through the sheerest of will power did he restrain himself from reaching for the sash belted loosely around her waist. He ached to draw her into his arms, to nestle her soft curves against the hard plains of his body and finally make real the dreams that had haunted his sleep for the past week.

Luckily, his faithful pet took that moment to greet him, leaping onto the couch and prancing over Luke's thighs. He stroked Cu's fur until the cat settled into a ball on his lap, successfully hiding some very telltale evidence.

"Let's just say finding my ex-wife naked in my bed was the last straw to a perfectly miserable five days." He took a deep breath, exhaling it in a rush. "I'm exhausted, Thea. Would you mind if I stayed in your guest room tonight? I'll deal with Julie tomorrow."

Thea nodded.

"One other thing."

"Yes?"

He offered her a sheepish grin. "Any chance of getting something to eat?"

While Thea scrambled Luke some eggs, he filled her in on the gist of the shouting match that had awakened her. "Julie thought they were taking a first-class sightseeing trip to Everest like some New Age jet setters. To her chagrin, the wealthy yoga stud wanted to rid himself of all his earthly possessions and settle down in Nepal permanently. Julie flipped out when she discovered the village he brought her to had only life's barest necessities."

"No Bloomingdale's?" she asked, popping a sliced bagel into the toaster.

Luke grinned. "No Bloomingdale's and no indoor plumbing."

"That pleases you, doesn't it?"

"Immensely."

Thea giggled. "And Julie didn't realize any of this before running off with him?"

"Julie has a knack for hearing what she wants to hear. Maybe she thought she could change his mind. Who knows? At any rate, once she realized she'd be rubbing elbows with Sherpas rather than Hollywood celebrities, she hopped on the first plane back to civilization. She's been spending her way across Europe for the past several months."

The bagels popped up from the toaster. Thea plucked them out and placed them on a plate, spreading each half with apple butter before adding the eggs and setting the plate in front of Luke. He attacked the food with relish.

"And just when was your last meal?" she asked, settling into the seat opposite him, her elbows propped on the table, her chin resting on her fists.

Luke glanced over at the stove clock. He answered around a mouthful of egg. "Sometime yesterday."

Thea tried to stifle a yawned. "Excuse me."

"Go back to bed. I'll clean this up."

She stood. "Good idea. You know where the guest room is. Good night, Luke."

"Good night, Thea. And thanks."

Thea headed out of the kitchen but paused at the doorway. "Luke?" She turned to face him. "Why did Julie come back here?"

"She's broke. Some women will do anything for money."

Thea cringed at the sneering contempt in his voice. She twisted her head away, hoping to mask the pain overwhelming her. She still hadn't figured out a satisfactory way to explain Trulee to him, and now Julie's arrival reinforced Luke's negative feelings about duplicitous women.

How could she ever convince him her chicanery had been committed out of love and responsibility, not hate and selfishness? Once he found out about Trulee, how could she keep him from lumping her with his ex-wife and his mother? Forcing out one last goodnight, she made her way down the hall, knowing she wouldn't sleep.

* * *

The next morning Luke first placed a call to his lawyer to verify his legal position, then tried to reason with Julie, but she had other ideas. When her feminine wiles failed to have the desired results on him, she resorted to threats. "I'll make your life a living hell."

"You already have."

"You owe me, Luke!"

"I owe you nothing. You're the one who walked out on me, remember? *After* wiping out several large bank accounts."

"Those accounts were in my name, too!"

"Not that you ever contributed a dime to them."

"You're a cheap son-of-a-bitch, Luke Bennett. New York's most eligible bachelor? Ha! I pity the woman who has the misfortune of winding up with you. Maybe I should warn them all."

Luke turned his back on her. Throwing his hands up in disgust, he crossed to the other side of the room. "I wish you would. I'd welcome the peace."

"Should I start with your plain Jane neighbor? That's where you spent the night, wasn't it?" Julie snorted. "You must be pretty desperate to look twice at her."

Luke spun around, bristling at Julie's assessment of Thea. He stared at the woman who used to be his wife and wondered how he could have been so blind to her coarseness and lack of character. "She's ten times more woman than you could ever hope to be."

Julie offered him a condescending smirk, her gaze drifting below his belt. "I always knew you were lacking in some areas, Luke. Now I know you're also blind."

"Not anymore," he muttered through gritted teeth.

Julie grabbed her purse and stalked toward the front door. "I'm checking into The Plaza. I'll send someone over for my bags."

"The Plaza? You were pleading poverty a moment ago." Luke eyed the handbag she clutched against her body. He could think of only one way Julie could afford a room at The Plaza. Unwittingly, he'd handed her that opportunity last night when he left his bags sitting in the foyer.

He knew his ex-wife and how low she was willing to stoop to get what she wanted. Thoughts of ripping that damn Fendi purse from her arm played around his brain, but in the end, reason and common sense won out. That and the vision of his lawyer cringing over assault charges. If Julie had taken his credit cards, a few quick phone calls would keep her from using them. Imagine her humiliation when the desk clerk at The Plaza refused every piece of plastic she handed him.

Luke strode to the front door and opened it. He'd better place a call to a locksmith, as well. It never occurred to him that she'd keep the keys to the apartment. On the day she left, she had claimed she never wanted anything more to do with him. But that was when she thought she was off to greener bank accounts. "Get out, and don't bother coming back. Ever."

Julie leveled two hate-filled eyes at him and tossed off one parting shot. "You'll regret this, Luke."

"I regret the day we met." He slammed the door behind her.

* * *

"If it weren't for women like you and Margaret, I'd lose all faith in the female sex."

Thea took a sip of her wine. They'd gone out to dinner, and he'd just filled her in on Julie's departure. "Margaret?"

"My secretary. Nice woman. You'd like her." Luke reached for the bottle of Chardonnay, refilled his glass, and topped off Thea's.

"And what about your partners' wives? You like Barbara and Diane, don't you?"

"The jury's still out on those two. I have a sneaking suspicion they're behind my being offered up as a sacrificial lamb."

"I don't understand." After all, she knew Hedda's campaign was Grace's brainchild. Diane and Barbara had nothing to do with it.

"I think they feel guilty about Julie and want to marry me off again as soon as possible to ease their consciences."

"Why?"

"There's a bit of history between the three of them. Julie is the daughter of Barbara's best friend and was Diane's college roommate."

"Ouch. Touchy situation."

"Indeed."

Thea dragged her spoon in circles around the inner edge of the soup bowl and stared blankly at her vichyssoise. The background murmurs of other diners were drowned out by the increasing roar building inside her head. Tom, Dick, and Harry had formed a heavy metal rock band. Tom pounded away on a set of drums. Dick played lead guitar, and Harry accompanied them on bass. All three shrieked the vocals, the discordant chords a perfect accompaniment to a conversation she dreaded but knew she had to pursue. "What makes Margaret and me different?" she asked.

"You both have character." He raised his wine glass to toast her. "A trait sorely lacking in my ex-wife and ninety-nine percent of the women I've had the misfortune to meet over the years."

Luke had just handed her the opening she needed to broach the subject of Trulee with him. Could she find the courage? She lifted her gaze from her soup and stared into his warm, trusting eyes. Inwardly, she cried. Guilt, fear and self-loathing consumed her. Outwardly she said, "Don't place me on a pedestal, Luke. I'm human. I have as many flaws as anyone else."

"Of course," he said. "We all do, but you have principles, and I know you well enough by now to know you'd never compromise them. You're a woman of integrity, Thea. A woman with scruples.

I admire that."

Tears gathered behind her eyes and in her throat. Her cheeks flushed. She squeezed her eyelids shut and swallowed hard, fighting back the emotional upheaval that threatened to erupt. Luke mistook her reaction. He reached across the table and covered her hand with his. "Don't be embarrassed. You deserve the compliment."

Thea opened her eyes and focused on their joined hands. She shook her head, feeling only sadness. She didn't deserve his praise. Her voice choked with emotion. "Life is not black and white, Luke. We may not always understand another person's motives, but that doesn't necessarily mean they're not justified. Sometimes decent people are forced into circumstances where they have to compromise their values for a greater good."

She lifted her chin, her eyes pleading with his. "Not all lies are due to a lack of integrity, and not all fraud is committed out of avarice. Some is perpetrated only after much soul-searching and at huge personal sacrifice."

His eyes widened with disbelief. "And you think this was the case with Julie? And my mother? I can't believe you're defending them."

"I'm not. I'm only asking you to keep an open mind." She paused to take a deep breath. "About other situations. Other people."

"Are you saying I'm close-minded?"

She shook her head once again. This was not going well. Luke had assumed a defensive attitude. She feared pursuing her cause any further, but at least she'd planted a seed. Hopefully, it would take root. With her luck? Fat chance. Attempting to force a lightness into her voice, she smiled at him. "You do occasionally jump to the wrong conclusions. I'm merely asking you to reserve judgment on people and their actions until you have all the facts."

"And you don't think I do that?"

Thea rubbed her healed wrist and offered him a sarcastic smirk. "I think you have a tendency to attack first and ask questions later."

Smiling ruefully, Luke nodded an admission of guilt. "I suppose I'll be apologizing for *that* mistake for the rest of my life?"

"Or the rest of our friendship, whichever comes first."

"Then I guess I'll be offering you *mea culpas* the remainder of my life, because I have no intention of losing your friendship, Dr. Althea Chandler." He raised his glass in another toast.

Thea prayed he'd remember those words when they squared off at opposite ends of the street at high noon.

* * *

Henrietta Hopper had built her journalistic career on several maxims. Although trite, she found they served her well. As Hedda Two, the name she adopted in honor of one of her illustrious newsmonger forebears, she had carved a successful career for herself as a society reporter. She believed all was fair in love and war. And from her years of experience in the world of Manhattan society, Hedda Two proved time and again, everything was *always* either love or war.

Another tried and true adage, known to any reporter worth her salt, was that all information was available for a price. Dig deep enough, scratch the right itch, grease the right palm, and no secret was safe. After what she'd observed at the bookstore Monday afternoon, the suspicions raised during her lunch with Trulee, and the information she'd just gleaned, she knew there was more than one secret lurking within this particular story.

With each intriguing tidbit unmasked, she discovered the hint of another spicy detail awaiting dissection. This conspiracy had enough layers to keep her in columns for a year.

"Thanks, Lucy. I owe you." She hung up the phone and reached for the book sitting on her desk. Opening it, she flipped to the appropriate page. A good reporter always verified her informant's tips. A wide smile of satisfaction spread across her face. She closed the book and leaned back in her chair, savoring the choice morsels she had purchased in exchange for a future favor. In this case, all it took was the promise of an invite to a forthcoming Brad Pitt movie premiere.

Her final axiom had served her well once more. Early in her career Henrietta had learned the value of befriending low-level assistants. She commiserated with them, gaining their respect and confidence. She let them know she knew how the world really operated. They did the work; their superiors gained the glory. Hence, when Henrietta wanted to know the real inside story, she placed a call to the overworked and under-appreciated peons, never the head honchos.

Only this time she'd boxed herself into a corner with a few white lies. If she printed the bombshell she just uncovered, she'd lose credibility with her readers.

On the other hand, her Luke Bennett campaign was dying a quick death. New York's most eligible bachelor was proving himself a less-than-cooperative subject. Rather than jumping aboard and enjoying the media attention, he'd done his best to squelch her efforts. The ingrate!

Henrietta knew she had to plan her next move with the utmost care. She was in the middle of negotiations with Fox for a weekly segment on the local news. She desperately needed to land the plum assignment—especially if *The Daily Post* folded. However, if her credibility came into question, she might as well kiss her network career goodbye before her first appearance. She hated having to sit on such a juicy story, but no one wanted a society gossip who reported fiction. And that's exactly what Hedda had done by bragging about her friendship with Trulee. Luckily, though, the two women privy to her *faux pas* were in no position to divulge it.

* * *

Thea's insight and sensitivity struck a chord with Luke, challenging him to think beyond the narrow scope of his experience. Two hateful women had clouded his views for too many years. Tonight Thea showed him that he alone possessed the power to stop them from controlling him.

As they strolled back toward their apartment building, he laced his fingers through hers and raised them to his lips. "Thank you."

"For what?"

"For having the courage to tell me I'm an opinionated, obstinate ass."

"I never said any such thing!"

Luke chuckled. "No, you were far more ladylike and diplomatic, but the meaning was the same."

They entered the building, Thea's fingers still entwined with his. Melvin smiled broadly at them. "Evening Mr. Bennett, Dr. Chandler."

"Good evening, Melvin."

"Perfect spring night, ain't it, sir?"

"Perfect," agreed Luke as he and Thea stepped into the waiting elevator.

Melvin's final proclamation came as the doors closed. "Yes, sir. Love is in the air tonight."

Luke turned to face Thea. Her cheeks blazed a deep crimson. She stared down at her feet, avoiding his gaze. With his free hand he drew his knuckles along her jaw line, lifting her chin until their eyes met. He rested his hand against her neck, feeling her quickening pulse. In her large violet eyes, he read a combination of need and uncertainty—emotions that mirrored his own state of turmoil. "I don't think either of us expected this to happen."

"Has anything happened?" she asked, her voice a breathless whisper.

Luke removed his glasses and slipped them into his jacket pocket. For the first time since moving into the building, he was grateful for the lumbering old relic of an elevator and the time it would take to make its way up to the twelfth floor. "Not yet, but it's about to."

FOURTEEN

Luke placed a palm alongside Thea's cheek and lowered his head, brushing his lips against hers. They trembled at his touch. He teased them with soft pecking nibbles before capturing her mouth in his and giving in to the ravenous hunger that had plagued him ever since his first taste of her.

Thea responded, parting her lips, inviting him to enter and explore. He accepted her invitation, his tongue slipping inside, roaming the velvety moist recesses beyond her lips, stroking and caressing. Thrusting deep, his tongue did to her mouth what another part of his anatomy strained to perform on another part of hers.

Cradling her head with both palms, he explored further, his lips wandering from the moist warmth of her mouth along the plains and contours of her cheeks and jaw and temples. He buried his face in her hair, inhaling the sweet vanilla and orange blossom scent he remembered from the first time he held her in his arms. He whispered her name over and over before returning to her mouth. He was in heaven, and he was in hell. He wanted her with an intensity that tortured every cell of his being.

Luke drew her closer against his body, his hands sliding from her cheeks, down her arms and around her back, drawing her into an embrace that imprinted the hardness of his desire against the softness of her belly. Thea moaned. She wrapped her arms around his waist and lost herself in a passion she had never before known. An aching need devoured her. Her breasts swelled and strained against the lacy cups of her bra. Her nipples pebbled, their hard peaks demanding the same attention from his lips and teeth and tongue that he devoted to her mouth. Warm, honey-like moisture flooded between her legs.

In the distance a soft bell pinged.

Luke broke off the kiss, leaving her hungry for the damp heat of his mouth against hers. Taking a step backwards, he ran the pads of his thumbs along her bruised, swollen lips. "Our floor." His hands traveled down the length of her arms. Linking one with hers, he led her out of the elevator and down the hall.

At her apartment he took the key from her hand and unlocked the door. She hesitated, remaining in the hallway. Luke stroked her cheek, searching her eyes for an invitation she still couldn't give him. Not until she had come clean to him about Doctor Trulee Lovejoy. And then she feared he would no longer want her.

"Am I going too fast?"

She bit down on her lower lip and nodded. "I...I'm sorry. I'm just not ready for this."

"I understand. It's too soon." His frustration showed in his eyes and the set of his mouth, but he bent down and gently kissed her cheek. "When you're ready, I'll be waiting."

"Thank you for understanding."

He offered her a wry smile. "Do I have a choice?" Before she could answer, he strode down the hall to his own apartment.

Thea slipped inside and quietly closed the door behind her. Leaning against the molding, she pressed her fingertips to her trembling lips and fought back a rush of tears. Although her words had made an impact on him tonight, was he wise enough to apply them to himself and her when the time came?

Will you be waiting, Luke? Will you still want to love me after you learn who I really am? Or will you hate me for how I've deceived you?

* * *

On Monday morning Luke sat at his desk, ignoring the stack of reports rising several inches in front of him. Pushing them aside, he leaned back in his chair, his hands clasped behind his head and propped his feet up on the desk. He couldn't remember the last time he'd felt so good.

Saturday night was an evening of startling revelations, the last hitting him hard as he returned alone to his apartment. His whirlwind courtship and disastrous marriage to Julie had been based purely on lust and his desperate need for a family of his own. Neither of them had loved the other. He finally realized that. Julie was merely the first to admit the obvious truth.

Things would be different with Thea. They shared the same values, and no matter how much he desired her, he was willing to wait as long as he needed to. He'd found his soul mate, and nothing was going to keep them apart.

"You'll never guess who's on the phone for you," said Margaret, poking her head inside his office.

Luke glanced over at her. Margaret stood in the doorway, one hand on her hip, the other poised on the doorframe. From the wry grin plastered across her face, he had a sneaking suspicion as to the caller's identity. His secretary had never liked his ex-wife. Too bad he hadn't listened to all her unsolicited advice after he'd introduced the two of them. Margaret pegged Julie from the start, and because she knew she could get away with it, she'd even had the audacity to say I-told-you-so after Julie walked out on him.

"If it's Julie, you can tell her I've given away all my money to the Hare Krishnas, shaved my head, and joined a monastery."

Margaret snickered. "You should have told her that the moment you met her. Look at the grief you'd have saved yourself."

Luke grimaced. He didn't want a tirade from Julie ruining his mood. "Thank you, Swami Hindsight. Tell her I'm in a meeting or something. Just get rid of her."

"I'd love to, but it's not Julie. It's Hedda Two, and she said it's urgent."

Luke groaned. He tore his glasses from his face and massaged his temples. "Why won't that irritating woman leave me alone?"

Margaret held out her arms, palms up and shrugged. "Because she needs someone to take JFK JR's place after his untimely death?"

Luke stared at his normally sane secretary and wondered if she, too, had succumbed to the gossip queen's daily dose of garbage. "That happened years ago. Besides, when was I ever in the same league as a Kennedy?"

"The day God gave you those sexy good looks." She spun on her heels. "Line two," she called over her shoulder as she headed back to her desk.

Sexy good looks? Luke lifted the receiver, his finger hesitating over the button. Did Hedda actually have the gall to think she could wheedle an interview out of him? Was she looking for an update on his relationship with Thea? From what he read in her columns, she wasn't too thrilled with his choice of *fiancée*. Whatever her motive, he resented the intrusion into his workday and intended to tell her so in no uncertain terms.

He stabbed at the button. "Bennett here."

"Lucas, darling," she gushed. "You are such a naughty boy, the two of you trying to fool me the way you did! But the cat's out of the bag now, sugar. I'm on to you and your phony fiancée."

Damn! How the hell did she find out? Barbara? Diane? One of them must have spilled the beans. As soon as Hedda breaks the news to her readers, her estrogen brigade will once again be out in force, chasing him like a pack of hounds after a fox. "Who told you?" he asked, feeling the sucker punch through the phone lines.

Hedda made a tsking sound. "Really, Luke! A reporter never reveals her sources!"

Luke muttered a few choice words under his breath.

"I'm sorry, darling, what was that you said?"

"I'm extremely busy, Hedda. Did you want something, or did you simply call to gloat?"

"Gloat?" Hedda chortled. "Heaven's no! Why would I gloat? I think it's wonderful. You and Trulee cooking up such a scheme! How delightful! How simply marvelous!" She laughed once more but this time it sounded more like a cackle. "How positively delicious! And ironic! Too bad it isn't true. Or maybe it is, and you just don't realize it yet. Considering all the other people she's fooled, I wouldn't put it past her to have a few ulterior motives concerning you. After all, she is single, and you are a great catch."

What the hell was she blabbering about? Surely, he hadn't heard her correctly, had he? "Me and *who?*"

"Why, Trulee, of course! Dr. Althea Trulee Lovejoy

Chandler!"

"*What?*" Now it was Luke's turn to laugh. He hadn't thought Hedda was that gullible, but obviously the woman was so desperate to save her career she'd buy into any nonsense tossed her way. "Are you out of your mind, woman? I hope you didn't pay too much for that audacious piece of fiction."

"Fiction?"

"Let me refresh your memory," said Luke. "When you accosted us at Le Cirque, you bragged about that quack being like a daughter to you. Are you so lousy a mother that you don't recognize your own daughter? She's been making personal appearances all over the place, if you've forgotten what she looks like. I've seen her on television, Hedda. Trulee Lovejoy looks *nothing* like Thea Chandler."

Several seconds of silence greeted Luke's indictment. Finally, Hedda replied, "I'll admit I *did* embellish the truth slightly concerning that, but you know as well as I do, Luke, that Dr. Trulee Lovejoy is the pen name of your Dr. Althea Chandler. There's no denying that fact. And we both know the woman posing as Trulee is Grace Wainwright, Althea Chandler's editor."

"That's the biggest load of horse crap to ever hit the streets of Manhattan, Hedda."

"Oh?"

He could hear the victory in her voice, and suddenly Luke wasn't so sure of himself. A cold foreboding crept up his spine.

"Then perhaps you'd like to explain to me why both of Trulee's books are copyrighted under the name A. L. Chandler."

Suddenly, Luke was eight years old again and staring at a piece of blue-lined paper stuck to the door of a harvest gold refrigerator. The note, written on the back of his last week's spelling test, hung from a magnet he'd given his mother for her birthday. It read *World's Greatest Mom.* The words of her goodbye letter were not nearly as loving.

"Here's the deal, Luke. I suspect you and Dr. Chandler cooked up this *engagement* to thwart my campaign to marry you off."

Luke grunted. "Not that you really care about my love life or lack of it."

"Of course not, darling. I did it for me, to raise my star higher in the celebrity firmament, but I needed a wealthy, handsome, eligible bachelor."

"Why me?"

"Believe me, had I known how uncooperative you'd be, I would have vetoed the suggestion and chosen someone else. Unfortunately, I didn't."

"How lucky for me."

"It's about time you realized it. If you weren't such an ingrate, you'd thank me for all the publicity I've given you and your brokerage firm. Not to mention your friend. Her book sales have tripled in the tri-state area since I started writing about her.

"Under the circumstances, I can't imagine why she'd agree to help you, but maybe she felt guilty. Or sorry for you. Or maybe she wants you for herself. Either way, I have too much on the line here. Here's what I'm proposing: You call the engagement off—in an exclusive interview with me—and I won't publish what I've uncovered."

Silence greeted her offer.

"Luke? Luke, are you still there?"

Luke stared blankly at the receiver in his hand.

"Luke!" Hedda emitted a sigh of annoyance. "I'll give you an hour to think it over. But only an hour. I have a deadline to meet."

The phone went dead. Still in a daze, Luke dropped the receiver onto his desk. Sitting perfectly still, he stared out across the room, seeing not the furnishings of his well-appointed office, but a torturous past that refused to die. Ice picks of intense pain stabbed at his temples. A knife slashed through his back. A sword pierced his heart. He took a deep breath, trying to force down the bile rising in his throat. Staggering to his feet, Luke placed one unsteady leg in front of the other and headed for the doorway. He had to get out of there.

"Luke? Are you all right?" Margaret stood and rounded her desk as he passed. He ignored the look of concern on her face and the hand that reached out to him. Brushing her aside, he continued his trance-like progression toward the bank of elevators.

Once outside, Luke headed north on Pearl Street toward Fulton. *She's wrong*, he kept telling himself as he strode purposefully toward the nearest bookstore. *She's wrong!* But deep down inside, the little eight-year-old boy, filled with hurt and anger and self-blame, knew otherwise. History was repeating itself. Again.

At the entrance to the bookstore, he paused, eyeing the display in the window. As a child, all his nightly prayers had gone unanswered. His mother never returned. Eventually, he'd ceased praying. He tore his gaze from the stack of pink-jacketed books, cursing at the tiny hearts that danced across their covers. Prayer or no prayer, his destiny was already set in type on a page in every one of those damn books. He opened the door and stepped inside.

* * *

Luke spent the remainder of the day and the better part of the night nursing one bourbon after another in a dimly lit corner of a hole in the wall. Instead of numbing his pain, the alcohol only intensified it until the festering wound consumed him. But his anger wasn't directed at Thea as much as it homed in on him. Against his better judgment and disregarding all past experience, he'd allowed himself to have feelings for another woman. And look where that got him! Again. Some fools never learned, and he was the biggest fool of all damn fools.

Finally, he stumbled out of the bar and hailed a cab, snarling his address at the turban-clad driver. Slumped in the back seat, he stared out the window and seethed at the city speeding past in a blur of shadows and lights.

Half an hour later he stood in the hallway outside Thea's door. How appropriate, he thought, listening to the strains of *Les Misérables* coming from the other side. Fantine's lament filled the still corridor, confirming what he already knew, that life—and in his case, yet another deceitful woman—had killed the dream he'd dreamed.

Luke balled his hand into a fist and pounded on Thea's door.

* * *

Thea exhaled a sigh of relief at the sound of Luke's knock. Buoyed by the lingering warmth of his kisses, she'd spent the remainder of the weekend convincing herself they cared enough for one another to weather the storm of her confession. Her courage hadn't flagged once all day, but as the hours crept further and further past dinnertime, she grew edgy. She wanted to get it over with, get the nightmarish admission beyond them so their relationship could move forward. Setting aside the book she'd tried reading for the past several hours, she removed Cupid from her lap and rose to let Luke into her apartment.

Her fingers trembled as she unbolted the lock and swung open the front door. Luke stood in the hallway, his face drained of color, his eyes sunken and empty. His hair was mussed, his glasses perched askew across the bridge of his nose. Dark stains splattered the navy and burgundy paisley tie that hung loose around his neck. Brown blotches peppered his white, partially buttoned shirt. He held his crumpled jacket under one arm.

Thea gasped. "Luke! What's wrong? What happened to you?" She grabbed his arm and tried to draw him into the apartment, but he refused to budge. Cupid darted into the hall, sniffed his master's shoes and emitted a scornful hiss before returning to Thea's side.

"Luke?" The scent of whiskey clung to his clothes and skin, but that didn't disturb her half as much as the blank stare with which he greeted her. Thea shuddered and tugged harder on his arm. "Please, come inside."

"Why?" His question came across as a hoarse whisper.

"Why? Because you need to sit down. What happened? Are you hurt?"

"Hurt?" The corners of his mouth curled up slightly, but the smile didn't extend to his eyes. A short, bitter laugh escaped from between his tightly pursed lips. "You could say that."

Thea scanned his body again. She saw no outward signs of injury to his person, just his clothing, and those were liquid in nature. "Are you drunk?"

"Not nearly enough."

His soft, monotone made no sense to her, but then again, she'd never before seen him under the influence of Jack Daniels. "Did Julie do something?"

He shook his head. "I expect backstabbing treachery from Julie."

If not Julie, then whom? What? He was speaking in senseless riddles. And why did he refuse to step inside the apartment? "Are you planning to stand out in the hallway all evening?"

"Does it matter?"

"Yes, it matters! What's going on?"

Luke sighed. His gaze grew even more distant, his demeanor resigned. "You know the answer to that, Thea. I think you've known from the day we met. If not before."

Bewilderment and a smattering of annoyance over his cryptic behavior began to crowd out her initial concern. This was not the way she had planned the evening. How could she offer her confession with Luke in such a peculiar mood? She threw her arms up and shook her head. "I don't know what you're talking about."

"Don't you?" Stepping over the threshold, he closed the door behind him and headed into the living room. Thea and Cupid followed, Thea stopping in the middle of the room. Luke continued to the far wall and began scanning her bookcase. Cupid jumped up onto a shelf and observed Luke.

"Here it is." Luke pulled a volume off the shelf. "Look familiar?" he asked, holding up a copy of *Hooking Mr. Right*.

An overpowering dread crept through her. *He knows!* Fighting her own misgivings, as well as an insane urge to flee, she stood her ground. "Of course it looks familiar. It's one of my research books. You know that."

"Ah, yes. Research." He flipped open the cover and slowly leafed through the pages. "Fascinating thing about books. Hardly anyone ever bothers to read the first few pages. We just skip over all that boring stuff. You know, title page? Dedication?" He paused, raising his head to meet her gaze, but his expression remained shuttered, and he never raised his voice above a soft whisper. "Copyright?"

No! This can't be happening! Please! She was going to tell him tonight. How could fate have played such a dirty trick on her? Her entire body trembled. She faltered, reaching for the back of the sofa to steady herself. She'd waited too long to tell him the truth. Now it was too late. He knew, and he hated her.

"Interesting thing about copyright," Luke continued, his voice remaining emotionless as he crossed the room toward her. "Did you know books are usually copyrighted under an author's legal name, not a pseudonym?" He raised his eyes from the page, daring her to challenge him. From his perch, Cupid raised his head and followed Luke.

Thea couldn't speak, couldn't think. Her brain had stalled on the word *copyright.* Somewhere in the back of her mind she remembered Grace having mentioned she could copyright under Trulee's name if she really wanted to remain anonymous, but she'd shrugged off the idea, deciding it wasn't necessary. Who the hell reads the copyright page of a book? She hadn't expected anyone to, let alone connect her with the generic-sounding A.L. Chandler. But Luke had.

"Take *Hooking Mr. Right* by Dr. Trulee Lovejoy, for instance," Luke continued, turning his attention back to the book. "According to this, the author is really...hmm, isn't that interesting?" He held the page up for her to see, pointing at the copyright line with his index finger. "Why don't you read what it says?"

Thea turned away.

"I don't suppose you need to see the words to know what they say, do you?" He snapped the book shut. Cupid yowled at the abrupt noise. He leapt from his perch and scampered across the room, planting himself between Luke and Thea.

"Copyright two thousand ten," Thea whispered over the lump in her throat. "A.L. Chandler."

"A.L. Chandler," Luke repeated, tossing the book onto the sofa. "Now who could that be?"

Thea turned back to face him, expecting to be met by a hate-filled glare, but both Luke's voice and features remained devoid of any emotion. She would have preferred anger. She deserved his hate. She was no different from Julie or his mother, and he was accepting her betrayal without a fight. His zombie-like state alarmed her more than any abusive tirade could have.

"Althea L. Chandler, maybe?" he continued. "What's the 'L' stand for? Liar?"

Thea winced. "Lisbeth."

"Lisbeth?" He shrugged. "I prefer liar." Luke sank into a chair and lowered his head into his hands. Cupid took up a position on the padded arm, his head bobbing back and forth as he studied first Luke, then Thea. "You really are something else, Dr. Althea Liar Chandler. Hell, you make Julie look like a rank amateur."

Her eyes filled with tears. "You have to let me explain, Luke. You don't understand."

"Oh, I understand. You're some pro. Really set me up, didn't you? Only you were smarter than the rest of Hedda's legion of desperate damsels. You knew they were all using your book, so you employed some reverse psychology. Pretended you weren't interested in me or any man. Even had me believing you weren't following me that first day, didn't you? And like the sucker I am, I fell for you and your I'm-not-interested act one hundred and ten percent."

Tears streamed down Thea's cheeks. "No, it wasn't like that.

You have to believe me!"

"Believe you? I *did* believe you. That was *my* big mistake. So tell me." He raised his head and stared at her. "What did you do to make your cohort turn on you?"

"C...cohort?" Thea's voice stumbled over the word. Someone *told* Luke about Trulee? Surely, not Grace! But who else knew?

"Hedda. Your partner in crime." He shook his head as if dealing with a recalcitrant toddler. "Don't deny it. I've had all day to figure it out."

He stood and began pacing back and forth across the room. "Amazing how a few bottles of bourbon can slice through the bullshit. Hedda admitted to me she lied, but she was lying about which lies she told, wasn't she? The two of you cooked this up from the start, scratching each other's backs to make a buck at my expense. You help her spur paper sales; she helps sell your books. A real quid pro quo, complete with a bonus prize—me."

"Luke, listen to yourself. You're not making any sense. What are you talking about?"

He stopped pacing and stared at her. "As if you don't know. And how convenient that I walked right into your little trap by confronting you that day in the lobby." He shook his head. "I'll wager you even made up all that bullshit about your sister and ex-fiancé. What did you do, pay some out-of-work actor to make that call to your answering machine? You're not even from San Francisco, are you? Where did you move from? SoHo? Chelsea?"

In her worst nightmares Thea hadn't expected to be plunged into such a bizarre scene. Luke's twisted, irrational logic baffled her. How could he possibly believe she and Hedda set out to entrap him? "Hedda?" she repeated.

Luke pierced her with that hollow stare of his. "Give it up,

Thea. You've worn out the innocent act."

Thea had a pretty good idea how Hedda discovered her secret. She'd seen Thea with Grace at the book signing. Afterwards, the gossipmonger simply used her numerous contacts to connect the dots. But did it really matter? The damage was done. Luke's mind was made up, believing some farfetched, alcohol-soaked conspiracy.

She collapsed onto the sofa and buried her head in her hands. Cupid traded the arm of the easy chair for her lap. "Yes, I wrote the books." She clutched the cat to her body and raised her head to plead her case. "But not for the reasons you think, and nothing else you've accused me of is true. I haven't conspired with Hedda. I never met the woman before the night you took me to Le Cirque."

Skepticism flashed across his face. "And I'm supposed to believe that after all your other lies?"

"I think you've already decided what you're going to believe, whether it's true or not. You won't listen to me, so what does it matter? It's over. Just go." She buried her face in Cupid's fur, her only solace the cat's deep, vibrating purr, and waited for the sound of the front door to close behind Luke. Forever.

Instead, she heard the rustle of clothing and felt his trousers brush against her legs. Thea raised her head. Luke stood directly in front of her, trapping her where she sat. His jacket lay on the floor beside his feet. He bent and reached across her for the discarded book, then settled himself onto the coffee table. Cupid raised his head and once again directed a penetrating gaze at Luke.

"How could I fall for a woman who writes this crap?" Luke shook his head and grimaced at the shocking pink, heart-adorned book cover. "Are you that good an actress, or am I that big an asshole?"

"Luke, please don't do this."

His brows knit together. His shoulders drooped. "Do what? I'm simply trying to understand why I keep making the same mistake over and over again. So what's your professional assessment of a man who's attracted to manipulative, deceitful women, doctor?"

"I'm not that kind of a doctor."

"No?" He sighed as he fanned the pages of *Hooking Mr. Right*. "With all the *advice* you dish out here? Could have fooled me." A doleful chuckle escaped from his throat. "Actually, you did fool me, didn't you?"

"It's not what you think."

He glanced up at her. "No, of course not. Where's the evidence, right? Remember playing hard-to-get, Thea? That little scene about not being ready for a new relationship?" He returned to the book. "What I'd like to know is how much of this trash is from personal research? Just how much of an expert—or is it *sexpert*—are you?"

Cupid hissed at him. Luke ignored the cat. Instead, he cast contempt-filled eyes, the first trace of emotion he'd shown, in her direction before returning to the book. "Like this chapter, *Fulfilling His Every Fantasy. The way to keep Mr. Right is to keep him begging for more. Never say no to your man, and he'll never be tempted to look elsewhere. Fantasy is healthy. Partake. Experiment. Enjoy. Anything goes as long as no one gets hurt.*"

Luke lowered the book. His face was contorted in disgust. "How could you debase yourself to write such retrogressive propaganda? You should be ashamed of yourself. You're a one-woman time machine bent on sending the entire female population back to the nineteen-fifties."

Thea couldn't defend herself against his indictment. She had accused herself of the same charge countless times, but she shuddered at the derision that edged its way into his carefully modulated words. "You don't understand. You have to let me explain."

"All the explanation I need is right here in black and white." He leaned in closer and continued to read. "Now, where was I? Oh, yes. Then, of course, you have your *Top Ten List*. I'm assuming these were derived from exhaustive research as well?"

Luke tossed the volume back onto the sofa. Startled, Cupid left Thea's lap to paw and sniff at the book.

"Did you have a different candidate for each or one special guy with whom you worked your way down the list? Whipped cream and whips? Chocolate sauce and handcuffs? Champagne and bubble bath? Looks like I missed out on an entirely different side of your culinary talents. But it's never too late, is it? Your kitchen is always open. I just never got to see the full menu, did I?"

He couldn't be serious! She'd written that list as a tongue-in-cheek joke, but the joke was on her ever since the book skyrocketed up the bestseller lists. Thea shook her head. "Sorry to disappoint you, but I'm all out of whipped cream."

Luke shrugged. "No matter. I'm not a big fan of whipped cream, anyway. Besides, I like my women with slightly less experience than a high-priced hooker."

Thea bit down on her lower lip to stem the sob threatening to explode from her throat. How ironic his words when weighed against the truth of her pathetic love life. Yes, she'd prostituted herself but not in the way he accused her. From the corner of her eye she noticed that even Cupid now looked at her with disdain.

With a snort, the cat bounded from the sofa. Tail raised, head held high, he strode from the room.

Thea returned her gaze to Luke's bloodshot, sunken eyes. If he never forgave her, she'd somehow survive and go on with her life. After all, she didn't deserve his forgiveness. She had deceived him. She had deceived the world. For money. But most of all, she'd deceived herself into believing her ruse was harmless. Luke was proof of how wrong she'd been.

She'd paid a steep prize. They both had. And it was all her fault. She saw the anger trapped beneath his shuttered demeanor. She suspected he wanted to lash out and hurt her in retaliation for the pain she'd caused him, but all he could muster were a few caustic insults, hurled not in a violent diatribe of spewed hate but with a resignation that showed he somehow blamed himself more than he blamed her.

And this was how she hurt him the most. Her actions reinforced his belief that caring about another human being only led down a road riddled with land mines. First his mother. Then Julie. Now her. She had destroyed far worse than any relationship they might have had. Luke was right. She'd inflicted much deeper wounds than any he'd suffered at the hands of his ex-wife.

Yet, even in his drunken state, even with barroom stench clinging to his hair and skin, even with the smell of bourbon on his breath, she yearned for his touch. She wanted him to take her in his arms and kiss her senseless. She wanted to feel the fireworks exploding behind her eyes, hear the bells pealing in her ears. Her fingers trembled from the need to reach out and caress his stubbled jaw and soothe his creased brow. Fresh tears filled her eyes. She loved this man who now hated her, but nothing she could do or say would ever make him trust her again—let alone love her.

"Yow!" From out of nowhere Cupid pounced, sinking his claws into Luke's shoulder and back. "Damn it, Cu!" Luke flailed his arms behind him, dislodging the cat from his shoulder blade and sending him sailing. Landing on the coffee table, Cupid arched his back, bared his teeth, and hissed at his master.

The sound of Luke's roar pierced through the jumble of emotions roiling inside Thea. Holding her breath, she watched as Luke glared at his pet. A tense silence gripped the apartment, broken only by the sound of the stereo and the bells still ringing in her ears.

Bells? By the time her brain registered the sound as her phone and not the manifestation of her own unfulfilled desires, the ringing was replaced by the sound of her own voice.

And then Madeline's.

"Althea, I know you're there. Pick up the phone!"

FIFTEEN

Reaching behind his shoulder, Luke felt the warm stickiness oozing from his gouged flesh. He withdrew his hand and stared at the smear of blood covering his fingertips. Even his cat had turned against him. As Thea grabbed for the phone, he stood to leave. There was nothing left for him here. Or anywhere. He'd finally learned his lesson. Never again would he make the mistake of caring for anyone or anything.

"Madeline, this really isn't a good time." Thea's voice quivered.

Luke stared at her. His alcoholic haze began to dissipate, replacing his pent-up anger with more self-loathing than he could bear. Everything had made so much sense as he sat in the bar analyzing and dissecting her multi-layered scheme. The more bourbon he poured down his throat, the more obvious her machinations had become. Now he wasn't so sure. He had expected her to fight back with all sorts of justifications and rationalizations, lash out at him with accusations of her own. She hadn't. When she begged to explain, he cut her off, and with little more than a whimper of protest, she'd crumbled into a defeated ball.

No matter what had happened between them, she didn't deserve the insults he'd hurled at her. He may not have raised his voice, but his behavior was inexcusable, all the same. An apology would be nothing more than empty platitudes. The damage was done. It didn't matter, though. As she'd said, it was over. For both of them. Silently cursing himself, he headed for the door.

"Having a bad day, Thea? I've got something that will cheer you up. Thanks to you, we're about to lose the house to foreclosure. Our family home, Thea! But you don't care about that, do you? All you care about is getting your sweet revenge. I never thought you'd stoop this low."

Luke halted abruptly at the sound of Madeline's stinging accusations coming through the answering machine. He couldn't believe he'd actually accused Thea of paying an actor to place calls to her answering machine. How much bourbon had he consumed to come up with such a farfetched theory? And no matter what he said earlier, Thea was no actress. She wore her every emotion wrapped around her like a custom-tailored suit. This call was real. He saw it in her eyes, heard it in her voice.

No matter how Thea had deceived him, in his heart he knew she was incapable of revenge. Vengeful women don't flee. They stay and get even. Then they leave, heads held high, lips curled in a satisfied smirk. Thea fled California broken-hearted and humiliated. Had she wanted her pound of flesh against her sister and ex-fiancé, she'd still be in San Francisco.

Standing in the foyer, Luke watched from the shadows and listened to the two sisters. A gentleman would have departed—or at least flipped off the answering machine. But Luke had already proved himself anything but a gentleman this evening.

"This has nothing to do with revenge, Madeline. Maybe if you opened your mail once in a while, you wouldn't be surprised by a visit from the city tax collector. The transfer papers from the lawyer were sent to you over two weeks ago."

"You know I don't have time to deal with the mail. You're supposed to handle things like that! And the bills. How do you expect me to pay the bills, Althea?"

Thea dropped the phone into her lap. She squeezed her eyelids shut. Her jaw trembled. Several large tears escaped from the corners of her eyes and slid down her cheeks, splashing onto her clenched hands.

Madeline continued to rant, demanding Thea return to San Francisco. Cu hopped onto the sofa and stalked the phone. He batted at the end producing the sound, then turned his attention to Thea's hands, licking away the salty tears still spilling from her eyes.

Thea took a deep breath, swiped at the continuing onslaught of tears, and raised the phone back to her ear. She kept her eyes closed. Her voice quavered as she spoke. "I'm not coming back. I signed the house over to you because you want it, and I don't."

"And what about everything else you promised to take care of? Should I expect a visit from the IRS and the hospital collection agency, as well?"

"No, you're not responsible for any of that. I said I'd take care of mother's other debts. The IRS won't take the house, but the city will if you don't pay the real estate tax. You don't have to worry about anything except the house, Madeline—if you want to keep it."

"You know I can't afford to keep the house by myself! Not

without you or Bill. I might just as well have let the damn place flood for all the good it did me. This is your way of getting even. Don't deny it."

Tears continued to stream down Thea's cheeks as she spoke. "No," she whispered, shaking her head.

"Of course, it is! Well, maybe if you weren't such a tight-assed virgin, Steve wouldn't have come to me in the first place!"

Luke couldn't believe his ears. *Virgin! The love expert?* He stared at Thea. Her eyes remained closed. She had no idea he was still in the apartment.

Thea choked back a heart-wrenching sob. "You could have turned him down, Madeline. You could have said no. It was only one more night."

"One more night?" Madeline laughed. "Oh, please, you can't be so naïve! That wasn't the first time. It was going to be the last!"

Thea crumbled. Her words, spoken between choking sobs, came across as nearly incoherent. "I sacrificed everything for you, Madeline. Everything." Dropping the phone, she lowered her head onto her knees and choked back a strangled cry.

Thea's words of Saturday night came back to poleax Luke. *Sometimes decent people are forced into situations where they have to compromise their values for a greater good.* She had pleaded with him not to pass judgment on others until he knew all the facts. She wasn't speaking in generalities, she'd been speaking about herself—Dr. Althea L. Chandler, alias Dr. Trulee Lovejoy—the *virgin* Doctor Love.

Luke was certain Thea's selfish, spoiled sister had no idea how much she'd sacrificed for her, although he was beginning to understand. Too late, the puzzle pieces fit into place. He might not have the specifics, but he had a pretty good idea of the circumstances that led Thea to compromise herself. And why she couldn't bring herself to tell him her secret. She knew how he'd react—exactly as he had. *You have a tendency to attack first and ask questions later.*

"Althea!" Madeline's shrill voice punctuated the air.

Luke silently stepped back into the living room, lifted the phone off the rug, and disconnected the call.

Thea raised her head and stared in horror at Luke. She fought to ignore the tugging need the sight of him triggered deep within her womb. She loved him, but whatever future they might have had was now irrevocably destroyed. She couldn't blame him. He might have handled things in a more mature fashion instead of first turning to a bottle, but given the extent of her deceit, she didn't even blame him for that. She'd shattered his trust in her, and knowing of Luke's past, she might as well have thrust a knife into his heart. Too cowardly to face the look of betrayal she knew she'd find in his eyes, she tore her gaze from his body and stared at her lap.

Althea *Liar* Chandler. If only she'd been up front with him from the very beginning...If only she hadn't been such a sniveling coward. Emptiness overwhelmed her. Emptiness and something else—an undefined uneasiness that slithered insidiously into her consciousness.

The realization hit like a tsunami, drowning her in one enormous wave of humiliation. *He'd heard!* Everything. Every syllable of Madeline's hateful diatribe, thanks to that damned answering machine.

A rush of heat surged up her neck and into her cheeks. Luke continued to stand silently in front of her. In the background the stereo filled the room with a love song that seemed obscenely out of place, given the circumstances. Knowing she couldn't handle whatever she might read on his face and in his eyes, she kept her head lowered, focusing on her trembling fists. She couldn't face him knowing what he thought of her. Not now. Not ever again. "Please leave."

"Thea, I...." He took a step closer. Cupid leaped between them. He arched his back and spat at Luke.

Clutching the sofa cushion with one hand, Thea held up her other hand, warding Luke off. She was already dying a slow death. If he touched her, she feared she'd fracture into a million pieces. "No! Just go. Leave me alone."

He turned and left the room. A moment later she heard the front door close behind him.

Luke paused in the doorway, his hand on the knob, his attention drawn to the song playing on the stereo. *Les Misérables*, still. He felt as though a lifetime had passed since he first stood in the hallway listening to the notes pouring out from under her door. How could he have destroyed so much between an overture and a finale?

He closed the door behind him, muffling the words of hope for a better tomorrow that struck at his heart. Maybe somewhere there was a place where people sang of a brighter future but only on a Broadway stage, not in real life.

Too late he realized how much he loved her. But that love had not been strong enough to ward off his suspicions and keep the pain of his past from sneaking in and sabotaging his future. Thea would never forgive him. Not now. Not after his accusatory stabs. And he could hardly blame her.

Beside himself with guilt, Luke made his way down the silent hall to his own empty apartment. In the space of one day, he'd gone from feeling like the king of the world to a slug beneath the monarch's feet. And he'd crushed another human being in his self-destructive wake.

* * *

No matter what she'd told Luke Bennett, Hedda had no intention of blowing the lid on Althea Chandler and Grace Wainwright. She had too much to lose in the way of credibility for a one-time headline that few people would devote more than a passing glance to. After all, the masses really didn't care about the identity of Dr. Trulee Lovejoy. They gobbled up her books when she hid from public view. They'd continue to hunger for them whether Trulee were Althea Chandler or Grace Wainwright or Yosemite Sam. Better to store away the information for future use as a bargaining chip.

Hedda would have loved to score an exclusive interview with Luke over the demise of his *engagement*, though. Her columns about New York's most eligible bachelor had created buzz around the city and the positive publicity she needed in her quest for an entertainment segment on the nightly news. Finally, after years of being ignored by the major networks, the head honchos were knocking on her door. And offering big bucks. Thanks to those columns.

She'd love to give a new jolt to the story by announcing Luke was once again available, but he hadn't succumbed to her not-so-subtle blackmail. All the more reason to suspect he and Dr. Chandler were in cahoots, one way or another, from the very beginning. Grace Wainwright had merely acted as a conduit when she presented Hedda with the publicity stunt idea.

Anyway, she knew before placing her call to Luke that any further columns about him would have to wait several weeks. The call was only to confirm her suspicions and possibly milk a bit more information out of him—not that he'd been very forthcoming in any of their previous encounters.

Tomorrow's column, as well as the next week's worth, were written days ago. Seven Hollywood mega-stars had arrived in Manhattan to film a blockbuster. She'd flown out to the coast to pre-interview each of them before their arrival and would be spending most of the next several weeks on location with them as they shot throughout the city. The Magnificent Seven, as she dubbed them in tomorrow's column, were far more important to her readership—and her career—than Luke Bennett and Dr. Trulee Lovejoy.

* * *

Not a word about him, Thea, or Trulee. Exhaling a lungful of relief, Luke tossed aside the morning edition of *The Daily Post*. Hedda had devoted her entire column to an interview with Brad Pitt, in town with half a dozen other celebrities to film a movie. In today's edition, Hedda made mention of subsequent columns featuring exclusive interviews with each of the other stars.

Luke hoped that meant he'd get a much-needed reprieve from the gossipmonger from hell. But he wasn't as concerned for himself as he was for Thea. What if, as she'd threatened, Hedda outed Thea as Trulee? He shuddered to think how the exposé might affect her.

He'd never called Hedda back, had never agreed to her extortion. And he hadn't heard from her again. Not that he would have known, had she tried to contact him. He spent the remainder of yesterday out of the office, first pouring bourbon down his gullet, then taking center stage in a waking nightmare of his own devising.

Now that he looked back on the events of yesterday with a more rational head, he couldn't figure out the reason behind Hedda's phone call to him. If she was planning to expose Thea as Trulee, why inform him ahead of time? Or did she suspect he was unaware of Thea's chicanery? Had she hoped that once she divulged Thea's secret, he'd walk out on her, thus keeping Hedda's trap-the-bachelor story alive a bit longer?

He glanced down at the discarded paper. Hedda knew before she called him that today's column, as well as the next six, were already written and scheduled. So why the subterfuge, veiled threats, and one-hour deadline when she never intended today's column to center around him and Thea? None of it made any sense to him. Unless Hedda's real intent all along was revenge against him for his lack of cooperation.

"Selfish bitch," he muttered at the paper. "You don't care how many lives you destroy to get what you want, do you?"

"Did you say something, Luke?"

He turned from his desk to find Margaret sticking her head around the doorway. He waved her away.

She stood firm. "You all right? You ran out of here looking really upset yesterday."

"I'm fine." He strode across the office and closed the door.

"Sure you are," she called through the heavy mahogany.

Luke knew he wasn't fooling her. In all the years Margaret had worked for him, he'd never closed the door between their offices.

He returned to his desk, collapsed into his chair, and buried his head in his hands. He'd spent a sleepless night sitting up in bed listening to the sound of Thea's muffled sobs on the other side of the wall. Several times he reached for the phone, hoping she'd listen to him, but she refused to answer and had turned off her machine.

Now, sitting at his desk, his head throbbing from a hangover that wasn't nearly punishment enough for his sins, he again tried calling her. He let the phone ring twelve times before he hung up, repeating the futile effort every ten or fifteen minutes throughout the day. By five-thirty he'd lost count of how many attempts he'd made.

When he arrived back at his apartment building later that evening, he confronted Melvin. "Have you seen Dr. Chandler today?"

"Can't say as I have, Mr. Bennett, but then again, I just came on duty a little while ago. Traded shifts with Gus 'cause he had to take his missus to visit her sick mama up in Poughkeepsie."

Luke reached into his pocket and pulled out a fifty-dollar bill. "If you see her leave, I want you to call me." He placed the money and one of his business cards in the doorman's hand. "Whether I'm here or at my office, understand?"

Melvin stuffed the fifty and the card into his jacket pocket and offered Luke a broad gap-toothed grin. "Sure 'nuff, sir."

"No matter what time it is,"

"You got it, Mr. Bennett."

* * *

A week went by, and Melvin never called. Luke offered a second fifty to Gus and one to Carlos, the other doormen, with the same lack of results. He could only surmise that Thea had gotten to the men earlier and with larger bribes. He knew she couldn't afford it, and it pained him to think she'd go to such lengths to keep from running into him.

She didn't answer her phone. She refused to come to the door when he knocked. Which he did every time he passed her apartment. If she left her apartment at all, she was apparently doing it when she knew she wouldn't run into him.

Luke knew she was home. He heard her in her bedroom at night, sometimes softly sobbing or carrying on a one-sided conversation with Cu. He wished he could hear well enough to make out her words.

As much as he missed his pet, he was grateful she at least had the comfort of the cat. Besides, Cu had taken sides, and Luke had lost. He doubted Cu would ever return, but Thea needed the cat more than he did. She had no one else to turn to. Occasionally, he heard her phone ring, but she never answered it.

Luke tried to submerse himself in work, but his attempts were proving less than successful. He wasn't sleeping or eating, and he knew he looked like hell. He didn't care.

Others, apparently, did.

"I think it's time you got whatever is eating away at you off your chest," said Sean. The firm's senior partner stood at the entrance of Luke's office, his arms crossed over his chest, his mouth set in a grim line.

From the day they first met, the sixty-year-old Sean Porter had been more father figure than partner to Luke. Although both men knew Sean could never fill the emptiness left by the death of Luke's own father, Sean came a close second.

Lifting his glasses, Luke massaged the bridge of his nose and grimaced. "It's a long, sordid tale."

"I'm in no hurry."

Luke waved him in. "All right. Close the door, and pull up a chair."

Sean headed for the bookcases along the side wall. "How about if I pour us each a stiff one first?" He reached for the decanter Luke kept for clients. Sean filled two cut crystal highballs each with three fingers worth of whiskey, then carried the drinks across the room. He handed one to Luke, placing the other on the far side of the desk.

Before he settled into the leather wing back opposite Luke, he returned to the bookcase and retrieved the decanter. "I have a feeling we're going to need this."

Luke lifted his glass, inspecting the golden liquid through the crystal prisms. "I don't know," he admitted as much to himself as Sean. "Maybe if I hadn't poured so much of this down my gullet last week, things might be different." He tore his gaze from the glass and eyed Sean. "Did you know I have a tendency to attack first and ask questions later?"

"I've heard that about you, but maybe you'd better start at the beginning."

One hour and half a decanter later, Luke had spilled his guts and laid bare his soul.

Sean sat back, cupping his hands behind his head and stretching his long legs out in front of him. He grinned at Luke. "Barbara knew the moment she saw the two of you together."

Luke slammed his glass onto his desk. "Knew what? That I'm such a Prince Charming?"

"Stop flogging yourself, Luke. The damage is done. Now you need to figure out a way to get that woman back in your life."

Luke snorted. "She doesn't want me, and I can't blame her."

"Don't be so sure."

"For God's sake, Sean! Haven't you listened to a word I've said? She won't even answer the friggin' phone, let alone the door!"

"She will. Eventually."

"When did you become a goddamn clairvoyant?"

Sean's lips turned up in a benevolent smile. "Not me, old man. My wife. Weren't you listening before? I told you she knew the moment she saw you and Thea together."

Luke exhaled a lungful of annoyance. "Knew what?"

"That the two of you were in love." He leaned forward in his chair and steepled his fingers. "Real love, Luke, not that phony pretend stuff you had going with Julie."

"Barbara knew, and we didn't?" Luke scoffed. "Not that I believe you, since we hardly knew each other at that point, but does it matter? Whatever might have been between us is dead, and I killed it."

"Don't be so quick to plan the funeral." Sean rose from his chair. "Meanwhile, I think you need to get away. Clear your head."

"I'm in no mood for a vacation."

"I wasn't suggesting one." He turned to leave. "But I am making a few changes in the schedule. I'm sending you to the coast next week instead of Jerry."

"Why?"

"That's where she's from, isn't it?"

"So?"

"So maybe you just might find some answers waiting for you in San Francisco."

* * *

As much as Thea would have liked to blame someone else for her grief—her parents for their blindness, her sister for her selfishness, Luke for his pigheaded obstinacy, she alone bore the responsibility for her actions. She knew right from wrong, lies from truth. She took the easy way out by allowing Grace to publish a manuscript never been meant for publication—at least not as a self-help book.

She certainly proved her doctoral thesis. In spades! Dr. Trulee Lovejoy was one of the biggest frauds ever to hit the pop-psychology genre.

Had she tried, she might have found another way of paying for her mother's medical care and staving off countless creditors. The bottom line was, she hadn't tried. Grace dangled that bag of gold under her nose, and Thea had grabbed it without any thought of repercussions.

And now her editor and friend, motivated by a keen desire to maintain her trendy Park Avenue standard of living and confronted with the same temptation, had transformed a wretched situation into a monstrous one. From the sidelines, Thea observed as an insecure Grace, scared to death at first of play-acting as Trulee, discovered and harnessed her inner actress. Over the ensuing days, from what Thea read in various print interviews and observed for herself on half a dozen talk shows, that lurking thespian persona had taken control of Grace like the most addictive of drugs. Grace was flying as high as the International Space Station. Too bad she couldn't write the damn books.

Other than a constant deluge of e-mails, she heard from Grace only once since that first book signing in Union Square. After her stint that evening on *Late Night*, Grace had spent the next few days doing interviews and making appearances on several morning news and talk shows. Then she'd hopped a plane to begin her cross-country promotional tour.

A week after Thea had walked out of Barnes & Noble, Grace called from Los Angeles. "God, Thea! I'm having a ball! I can't believe you didn't want any part of this. You wouldn't believe the celebrities I've met! You have no idea what you're missing. Last night I had dinner with Whoopi Goldberg and Tom Hanks. The three of us were guests on *The Tonight Show*, and they invited me to join them for dinner after the taping. Can you believe it?"

Thea snuggled closer to Cu, immediately regretting her decision to install Caller ID. She splurged on the service only because she knew she couldn't keep from answering her phone forever. Caller ID enabled her to monitor incoming calls without the torment of hearing certain voices.

She let Grace ramble on without paying much attention. Thea could care less about Whoopi Goldberg and Tom Hanks. "So it all worked out," was all she managed in the way of a congratulatory acknowledgement.

"Yes, incredible, isn't it? Who would have thought I'd have a talent for this? Remember how scared I was at that first book signing?"

"Hmm."

"So how's the next book coming?"

"It's coming," she lied.

"I'm certain *Mr. Right or Mr. Wrong?* is going to be your most successful book yet. People keep bombarding me with questions about it. Have you gotten the suggestions I e-mailed you?"

"All forty-two of them." Once Grace had divulged the title and topic of Trulee's next book, her fans began offering up countless Mr. Wrong woes at each of Grace's personal appearances. Grace passed them all along to Thea with suggestions for various chapters. Thea dutifully printed out each missive and stacked the pages on the corner of her desk. She hadn't read any of them, let alone written a damn word.

After a week of crying her heart out and consuming more pints of Ben & Jerry's than she cared to admit, Thea stuffed her grief into her emotional strong box and locked it away. She then commanded Tom, Dick, and Harry to steer clear of the cache. The three devilish tummy acrobats had been uncharacteristically subdued since she ordered Luke from her apartment. Either they were immersed in plotting some sinister upheaval, or they'd drowned in the deluge of her nonstop tears. Although she hoped for the latter, she feared the former. The symbiotic trio had been a part of her for too long.

Thea padded around the silent apartment in a ratty pair of sweats and bare feet, not even bothering to comb her hair. Knowing she looked like hell, she judiciously averted her gaze whenever she passed a mirror. She already felt miserable. No need confirming her suspicions. "As long as you don't mind," she told Cupid. "Being that you're my one and only friend, I certainly wouldn't want the sight of me frightening you away."

The cat cast her a disdainful glance before heading for his litter pan. Obviously, he wasn't keen on being seen in the company of a bedraggled frump, but since there was no one around to notice, he remained by her side. Thea kept her bedroom French doors cracked open in case he changed his mind and wanted to return to Luke, but the cat never once so much as ventured onto the balcony.

Thea swept her tangled hair from her face and reached for the contract sitting on her desk. She paced back and forth across the small office, rereading the paragraph she'd already committed to memory.

Two vying truths waged war within her. Morally, she was bound to honor the terms of her contract. Besides, if she reneged on the remaining book, she'd be forced to return the advance she'd already spent. Yet, she could no longer bring herself to spew Trulee's chicanery. Forget Grace's announcement about the title of the next book. There would be no *Mr. Right or Mr. Wrong?* And definitely no *Dear Trulee.* Never again would Thea compromise her moral principles. She'd already paid far too steep a price.

Although tempted to consult with her attorney, she decided against placing the call. So far, and she couldn't fathom why, Hedda had refrained from divulging her secret. Since the rest of the country was in the process of embracing Grace as Dr. Trulee Lovejoy, Thea saw no point in tempting fate by blurting the truth out to someone else—even if he *was* bound by professional constraints.

From what she could see, the wording in the contract appeared straightforward. She owed her publisher one more book penned by Dr. Trulee Lovejoy. Nowhere did it mention anything as to subject matter or content of that book.

In between the crying jags and ice cream binges and constant e-mails from Grace, a germ of a solution began to take root at the edges of Thea's mind. She had an idea how she might satisfy the terms of her contract without further compromising herself. Ironically, Luke had planted the seed.

* * *

Luke stood on the sidewalk in front of the venerable Pacific Heights structure. Locating the house had proved as easy as logging onto the San Francisco telephone directory. Dr. A. L. Chandler no longer resided in the city, but her listing remained.

Although the San Francisco branch of Porter-Sachs-Bennett ran like a well-oiled machine, and the monthly visits by one of the partners were more formality than necessity, Luke still had responsibilities that kept him busy through the week. He was forced to leave his visit to Thea's sister until Saturday morning.

He arrived at dawn, not wanting to risk missing her. Standing across the street, he alternately studied the house and checked his watch. On a street of grandly painted Victorians, the Chandler house stood out for its understated elegance. The unpainted cedar siding was weathered gray from exposure to years of the salt breeze blowing in from the bay. The window sashes, porch railings and gingerbread were painted white, the shutters, porch deck and door a deep navy blue, although all were in sore need of a fresh coat.

Luke checked his watch once more. The street was beginning to come alive. In the distance he heard the clang of cable cars. A light glowed from a second-floor window. Someone had awakened in the house across the street.

Luke filled his lungs with air, forcing the breath out in a rush. Within that house lived a brilliant but spoiled woman. Did she hold the answers that might give him a second chance with Thea, or was he on a fool's journey? He harbored no illusions, but he refused to give up hope.

By eight-thirty he could wait no longer. Squaring his shoulders, he strode down the walkway and up the half-dozen steps to the front door. Taking one final deep breath, he rang the bell.

A moment later the door swung open. The woman standing on the other side eyed him suspiciously. He would have recognized her anywhere. Madeline was a younger, blonde version of her sister, but she lacked Thea's magnificent violet eyes. Madeline's eyes were a glacial blue—harsh and hostile. Her remaining features, although identical in appearance to her sister's, held a disturbing testiness he'd never seen in Thea.

"Don't you damn vultures ever let up?"

"I beg your pardon?"

"Petty bureaucrats! I'll bet you're even collecting overtime to harass me on a Saturday. Well you're too late! I paid the tax bill yesterday. Go hassle some other poor soul." She started to slam the door in Luke's face, but he grabbed it from her and stepped inside. "What do you think you're doing?" she screamed. "Get out!"

"Are you Madeline Chandler?" he asked, keeping his voice as calm as possible and knowing damn well she couldn't be anyone but Madeline.

She crossed her arms over her chest and jutted out her chin. "Who wants to know?"

"My name is Luke Bennett. I'm a friend of your sister's from New York."

Immediately, Madeline's combative posture deflated. Worry knit her brows together. Her lower lip trembled. "Is Althea all right? I've been so worried."

"Was at the door, darling?"

Luke swung his head around. The voice came from the top of the stairs where a man, dressed only in a pair of khaki shorts stood. A towel was draped across his shoulders, his chest and jet-black hair still glistening from a recent shower. He bounded down the steps, taking them two at a time.

Joining them in the foyer, he wrapped his arm around Madeline's shoulders. "Who's this?"

Luke's fists curled into two tight balls. All the anger, guilt, and frustration of the past two weeks immediately transformed into a consuming rage that traveled up his body and into his fists. This had to be Steve, the ex-fiancé—the man who slept with Thea's sister the night before her wedding. And here they were living openly together in what should rightfully be Thea's home, while she struggled to pay her mother's medical bills!

Luke turned to Steve. "This is from your ex-fiancée," he said.

"She's too well-bred to deliver it herself. Fortunately, I'm not."

In the next instant Luke's fist made contact with the man's jaw, sending him careening backwards into the steps. His head hit the tread with a dull thud.

Madeline screamed. "Bill!"

SIXTEEN

"Bill! Oh my God!" Madeline ran to the man sprawled on his back across the bottom third of the staircase and bent down beside him. "You're crazy!" she shouted at Luke over her shoulder.

"Bill?!" Luke stared at the dazed man. "You're not Steve?"

"Of course he's not Steve!" Madeline glared at Luke. She cradled her husband's head in her lap. "Are you all right, darling?"

Bill rubbed his jaw with one hand. The other reached behind his head. He winced. "I'll survive." He turned his attention to Luke. "I don't know who you are, pal, but with an uppercut like that I sure as hell wish you'd been around when *I* confronted that sonofabitch."

"I'm sorry." Luke extended his hand to help Bill to his feet. "According to Thea, I have this habit of attacking first and asking questions later." He grimaced. "Looks like she's right. I did it again. Only I've never used my fists before." Luke flexed his hand, then extended it once more. "Luke Bennett."

"Bill Jennings," said Bill, shaking Luke's hand. "Pleased to meet you." He opened his mouth and moved his jaw from side to side. "I think."

"Thea was right about a lot of things," said Madeline, wrapping her arm around her husband's waist. "I wish I could tell her that."

"She told me the two of you were getting a divorce," said Luke, puzzled to see Madeline and Bill together. "Naturally, I assumed...."

"That Steve had moved in with me?" asked Madeline, finishing his sentence for him.

"Well, under the circumstances...."

Madeline blushed. "I made some terrible mistakes, Mr. Bennett, mistakes which wound up hurting the two people I love the most in the world." Madeline nestled closer under her husband's arm and gazed up at him before turning back to Luke. "But then I woke up. And grew up." She offered Bill a hopeful smile. "Right?"

He snorted a chuckle before planting a kiss on top of her head. "Let's say you're working on it and leave it at that."

Madeline chewed on her lip, as if processing her husband's response before continuing, "Anyway, it's all because of Thea. She needs to know that, but she refuses to speak to me."

Luke studied the sister he had decided sight unseen to blame for everything. His only reason for coming to see Madeline was to wring details from her. He needed to know what happened in the Chandler family that had compelled Thea to take on the identity of a person contrary to every principle she held dear. He already knew it had something to do with family finances and their mother's health, but he needed to know the specifics. Maybe then he'd figure out some way to make amends for his behavior.

He came having made up his mind to hate Madeline Chandler

the way he hated Julie. And his mother. But the icy arrogance he first saw in Madeline's eyes and on her face had given way to a contrition that now echoed in her voice. Only he had no way of knowing how genuine were her regrets.

Luke grimaced. He certainly had a history of jumping to the wrong conclusions with Chandler women, but something told him he'd made a mistake in his initial assessment of Madeline. "We need to talk," he told her.

Madeline looked questioningly at Bill.

He answered with a light kiss to her temple. "Why don't you start a pot of coffee, darling? I'll grab a shirt. Then we'll find out why Mr. Bennett is here."

* * *

"You never answered my question," said Madeline as she measured several scoops of coffee into a filter. She glanced over her shoulder at Luke, her eyes filled with anxiety. "Is my sister all right?"

Luke hesitated. He had no intention of divulging the details of his last encounter with Thea. He'd give anything to erase that evening and his less than honorable behavior. But apparently that night was also Madeline's last contact with her sister. "She's extremely upset at the moment," he finally answered.

"With me." Madeline sighed and turned back to the coffee maker. She poured the water into the reservoir. Her hand shook, and she spilled some of it on the counter. Her shoulders slumped as she reached for a sponge. "She hung up on me over two weeks ago. I haven't been able to reach her since. She won't answer her phone, and she's turned off the answering machine. I can't even leave a message."

"*I* hung up on you that night," said Luke.

Madeline spun around. "You? Why?"

Luke decided there was no point in mincing words. Madeline might now be filled with remorse, but he knew of her past behavior, and he wanted to make certain she knew he knew. "Because your sister had been through a severely traumatic experience that night and didn't need any of your selfish nonsense adding to it."

Madeline flipped the switch on the coffee maker, then took a seat opposite Luke. She folded her hands on the table and stared at them for several long seconds before speaking. "It's all my fault. Everything." She raised her chin. Her eyes glistened with unshed tears. "All my life I was jealous of my sister. She had the freedom to do what she wanted. I was smothered and controlled by my parents, never allowed to have a normal childhood.

"Thea could run off and climb a tree if she wanted to. She might get a scolding for it afterwards. Mother considered such behavior unladylike, but still, she climbed that tree. And I hated her for it. For having the life I wanted.

"Have you ever climbed a tree, Mr. Bennett? Of course, you have," she answered for him. "All children get to climb trees. Except me."

She took a deep breath and pierced him with her icy blue eyes. "Know what Christmas was like in our house?"

He shook his head.

"Thea received Madame Alexander dolls. I got books. The closest I ever came to receiving a toy was the time Mother and Father gave me a set of Mensa puzzles." Her mouth tightened into a thin line. Luke could see she was trying to keep her lower lip from trembling. She wasn't succeeding.

"When our mother died, I thought I'd finally have the freedom to live my own life, but...."

"But her misguided husband and sister thought they knew better," said Bill, entering the kitchen. He pulled out a chair and joined Madeline and Luke at the table. "To put it bluntly, we continued to treat Madeline like a gifted child, running her life in much the same way Camilla and Frederick had."

Bill patted Madeline's hand. "Good intentions aside, Madeline's parents created a selfish, self-centered monster. Thea, on the instructions of her parents, acted like an enabler. And I...well, being twelve years older than Madeline, I'm afraid at times, she saw me more as a father figure than a husband, and I did little to discourage that. She needed taking care of; I took care of her."

"One day I decided I'd had enough," said Madeline. "It's one thing having your parents control your life when you're a child. But when it's your sister and husband..."

"And in one poorly thought through decision," said Bill, "Madeline lashed out at us in the most hurtful way possible. By taking up with Steve, she found the one way that would drive us both from her life."

Luke turned to Madeline. "Then you wanted Thea to catch you that night?"

She nodded. "I hoped she'd find out sooner, but she was so damn trusting. Once she discovered us, I realized how wrong I'd been. When I no longer had my husband and sister to depend on, I felt worthless and incapable of surviving on my own. Isn't that ironic? I have an I.Q. that flies off the charts, and I didn't even know how to do a load of laundry! I begged Bill and Althea to come back, but I'd hurt them both so deeply that they refused. I could hardly blame them."

"What about Steve?" asked Luke.

Madeline cringed. "What a piece of work! That bastard started coming on to me from the moment he and Thea announced their engagement. He knew exactly what I craved and played on my insecurities. He treated me like a woman, not a child. And I enjoyed it. So I encouraged him. At first, it was like this big joke I was playing on Thea and Bill. Here they thought they were controlling me, and look what I was doing behind their backs, you know?"

Luke nodded, but he found it difficult to accept Madeline's childish rationale for such a treacherous act of betrayal.

"Steve and I used each other for different reasons," continued Madeline, "but if really loved my sister, he never would have cheated on her." An ironic laugh escaped through her lips. "In a way I probably did Thea the biggest favor of her life. Steve Ross never loved anyone but himself." She rose from the table to pour the coffee. "How do you take yours, Mr. Bennett?"

"Black." Luke studied Madeline as she filled the cups, then brought two of them to the table, handing one to Bill and one to him. She removed a container of milk from the refrigerator and added a few drops to her own cup before rejoining them at the table.

Over their leisurely dinners Thea had gradually told Luke of her childhood. After discovering Madeline's abilities, Thea's parents virtually ignored their firstborn except to instill an unreasonable burden of responsibility on the young girl. Thea grew up resentful and jealous of the sister who became her parents' prime focus. Meanwhile, the object of their adulation harbored her own resentments.

Luke turned his attention to Bill. "Thea said you filed for divorce. What made you change your mind?"

Bill reached across the table and took hold of his wife's hand.

"Ever been in love, Bennett?"

"Once."

"Ever lose that love?"

A knot tightened in Luke's gut. Another choked his vocal cords. He nodded.

"Then you know what it feels like to be half a person." Bill picked up his coffee cup and took a long swallow. "It's the most horrible feeling in the world." He set the mug down in front of him and glanced toward Madeline. "You go through the motions of living, but inside you're dying a slow, torturous death."

"And you'd sell your soul for a second chance to make things right," added Madeline.

Bill squeezed her hand. "God knows, Madeline has her faults, but after my initial anger subsided, I came to realize I'd rather live with those maddening faults than without her. Still, I wasn't completely crazy. I needed her to recognize that she had to meet me halfway if we were going to make this work. Things aren't as rosy as they may appear to you. We're seeing a marriage counselor. Taking one day at a time. We have a lot of work ahead of us."

"*I* have a lot of work ahead of *me*," said Madeline. "I'm the one with the problem. Bill's a saint. Tell him what I did."

Bill chuckled. "In case you haven't already figured it out, Madeline is very stubborn and used to getting her own way."

"Two of the many things I'm working to change," she said.

"She wanted me back," said Bill, "and she wasn't going to take no for an answer, no matter how many times I hung up on her. She parked herself at my front door a week and a half ago and refused to leave until I listened to her. At first, I ignored her, going so far as to step over her body whenever I came or went."

"I stayed there for three days," said Madeline, "leaving only to use a public restroom from time to time and grab some fast food."

"Finally, I took pity on her and allowed her into the apartment. We spent the next twenty-four hours talking." He smiled at his wife. "Actually, she did most of the talking. I listened."

Madeline sighed. "I think it was the first time in my life that anyone ever listened to something I said that wasn't related to quarks or neutrinos or black holes."

"I refused to listen," mumbled Luke.

Madeline and Bill turned their gazes from each other to him. "That's why you're here, isn't it?" asked Madeline. "You're in love with Althea."

Luke nodded. He wondered how many of life's heartaches might have been prevented if the people involved had spent their time building bridges between each other rather than walls of separation. Had a similar scenario torn his parents apart? Would his mother have stayed had his father only listened to her? Had she spent years crying out to be heard until someone else finally answered, someone other than her husband?

Luke could only conjecture. He'd never know the reasons behind his mother's desertion. His memories of her were vague and colored by years of his own resentment and his father's bitterness. For the first time he tried to imagine her pain. He still couldn't accept the fact that she abandoned him, but maybe there was more to the story than what he remembered or his father told him. Or maybe, as his father had repeatedly hammered into him, she was nothing more than an opportunistic gold digger. He'd never know the truth, but until this moment, he never considered there might be two sides to his own childhood tragedy.

"What happened?" asked Madeline. "Why are you here?"

"I need your help."

"In what way?"

"Tell me why your sister was forced to make a pact with the devil. Why did she need money so desperately?"

"A pact with the devil?" Madeline eyed him with bewilderment. "I don't understand what you're talking about. What did she do?"

Luke stood and strode around the table to the counter. He refilled his coffee cup, then topped off Madeline's and Bill's before returning to his chair. "Ever hear of Dr. Trulee Lovejoy?"

Madeline blushed. She lowered her gaze and blew into her steaming mug. "I bought one of her books to figure out how to get Bill back." She cast her husband a sideways glance and bit her lower lip. "I was getting desperate."

One puzzle piece fell into place for Luke. "Then you have no idea who Trulee Lovejoy really is?"

Madeline turned her attention back to Luke. She nodded, her blonde curls bouncing against her shoulders. "Of course, I do. She even autographed my book when I bought it. She was in town for a promotional tour."

"That's not Trulee Lovejoy," said Luke. "Her name is Grace Wainwright."

Madeline shrugged. "So she uses a pseudonym. Lots of authors do that, don't they?"

"She's not the author. She's the author's editor. A shill posing as the author."

"What's this got to do with Thea?" asked Bill.

"Everything. Dr. Trulee Lovejoy is the pen name of Dr. Althea L. Chandler."

"Good God!" cried Bill. "You can't be serious! Thea would never write such drivel. Her dissertation was based on debunking quacks like that."

"I know," said Luke. "So what happened?"

Madeline looked at Bill. Bill looked at Madeline. "Martin Kirby," they said in unison.

Luke had never heard Thea mention the name. "Who?"

Madeline began to sob. "Oh God, Bill. Now I understand what Thea meant when she said she sacrificed everything for me. I had no idea. I never questioned where the money came from. We were both so worried about mother's health. No one ever asked my opinion or told me more than they thought I needed to know. Thea said she'd take care of everything, and she did. I never gave it another thought. Not at the time."

"Who's Martin Kirby?" repeated Luke.

Madeline sniffed back her tears. "The bastard who ran off with our money. I knew he'd swindled mother and drained our trust funds, but I had no idea how serious things were until both Thea and Bill were gone. He took everything, and no one ever told me."

Bill shrugged an apology. "As I said, Bennett, we treated her like a child."

"What happened?"

Bill deferred to his wife. "Do you want to tell him, or should I?"

"You can." She snuffled back more tears.

Bill cleared his throat and spoke directly to Luke. "Frederick Chandler, Thea and Madeline's father, was a nineteenth century sort of guy. He didn't believe women were capable of handling money properly."

"He probably came to that conclusion watching my mother shop," said Madeline. Then she offered her husband a sheepish grin and added, "And me."

266

"Probably," agreed Bill. "When Frederick died twelve years ago, his will stipulated that his wife choose a financial adviser to handle the estate and oversee their daughters' trust funds. He gave her the names of three business associates to choose from. Unfortunately, Camilla made the worst possible choice—Martin Kirby. In all fairness I'm sure Frederick never knew Kirby's true nature. He wanted his family taken care of after his death."

"He took care of us, all right," said Madeline, her voice filled with bitterness.

"Seven years later," continued Bill, "Kirby had bled the accounts nearly dry. He fled the country, leaving in his wake a mountain of debt, including several years' worth of federal taxes which had been prepared by him and signed by Camilla and her daughters but never filed and paid."

Luke blew out a lungful of disgust, a few choice expletives riding the wave of his exhaled breath.

"As you can imagine," said Bill, "the IRS, ever the sympathetic branch of the government that they are, had little compassion for the family's plight. They demanded the back taxes plus interest and penalties on the income from the stolen funds."

"Shortly afterwards," said Madeline, "mother was diagnosed with cancer. It wasn't until after she died that I learned Kirby had ceased paying our health insurance premiums two years earlier. Thea was shouldering all of mother's medical bills along with paying off liens on the house and the IRS." She sniffed back a fresh onslaught of tears. "I never questioned where the money came from."

"When Madeline and I married," said Bill, "I paid off the balance of the taxes due on her trust. After Camilla died, the three of us remained in the house, sharing the upkeep equally. Thea continued paying off Camilla's extensive debts as well as her own."

"Bill offered to help," said Madeline, "but Althea insisted he'd already contributed more than enough to a debt that wasn't his."

Luke was able to piece the rest together. With her mother seriously ill and the IRS threatening to seize the family home, Thea sacrificed her professional integrity to save her family. If word ever got out that Dr. Althea Chandler, respected Berkeley sociologist, was the psychobabble doctor of love, her career would be toast.

And now Hedda had discovered Thea's secret!

Luke lowered his forehead onto his palms. Thea tried to tell him that night. If only he hadn't been so blinded by anger and hate....How could he not see that his wonderful Thea would never compromise herself unless she felt she had no other choice—and only then, not for herself, but for others. She'd even told him as much. *I'm merely asking you to reserve judgment on people and their actions until you have all the facts.*

Luke groaned. Madeline reached out and placed her hand on his shoulder. "I want nothing but happiness for my sister, Mr. Bennett. I know I said I hated her, but those were the words of a confused, lonely, angry child. I love my sister. And after what you've just told us, I owe her more than I could ever repay in a hundred lifetimes. Please, tell me how I can help."

Luke thought for a moment. "Come back to New York with me today."

Madeline's eyes widened. "New York? Now? I can't. Not now."

Luke grew angry. "You said you'd do anything to help. Or did you mean anything, as long as it wasn't an inconvenience?"

"No, of course not but I can't go to New York. You don't

understand. Not now. Not when I've finally...Bill?" She turned pleading eyes to her husband. "How can I go to New York *now*?"

Her husband frowned at her. "How can you not go, Madeline?"

* * *

Thea pulled the sheets of paper from the printer, tamped them into a neat stack, and placed the pile on an empty corner of her cluttered desk. Scowling, she eyed the two hundred and eighty-seven pages that represented her third and final Dr. Trulee Lovejoy advice book. She inhaled a ragged breath, slowly releasing it.

She'd fulfilled her contractual obligation—as long as Grace bought into the unique twist to the third book. If not, she'd have to find some way of repaying the advance. As far as she was concerned, Trulee Lovejoy was now dead, and Thea would dig ditches or shovel sludge before she'd resurrect the alter ego who'd caused so much heartache.

Thea had no idea how Grace would react to the final book. She was expecting *Mr. Right or Mr. Wrong?* Thea had given her no reason to believe she'd receive anything but *Mr. Right or Mr. Wrong?* She'd led Grace to assume she'd been typing away at *Mr. Right or Mr. Wrong?* from the moment Grace, as Trulee, had gone public with the title.

"So I'm a coward," she told Cupid. "If Grace is so set on *Mr. Right or Mr. Wrong?*, let her write the damn book herself." Grace might disagree, but from what Thea had observed recently, she had no doubt Grace *could* write as Trulee. Grace had *become* Trulee. When Thea caught Grace on TV, she barely recognized her editor and friend.

Cupid sidled up against her ankles and growled his agreement.

Or maybe he was just hungry. With Cupid, it was often hard to tell. The cat was always hungry, but he also possessed an uncanny sense of understanding in those amber eyes of his.

She grimaced at him. "I know. I didn't even try to write *Mr. Right or Mr. Wrong?*, but can you blame me?"

Cupid cocked his head and stared up at her as if waiting for further explanation.

Thea smacked her arms against her thighs. "I couldn't bring myself to do it, okay? Some people take longer than others to develop backbone." In the space of the past few weeks, she'd uncovered too many disturbing truths about herself. Trulee had always been a reluctant part of her, someone she was forced to become. But still, she and she alone made the decision to become Trulee.

At the time she thought she had no alternative. Too late she realized there are always choices, always a Door Number One and a Door Number Two. Life was no different than *Let's Make a Deal*. Grace, the Monty Hall of the publishing world, waved the easy cash under her nose, and Thea, lacking the courage to choose the unknown, had grabbed it. Never again. As far as she was concerned, Dr. Trulee Lovejoy was six feet under, and going to stay there.

Fearing Grace's reaction, Thea remained as evasive as possible about the book whenever she communicated with Grace. She rarely answered her phone, seldom returned calls. So most of their communication consisted of e-mails. Thea preferred it that way. She felt more in control when she could weigh her thoughts before committing them to cyberspace. On the phone she might say something she'd later regret. Or she might break down and start blubbering about Luke. She wasn't sure which she feared more.

"Not much of a backbone," she mumbled under her breath as she stared at the manuscript her editor wasn't expecting. "More like a wobbly column of cottage cheese. Guess I still have a way to go, huh?"

Cupid meowed.

Keeping to herself, ensconced in her apartment, Cupid had become Thea's only companion. Much of the day the cat slept nestled in her lap as she typed away at the computer. Occasionally, he hopped onto the monitor and playfully swatted at her fingers as they sped across the keys. At night, snuggled within the curve of her body, his soft purrs helped fend off the loneliness that pervaded her bedroom.

The nights were by far the worst. Sleep never came quickly, and when it did, her dreams and the man in them—the man whose head lay only feet away on the opposite side of the wall—tortured her. During the day she kept busy, forcing Luke from her thoughts, but at night he filled her head with fantasies of what might have been if she'd only possessed the courage—and backbone—to be honest about herself.

Thea secured the manuscript with a rubber band and dropped it into her canvas tote. Placing the tote back on her desk, she tucked the bag's opening underneath the weight of the pages. "To keep you out," she told Cupid as he jumped up onto the desk and batted the canvas. Unable to gain entry, he snorted at the bag, then leaped to the floor and followed her from the office into her bedroom.

Thea stripped off her ratty T-shirt and denim shorts and slipped into a pair of white linen trousers and a black silk camp shirt, additional purchases from a second trip she'd made to Repeat Performance, back during what now seemed like another lifetime. She took several quick brush strokes to her hair, scooping the strands into a ponytail she secured with a black scrunchy.

Cupid sat perched on the toilet tank, carefully observing her every move. Thea slumped onto the lid of the commode and stroked his fur. "It's D-Day."

He responded with a blank stare.

"I'm glad one of us isn't concerned. Too bad Tom, Dick, and Harry can't cop your attitude." Her tummy acrobats had returned with a vengeance, transforming her intestines into an internal version of a combination Sooperdooperlooper, Montezooma's Revenge, and Xcelerator. Not a pleasant experience for someone prone to motion sickness from merry-go-rounds, let alone world-famous roller coasters.

Cupid yawned his disinterest and began to groom his nether regions. Thea looked away. "Don't enjoy yourself too much."

On her way down the hall, she grabbed her tote from the office and removed a dish from the refrigerator. Then, with one final inhalation of courage, she headed out the door to her late Friday afternoon meeting with Grace.

* * *

Forty minutes later Thea sat across from Grace as her editor glared at the manuscript.

"This isn't *Mr. Right or Mr. Wrong?*"

"No, but it fulfills my contractual obligations."

Grace glanced up from the pages, a deep scowl etched across her face. "Does it?"

"I believe so." Thea popped open the Tupperware container. "Here. Have a brownie."

Grace smirked at her. "Trying to sweeten me up for the kill?"

Thea offered her a slight grin. "Couldn't hurt."

Grace lifted a brownie from the container and sighed. "You've really put me in an awkward position, Thea. For the past few weeks I've been touring the country, touting your next book. This isn't it."

"Yes, it is, Grace."

"No, your next book is supposed to be *Mr. Right or Mr. Wrong?*"

"I never agreed to that."

"But you led me to believe you were working on it." She popped the brownie into her mouth and stared over her reading glasses at Thea as she chewed.

Thea squirmed. She couldn't deny she'd misled Grace with cryptic answers to her various questions about the status of the book. "I know. I have no excuse for that. I should have been up front with you, but...." She shrugged. "Chalk it up to weak backbone."

Grace and Thea stared at each other across Grace's cluttered desk for several seconds until Grace broke the standoff with a deflated sigh. "I'm sorry. I know it's been a rough few months for you, and I sure as hell didn't help by ambushing you with yet another complication."

"You could say that."

"I couldn't help myself. I just fell into the role of Trulee. Half the time I wasn't even aware of what I was saying. It was like I developed a split personality, and before I knew it, she completely took over."

"I know. I watched it happen."

Grace chortled. "Hidden talent, huh? Who knew? But this..." She nodded in the direction of the manuscript. "No way could I pull something like this off on the talk-show circuit. I'd be exposed as a fraud in no time."

The same worry consumed Thea. With Grace's overwhelming success on the talk shows, Wordsmith would insist on another round of on-air publicity for Trulee's latest book. Only this time, given the nature of the book, Grace would have to do much more than simply chat with the host and answer questions from the audience. Thea wasn't willing to give up, though. "We'll think of something."

"Think fast." Grace bit into another brownie. "These are really good."

Thea smiled. "Thanks."

Grace tapped the manuscript with her pencil and talked around the mouthful. "I don't know how the suits upstairs are going to react to this. Especially The Icebergs. But considering how hot Trulee is now...who knows?" She shook her head and smiled at Thea. "I'll see what I can do. That's all I can promise. Remember, they're also expecting *Mr. Right or Mr. Wrong?* Marketing and sales are already kicking around cover ideas and developing promo for it."

Thea winced. She hadn't thought about that. Lots of wasted time and dollars for a company already bleeding gallons of red ink, and once again, the suits would point their collective fingers of blame at Grace. The fault belonged to Thea. She should have told Grace about the direction of the new book from the moment she sat down to write it, not surprise her with it this morning.

Thea stood and looped her purse and the empty tote over her shoulder. "Take the brownies upstairs with you," she said before leaving the office.

Thea spent the next several hours wandering around the city. With her fate entwined in those two hundred and eighty-seven pages, she tried not to think about the future. If the head honchos of Wordsmith Press rejected the book, she'd lose her apartment. Even if the new book was a success and all her debts were settled, she'd never be able to go back to the classroom.

Thea believed it was only a matter of time before Hedda renewed her Luke campaign and divulged Thea's secret to the world. Once exposed, she knew she'd be shunned by every academic institution from the Golden Gate to the Brooklyn Bridge. She didn't care, though. Somewhere along the line she'd discovered another truth about herself: she really didn't like living the life of a sociology professor. She hadn't chosen her given profession. It was chosen for her—by a father who thought he knew what was best for his daughters and didn't trust them to choose their own paths in life.

* * *

By the time Thea returned to her apartment, she had worked herself into a deep depression that continued throughout the next day. "What a god-awful mess I've created," she told Cupid, flopping onto the sofa later that evening. Tears spilled down her cheeks. She'd given up trying to control them. Grabbing a bright purple floral pillow, she hugged it to her chest and silently berated herself for the muddle she'd made of her life. And Luke's. He trusted her, and she deceived him like his mother and wife before her. Her motives had been pure and unselfish, but somewhere down the road of good intentions, she drove her life into a ditch. And there wasn't a tow truck in sight.

Cupid jumped onto her lap and began licking her face. Thea wrapped her arm around the cat and drew him against her body. She needed the comfort of another living being. The cat accepted her for who she was, major character flaws and all. "You sure you want to be seen with such a screw-up?"

He squeezed his eyes shut and responded with a loud, contented purr. Thea frowned. "Scratch behind your ear, and you'll agree to anything, right? Well, I need a miracle, Cupid, not a yes-cat."

She threw her head back against the sofa and sighed. "Look at me! I'm reduced to having conversations with a cat!" A huge lump swelled in her throat. The tears continued to stream down her cheeks. In just a few short weeks she'd morphed into her greatest fear, the spinster with only a cat for a companion. She glanced down at the T-shirt. "And I'm even wearing lavender!" she cried, startling the cat.

The buzz of the lobby intercom interrupted her self-flagellation and forced her to her feet. Wiping her cheeks with the hem of her rumpled shirt, she shuffled into the foyer, inhaling several deep breaths before depressing the talk button. "Yes?"

Melvin's sonorous voice boomed through the speaker. "Your brother-in-law is in the lobby, Dr. Chandler."

"Bill?" Thea glanced down at herself. Dressed in her worn T-shirt and faded cut-offs, she hardly looked presentable. She studied her reflection in the hall mirror and shuddered. Puffy dark patches ringed her bloodshot eyes. She was in no shape for company. Still, it was Bill. He'd understand, and considering the recent abrupt changes in his own life, she hardly expected him to look much better.

She pressed the speaker button again. "Send him up, please." Then she raced into the bathroom, splashed cold water on her face, and gave her hair a quick brushing. She returned to the foyer in time to hear Bill's knock.

Thea pasted a smile on her face, then swung open the door.

"Bill, what a pleasant—" The remainder of her sentence died on her lips.

SEVENTEEN

"Hello, Althea."

Unable to speak, Thea stared dumbstruck at the sight of her sister before her gaze shifted to the man she expected to find standing alone on the other side of her door. Bill's arm draped protectively around his wife's shoulders, but his brown eyes were focused entirely on Thea. "May we come in?" he asked.

Thea glanced back at Madeline. "Please?" her sister added, her spoiled brat whine completely absent from her voice. In its place Thea caught an inflection that she could only identify as a mix of sorrow and regret. The sound, an echo of her own battered emotions, tugged at her.

Confused by the sudden change in her sister's demeanor and speechless at the sight of her brother-in-law with his arm around his unfaithful wife, Thea glanced down at Cupid. The cat had staked a sentry position at her feet. Head cocked, he eyed Bill and Madeline as if sizing them up.

"I'm sorry we tricked you," said Bill. "Madeline was convinced you wouldn't see her if she came alone."

"You have every right to hate me," said Madeline, "but I'm begging you, Thea, please, listen to me first. Then, if you never want to see me again...." Choking back the rest of her sentence, Madeline averted her eyes. Bill drew her closer against his body.

Thea stared in amazement. The last time she spoke with her sister Bill had filed for divorce. Now he stood at Thea's front door comforting and protecting the woman who'd wronged him.

With Cupid leading the way, she ushered them into the living room. Nothing her sister could say would change the past or rebuild Thea's crumbled life, but her sense of family was too ingrained to deny Madeline the opportunity to speak.

Thea thought of how Luke had hurt her, not by his accusations, but by denying her a chance to explain her actions. She might be incapable of granting her sister absolution for her sins, but she would listen to Madeline explain why she committed them—if that was her reason for traveling three thousand miles across the continent.

Thea offered Madeline and Bill the sofa. She settled into one of the chairs on the opposite side of the coffee table. Her sister sat perched on the edge of the couch, her posture tense, her hands knotted in her lap. Bill's hand rested loosely on his wife's knee.

Madeline cleared her throat. "I...I'm not certain exactly how to begin," she said, staring at the floor. "There's so much I need to say to you. All I ask is that you let me finish before you respond to any of it." She glanced over at Thea, expectantly.

Thea nodded. "Go ahead."

"I know you're not going to believe this, but all my life I've been jealous of you, Thea."

"How —?"

Bill held up his hand. "Please, you promised to let Madeline speak."

Thea clamped her lips together, squelching her disbelief. Leaning back in her chair, she nodded and motioned her sister to continue.

As Madeline spoke, her slow and painful words and halting sentences stripped away years of misconceptions. For the first time Thea saw their shared childhood through the eyes of the gifted daughter who only wished to be as normal as her older sister.

Thea had long ago accepted the fact that her well-meaning parents did Madeline a tremendous disservice by spoiling her. But what she hadn't understood, until now, was the role first she, then Bill played as enablers after her parents' deaths. Camilla and Frederick had denied Madeline a childhood; she and Bill had denied her an adulthood.

"Part of growing up is learning to take responsibility for your own actions," said Madeline. "And mistakes. Most children sever the apron strings with little snips here and there, but Mother and Father didn't let me grow up, and after they were gone, neither would you and Bill. I felt suffocated. Angry. I rebelled. I know that doesn't justify what I did, and I'm not asking for forgiveness, only understanding. I lopped off that apron knot with a hatchet when I should have picked up a butter knife.

"I'm sorry," she cried, tears streaming down her cheeks. "For everything. For being selfish. And petulant. And nasty. And demanding. I don't know if I can change twenty-four years of bitchy behavior, but I'm trying because I don't like who I am and what I've done." Madeline paused, drawing in a deep breath.

Bill reached over and covered her hands with his, squeezing them gently. "It's all right, darling. You're doing just fine."

She offered him a faint smile, then cast a pleading look in Thea's direction. "But most of all I'm sorry for all the hurt I caused you by my misguided efforts to gain my freedom. Unfortunately, I learned too late that freedom is meaningless if it's at the expense of those you love."

Thea was at a loss for words. She'd never seen this gentler, thoughtful side of her sister. Didn't even know it existed. Inside her, she felt Tom, Dick, and Harry tossing grappling hooks into her heart. With spiked boots they began their climb, their ascent tugging on her heartstrings. A flood of tears gathered behind her eyes, and she bit down to still her own quivering lip.

Madeline was all the family she had. As wrong as Camilla and Frederick had been about so many things, they had been right about one. About family. Family stood by to prop you up when you faltered, to pick up the pieces when you shattered, to offer comfort when you hurt. Family let you explain. Family listened. And family gave you a second chance when no one else would.

How could she blame Madeline for her actions when she'd inadvertently helped create the situation that provoked them? Madeline had acted out of self-preservation, not spite. She might have chosen a kinder method to force the issue of her independence, but under the circumstances, would anything less drastic have produced the desired results? Possibly, but Thea doubted it.

Tired of the emptiness and loneliness of her life, Thea stood and held out her arms to her little sister. "I love you, Madeline, and I understand. I forgive you."

Madeline flew into Thea's arms, their tears and words and laughter mingling in joyful concord.

"There's one more thing we need to discuss," said Madeline,

pulling back.

"What's that?"

Madeline held her at arms' length, her brow knit in a thoughtful scowl. "Trulee Lovejoy."

Thea took a step back, reaching for the arm of the chair. Her other hand flew to her mouth muffling a whimper. "How did you find out?"

"We'll go into that later," said Madeline. "Why did you do it?"

Thea tossed her hands up in the air, then slapped them against her thighs. She had asked herself this same question countless times over the last few years. "You're not the only one who made mistakes, Madeline. At the time I thought I had no choice. Mother was ill. We had no money. I saw a chance to solve our problems, and I grabbed it."

Bill spoke for the first time. "I offered to help you, Thea. Why did you turn me down? You sacrificed so much. Principles. Integrity. If word of this gets out, you may as well kiss your academic career goodbye."

Sprawled across the back of the sofa, Cupid meowed in agreement. Thea winced. She and the cat both realized she'd lost far more. Principles? Career? None of that mattered half as much as the loss of the man in the next apartment. She'd sacrifice anything and everything to win back his respect. And his love.

"It was too late," she told her brother-in-law. "I'd already signed a three-book contract."

"Too late for some things, perhaps, but maybe not for everything." Bill glanced at his watch, then stood and turned to his wife. "It's time," he said.

Thea clutched Madeline's hand. "Time? To go? But you just got here! We have so much to talk about."

Madeline kissed Thea's cheek. "I can't. There'll be other times. Soon. I promise." She withdrew her hand from Thea's grasp.

"You mean to tell me you flew three thousand miles for a ten-minute conversation?"

"You don't think it was worth it?" asked Madeline.

"Yes, of course, but...."

Madeline smiled at her. "I wish I could stay. I want to more than you can imagine, but I have responsibilities—thanks to your kick to my butt, dear sister, and I don't think Starr Labs would be too pleased if I didn't show up for my first day of work Monday morning."

Thea gaped at her sister. "Your what?"

"You're looking at Starr's newest star," said Bill, beaming at his wife. "Madeline accepted a position to head up their astrophysics department."

Thea looked at her sister with newfound admiration and respect. "I'm impressed. And shocked."

Madeline blushed. "I have you to thank, Althea. Or blame. I needed to earn more money to support that money-guzzling Victorian monstrosity." She stared at her feet and mumbled, "Besides, I couldn't continue working with Steve."

Thea stiffened at the mention of her ex-fiancé's name, but all she said was, "You could have sold the house."

"Never. I love that old monster. There was more to it, though. I'm beginning to realize that our lives are what we make of them, and if I'm dissatisfied with mine, I have to work to change it—in a positive way.

"My unhappiness stemmed from others always making my decisions for me. Father is long dead. It was time to bury his paranoia along with him."

"He always worried some large corporation would take advantage of your genius," Thea reminded her sister.

Madeline smirked. "After all I've been through, do you really think I'd allow that?"

Bill cleared his throat. "I really hate to rush you, darling, but —
"

"I know. I'm coming." She gave Thea one final hug. "We have a plane to catch, and you have a life to put back on track."

No, thought Thea. That train not only derailed, it plummeted down a ravine. Only Madeline didn't have to know the details of the wreck. Not yet, at least. Besides, Thea was still too raw to discuss Luke with anyone. She stooped and lifted Cupid into her arms.

"That is one ugly cat," said Bill with a chuckle. "Where did you ever find him?"

"He found me," said Thea. Defending the cat in her arms, she added, "And he's not ugly. He's unique."

Cupid turned his head in Bill's direction and hissed.

"Well, he's not much on looks or personality, but nonetheless, I'd say he's a definite improvement over Steve." Bill tucked his wife under his arm and headed for the front door.

Madeline glanced back over her shoulder, her eyes filled with apology.

"Don't," said Thea, following behind. "He wasn't worth it. I know that now."

"But someone else is," said Bill swinging open the apartment door.

Thea gasped at the sight of Luke. He stood in a rumpled suit, his tie askew, several days' worth of stubble shadowing his jaw. His pale blue eyes, sunken and hollow, mirrored her own misery.

Cupid jumped from her arms and approached his master. Arching his back, he confronted Luke as if demanding to know his intentions.

Bill bent down and kissed Thea's cheek. "Good luck," he whispered.

Thea turned on Madeline. "*He* told you about Trulee, didn't he?"

Madeline nodded. "Because he loves you, Thea."

Before she realized what was happening, Bill and Madeline stepped into the hall and Luke entered her apartment, closing the door behind him.

Luke hadn't slept in days. He had little hope that Thea would give him a second chance. He had wronged her too severely. Still, he clung to a slim thread, but when he stared into the eyes of the woman he drove away, he felt any lingering optimism soundly squelched. She hated him, and he hardly blamed her.

He sighed in resignation. All he could do now was offer an apology and remove himself from her life. Permanently. He took a hesitant step closer. Cu hissed. Luke glanced down at his former pet. Sitting back on his haunches, Cu met his gaze, his amber eyes daring Luke to continue.

Waving his arms in frustration, Luke glared at the cat, then spoke. "Everything you ever said about me is true." His voice choked with remorse. "I'm an insensitive, close-minded fool who acts before he thinks. I don't blame you for hating me. I hate myself for what I put you through, for the accusations I made."

He paused, his eyes beseeching her one last time before he hung his head and spoke his final words to the floor. "I'd do anything to turn back the clock and start over, Thea, but I know that's impossible. I can't expect your forgiveness. And I know I don't deserve it."

Silence greeted his repentant confession. Unwilling to bear the hate he knew he'd find on her face, he turned to leave. As he reached for the doorknob, a muffled moan stopped him short. Turning around, he saw she was fighting to keep from crying. Her eyes glistened with unshed tears. Her clenched fists pressed against her lips. The last thing in the world he wanted was to cause her more pain, but that's what he seemed to be doing.

He yearned to scoop her up in his arms and kiss away the hurt, but he feared if he reached out to touch her, she'd shatter. Instead, he tried to comfort her with more words. "I only wanted you to know how sorry I am. Not only for what happened that night but for not trusting you and not giving you the opportunity to explain."

He raked his hands through his hair. His head told him he was only making a bad situation worse, but his heart refused to give up. In desperation he continued. "I know about Martin Kirby. And your mother's illness."

One large tear escaped the confines of her lower lid. Luke followed its slow descent. As the drop of moisture slid down her cheek and splashed onto her rumpled T-shirt, rational thought gave way to a flood of emotion. This was the woman he loved, and he'd surmount any obstacle to keep from losing her—even if *she* were that obstacle.

He took a step closer. Cu rose and arched his back. Choppy multi-colored hairs stood at attention. Another hiss, this one louder and more menacing than the first, sprang from between the cat's bared teeth. Luke ignored him. "You tried to tell me, didn't you? You tried, but I refused to listen."

Thea nodded. Luke saw his own misery reflected in her watery violet eyes. Misery and regret. Not hate. Encouraged, he reached across the short distance separating their bodies and captured a fresh tear, his index finger skimming across her soft cheek.

Luke stared at the teardrop perched on the tip of his finger. It burned him like acid, searing his heart, decimating his spirit. His words filled with anguish. "I was so angry. I thought we were friends. More than friends. Soul mates." He glanced up at her, his words now tumbling from his lips. "I fell in love with you, damn it, and then it was happening all over again. The hurt. The betrayal. All I wanted to do was hurt you back."

Thea nodded. "But not just me," she said in a voice little more than a whisper.

No, not just you. Luke lowered his head, shaking it slowly. "I wanted you to pay for everything." Disgust and self-loathing welled up inside him. "For Julie. For Hedda Two."

"And your mother."

Luke lifted his head. Their eyes met. "And my mother."

Cu meowed as if in agreement. Luke glanced down at his former pet. The cat had retreated from his attack stance. Sitting back on his haunches, he studied the situation. Although he eyed Luke with suspicion, he no longer looked ready to pounce.

Luke reached for Thea's hand. "Right or wrong was always based on my perspective, my preconceptions. It's taken me far too long, but I now realize things aren't always what they seem on the surface. Life is an infinite palette of grays, not merely the black or white of my limited vision."

Thea sniffed back a fresh flood of tears. "Luke, I'm so sorry," she cried, her words catching in her throat. "I was only trying to help my family. I never thought how I might be hurting someone else. Hurting you. I took the easy way out. The end doesn't justify the means."

Luke released her hand and cupped her cheeks, tilting her face up toward his. "Don't. You have nothing to apologize for. If I weren't such a blind ass, I would have realized that sooner. Your sacrifice was far from easy, Thea. We both know that. Give yourself some credit. Sometimes the end does justify the means. I only wish I'd figured that out before I hurt you. I'm the one who committed the unforgivable, not you."

Thea reached up and touched his cheek, her fingers trembling. "But I do forgive you," she whispered.

"I don't deserve your forgiveness. How can you stand to look at me, let alone forgive me?"

"Because I love you."

For a split second both time and Luke stood still. Slowly the impact of her words settled within him, spreading through his body like the warmth of a welcoming hearth fire on a wintry day. "You love me?" When Thea nodded, her lips curving upward in a hesitant smile, he said the words once again, this time with more conviction "You love me!"

"Yes."

He swept her into his arms. "I love you!"

"Yes." The word tumbled from her lips through a combination of laughter and tears. "Oh, yes!"

He lowered his head, capturing her mouth with his, kissing her in that toe-curling, mind-numbing, gravity-defying way that infused her with joy and hope and a tugging need.

Thea moaned with pleasure as Luke explored her mouth, nibbling her lips with his teeth, raking his tongue across her palate. He paused to fill his lungs, then exhaled a declaration of love. His fingers traced along her jaw line, up to her temples, across her forehead, down the bridge of her nose, forging a path for his lips to follow. His mouth caressed first one cheek, then the other. His fingers wove through her hair, dancing an erotic massage across her scalp and down her neck.

Thea burned with the need to touch him. She rubbed her palms along his stubble-covered jaw and neck, reveling in the tingling roughness, but it wasn't enough. She needed to feel more of him. All of him. Flesh to flesh.

She yanked at his loosened tie, exposing the row of small white buttons that traveled from his collar and disappeared below his waistband. Her fingers flew to the top button. Luke plunged his tongue deep within her mouth, igniting a desire that spread like brush fire straight to her womb. She shuddered with need as her fingers fought blindly with the buttons. Slowly, the fasteners gave way, exposing the dusting of dark blond hair that covered his chest. She raked her fingers through the springy curls.

She yanked at his shirt, releasing the tails from his pants, then slid her hands up and down his firm torso. Placing her cheek over his left nipple, she felt the rapid staccato of his heart. Gingerly, she skimmed first her fingertips and then her lips across the hard tip.

Luke groaned. "Do you realize what you're doing to me?" he whispered, his voice hoarse with desire. He slipped his hands under her shirt and deftly flicked open the front clasp of her bra. Her breasts spilled free, tumbling into his waiting palms. With his thumb and forefinger, he captured a nipple in each hand, rolling them to marble hardness.

Thea moaned. Her entire body was now on fire, every nerve ending straining for his soothing touch. "Yes," she said. "Oh, yes." She fumbled with his belt buckle.

Luke reached for her wrist, stilling her fingers. She looked up at him, her eyes filled with uncertainty, her brow creased with worry. "Before we go any further," he said, "tell me this is what you want."

"It is."

He took a deep breath and shook his head. "I don't want to hurt you, Thea. I couldn't live with myself if I woke up tomorrow and found you filled with regret over what we did tonight."

The apprehension smoothed from her brow. Her lips curved up in a sweet smile. "I could never regret loving you." She glanced down at his belt buckle then back up at him. Her smoky amethyst eyes twinkled with devilment. "May I continue?"

Luke raised both eyebrows. His sweet, naïve Dr. Chandler was full of surprises. Well, so was he, and he intended to spend the rest of their lives introducing her to all of them. Swinging her up into his arms, he strode down the hallway. "Absolutely not," he said. "Not until we find a bed."

As he drew closer to her bedroom, visions of their last encounter threatened the joyful anticipation filling his heart. He gathered her closer to his chest, hoping to protect her from the dark specter and his own shame. "I'm so sorry for the pain I caused you."

"I know." Her voice echoed the love and trust he saw in her eyes.

Luke sighed. "I don't deserve you," he said.

"Too bad, Bennett. You're stuck with me."

He lowered her onto the bed. Cu hopped up beside her. "No way, pal." Luke scooped the cat into his arms and deposited him out in the hall. "Get your own woman." He slammed the door in the cat's face.

Cu howled his displeasure.

Luke snorted.

Thea giggled. "How cruel!"

"Hell, I have no intention of sharing you with anyone, let alone a jealous alley cat." He sat down on the edge of the bed and brushed aside the strands of hair that had fallen across her face. "This party's just for two."

"But if it weren't for Cupid —"

Luke's index finger skimmed across her lower lip. "Shh. He's just a cat, Thea, not the reincarnation of some mythological Greek god." His finger trailed along her chin and down her neck, settling over her excited pulse. The rapid beat shot waves of electricity from the tip of his finger to every nerve ending from his scalp to his toes.

"Roman." The word fought its way through her short, rapid breaths. Her eyes told him the same fierce charge that had captured him engulfed her.

Luke grinned. Greek. Roman. Hell, the cat could be an Etruscan fairy godfather for all he cared. If Thea wanted to give Cu matchmaking credit, who was he to argue? Especially when that succulent mouth of hers was beckoning.

Like a magnet, his lips were drawn to hers once more, his tongue thrusting, roaming, savoring. He doubted heaven could be as sweet. "I don't know what I've done to deserve you, but I swear I'll love you forever."

The resonance of his voice, the intensity of his words wrapped around Thea like a warm comforter. "Forever," she said, repeating the pledge.

He removed her clothes slowly, exploring every inch of her flesh with a lingering gaze, lingering fingers, lingering lips, working his way down her body. His hands parted her legs. His lips trailed a line of fervent kisses from the back of her knees across the sensitive flesh of her inner thighs. His fingers raked through her dewy curls, then explored further, searching for and finding the most sensual of spots. Thea writhed with pleasure. Trembling pleasure. Fiery pleasure. "Oh, my God," she moaned, realizing his tongue had replaced his fingers. "Oh, Luke!"

Thea squeezed her eyes shut, her body roiling with the most excruciating pleasure she'd ever known. Tidal waves of dizzying sensation washed over her, each one more powerful than the last. *This can't really be happening*, she told herself. *Nothing could be this wonderful.* But it was. Every glorious moment of it. Of him.

She drifted back to earth slowly. Opening her eyes, she found him watching her, a soft smile playing at the corners of his mouth. "That was just the appetizer, my love."

Thea shook her head, her voice ragged with emotion. "It couldn't possibly get any better."

"Trust me." Luke stood to remove his clothes.

"Let me." Thea knelt on the side of the bed and pushed his shirt over his shoulders and off his arms. With fingers still shaking from the aftermath of her explosive climax, she unfastened his belt buckle and slipped the metal hook from the eye above his fly. Placing her palm against the taut fabric, she felt the hot throbbing strain of him through the gabardine. Her fingers traced around the outline of the bulge, her lips quivering at the length and breadth of him. Lowering her head, her mouth replaced her fingers, leaving a damp tracing of kisses along his fabric-sheathed shaft.

Luke sucked in a lungful of air and groaned.

Thea lifted her chin. "You don't like this?"

Luke grasped her head with both hands, combing his fingers

through her hair. "Sweetheart, you're killing me." His teeth clenched teeth, his fists filled with handfuls of her hair.

"Oh, then I should stop?"

"God, no!"

Thea offered him a wicked grin and reached for his zipper. "I didn't think so."

Luke was so engorged with desire that she struggled to force the zipper pull down. It didn't help that her own body was throbbing for the *entree* he'd hinted at, although she couldn't imagine anything feeling better than the *appetizer* he'd already served her. Finally, in frustration she grasped the tab with her teeth and yanked.

Luke sprung free. She pushed his pants down over his hips. Slipping her hands under the waistband of his briefs, she forced them down past his knees where they dropped to join the pants pooled around his ankles. Luke stepped out of the clothes, kicking them to the side.

Thea stared at the thick, straight shaft, mesmerized by it. With hesitant fingers she gingerly explored its length and thickness. Dipping her head, her hair skimming his belly, she flicked her tongue across the tip before wrapping her lips around him.

Luke sucked air down his parched throat. His breathing quickened. Closing his eyes, he allowed himself a moment's pleasure before he drew on his last vestige of self-control and gently separated them. As much as he wanted her sweet lips around him, he had to wait. He owed her much more.

"Later, sweetheart." He gently eased her back onto the pillows. Stretching out beside her, he teased the rigid peaks of her nipples with hungering lips. While his hands explored every supple curve and sloping plane of her body, his heart reveled in the sound of her soft moans.

He straddled her thighs, his eyes trapping hers in an intense gaze. "I'll try not to hurt you."

"You won't."

He brushed the tip of his shaft against her slick opening. Thea raised her hips to meet him. "Slowly, sweetheart, slowly," he whispered, taking her in inches. Thea met his slow thrusts, encouraging him to press farther inside her. He bent and kissed her eyelids. She wrapped her legs around him, and he deepened his penetration, a little farther with each gentle foray until he heard her gasp of pain. He froze inside her. Withdrawing, he raised his head and reached for her.

"No, please," she cried. "Don't ever stop."

Luke gazed into eyes wild with desire and smiled. He buried himself fully inside her, taking long, slow thrusts at first, feeling her tighten and tremble around him as he steadily increased his rhythm and pressure until it grew to a frenzy and had pushed them both to beyond oblivion.

A short time later, Thea nestled against Luke, their legs braided together, the fingers of one of her hands splayed across his chest. "I never expected it to be this wonderful."

Luke planted a series of kisses across her brow. "With all the research you've done?"

"No book in the world could accurately describe what you just did to me."

Luke chuckled. "I'm that good, huh?"

Thea's brows knit together. "Well, keep in mind I can't make any comparisons." She offered him a dreamy-eyed smirk. "Tell you what, I'll let you know after dessert."

Luke cradled her in his arms, slowly stroking her limbs and

torso. She was right. Words couldn't do justice to what he'd experienced with her. Nothing had ever felt so right. And he *could* make comparisons. He cringed when he thought how close he'd come to never knowing such bliss. "I wish I'd listened to what you were trying to tell me," he said, still unable to put his past transgression behind him. "I would have understood your reason for writing the books."

Thea shook her head. "No, I'm not sure you would have. Not then. I realize now, that's why I kept hesitating. Every time I tried to explain, you'd say or do something that warned me from continuing." She paused, her voice filling with emotion. "I was so afraid of losing you. And then I waited too long, and I did lose you."

Luke propped himself up on one elbow and stroked her cheek. She was so beautiful, so understanding, so selfless. How could he have thought ill of her? But she was right. As much as he'd like to believe he would have understood and accepted her dual identity, he knew it wasn't true. It had taken nearly losing her to knock some sense into him. "I was pretty damned arrogant, wasn't I?"

"You felt threatened."

Luke raised an eyebrow in question.

Thea traced the arch with a finger, smoothing away the lines of concern. "You had lost control of your life and privacy thanks to Hedda Two, and you were already vulnerable from Julie's betrayal. When Hedda recommended my books, you directed all your hostility toward Trulee. In your mind she became the real enemy. *I* became the real enemy."

"But I did come to accept I was irrationally transferring my anger over Hedda to Trulee. You pointed that out to me. I realized you were right, and I accepted it."

"But your subconscious never let go of the idea. I could see that whenever I tried to confess to you." She lifted his hand to her face, pressing his palm to her cheek. Sadness filled her eyes. "Oh, Luke. Don't you see? No matter how hard I tried, I couldn't find the right words to break through to you. And the longer I waited, the harder it became.

"Finally, I realized that nothing I said would keep you from hating me if the truth came out. I had to hide Trulee from you. I'd done such a good job of hiding her from everyone else, that I didn't think I'd have a problem. But you were different. I didn't want to lie to you."

She sighed. "Then, when I finally worked up the courage to tell you, it was too late. You'd already found out."

She lowered his hand back onto the bed. "I created the monster, and *she* wound up nearly destroying me. Nearly destroying us. Not you. You were just another victim of *my* arrogance. I thought I could solve every problem, control every situation." She turned away from him and buried her head in the pillow. "What a great job I did of screwing things up! I controlled my sister right into an adulterous affair. Controlled myself out of a career. Controlled you into...into...." The remainder of her sentence died in a shudder of remorse.

"No more, Thea." Luke stroked her back, his fingers trailing along the velvety curve of her spine. "No more regrets. From either of us." He swept her hair up onto the pillow and lowered his head, planting soft kisses across her shoulders and neck. "Only love from now on."

EPILOGUE

Thea leaned back in her chair and surveyed the snaking queue wrapping around several bookcases and out the door of the bookstore. Taking a deep breath, she shook the stiffness from her hand before greeting the next woman in line.

"I have three daughters and seven nieces," said the woman, bubbling with enthusiasm. "I've given them each a copy of your book." She winked at Thea. "This one's for me."

"I hope it brings you hours of pleasure," said Thea, autographing the inside cover.

"*I* hope it lights a fire in my lug of a husband," answered the woman.

Thea glanced across the crowded store, following the woman's gaze to a middle-aged man, his face set in a bored scowl, slouching against a table of calendars. "Try the chocolate apricot flambé with chopped pistachios," she suggested, returning the woman's conspiratorial wink. "Guaranteed to bring him to his knees."

"I'll vouch for that," said Luke, coming up from behind. He

leaned down, planting a kiss on the top of his wife's head and an extra-large cup of decaf cappuccino on the table in front of her. He handed a second cup to Grace who sat beside Thea. Luke motioned to the long line. "Thought you ladies might need some fuel."

"I'm running on endorphins," said Thea. And she was. Life couldn't get any better. *Love Recipes: Secrets from Trulee's Kitchen* by Dr. Althea Chandler-Bennett, was a runaway bestseller, surpassing the sales figures of both *Finding Mr. Right* and *Hooking Mr. Right*.

Grace had followed Thea's suggestion and plied The Icebergs with Thea's brownies before presenting the manuscript to them. The sinful chocolate morsels cast a magic spell over the skinflints.

"You sure these aren't Alice B. Toklas brownies?" asked Grace when she gave Thea the good news.

"What do you mean?"

"You didn't add some secret ingredient not mentioned in the recipe, did you? Something that might mellow out those hard-nosed bastards?"

Realization slowly dawned in Thea. "You mean...? Of course not! How could you even suggest such a thing?"

"Because apparently, not only is the way to a man's heart through his stomach, but it's also the way to his wallet. Not a single one of them objected to the change in concept."

"What about all the time and money they've already devoted to *Mr. Right or Mr. Wrong?*"

Grace shrugged. "Not a mention of it. Other than to say they still expect me to sign you to a new contract and get you to write it next."

"Not a chance in hell, Grace."

"I know that."

"So now what? They'll still fire you, won't they?"

Grace winked at her. "Not a chance in hell."

"But —"

Grace held up her hand. "Hush, Thea. I'm about to make you an offer you can't refuse."

"I doubt that."

"Hear me out."

Knowing a potential gold mine when it fell in her lap, Grace presented the proposal to her reluctant author. As she surmised, Thea couldn't refuse. Grace agreed to take over the writing of the Trulee Lovejoy advice books as long as Thea agreed to act as an unnamed consultant when needed. In exchange, she signed Thea to a second three-book contract, this time to write cookbooks.

A month after *Love Recipes: Secrets from Trulee's Kitchen* hit the stores, Grace negotiated a half-hour cooking show on PBS. *Love Recipes*, hosted by Dr. Trulee Lovejoy and Althea Chandler-Bennett, was quickly picked up by affiliate stations throughout the country. Endorsement opportunities poured in daily, and Grace's financial problems disappeared.

And Hedda? Thea no longer feared what would happen if the gossipmonger divulged her secrets. She didn't care. She had no desire to return to a career she now realized she never really wanted.

Besides, Grace had taken care of Hedda. She offered the gossip columnist a heady advance to write her memoirs. Being a savvy businesswoman, Hedda realized she had far more to gain by making Grace her newest best friend than by pissing her off by blabbing Trulee's secrets.

For the first time in her life Thea was pursuing her own dreams and loving every minute of it. She now realized her parents had orchestrated her life as much as they had Madeline's. Being the obedient daughter, she marched along the road they chose for her without question—until an encounter with an angry man and his punk-rock stray had plunged her down a rabbit hole of wonder.

On the dedication page of her new cookbook she'd written, "*This above all else—to thine own self be true. Thank you, Luke and Cupid, for showing me the way.*"

A fluttering cascade of pleasure bubbled inside her. Thea gasped in delight, still not used to the exciting, new sensation. She placed her hand protectively over her abdomen. Tom, Dick, and Harry were gone, permanently banished from her body and soul. In their place, a new life now grew.

"It's almost over," whispered Luke, brushing her ear with his lips. "Hang in there, sweetheart."

Although she realized he was referring to the book signing, she smiled to herself and responded, "No, Luke, it's just beginning."

And it was.

THEA'S RECIPES

Dr. Trulee Lovejoy's To Die For Flambé
(Serves 4 to 6)

Ingredients:
1/4 cup apricot jam
3 tablespoons sugar
1/2 cup water
2 lbs. fresh apricots, peeled and sliced
1 teaspoon fresh lemon juice
1/4 cup brandy
1/2 cup shelled, finely chopped pistachios
1 quart vanilla ice cream
chocolate sauce

Combine jam, sugar and water in a chafing dish. Simmer over low heat until syrupy (approximately 5 minutes). Add apricots. Continue cooking over low heat until tender (approximately 3 minutes). Stir in lemon juice. Heat brandy in saucepan. Pour over apricots and ignite. When flame has died off, spoon apricots over individual servings of ice cream. Drizzle chocolate sauce over apricots. Garnish with chopped pistachios.

Thea's Double Chocolate Cherry Cream Cheese Brownies
(Serves 8 to 10—or one, depending on mood)

Ingredients:
4 ounces semi-sweet chocolate
1/4 cup unsalted butter
1 cup sugar
3 large eggs
1 teaspoon vanilla
1/2 cup plus 1 Tablespoon flour
4 ounces cream cheese, softened
1 cup semi-sweet chocolate chips
4 ounces cherry preserves

Melt chocolate and margarine in microwave at HIGH for two minutes, stirring frequently until chocolate is completely melted. Set aside to cool. Stir 3/4 cup of sugar into melted chocolate. Blend in two eggs and vanilla. Add 1/2 cup of flour, stirring well until well blended. Spread into greased 9-inch square pan.

Using a blender, mix cream cheese, remaining sugar, egg, and flour until smooth. Fold in chocolate chips. Spoon over brownie mixture. Spoon cherry preserves over cream cheese mixture. Run a knife through batter to swirl mixtures. Bake at 350 degrees for 35 to 40 minutes. Cool in pan. Cut into squares or bars.

Thea's Caesar Dressing
(Serves 2)

Ingredients:
1 small clove garlic
1/2 tablespoon Worcestershire sauce
1/2 teaspoon Dijon mustard
3 tablespoons wine vinegar
1 small coddled egg
1 tablespoon olive oil
1/2 teaspoon oregano
juice of 1 lemon
3 tablespoons freshly grated Parmesan cheese
dash of salt and pepper
1 head romaine lettuce torn into bite-size pieces
1 cup croutons

Crush the garlic. Add the Worcestershire sauce, mustard, egg and vinegar, whisking ingredients together. Continue whisking, adding oil, oregano, salt, pepper, lemon juice, and Parmesan cheese one at a time until all ingredients are mixed together well. Toss in croutons. Pour dressing over lettuce.

Thea's Veal Parmesan with Mushrooms and Baby Spinach
(Serves 2)

Ingredients:
1/2 cup finely chopped fresh mushrooms
1/2 cup finely chopped fresh baby spinach
1/2 cup finely chopped fresh tomato

1/4 cup finely chopped onion
1 clove garlic, minced
1 cup ricotta cheese
1-1/2 pounds veal cutlets
olive oil
1 cup marinara sauce
freshly grated Parmesan cheese

Mix mushrooms, spinach, tomato, onion and garlic together. Fold in ricotta cheese. Set aside.

Place veal between sheets of wax paper and pound lightly to flatten. Lay cutlets on flat surface. Sprinkle with olive oil. Spoon vegetable-ricotta mixture onto center of each cutlet. Roll cutlets and secure with toothpicks. Brown in oil on all sides. Remove from pan and drain on paper towels. Spoon a small amount of marinara sauce in bottom of baking dish. Arrange cutlet rolls in dish. Remove toothpicks. Pour remaining sauce over cutlets. Sprinkle generously with Parmesan cheese. Bake at 350 degrees 20-25 minutes.

Thea's Veggie Omelet
(Serves 1)

Ingredients:
1/4 cup coarsely chopped tomato
1/4 cup sliced mushrooms
1 tablespoon minced onions
1 tablespoon minced sweet peppers
1 teaspoon Worcestershire sauce

dash of salt and pepper
3 eggs
1 tablespoon olive oil
1 teaspoon fresh-snipped dill

Combine vegetables, Worcestershire sauce and seasoning, mixing well to coat. Set aside.

Whisk eggs until whites and yolks are well blended. Heat oil in omelet pan until hot. Pour eggs into pan. Slide pan over heat to spread eggs, stirring quickly with fork as eggs thicken. Let eggs stand over heat a few seconds to brown on bottom. Spoon vegetable mixture over egg. Run fork under edges of egg to loosen. Fold opposite edges of egg to center, overlapping and slide onto plate. Sprinkle with fresh dill.

Thea's Onion Dill French Bread
(Yield: two loaves)

Ingredients:
5 cups bread flour
2 cups whole-wheat flour
2 tablespoons honey
2 packets yeast
2-1/2 cups warm water
1 tablespoon salt
1 tablespoon dill
1 tablespoon dried minced onion
1/4 cup cornmeal

Combine flour, salt, yeast, dill, onions, and honey in bowl. Pour in warm water. Kneed with dough hook three to four minutes or stir by hand until all ingredients are well mixed. Remove dough to a floured surface and kneed by hand for ten minutes. Place in covered bowl. Allow to rise one hour. Punch down the dough and separate into two equal parts. Roll out each half to 1/2 inch thickness. Then roll into a tight, long loaf, pinching the ends. Place loaves on cornmeal sprinkled cookie sheet. Cover with wax paper and allow to rise one hour. Make four slits along the top of each loaf. Bake at 425 degrees for 25 minutes. Place loaves on cooling rack to cool.

Thea's Seafood Bouillabaisse
(Serves 2)

Ingredients:
2 tablespoons olive oil
1/2 cup chopped onions
2 minced garlic cloves
1/4 cup chopped parsley
2 tomatoes, peeled, seeded and chopped
1/4 cup chopped celery
1 bay leaf
1/2 teaspoon lemon zest
1/2 tablespoon salt
1/4 teaspoon thyme
1/4 teaspoon marjoram
2 cups water
3/4 cup dry white wine
1/2 pound lobster meat

1/2 pound shelled shrimp
1/2 pound crabmeat
1/2 pound scallops

Sauté onions and garlic in oil until tender. Add all other ingredients except wine and fish. Simmer covered for two hours, stirring occasionally. Add wine. Simmer uncovered for ten minutes. Add fish. Simmer ten to fifteen minutes until fish is cooked.

Thea's Steak Diane
(Serves 2)

Ingredients:
2 fillet mignons
salt
2 tablespoons olive oil
1 clove crushed garlic
2 teaspoons Dijon mustard
1/2 pound sliced fresh mushrooms
1 medium onion, chopped
1 tablespoon fresh minced chives
1 tablespoon Worcestershire sauce
1 tablespoon brandy
2 tablespoons sour cream
1 tablespoon fresh minced parsley

Season steak with salt. Heat oil and garlic in skillet. Brown meat one minute on each side. Remove meat. Add mustard, mushrooms, onions, chives, and Worcestershire sauce to skillet.

Sauté over medium heat one minute. Return steak to skillet, cooking approximately three minutes per side for medium-rare. Remove steak to serving platter. Keep warm.

Add brandy to skillet. Simmer one minute. Remove skillet from heat. Stir in sour cream. Pour over steak.

Thea's Shrimp and Broccoli Scampi
(Serves 2)

Ingredients:
1/2 pound linguini
1 pound peeled, deveined medium shrimp
1/2 cup unsalted butter
2 cloves minced garlic
1/2 cup white wine
juice of one lemon
1 cup cut-up fresh broccoli

Cook linguini until al dente while sautéing shrimp. Drain and set aside when cooked.

Melt butter in large skillet over medium heat. Add garlic, broccoli, and shrimp. Sauté four to five minutes. Add wine and lemon juice. Continue sautéing until shrimp is cooked, approximately three minutes.

Divide pasta into two bowls. Pour shrimp and broccoli over pasta.

Finding Mr. Right

A Short Story Sequel to
Hooking Mr. Right

ONE

January 2nd

"We'll do a Valentine's Day theme for the first two shows of the month." Producer Becket Delaney handed the February program schedule to Dr. Trulee Lovejoy and Thea Chandler-Bennett, co-hosts of *Love Recipes*.

"No, we won't." Grace shoved the sheet of paper aside without looking at it. "I hate Valentine's Day."

"You're Dr. Trulee Lovejoy," said Beck, "bestselling author of all those how-to-catch-a-guy books. How can you possibly hate Valentine's Day?"

Because she really wasn't Dr. Trulee Lovejoy. She was Grace Wainwright, imposter. Then again, so was the real Dr. Trulee Lovejoy. Talk about a tangled web!

When Thea Chandler, writing under the pen name Dr. Trulee

Lovejoy, had refused to promote her popular self-help books, Grace had no choice but to step into the limelight and take on the persona of the faux relationship expert. Her job was on the line. With two kids in college and a deadbeat ex, she couldn't afford to lose her editorial position at Wordsmith Press.

The bean counters at the publishing house had made it clear that's exactly what would happen to Grace if Dr. Trulee Lovejoy didn't agree to a book tour and media blitz. But Thea had compelling reasons for keeping her identity secret and refused to take part in the publicity campaign.

So Grace became Trulee, embarking on the requisite interviews, book signings, and talk show appearances. In retrospect she'd do it all again. That one decision had taken her from within steps of the unemployment line to bestselling author and daytime television star. Thea, who first opposed the subterfuge, became Grace's reluctant partner-in-crime, keeping Grace's secret, just as Grace had kept hers for years.

Now Grace, with occasional input from Thea, wrote the Trulee Lovejoy books, and Thea, the former reluctant love expert, was free to pursue her true passion—cooking. Thea's first cookbook, *Love Recipes: Secrets from Trulee's Kitchen*, became an overnight success. A month after the book hit store shelves, Grace had negotiated a half-hour cooking show for them on PBS. *Love Recipes* now appeared on affiliate stations coast-to-coast.

Tangled web, indeed!

"I'm not all that fond of Valentine's Day, either," continued her producer, "but tradition dictates and our sponsors demand that cooking shows feature holiday recipes. Turkey and cranberry dishes for Thanksgiving. Cherry pies on Washington's birthday. Ham at Easter. Romantic dinners and to-die-for chocolate desserts for Valentine's Day."

"He has a point," said Thea.

"Screw tradition," said Grace. Valentine's Day brought back the most painful memory of her life. For the past ten years she'd dealt with the day by calling in sick and throwing a pity party for two. Her only invited guest? Jack Daniels.

"We're doing a Valentine's Day show," said Beck, "whether you like it or not. End of discussion."

"If you insist." Grace scowled at Beck, then turned to Thea. "Got any recipes for heart-shaped arsenic cookies?"

"What's your problem with Valentine's Day?" asked Thea once she and Grace left Beck's midtown Manhattan office.

Grace sighed. "Long story."

"I have time."

"I'll need a drink to get me through it."

"One margarita coming up." Thea steered her toward an upscale pub on the corner of Ninth Avenue and 50th Street.

"This tale requires something stronger than a margarita," said Grace. "And definitely more than one drink."

"Lucky for you it's happy hour."

"Don't you have to get home to your hunky husband and that darling baby?"

"Luke is in Atlanta on business, and the nanny doesn't expect me for another couple of hours. So I'm all ears."

They found an unoccupied table in a back corner of the dimly lit bar. Grace waited to spill her guts until their drinks arrived—a double scotch on the rocks for her, a frozen raspberry margarita for Thea. "Brace yourself for another Dick-head story," she said, referring to her ex-husband.

"Now why am I not surprised this has something to do with

him?"

Grace scowled into her glass, then took a long swig to work up some courage. "We had a tradition on Valentine's Day, dining at the restaurant where we spent our first date. Ten years ago, a week before Valentine's Day, I found a receipt from Tiffany's in his pants pocket."

Thea raised her eyebrows.

Grace held up her hands. "I wasn't snooping. Honest. I was taking clothes to the cleaner, and the jerk never remembered to empty his pockets before tossing clothes in the hamper."

Thea nodded. "Go on."

"Lucky me, I thought. But then late afternoon on the fourteenth Dick-head calls to say he's had a client emergency and has to work late. He cancelled our reservation."

"I can see where this is going," said Thea.

"I couldn't. Not at the time. I decided to place a take-out order. If he couldn't come to the restaurant, I'd bring the restaurant to him. After all, he had to eat, right? Imagine my surprise when I arrived to pick up the food and discovered him all up-close and extremely personal with some skank just shy of jailbait."

"Ouch."

"Oh, that's not the worst of it. While I'm staring across the room at him, not believing my eyes, he whips out a robin's egg blue box from his pocket and hands it to her."

"Double-ouch. Did he see you?"

"Not until I marched up to their table and dumped an order of steaming Shrimp Bolognese on his lap. I stormed home, locked him out of the apartment, and filed for divorce the next morning."

She drained her scotch, then slammed her empty glass on the table. "And now you know why I hate Valentine's Day."

* * *

If Beck Delaney ruled the world, he'd cancel Valentine's Day. Scratch that. He'd cancel *all* holidays. They only reminded him of everything stolen from him five years ago. Unfortunately, not only didn't he rule the world, he didn't even have total control of his own television productions. Gourmade, a major sponsor of *Love Recipes*, expected a Valentine's Day theme to help sell their pricey confections.

Beck didn't know why Trulee Lovejoy, otherwise known as Dr. Love, hated the one day of the year set aside for lovers. It made no sense, given the type of books she wrote. Not that he cared.

He knew little about his star other than she wrote books that women swore by. *Love Recipes* was PBS's highest rated daytime show after all the kids' programming, and that's what mattered to Beck. The bottom line ruled.

He suspected Trulee Lovejoy was a pen name—what parents in their right minds would name their daughter Trulee Lovejoy?—but she'd never said, and he hadn't asked. Beck believed in keeping the workplace purely professional.

He pegged Dr. Love at somewhere around his age, perhaps a few years younger, which would put her between her late thirties and early forties. With curves in all the right places and hair the color of honey, she looked damn good for a woman on the cusp of middle age. Every male head turned whenever she entered the offices or studio. Every male but one. His libido had died a long time ago.

* * *

Grace flagged down the waitress and ordered another double, her third.

"And an order of chicken quesadillas," added Thea.

"I'm not hungry," said Grace.

"I don't care. You need food to sop up all that alcohol."

Grace drained the last drops from her glass. "Whatever you say, mother."

"When was the last time you went on a date?"

"Since the divorce?" Grace heaved a sigh. "Never."

Thea's jaw dropped. "Not once in ten years?"

Grace shrugged. "No time. Between working fifty hour weeks and single parenting, any free time is spent doing laundry. Grocery shopping. Cooking. Sleeping. And that was before I had to step in and become you."

"And for that you'll forever have my undying gratitude."

"I know." Grace smirked. "You owe me big time. However, you also scored the last man in the city worth having. Unless Luke Bennett has a clone hiding under some unturned rock in Central Park, I'm not interested. The rest of the species are either jerks, gay, or already taken. Or already taken gay jerks."

"What about Beck?"

Grace laughed. "He falls into at least one of those categories, possibly more." Although she had to admit Becket Delaney ticked off all her must-have boxes when it came to looks. She'd always been a sucker for tall hunks with dark, wavy-hair à la Patrick Dempsey. Beck looked enough like Patrick that when they first met, she'd nearly suffered whiplash executing a doubletake.

"He's taken?" asked Thea.

Grace shrugged. "He falls into the jerk category. Plus, I think he's gay. Ever notice there are no pictures of a wife or girlfriend in his office? Has he ever mentioned one to you? He hasn't to me."

Thea laughed. "That's pretty flimsy evidence. You never talk about your social life. Does that make you a lesbian?"

The waitress arrived with their quesadillas, and Grace waited until she left to respond. "I don't talk about my social life because I don't have one."

"Maybe Beck doesn't, either. I think you need to get to know him better."

"Why? Are you setting up a matchmaking business?"

"Because it's time you moved on, Grace. Your hatred of Dickhead is keeping you from living your life. Ten years is long enough to wallow in self-pity. You need to make new memories to rid yourself of those old, painful ones."

Grace bit into a quesadilla and waved away the suggestion. "Not interested," she said around a mouthful of food. "One decimated heart per lifetime is enough for any woman, especially me."

"Such an un-Trulee-like philosophy. Better keep it to yourself."

"Don't worry. I know what's paying for those hefty tuition bills."

"Good to know." Thea grabbed a quesadilla. "You do realize if I'd espoused that philosophy, Luke and I would never have gotten together."

"There's always one exception that proves every rule."

Even though she'd told Thea she wasn't hungry, Grace had no trouble polishing off her half of the quesadillas. After she finished, she tossed her napkin onto her empty plate. "I hate to eat and run, but I need to finish editing a manuscript this evening."

"Go. I've got the bill."

"Thanks. My treat next time." Grace reached for her purse and laptop. "Crap! I left my computer in Beck's office."

"Call him. He may still be there."

Grace whipped out her cell phone and scrolled down her contacts list until she found Beck's number. He answered on the third ring. "Beck? It's Gr—uhm...Trulee. Did I leave my laptop in your office?"

"Hold on. I'll check." A moment later he said, "Found it. I'll be here for at least another hour if you want to stop by for it."

"Thanks. I'm on my way."

Ten minutes later Grace stepped into Beck's office and immediately spotted her leather laptop case where she'd left it on the floor next to one of the two chairs flanking his desk. She strode across the room. "Am I ever glad you're still here. I have a ton of work to finish up tonight." As she stooped to grab the case, the lights went out.

TWO

"What the—?" Beck turned to look out the window. An overcast sky blocked the moon and stars. Only the headlights and taillights of the cars on the street below broke through the inky blackness that engulfed the city. All of Manhattan, from what he could see of it, had lost power. "This can't be good," he said.

"Tell me about it," said Grace. "We're thirty-four floors up. I'm certainly not excited about traipsing down all those stairs in heels in the dark."

"You shouldn't even consider trying it. What if you trip?" He squinted into the night. "It's not snowing, so it can't be weather-related. I'd think whatever caused the outage should be corrected soon."

"You haven't lived here long, have you?"

"A few years. Why?"

"Not long enough. Ten-and-a-half years ago all of New York, seven other states, and parts of Canada lost power for two days."

"From a storm?"

"In a manner of speaking. A combination of untrimmed trees in Ohio and a software bug in the electrical grid created a cascading failure—a perfect storm, so to speak."

"How do you remember such details?"

"Trust me, when you're stuck twenty stories up in the dark for nearly forty-eight hours with two bored kids, one really pissed off husband, and no air-conditioning during one of the hottest weeks of the year, you remember every freaking detail of the nightmare. At least we don't have to worry about heat stroke this time. Although I suppose we could freeze to death."

"How optimistic of you. Wouldn't the electric company have taken steps to prevent something like that from occurring a second time?"

"Probably."

"Which means this outage is most likely caused by something else."

"Like what? Hackers?"

"Possibly. Cyber-attacks are growing among terrorists." Beck turned on his phone, bathing the room in a muted glow. "No service. Not a good sign."

"I'm guessing you don't have any candles," said Grace.

"Not a standard issue office supply around here." He used the light of the phone to guide them both across the room to the small sofa he camped out on during those nights when he couldn't bear returning to his empty apartment. "We might as well make ourselves comfortable." He settled into one corner while she seated herself at the other end. "So who are you, really?" he asked.

* * *

Could Beck see the heat rise up her neck and into her face? "You should conserve your battery," said Grace.

He switched his phone off, plunging the room into darkness. "Is that your way of avoiding the question?"

She waited until her eyes adjusted to the blackness. She could barely make out the dim silhouette sitting a few feet away from her. "You know who I am—Trulee Lovejoy."

"When you called, you started to introduce yourself as someone else."

"You must have had poor cell reception."

"Trulee Lovejoy can't be your real name."

"What's wrong with Trulee Lovejoy?"

"Lovejoy I can buy. It's not the most common of surnames, but it is a legitimate one. However coupled with Trulee, it becomes a joke. Like Kanye West naming his daughter North. Poor kid."

"And yet he did. Celebrities often give their kids odd names."

"Were your parents celebrities?"

"Does it matter?"

"You still haven't answered my original question."

Grace debated whether or not to divulge the truth to Beck. Did it really matter if he knew her legal name? She released a deep sigh. "My real name is Grace Wainwright."

"Why Trulee Lovejoy?"

"I needed a pen name, and it works for the books." He didn't need to know that the pen name was originally chosen for Thea, not her.

"What does your husband think about those how-to-snare-a-guy books you write?"

"I'm divorced."

"Because of the books?"

"Because of his penchant for jailbait."

"Sorry."

"That makes four of us."

"Four?"

"You, me, and my daughters. There's a certain ick factor involved when your father shacks up with someone young enough to be one of your classmates."

"Understandable. Can I assume your divorce has something to do with your hatred of Valentine's Day?"

All that alcohol she'd consumed with Thea might have loosened her tongue, but she wasn't about to divulge her Valentine's Day humiliation to a man she barely knew. "You can assume anything you want. I'm not answering any more questions until you dish up some answers of your own."

"Like?"

"Like why you're not very keen on Valentine's Day, either."

"I'd rather not say."

"No fair."

"It's personal."

Grace slammed her fist onto the sofa cushion. "So are the questions you're asking me, Beck."

"Let's just say I'm not fond of holidays in general."

"Is your real name Ebenezer Scrooge?"

He had the audacity to chuckle. "Guilty as charged. Are you hungry? I'm going to root around the other offices to see if I can find some food for us."

Grace felt him rise from the sofa. "That was a less-than-subtle way of changing the subject."

"I'm devious that way. Still, I am hungry. I'll be back."

As she heard him head down the hall, she wondered about the secrets Becket Delaney kept bottled up inside that hunky body of his. Their banter would grow old quickly, and if the power didn't come back on soon, a long night stretched before them. How would they fill those boring hours once they both grew tired of small talk?

She decided she'd ignore him and get some work done. Grace reached for her laptop. She'd charged her battery earlier in the day. That gave her at least four or five hours of juice, plenty of time to finish those manuscript edits. Hopefully, by then the power would be restored.

* * *

Foraging around unlocked offices in the dark netted Beck the remains of a birthday cake from a party earlier in the day, an unopened bag of pretzels, a dish of M&M's, and half a bottle of Johnnie Walker Blue Label.

"At least we won't go hungry," he said, reentering his office. Aided by the light from Grace's computer, he deposited the stash on the coffee table in front of the sofa. "This should see us through to breakfast tomorrow. If the power is still out at that point, at least I'll have daylight to aid me in my search for more provisions."

Grace picked up the platter with the cake and removed the plastic wrap. "Forks?"

"Couldn't find any. We'll have to use our fingers." He reached over, broke off a wedge of cake, and held it up to Grace's mouth, smearing chocolate icing across her lips. "Open up."

When Grace opened her mouth, Beck deposited the cake onto her tongue. "Hmm, delicious," she said. Her tongue darted around her lips and the edges of her mouth, scooping up the chocolate.

"You missed some." He ran his index finger along the corner of her mouth, then pressed it between her slightly opened lips.

Big mistake. When Grace sucked the chocolate from the tip of his finger, a certain part of his anatomy sprang to life—for the first time in years. He scooted away from her and grabbed the bottle of Johnnie Walker. Instead of dampening his sudden appetite, the large swig only heightened his growing discomfort.

He tried small talk to move his mind off the bulge in his pants. "What are you working on?"

"My day job." She lowered the laptop lid, plunging them back into darkness. "And that's all you get until you cough up some info on yourself." A moment later Beck felt her finger skim chocolate icing across his lips. "Touché," she said.

Was she coming on to him? Wait. Hadn't he just made the first move? One that had surprised the hell out of him? Beck licked the icing from his lips and debated his next move. His head told him one thing, the area below his belt, alive for the first time in years, argued for a different course of action. His head lost the battle.

* * *

Had the blackout stripped Grace of all inhibitions, allowing some alien, seductive vixen to take over her body? Such behavior was totally out of character for her. Although, she had to admit, a part of her didn't want to stop. All of a sudden heat pooled in previously glacial parts of her body. She'd lived like a nun so long that the sensations startled her.

Beck inched closer, his breath tickling her cheek. "Grace?"

"Hmm?"

"What are we doing?"

"I'm not sure."

"Do you want to stop?"

Did she? Two thoughts sprang to mind: Becket Delaney was definitely not gay, and she absolutely didn't want him to stop whatever he'd started. She drew in a shaky breath. "I don't think so."

He wrapped his hand around the nape of her neck and drew her closer, capturing her lips with his. Other than pecks on the cheek from her kids, no one had kissed her in ten years. Suddenly Grace realized how starved she was for intimacy. She leaned into Beck and kissed him back. Hard. With a desperation that shocked her. He responded in a way that sucked the air from her lungs and shot waves of need rocketing through her body.

He slid her down onto the cushions and covered her body with his. His hands caressed her scalp, her cheeks, her neck. He shifted his weight, lowered one hand from her head, and stretched out his arm. A moment later he trailed his chocolate icing-covered fingers from the hollow of her neck down into her cleavage. With his lips and tongue he kissed away every last morsel.

Grace arched into him. Desperate for more, she began her own exploration. She unbuttoned his shirt and freed it from his waistband. Her fingers played across each rippling muscle of his bare chest, her lips following. "Needs chocolate," she murmured.

She reached out to swipe a finger of icing and painted it over his nipples. When she wrapped her lips around a hardened nub and sucked, he moaned his own need. "I want you."

Acting more wanton than she'd ever behaved in her life, Grace grabbed for his belt buckle. "I need you. Now."

They frenetically stripped off each other's clothes, tossing garments into the dark until not a strip of fabric separated his skin from hers.

Beck paused above her. "Are you sure?"

She answered by drawing him inside her.

They made love three times, each coupling more explosive than the last.

"I hope the power never comes back on," she said when finally spent, they rested in each other's arms.

He nuzzled her neck. "I could live with that."

A roar from Beck's stomach broke the mood.

* * *

Grace laughed. "We should finish the cake."

"That's what got us going in the first place."

"Maybe we should switch to the pretzels?"

Beck reached around in the dark until his hand landed on the bag. He ripped it open and pulled out two pretzels, handing one to Grace and popping the other into his mouth.

Only the sound of munching pretzels broke the silence that settled over the room. Beck puzzled through the thoughts and emotions bombarding him. He never expected to make love to another woman. He expected guilt to consume him if he ever tried. Yet he felt no guilt after making love to Grace. A sense of peace had settled over him. And freedom. Maybe all he'd needed was finding the right woman to rid him of the shackles of his past.

He wrapped his arm around her shoulders, drew her closer, and inhaled a shaky breath. For the first time since the incident, he felt ready to talk about it. "They were killed on Valentine's Day," he said.

"Who?"

He swallowed the lump that had formed in his throat before continuing. "My wife and two kids. Five years ago. They were on their way home from school when a seventeen-year-old ran a red light. He'd been texting while driving. Never saw the light change."

"Oh, Beck!"

"He walked away with barely a scratch. My family died at the scene. All holidays are hard on me, but Valentine's Day is the worst. Every year since, the moment I see hearts and cherubs popping up all over the place, I sink into a deep funk that lasts for weeks."

Beck leaned forward and fumbled around on the coffee table until he found his phone. He switched it on to provide light to find the bottle of scotch, then leaned back against the cushions and took a long swig. When he turned to offer Grace the bottle, he noticed the tears streaming down her face. He wiped them away with the pads of his thumbs.

"My reason for hating Valentine's Day is so insignificant compared to yours."

"Tell me anyway."

* * *

Grace sniffed back a few more threatening tears. She'd carried the pain of betrayal with her for ten years, but Dick-head had killed any love she had for him the moment she discovered him cheating on her.

Beck's loves had literally been torn from him. How could she possibly compare her loss to his? Still, she owed him an explanation after he'd bared his soul to her. "Long story short? I discovered my ex with another woman—on Valentine's Day."

She snuggled deeper into Beck's chest, heaved a sigh, and closed her eyes.

THREE

Grace woke the next morning to find herself spooned against a warm, muscular body. His arms holding her snuggly, she felt the steady rise and fall of his chest against her back. Not an unpleasant sensation but not one she'd experienced in a very long time. Behind her eyelids, she sensed sunlight streaming into the room. It took a moment for her brain to focus before she remembered where she was, what she'd done the night before, and with whom.

Had the sex really been as spectacular as she thought, or were her feelings influenced by her ten-year, self-imposed abstinence? Try as she might, she couldn't remember ever experiencing such satisfaction from Dick-head, not even when they were in the heady early days of their romance, back when she thought those marriage vows meant something to him. Now, here she was the morning after the night before, pondering exactly what last night meant to her and wondering what it meant to Beck.

The morning after the night before. That brought her out of her reverie and to her senses. She hadn't experienced one of those in decades. And never in an office building with a coworker, let alone her producer. Talk about awkward! Maybe if she fell back to sleep, she'd wake up alone in her own bed.

However, with her brain racing, she found it impossible to sink back into the oblivion of sleep. She finally pried her eyes open and assessed her surroundings. Various items of clothing—hers and Beck's—lay in haphazard disarray, scattered across the carpeting. Her bra draped off the coffee table in front of the sofa. Somehow one of her shoes had managed to wind up halfway across the room.

She scanned the rest of the office. On a bookshelf to her left she noticed a digital clock blinking a series of zeroes. They had power! Grace slipped her arm out from under Beck's embrace and reached for his cell phone to check the time. Six-thirty. In less than an hour people would begin streaming into the building. And here they were, sprawled naked on his office sofa.

She squirmed around to face him and nudged his shoulder. "Beck, wake up."

"I'm awake," he mumbled, pulling her closer.

So was a certain part of his anatomy that had sprung to life against her belly, but she couldn't think about that now. And neither should he. She pushed away from him. "No time for that. The power's back on. We need to get out of here before anyone arrives."

His eyes sprang open. He took one look at her and smiled. "Good morning, Grace."

She smiled back but said, "It won't be if we don't get out of here."

He leaned over and kissed the tip of her nose. "Afraid of office gossip?"

"More afraid of you losing your job. I'm sure the network must have some rule against sex on the office sofa."

"Not sure but now that the power is back on, I could look it up in the company handbook."

She swatted his arm. "Get dressed."

"Don't be a killjoy." He pulled her into his arms and kissed her. Her breasts tingled. Need blossomed below her belly. "We can't," she moaned, unable to deny her body.

"Sure we can. Where's your sense of adventure?"

* * *

Half an hour later, fully sated, Grace and Beck slipped out the service entrance at the side of the building and headed down the street to a café for breakfast.

Beck sat across the table from Grace and attacked a stack of blueberry pancakes while she concentrated on her veggie omelet. The food, along with the noise from the crowded café, gave them both an excuse not to speak much, which he viewed as a good thing at the moment. In the light of day and away from the office, he wasn't sure what to say to her.

What he did know was that last night had changed his life. However, had they'd shared a one-night stand or the start of a relationship? He had no idea how to broach the subject with her. Last night they both opened up to each other, sharing deep wounds from their past after coming together in explosive passion. Was it only about the sex, or was there more to their blackout encounter? Did they walk away after breakfast and pretend nothing had happened or find some way to build on the experience?

He'd dated little in high school and married his college sweetheart. Nothing in his past prepared him for this moment. He'd never had a one-night stand, never had an encounter with someone he barely knew.

After they finished eating and were both sipping coffee, their eyes met over the rims of their mugs. The doubt in her eyes told him she struggled with the same issues that plagued him this morning. Finally, he set his mug on the table and said, "There's an elephant in the room."

She nodded. "An enormous one." Grace took a deep breath. "But is it named Regret? Or Possibility?"

"I'm thinking he looks more like a Possibility."

The corners of her mouth turned upward, and the worry left her eyes. "I was hoping you'd say that."

He reached across the table and tooboth of her hands in his.

FOUR

February 10th

"That's a wrap," said Beck at the conclusion of the taping for the second of the two *Love Recipes* Valentine's Day shows. "Great job, everyone." He nodded to Grace and Thea before following his director off the set.

"See?" Thea elbowed Grace in the ribs. "You made it through the tapings without needing a single heart-shaped arsenic cookie."

"I had your help."

"Not to mention someone else's. I see you took my advice."

"What advice?"

"That you should get to know Beck better."

Busted! Grace felt the heat rise to her cheeks. With so much baggage between them, she and Beck had decided to keep their budding romance a secret for the time being, even from Thea. After so many years of emotional isolation, they both first needed to make certain they were experiencing love and not just hormones run amok after years of imprisonment.

"Did you think I wouldn't notice?" asked Thea. "The rest of the crew might be clueless, but I've known you far too long, Grace."

Grace forced a nervous chuckle. "Can't pull anything over on you, can I?"

"Hey, I *am* the original Dr. Trulee Lovejoy, or have you forgotten?"

"How could I forget?"

"Well, then? Anything you'd like to share with me?"

Grace shrugged. "I was only following doctor's orders."

"I'll send you a bill."

Grace and Beck had spent so many nights together over the past month that they had begun discussing moving in together. For two people who had eschewed sex, not to mention romance, for so many years, they were certainly making up for lost time. *Hormones or true love?* Only time would tell.

Getting through today's tapings had been a huge hurdle for both of them. The ghost of two prior Valentine's days—one hers, one his—loomed large throughout the show's rehearsals and taping. She saw it on his face and knew he saw it on hers whenever their eyes met.

Getting through Valentine's Day four days from now would be an even greater hurdle. They had vowed to do it together, to be there for each other. Grace promised herself she wouldn't let Beck sink into depression during the day. He had assured her that he, not Jack Daniels, would be her Valentine's Day date this year. No pity party for either of them—no matter what it took.

"I brought you something," said Thea. She pulled a small pink gift bag from her tote and handed it to Grace.

"A Valentine's gift?"

"Of course not. I know how you feel about Valentine's Day. Think of it as a Congratulations-on-Your-New-Relationship gift."

Grace peeked into the bag and blushed. "You were very sure of yourself, weren't you?"

* * *

Four days later Beck arrived at Grace's apartment, his arms laden with a large bag of Chinese take-out and a signature robin's egg blue Tiffany gift bag, a reminder of her greatest humiliation. But of course, Beck wouldn't know that. She'd never told him the full story of that night ten years ago.

Grace eyed the bag with trepidation, hoping Beck hadn't decided to deal with the day by proposing. It was way too soon to be talking marriage. But if that were his intention, wouldn't he have a small box in his pocket rather than walking in with a large gift bag? "What's that?" she asked, pointing to the bag.

He placed the food on her kitchen counter and walked her over to the sofa. Once they were both seated, he handed her the gift bag. "Something I thought you should have. Think of it as a souvenir of a very special night."

Grace reached inside the bag and withdrew a large robin's egg blue box tied with a white silk ribbon. She pulled on one of the ribbon ends, undoing the bow, then lifted the box lid. Under layers of white tissue paper she discovered a blown glass elephant. She lifted it out of the box. Flowing cursive letters etched along the elephant's upturned trunk spelled out *Possibility*. "Our personal elephant in the room," she said.

"Reminding us that our future together is full of possibilities."

"I like that." She leaned over and kissed him.

One thing led to another, and in no time they were both naked, dinner forgotten. "Wait," said Grace. "I have a gift for you."

"You're all the gift I need."

"Trust me, you're really going to want to open this."

"Now?"

"Now." She scooted off the sofa and into the kitchen where she removed Thea's gift from the microwave. After screwing the lid back on, she placed the jar in the pink gift bag. Returning to the living room, she handed Beck the bag.

He reached in and pulled out the warm jar. "Chocolate?"

"Not just any chocolate. Read the label."

Beck held the jar up and read aloud, "*Trulee Delectable Chocolate Body Paint.*" He threw his head back and roared with laughter. "Got a paint brush?"

"

Trulee Delectable Chocolate Body Paint
(also good on ice cream, fruit, and cake)

Ingredients:
4 oz. butter
5 oz. unsweetened chocolate
12 oz. evaporated milk
1 lb. confectioner's sugar
1/2 teaspoon almond or peppermint extract

Melt butter and chocolate on top of a double boier. Remove from heat. Beat in evaporated milk, then confectioer's sugar. Return to double boiler and continue to heat for 10 to 15 inutes, stirring occasionally, until mixture thickens. Stir in extract once mixture has thickened.

Serve warm or cold. Refrigate or freeze leftovers.

ABOUT THE AUTHOR

USA Today and Amazon bestselling and award-winning author Lois Winston writes mystery, romance, romantic suspense, chick lit, women's fiction, children's chapter books, and nonfiction. *Kirkus Reviews* dubbed her critically acclaimed Anastasia Pollack Crafting Mystery series, "North Jersey's more mature answer to Stephanie Plum." In addition, Lois is an award-winning craft and needlework designer who often draws much of her source material for both her characters and plots from her experiences in the crafts industry.

Connect with Lois at her website, www.loiswinston.com, where you can learn more about her and her books, sign up for her newsletter, and find links to follow her on social media.